American
Fiction

❀❀❀

Volume Twelve

American Fiction

❀❀❀

Volume Twelve
the best unpublished stories by emerging writers

Josip Novakovich, Guest Judge
Kristen Tsetsi and Bruce Pratt, Editors
Bayard Godsave, Assistant Editor

n e w
RIVERS
PRESS
MSUM

Cover design by Sarah DeGooyer
Interior design by Daniel A. Shudlick

The publication of *American Fiction* Volume 12 is made possible by the generous support of the McKnight Foundation, Clint McCown, and other contributors to New Rivers Press.

For academic permission or copyright clearance please contact
Frederick T. Courtright at 570-839-7477 or permdude@eclipse.net.

New Rivers Press is a nonprofit literary press associated with
Minnesota State University Moorhead.

Alan Davis, Co-Director and Senior Editor
Suzzanne Kelley, Co-Director and Managing Editor
Wayne Gudmundson, Consultant
Allen Sheets, Art Director
Thom Tammaro, Poetry Editor
Kevin Carollo, MVP Poetry Coordinator

The editors of *American Fiction* Volume 12 thank Jessica Johnson, Steve Lauder, and Mary Pauer for their assistance.

Publishing Interns:
David DeFusco, Andreana Gustafson, Katelin Hansen,
Noah M. Kleckner, Daniel A. Shudlick, Sarah Z. Sleeper, Alicia Strnad

American Fiction, Volume 12 Book Team:
Ian Cole, Melynda Heying, Bethany Hill, Sarah Z. Sleeper,
Samantha Woods

New Rivers Press
c/o MSUM
1104 7th Avenue South
Moorhead, MN 56563
www.newriverspress.com

CONTENTS

✿ ✿ ✿

INTRODUCTION

Seventeen years ago I had a wonderful experience with the *American Fiction* anthology. Tim O'Brien line edited a story of mine. It didn't make it to the select three, but it didn't matter. I was proud that it was in the anthology and that Tim O'Brien had read it carefully.

I was delighted to be asked to select the winners and to review the anthology this year, and the way I felt about it when I was on the other side of the table is the way all eighteen finalists ought to feel about being included in this anthology. The stories are so fine that they are all winners.

There are so many writers and writing programs today that American writing is, in general, functioning at a high level, but I think it is fair, as a result, to ask the question, is there such a thing as a workshop story? I could answer, sure, some of these are, perhaps a third (Where else would people use verbs like *sashay* and *traipse?*), but all the better, because there's less editing to do. In the world of painting, it's a damning thing to be an autodidact rather than an academically trained painter, so why should it be the reverse in writing?

There is something strongly American in most of these stories. In some, you will find particularly fine scene-making, quintessential American cultural and cinematic talent in fiction, and others rely more on telling and poetics, so I cannot completely generalize, but one thing that struck me is that it seems that more than a third of the stories are written by immigrants or children of recent immigrants, which reflects what America is—not only itself, but also the world with its currents and peregrinations.

Two of our winners come from immigrant culture. As an immigrant, perhaps I favor stories with a culture clash. Through my aesthetics, seeking poetry in fiction and favoring a general overstepping of boundaries (especially genre boundaries), I have selected the winners perhaps subjectively, and with another set of predilections, I would have perhaps selected other stories. On the other hand, these stories are wonderful in many respects, with or without me reading them, so my somewhat idiosyncratic angles in no way detract from them. They are truly marvelous.

"The Polar Bear Swim" by Dika Lam. In this story, a Chinese immigrant kid in Canada, tired of being an alien, decides to convert to a native, an Eskimo (only to learn that she got that wrong, Inuit would be appropriate), and tells stories to substantiate her imaginary identity: "I told Jessie Lawson that my real mum, up in Yellowknife, once caught a polar bear feasting on our Christmas lights—she heard the bulbs crunching. I told Sophie Lafleur and Gordie McLachlan about the time my gang of sled dogs ran away—they were lost in the tundra for weeks, and when they came back, dancing bloody footprints on the snow, their eyes were glowing like jellyfish." The writing throughout is brilliant, and we are willing to go with the author anywhere—even into icy water.

"Jody's Solo" by Rachel Furey. This touching story about an anorexic girl who has to give up her spot as a soloist is told by the soloist's less talented sibling with a great deal of humor and mischief. Rachel writes in a painterly way, vividly: "When Jody fainted, I was lost in the glow of the tubas and trombones. We'd just taken the stage for the first of our dress rehearsals for the fall concert, and above me, domed lights dangled like glass ornaments suspended from a tree. The entire brass section took on a shine that made them seem brand new instruments—not the old, dented creatures that had sat in our dim practice room for years. From my position behind the bass drum, the flutes shone like icicles. The trumpets looked prepared for a fine processional. Even my mallet had taken on a newfound glow." Rachel puts me right there, in the orchestra, ready to observe with trepidation the thin red line of blood coming from Jody's nostrils. This is amazing writing.

"Jacinto's Teeth" by Theresa Duve Morales. A boy, who misses his two front teeth and loves playing soccer, frequently has to run away from the police during curfews. He gets tickets and invitation to go to the United States, but he doesn't want to escape the civil war in Guatamala because he is in love with a girl who watches his games. The contrast between childhood happiness and what's going on in the country at the same time is startling: "At the same time he was playing soccer in the street, 100 kilometers to the northwest in the highlands of Huehuetenango, Tomás Machic was returning home after attending a union meeting with fellow farm workers. He entered his front door to find three militiamen at his kitchen table, eating the *tamales blancos con chile* that his wife had prepared for his dinner. She lay dead at their feet next to the bodies of his son and nephew. As Jacinto spun the ball around . . ." Theresa spins her tale skilfully, weaving the mundane details with the threatening political scene, evolving powerful suspense.

For honorable mentions, I have selected "Talk" by Chris Belden—a humorous story about a radio talk-show host who has a mute son and who rarely talks, himself, while at home, as well as "John the Revelator" by Sean Conway, a burlesque in which a bar-owner, a former convict, trusts only former convicts to work for him.

The stories in this anthology explore a variety of human experiences in a variety of styles, displaying the amazing vitality in the current American short story. It makes for lively reading, and while editors generally detest the short story as a form, a good collection of stories, like this one, can beat most novels in terms of freshness, change of pace, and emotional range, moving through the sheer wealth of human experience. I am not sure why in our ADD culture the short story has not become the primary literary form (or at least an equal to the novel), or why it should be so despised by the market. Anyway, this is not an occasion to bitch, but rather to celebrate the wonders of new American short stories. Have fun!

—Josip Novakovich

Photo by Margo Rabb

DIKA LAM's fiction has appeared in *One Story, Scribner's Best of the Fiction Workshops*, and *This is Not Chick Lit*. She was a New York Times Fellow in the MFA program at New York University, a Tennessee Williams Scholar at the Sewanee Writers' Conference, and winner of the Bronx Writers' Center Chapter One Fiction Competition. Lam was born in Canada and lives in Chicago.

THE POLAR BEAR SWIM
Dika Lam

I've converted to Eskimo. It's official.

My mum and I moved to northern Ontario in June, when trilliums whitened the woods like serviettes at a fancy supper, and blackflies terrorized my scalp until it bled. Way before the fall semester, before any of the kids in grade nine could pry, I wowed them with tales of the permafrost. I told Jessie Lawson that my real mum, up in Yellowknife, once caught a polar bear feasting on our Christmas lights—she heard the bulbs crunching like popcorn, then saw flashes of color lighting up its fur from the inside. I told Lori DiPietro that during a storm that trapped our family in an igloo for moons and moons, my dad carved one hundred walruses out of soapstone, each sculpture no bigger than the paw of a hare. I told Sophie Lafleur and Gordie McLachlan about the time my gang of sled dogs ran away—they were lost in the tundra for weeks, and when they came back, dancing bloody footprints on the snow, their eyes were glowing like jellyfish and all the hair on their bodies had been scared right off.

On the globe, I indicated the Northwest Territories with a sweep of my hand. "Way up here," I said, "is where I was born."

For backup, I looked to the portrait of Queen Elizabeth II above the blackboard, right next to the signed photo of the prime minister of Canada. This was the young Queen E, back when she was hot. She was wearing her tiara and looked royally victorious.

When my classmates heard a different story, namely that my mother, Louise Pelletier, trekked to China to adopt a little girl thirteen years ago, I whispered, "That's what they'd like you to think. I'm an orphan.

My mum went to the Arctic to see the aurora borealis and found me instead. Papoose and all."

Truth is, I was found in a tub of bok choy in an open-air market in Guangzhou, China, when I was nine months old. Whoever dropped me off included accessories—a silk pouch full of coins and a jade ring. Mum is always reminding me how valuable that ring must have been to the person who left it there. There was no note.

To hear her tell it, when Louise Pelletier flew to China, she did not see the aurora borealis, only a sky the color of raw shrimp. The agency crammed the adoptive parents into a hotel, these almost-mums-and-dads doing time in the lobby and itching to feel a child in their arms.

"So there I was, waiting for the orphanage to bring you to me, when I met a couple from Saskatchewan, really nice folks, teachers." (At this, Mum rolled her eyes.) "They'd brought a suitcase full of peanut butter and Tang and were handing out crackers. They even brought their own silverware. Anyway, they had just gotten their daughter. She was so beautiful. Maybe six months old. She'd been swaddled so tight, she looked like the Michelin man. But her hair was soaking wet. So I asked the couple about it and they said, cheery as sunflowers, 'Oh, we just baptized the little heathen in the bathroom sink.'"

From then on, whenever I was bad, my mother would bring her up as a joke. *If you don't clean your room, I'll send you to Saskatoon to live with the Little Heathen. You think I'm being reactionary for making you eat tofu, imagine what the Little Heathen is going through!*

I did not imagine. I did not have to. The Little Heathen first appeared to me at a ski resort when I was six years old. I had fallen off the T-bar and was sulking in the lodge, waiting for Mum to bring me some ice, when a strange girl sidled up to me. She was rocking a dress that looked like a quilt, her face hidden by an enormous blue bonnet. At first, I thought she was some dress-up kid who just happened to look like Mum's ancient Holly Hobbie doll until she said, "Hello my sister. Can I borrow your ring?"

Over the years, the Little Heathen visited regularly, usually in the locker room after we'd lost a soccer game, or in my bedroom when I was studying for a test. Her hair was always wet. She'd eagerly update me on her latest grievances: *I'm not allowed to go online. My parents homeschool me. On Youth Group Movie Night, we watched* Romeo and Juliet, *and they fast-forwarded through all the naughty parts.* I once found her mimicking my favorite pastime in the school library, reading all about critters in *National Geographic.* "Did you know that cuttlefish are shape-shifters?"

she said, the yellow spine of the magazine winking as she slotted it into a needlepoint bag. "At night, they can camouflage themselves as rock."

So on the first day of my new school in my new town, I was not surprised to spot her on my bike in the driveway. She was wearing a prairie dress with a high lace collar, and the length of the skirt made it difficult for her to balance. She rode in a wide circle, the front wheel jerking from side to side. "You want my advice?" she said, though I didn't want anything from her. "Go Eskimo, my sister. If you're native, no one will say you don't belong here."

❊ ❊ ❊

In December, our gym teacher Mr. Borislava throws us outside for "independent fitness," where we loiter against the high school building with our MP3 players on like we're waiting for someone to start a game of murderball and put us all out of our misery. It's so freezing, our attempts at snow angels don't even make a dent. We're really supposed to have separate gym classes for girls and boys, but there have been budget cuts, and Mr. Borislava hasn't been right in the noggin since all the painkillers from his shoulder surgery.

Sophie Lafleur has sneaked into the conservation area to try her first smoke all over again while the rest of us are content to watch our breaths die in great grey veils. I'm regretting my imitation mammoth-hair boots. Tiny ball bearings made of ice are stuck to the fur like burrs, and I constantly have to comb them off the way Lori DiPietro picks the fuzz from her sweater with a roughed-up protractor.

Behind the school, old snow lives on the boulders in the gully like underwear left to fend for itself. Among the pines lurk skiers, hikers, and the ruins of a fort where the body of a baby was found last summer. So says Craig Mitchell, who set his ski boot on fire last week while trying to hide a joint from his dad. Craig's dad is Constable Mitchell, who has a thing for my mother, maybe because she's a single mother, and he's a single father, and despite the fact she talked his ear off about composting and organic beer during Halloween when he was trying to give out candy. (When I was still young enough to go trick-or-treating, Mum would let me keep only one Jersey Milk and one Sweet Marie before taking the bag away.)

Constable Mitchell has asked my mother to the Bon Hiver Winter Carnival. Though I'm sure he's most interested in the Miss Bon Hiver Pageant, the best thing about the carnival is the Polar Bear

Swim, when maniacs plunge into the St. Joe's River to show winter it cannot beat them. I'm obsessed with it, maybe because I can't really swim, though Mum always meant to teach me. She says the water in public pools is teeming with chemicals. I do not shudder at the thought of the Polar Bear Swim, but I do shudder at the thought of having Craig Mitchell for a brother.

Though my mother does not know it, I am training for *both* events: Whenever Craig yanks his eyes into slits, I say, "You know, Craig, I can always get plastic surgery. But you'll always be retarded." When I take a bath, I run the water so cold, even my shrieks are blue. I give shoplifted mickeys of rye to Sophie Lafleur in exchange for twenty-minute doggy paddles in her indoor pool. Sophie's parents, who are never home, are both surgeons. When she's not mixing Bloody Caesars at a wet bar that's really a closet, Sophie herself is an excellent swim teacher.

❀ ❀ ❀

Just before Christmas, Sherry Ann Bedell challenges me. Her hair is the color of the red-brick wall separating the rink from the fallow baseball diamond, and her greatest desire is to make a power play for Gordie McLachlan's Pee Wee hockey jacket. Sherry Ann knows a lot about our national pastime because her mum and dad have become house parents; they're billeting a star hockey player for the Lock City Wolves, our local Ontario Hockey League team. He's a seventeen-year-old from Hamilton named Patrick St. Amand, and his dimples leave us all dumb. Sherry Ann is supposed to treat him like a big brother but she calls him "the immigrant" behind his back. Everyone says she's crushing so hard on Patrick that she can't sleep knowing he's hanging out in his boxer shorts in the next room. I also happen to know that when Sherry Ann is thinking too much about Patrick, she snacks on cherry ChapStick down in the gully, and if she irks me, I plan to use this secret intelligence. Sherry Ann's mum is a *dental hygienist*.

At our lockers, she says, "Aren't you guys supposed to have one hundred words for snow? Can you tell us *one*?" Sherry Ann hates that the other kids have started defecting to my table in the cafeteria.

I study the puffy jacket on display in her locker. Her red toque leers out of the pocket like a tongue because she has decided it's uncool to wear a hat. I sigh long and loud. "Sherry Ann, that's such a lie. We have, like, four, and because you are so ignorant, I am not going to tell you."

"You're a liar," she says, her teeth pink and waxy. "What do you know about the Arctic?" She pronounces it *Artic*, but I let it slide, even though Mr. Little reminds us there's a letter in there we're not supposed to ignore. Mr. Little is teaching us geography via a class-wide game of Risk—the construction-paper version of the world, bristling with pushpins, eats up one whole wall of the room. We play the computer version too, but it's retro-cool to have a handmade map spread in front of you. Sherry Ann is England; Laurent Belair, the skinniest guy in our grade, is Chile; Jessie and I are Russia. Jessie has grand plans to conquer Japan and spends a lot of time drawing battle plans on the inner flap of his binder. Nobody bothers him because he's the best artist in the class, and if you're not careful, you could see your ugly twin painted on the cinderblock wall of the Zellers on Great Loon Road.

I only wish I were as untouchable. But I'm getting there. I am golden. The other kids hang on my every joke. Last weekend, I was invited to the Esposito Club with Lori DiPietro and we played bocce.

Golden, that is, until the New Year.

❉ ❉ ❉

"Kids, I'd like you to welcome the latest addition to Batchewana Collegiate," says Mr. Little.

The new kid is shorter than Sherry Ann but so solid, he looks like he could beat you up with his eyeballs. His hair and my hair are twins, like outer space without the stars. His skin, naturally tan, stretches over the apples of his cheeks. He is not wearing mammoth-fur boots. He is wearing a red-and-black-checked flannel jacket.

"Please welcome Erik Qimirpik, from the Northwest Territories."

Twenty sets of eyes are mosquito-pricking my skin.

Kill me now.

Erik Qimirpik!

Later, I will find out all about him. Erik Qimirpik, who grew up around signs that said, PLEASE DO NOT SKIN YOUR CARIBOU HERE. IT ATTRACTS BEARS. Erik Qimirpik, who knows what it's like to sleep under the midnight sun. Erik Qimirpik, for whom "down south" does not mean Toronto but means where we are right now. Erik Qimirpik, who says he was born on a kayak. Erik Qimirpik. A real. Live. Eskimo. What is he doing here? Shouldn't he be with his people? I can hear Sherry Ann throwing her triumph across the room like a spear with my name on it.

Erik takes a seat next to me. He suffers through a lesson on the explorers Radisson and Groseilliers.

"See, kids? Radisson," says Mr. Little, banging his metre stick against the tile. "Not just a hotel."

At recess, I fake a bellyache and run to the bus stop as fast as possible. I am in full retreat now, like when Thailand failed to conquer India in Risk.

❀ ❀ ❀

The bus is slow today. It crawls past the Ojibwa reserve, past the casino and the highway, and down to my mum's health food store on King Street. She grew up right here in Lock City, eating Kraft Dinner for breakfast, and now she's back where she started, like a steelhead trout coming home to spawn. Mum has a master's in nutrition from Guelph. We moved up north for the cleaner air, she insists, though the first time we drove through, we rolled up the car windows to block the farts from the pulp and paper mill. I remember the smokestacks of Algonquin Steel giving me the finger. My grandpa died right before we moved, and now we live in his house; I never knew him that well, but I wonder if it was the steel plant that made him sick.

I saunter into the store, hoping Mum will think it's already three o'clock, but she says, "Why aren't you in school?" When she hears about my tummy, she hugs me and strokes my hair until I pull away, embarrassed. She gives me some ginger candy with a panda on the wrapper and goes back to sorting containers of milk thistle extract. Behind her, coenzyme Q-10 shares a shelf with hemp protein.

"Chantal, I just want to remind you," she says, waving a jar of ginkgo biloba, "this is not candy, so I don't want you sharing this stuff with your friends."

But there is no danger of that. Because their dads do shift work at the steel plant, my classmates eat supper at four-thirty in the afternoon. I can't join them in evening activities because I usually help my mum with dinner around seven-thirty (eggplant Parmesan or ratatouille), and then we sit down to eat when everyone else is hanging out. I know for a fact that our French mealtime is murdering my social life.

After two more ginger candies, I say, "When are we moving back to Ottawa?" Back in the nation's capital, we knew some other families that had adopted kids from China. We used to celebrate Chinese New Year together. My stomach is beginning to hurt for real.

Mum knits her eyebrows into a shapely caterpillar. It's the same look she gave me when we first moved here, after an incident at the Lock City Mall. It all started when she dropped me off at the bookstore, and I wandered off in search of doughnuts—which was when a lady in the food court mistook me for an exchange student and said, "Welcome to our country!" I retaliated by sitting on a coin-operated pony and accosting everyone who passed. "*Guten tag!*" I yelled. "Hey, are you Russian? You Greek?"

Mall security turned me over to Constable Mitchell when I wouldn't tell them who my mother was. That's how they met.

On the ride home that afternoon, Mum asked quietly, "Chantal? Why did you say those things?"

I confessed that people were always coming up to *me* and saying, *Konichiwa!* Or, *do you speak Korean*, or *you must know karate*. "Why do they get to ask all the stupid questions?" I asked.

"I see," she said. My mother looked hurt and lost at the same time, like she'd just been run over by a car in a foreign country.

Today, she closes the store early and we stroll along the canal that separates us from the States, the Friendship Bridge arcing above our heads. We lick popsicles made of 100 percent orange juice as the freighters parade through the locks, rusty mountains rising and falling, sliding from one Great Lake to another. "When I was sixteen," she says, "I used to come here with my boyfriend and make out."

It's easy to imagine Mum when she was young (from behind, people used to mistake her for a boy, her dirty-blond hair ending below her ears), but I can't see her ever doing anything like that. I think of Erik's cheekbones; I picture smooching him underwater and almost choke on my popsicle.

"You're smiling," she says. "Oh, I'm so glad to see it." She takes off her glasses to hug me, and I burrow into her cardigan, throwing myself around the kite of bones that holds her together. We often joke that we look alike because we have the same skeleton.

❀ ❀ ❀

The next day, the Little Heathen walks to school with me. She's munching on the frozen ends of her hair. "You gotta help me," she says. "My parents grounded me for sending a text on a neighbor's phone. You gotta come out west and take me away." The legs of her snowpants swish against each other.

"I've got my own problems," I say. I cut through the conservation area to approach Batchewana from the rear flank. A line of white pines marks the boundary between the forest preserve and the soccer field. "If you're grounded," I say, "what are you doing here?"

"Look," she says, holding up a bar of Cadbury Flakes. "Your favorite." This isn't the first time she's tempted me with the sweet stuff—last week, it was a box of Froot Loops.

"No thanks," I say, my tongue moist. The snow on the trail has been packed down by skiers; she walks in the long stripe left by a ski, one foot in front of the other. I walk in the middle, my boots making that crunching noise I love. Clean and squeaky, it always makes me feel strong. It makes me walk faster. Tree roots and tiny branches ping out of the path, struggling back to life after being flattened.

Trying to shake her off, I veer toward the middle of the conservation area, where the baby was found. When we first arrived in town, Mum and I explored all the trails until we located the old fort. The clearing opened up like the sun had exploded; buttercups and dandelions everywhere, grasses tickling my knees. In the middle loomed the stockade, just stranded there like a belt made of driftwood. After Craig Mitchell mentioned the body of the baby, I went back to the spot and looked for clues. I don't know what I expected to see: a bag of coins? a jade ring? I ended up taking a box of gummy bears out of my pocket and leaving it inside the blockhouse. It didn't seem so lonely then.

Now, in winter, the fort looks bigger. As soon as I step off the trail, the snow buries me up to my calves.

"Gimme those Cadbury Flakes," I say to the Little Heathen, high-stepping one boot in front of the other.

"We're not going to leave it for the baby, are we?" she asks. I hate that she's using the royal *we*. Queen E would not approve.

As I hike over to the fort, I hear her chuffing through the snow behind me. She is ruining my crunching noise. "At least your birth parents cared enough to leave you a little money!" she cries. "The orphanage found me on the doorstep with a big pile of nothing!"

❁ ❁ ❁

One afternoon, as we're filing out of school, Sherry Ann gets down to business. (We were all at the hockey game last night, where Patrick scored a shorthanded goal and the entire town gave him a standing ovation.) Right in front of me, right in front of Lori DiPietro and Jessie

Lawson and Laurent Belair, she goes up to Erik and touches him gently, on the arm, with her bare yet manicured hand. (This week, it's uncool to wear mittens or gloves of any kind.) Erik stops eating his PowerBar and looks down at his sleeve. "Yeah?" he says.

I pretend to stare at the outdoor rink just down the slope, where some of the students are playing jam-can curling with old bottles of Javex that have been emptied and weighted with sand. Craig Mitchell pulls his arm back and throws the stone with surprising grace. Gordie McLachlan, broom in hand, gets in front and sweeps the rink furiously, prolonging the glide. Subzero shuffleboard.

I start to move toward the game, my fists closing inside my pockets, when Sherry Ann's voice throws me out onto the ice. "Erik, Chantal here says she's one of you. That she's from Yellowknife. That she's eaten walrus flipper. That her mum and dad fell into Great Slave Lake when she was a baby."

The Javex bottle is still coasting; the whiskers of Gordie's broom are hurrying, hurrying. I don't know if the stone is going to make it.

Erik's eyes, double oil spills, study me. He has been fully powered by the PowerBar, but what I see there is a gentle recognition.

"Yeah?"

I try to nod and not nod at the same time. Sherry Ann whips out her cell and snaps a picture of us. I know this little face-off will be posted on the Internet in about sixty seconds. Her caption will read, "Two natives!" Sherry Ann's smile is a blinding explosion threatening to collapse the mine of lies I have dug for myself.

Erik studies my nods for a while. Rinkside, the Javex bottles are being retrieved, ready to be thrown again.

"Yeah," he says. "Good to meet you."

Sherry Ann's phone snaps shut.

❀ ❀ ❀

The next time I head to the fort, I spy the Little Heathen on the rink. She's dressed like a Victorian lady, her long tartan skirt fluttering around her ankles as she cuts figure eights into the ice.

"You just met him. He's not your brother." She, also, is too cool for mittens. Her blades are the sound of her jealousy being honed.

"Hallelujah for that," I say.

"Don't forget that you and I shared a crib at the orphanage. Doesn't that count for something?" She picks up speed, her hair streaming upward, one long twirl from a Coke bottle.

9

I keep walking.

Barbie's little sister, Skipper, is bouncing around in my packsack—another gift for the baby. As I duck under the arch cut into the stockade, thinking about how sucky it would be to have Barbie as a big sister, I see a cigarette hit the snow over by the blockhouse. At first I think it's Sophie Lafleur, until I spy the red-and-black-checked flannel jacket.

Erik's hair is hanging in his face, wing-like. He coughs, giving the cigarette butt the evil eye. "By the way," he says, "it's Inuit."

"What?" I say.

"It's INUIT, not Eskimo."

"I know," I say, looking up at the sky. I tend to look up when other people would look down. There's so much more to see up there, and that way, you don't have to focus on your shoes. You don't have to see any part of yourself.

The snow outside the blockhouse has been trampled into three shades of ugly. Erik begins to form a snowball with his bare hands. He makes a gentle pat-pat motion, and my stomach tilts back and forth like he's molding me too.

"Also, I grew up in a house, not an igloo."

"OK," I say.

"Listen, Chan–"

"My name is Chantal–"

"Let's call you Chan. I've heard you telling stories. You want to tell a real story? You need to have some hunters in it. Lots of hunters. And ptarmigan. You need to mention bears that take off their skins and walk around like human beings. You need to talk about bravery." He hurls the snowball over the fence.

I pause, thinking he's going to share a tale with me, but all he does is wipe his hands on his jeans. He lights another cigarette and the match falls into the snow, burning a hole. He's now so close I'm practically sharing the smoke. I turn to the side and cough like I'm dying on TV. We could be sitting around a campfire. He takes two drags, then the cigarette sails over the fence too, as if it's going after the snowball. He ducks through the blockhouse door and I follow, the packsack light on my back. Inside, dead leaves cower in the corners of the plank floor. My previous Cadbury offering is nowhere to be found. The ceiling of the blockhouse is so low that Erik morphs into a giant; he expands before my very eyes like those toy capsules that, when dropped in water, turn into sponges shaped like dinosaurs.

Before my brain knows what my mouth is planning, I say, "What are you doing in Ontario, anyway?"

Erik swings his arms like he's warming up before gym. His biceps are what my mum would call "great guns." He says, "You first. What are *you* doing here?"

"I'm from a hotel in China."

"See, kids? Not just a hotel!" His imitation of Mr. Little is dead on. We are laughing together. We are two Inuit laughing.

Erik stops. "Yeah well, my dad was transferred here. Government job."

He leans up against the rough log walls and I want to tell him that he should watch out or he'll get a splinter. That's what the Little Heathen would say, anyway.

With no warning, his hand shoots out and brushes my head. It's the softest thing that's ever happened to me.

"What was that?" I say. My hair is tingling. I'm afraid to look at him.

"Cobweb," he says. His arms begin to close around me and it's like I'm made of smoke. I shut my eyes; his breath tickles my cheek; I think about all the times I've practiced kissing a Sesame Street Ernie puppet, wondering where to put my tongue. I hear a zipper unzipping.

"What's this?" he asks. He's removed the vintage Skipper from my packsack and is holding the doll by her hair.

"It's a Growing Up Skipper," I say, my voice full of pebbles. "If you move her arm, her boobs grow."

"Get outta town," he says, pumping her weeny bicep up and down. "Hey, too bad this doesn't work on real girls!"

My face is on fire. My flat chest is tight. Out of the corner of my eye, I can see through the cutout in the blockhouse wall that passes for a window. The Little Heathen is framed there, the Cadbury Flakes in her hand. She waves.

"Please leave," I mumble.

"What?" Erik's eyes follow mine, but they don't change. The Little Heathen shoves the chocolate into her mouth.

"No, not you. I'm sorry!" I say, but the moment has already popped.

"Chan, my sister," he says. "Aren't you too old for dolls?" He leans down and plants one right on Skipper's lips.

❖ ❖ ❖

It's gym time again. We're supposed to be snowshoeing, but we can't move. Today, the snow is a horizontal beating; Gordie McLachlan tried to sneak back inside but Mr. Borislava told him to be a man. Being a man apparently means huddling together like emperor penguins.

True to form, Mr. Borislava hopped ahead of us into the woods and failed to notice that nobody was following. We try to loiter against the wall in our usual firing-squad formation, but the equipment glued to our legs makes nonchalance impossible. Sherry Ann Bedell is shoving tubes of ChapStick into her pocket. She is loaded for moose. Sources have informed us that Sherry Ann caught Patrick walking back from the shower naked last night. She'll never get over it. She has even forgotten to make her weekly fashion statement, which means that all the girls are at a loss for what to wear.

The snow finally turns vertical again, a signal to unstrap our snowshoes. Mr. Borislava is panicking his way out of the trees when Sherry Ann says, "Chan, tell us a story."

I am all out of stories. Ever since Erik showed up, the thought of him has swallowed up valuable mental real estate.

"What's the matter? Not enough room in your brain?" she says, not realizing how close she is to the truth.

I say, "Have you heard the one about the redhead who was born into a village in the Yukon? Her hair was so hot, it melted the igloo while she was sleeping, and her whole family was washed out to sea."

"Screw off, Chantal!" Her voice makes me jump. Though she's yelling into the hood of her fur-lined parka to conserve energy, I have never heard Sherry Ann this loud and this pissed. I quickly look to my cronies to see if anyone's planning to intervene, but everyone's too cold to take sides.

Just then, Erik's voice rings out like a bright coat in a blizzard.

There once lived an old woman and her orphan grandson Kautaluk. There was no one to protect them, so he was tormented constantly. There was no one to hunt for them, so they had to eat other people's leftovers. Then one night, the Great Spirit gave the boy the gift of enormous strength. Overnight, he threw boulders in front of the houses of the villagers who abused him. The people were frightened but he didn't say a word.

The next time the Great Spirit visited, Kautaluk learned that a white bear and her two cubs were approaching the village. The boy surprised everyone that day by outrunning the other hunters and killing the three bears by slamming them against the ice with his bare hands. Finally, everyone began to respect him, but when it came time to take a wife, he decided to demonstrate his powers once and for all. He chose to marry the daughter of his worst enemy. And overnight, he booby-trapped the igloos of the cruelest neighbors

12

by balancing trees above their doorways. In the end, his enemies ran away in fear. But those who had always been kind to him and his grandmother were allowed to stay.

There is something about Erik's voice that stretches time—that makes you remember your own stories and the stories of your parents and the stories of your parents' parents. As soon as he opens his mouth, he can't stop, telling about the woman who turned into a walking skeleton, about the ghost hunter who took a ghost wife and disappeared into a bowl of water. I understand immediately that his myths are the real deal; I also understand that he will never come close to kissing me again.

❁ ❁ ❁

Within a matter of weeks, Erik is the most popular guy in school. Patrick St. Amand (Patrick St. Amand!) lends him a hockey stick and they play shinny behind Canadian Tire. He hangs out in basement rec rooms all over town, high-scoring all the video games with Jessie Lawson and Laurent Belair. He goes snowmobiling with Gordie McLachlan. He hooks Craig Mitchell's huskies up to an old wooden toboggan and they fly through the forest preserve, laughing and barking. Sophie Lafleur's father even claps him on the back and says, "Son, I know it's not as exciting as harpooning seal, but come deer season, I want you along."

I am not surprised when a small fire breaks out in the blockhouse one afternoon, and a quick-thinking pupil from our school smothers the flames with a deconstructed snowman. It's all over the newspapers; it's on local TV; it's Erik, of course. To hear him tell it, you can practically feel the inferno on your cheeks. The Little Heathen confirms my suspicions: "*He* started the fire you know, by accident. It's true what my parents say; smoking will kill you." But it's not arson that bothers me. What bothers me is that Erik was at the blockhouse with Sophie Lafleur.

Pretty soon, everyone is asking him the same question:

"So, Qimirpik, you going to do the Polar Bear Swim? You could kick butt."

"Qimirpik, compared to what you're used to, this'll be the Florida Swim!"

And Erik just nods and grins, wearing his red-and-black-checked jacket like a superhero cape.

❊ ❊ ❊

The Polar Bear Swim takes place on a blurry river guarded by pines. A couple hundred people stand around a rectangle of open water that's been punched out of the ice and lined with cloth. One by one, they cannonball into the hole, men in shorts and toques, women in bikinis, two-legged icicles screaming as they drag themselves up the ladder and out the other side. One guy comes dressed as Superman; another one wears a kilt and carries a plastic sword. A lot of folks arrive in teams, sporting identical costumes.

The search-and-rescue workers mill around in orange jumpsuits, just in case, flurries starting to come down like dandruff. The newly crowned carnival queen, wrapped in a fur coat and sash, sells hot chocolate from a tent. It is a balmy minus five degrees Celsius.

Mum nods when I tell her I'm going to get a cup. I don't even need to give her my usual speech about chocolate's beneficial antioxidants. She's too busy gabbing with Constable Mitchell, who's sending her love beams through his eyes. I wonder if she notices. What she definitely doesn't notice is that underneath my street clothes, I'm wearing her old bathing suit. It barely fits because I don't have the bazooms to fill it out, but I've clipped the extra fabric with a clothes-peg. (Before you can participate in the swim, you have to get a written letter of consent from your parents, but I know my mum would never allow it.)

I stroll to the carnival tent, peeking at the liquid grave in the distance. Splash! Scream! Splash! Scream! At some point, Erik shows up and all the kids mob him. He catches me staring and I gaze up at the white sky, the clouds as invisible as I feel. *Just wait*, I think, *until you all see me become a polar bear.*

Gordie McLachlan's cousin Bronwyn takes the stage with her fiddle; she is semi-famous, playing at ceilidhs out in Nova Scotia. As her bow moves over the strings, she taps her boot, her breaths coming out of her in musical puffs. The town cheers.

Over by the hot chocolate, Erik finds me. His eyes are sick. His copper cheeks are pale. Under his red-and-black-checked jacket is a homemade T-shirt that reads, "Meet You At the North Pole." The words look like they were scrawled with lipstick.

"Chan," he says.

Forgetting that I'm not supposed to care, I ask, "What's the matter with you? Do you have the flu?"

"No, listen to me—" He grabs my arm, and I'm tingling all over again.

"When are you going in the water?" I ask. "Where are your folks?"

"They're out of town," he says. "I'm staying at Jessie's." His arm tightens; his eyes are whispering but I can't read them.

"Erik!" Sherry Ann Bedell is standing by the shore, her hands cupped to her mouth. "Are you ready?" She swivels toward me so I can get a good look, and my heart plummets through the ice when I see she's wearing the exact same T-shirt as he is.

"Oh," I say. "Oh. Of course."

"Chan–"

"See you at the North Pole," I say, and though it kills me not to be touching him, I pull away.

Erik! Erik! Erik! All of Lock City is chanting: the students and teachers from Batchewana, the skips from the curling club, the old fogies from the Croatian rest home, the *padres* from the Esposito Club. I can't help but watch as he and Sherry Ann head up to the big wound in the ice; they stop about ten metres away so they can get a running start. She goes first, screaming, her hair a long lick of fire; Erik, taking his time, keeps glancing back in my direction, his body suddenly fragile as he sheds his jacket. The spectators line either side of the path, applauding, but there he stalls, trembling in his girly T-shirt. The search-and-rescue guys are MIA. Way over by the bandstand, the emergency divers have searched out the fiddler and are getting their foreheads autographed.

The Little Heathen pops up next to me in a Russian hat. She looks awful. Though her fists are hidden inside a fur muff, I can tell she's wringing her hands. Her eyes are watermelon seeds. Her cheekbones are threatening to burst right through her skin.

"I'm on hunger strike," she volunteers. "My parents are threatening to send me to this weird summer camp. But don't worry about me— look at him."

She analyzes Erik as he swings his arms, jumping up and down. The great guns don't look so dangerous from where I'm standing. Erik backs up all the way to the end of the runway and—stumbling for the first couple of steps—breaks into a sprint.

I know the truth before she even says it, before the Little Heathen looks me right in the eye and says, "You know he's a fraud. You. Know. He. Can't. Swim."

It's all the story I need.

I shed my fleece, ripping off my sweater and dropping my jeans. My breath hits the air in plumes, the cold slamming open every door in

my chest, my heartbeat fighting with the roar of the crowd as the carnival mascot, a bear in overalls, bungles the two-step for laughs. There
is nothing funny about it. Erik will go down fast; he will sink like an
enchanted boulder.

My mother yells my name as I run, my legs pumping, the sun
throwing foil in my eyes, the ground as mean as concrete as I dash
across the solid water, the Great Spirit inside me! But I don't really hear
her—I do not answer to Chantal anymore. I do not answer to anybody.
I am invincible as I take flight, knowing—like those endangered turtle
hatchlings that are born on the beach and scramble to the sea before
they're gobbled up by predators—I have just one chance to succeed.
There are worse things to be than a polar bear. Did you know that under
their fur, their skin is black? Did you know they can swim for over a
hundred kilometres before stopping?

Photo by Nancy Redman-Furey

RACHEL FUREY received her MFA from Southern Illinois University and is currently a PhD student at Texas Tech. Her work has appeared in *Freight Stories* and *Hunger Mountain*. She is winner of *Sycamore Review*'s Wabash Prize for Fiction and *Crab Orchard Review*'s Charles Johnson Student Fiction Award.

Jody's Solo
Rachel Furey

When Jody fainted, I was lost in the glow of the tubas and trombones. We'd just taken the stage for the first of our dress rehearsals for the fall concert, and above me, domed lights dangled like glass ornaments suspended from a tree. The entire brass section took on a shine that made them seem like brand new instruments—not the old, dented creatures that had sat in our dim practice room for years. From my position behind the bass drum, the flutes shone like icicles. The trumpets looked prepared for a fine processional. Even my mallet had taken on a newfound glow.

In the middle of our first song, Bethany, lead flutist, lowered her instrument, and my gaze drifted to her chair. She sat just a couple feet from our band director's podium. But Mr. Scotts wasn't there. I could make out only the back of his shirt, his rear end in the air while he bent over. I thought maybe he'd dropped his baton and, in his attempt to retrieve it, was now flashing crack to an audience of empty chairs.

But when he stood up, Jody was in his arms. Her head was kicked back over his shoulder. A thin line of blood flowed from her lip. Later, people would ask me if, as Jody's twin, I had felt it—felt my lip hit the cool metal of the music stand or my knee bang into the stage. Maybe if the lights hadn't been so bright I would have.

I expected Jody to open her eyes at any moment—maybe reach a hand up to tickle Mr. Scotts in the armpit, if she dared. But Jody held still. The domed lights hanging above me grew hotter. Jody's face grew paler and she looked like someone else entirely. Not the girl who had held my hand on our first day of kindergarten when the automatic doors at the school's entrance frightened me. Not the girl who had once kneed Benjamin Waller in the groin after he called me four-eyes.

I was swept back to the Saturday afternoon I rose from a nap to find Jody balanced on the kitchen counter, Mom hugging Jody toward her body while cradling the phone with her other hand. Jody had been pink, lifeless. Her legs had dangled down against the cabinet doors, where I'd focused on an untied shoelace. She'd learned how to tie them the previous week, and because I hadn't yet, she'd taken every opportunity to remind me of that. Although I didn't yet understand what the word allergy meant—what anaphylaxis was—the untied shoestring signaled something was horribly wrong.

Under the stage lights, Jody didn't look pink. Her body wasn't swelling. In fact, her face was particularly angular, her collarbone particularly prominent—almost as if she were a sculpture with corners someone had forgotten to smooth. The line of blood began to roll down her neck. The glow from the brass section made me dizzy, and I dropped my mallet. Bethany scuttled off to call 911.

Jody and I had joked about how Mr. Scotts was germ-phobic. He kept a bottle of hand sanitizer on his music stand and wore a medical mask when one of the flute players was coming down with a cold. And yet there he stood, Jody in his arms, the hot stage lights making sweat rise on his forehead, and the blood from Jody's lip slowly dripping onto his own white shirt. It spread out the way water does on a towel, those small drips of blood blossoming into something larger, falling in such a pattern that if you looked at him from the side you would have thought the shirt was meant to be like that all along. He didn't say a word, and no one in the band came forward. Mostly, they played with the keys on their instruments the same way I shuffled my fingers inside my pockets. Jody never would have forgiven me if I'd gone to her, if I'd ruined her chance to drip blood onto Mr. Scotts's freshly pressed shirt.

As her twin, I earned a spot in the ambulance beside her and watched while the medics dabbed at the blood and checked her vital signs. I hit the record button on my cell phone so that later she could see the beautiful brown curls of the medic tending to her lip, his adept handiwork even as the ambulance careened over rises in the road. I showed her the other medic, too, the one with a beer gut and balding head, the one who kept watch on her pulse. He must have been self-conscious. Two minutes in, he raised a hand and said, "This isn't the place for that," holding a stare so serious I nearly broke down to tears. I ended the video.

The hospital waiting room was a swirling of smells: hand sanitizer, lotioned tissues, and the scent of crisp fall leaves that rode in on overcoats. I squinted in the harsh light, wishing I had ear plugs to drown out the sound of the woman gnawing on her nails beside me. While I answered a nurse's questions regarding Mom's work number, my mind blanked after the area code. I saw the numbers in pieces, like on a digital clock.

"It could be a three or a five," I told the nurse. "But definitely not a seven."

She patted my knee. "I'll try again in a few minutes," she said.

Moments later, I heard her on the phone, calling the school, getting the number I had forgotten, the number I later realized had been on my cell phone all along.

When I was finally released from my seat in the hospital hallway and allowed to enter Jody's room, a different nurse accompanied me.

"The IV contains nutrients," she said, "don't be scared by that."

But the fact that she had to say it meant that I was.

She showed me to a seat beside Jody's bed, and I took the hand attached to the arm free of tubes, giving it a gentle squeeze. Jody's lip was swollen and stitched, cleaned of blood, but so large it looked like it might pop. Her face was the color of freshly fallen snow, and the hospital gown was a pale pink that made me sick to my stomach. It wasn't a color Jody ever would have worn. We thought of pink as a color for girls who played with Barbies and planned out their prom dresses months in advance.

I was keeping watch on the doctor, who had entered the room to read over Jody's clipboard and check her IV, when Jody finally opened her eyes. She gazed over at the doctor and then back at me. With her arm not full of tubes, she elbowed me in the stomach. "Fat ass," she whispered, eyeing the doctor. It was the first thing I'd heard her say since our conversation at lunch, when she had told me she was eighty-seven percent sure the cafeteria worker with a pink hairnet—the one missing a front tooth—was out to get her. The cafeteria worker's niece ran cross-country for a neighboring school and never raced nearly as well as Jody did. In Jody's mind, poisoned food was how the cafeteria worker struck revenge. Jody had eaten only one bite of the afternoon's tuna casserole before tipping the contents of her tray into a trash can. She had been doing a lot of that lately.

I doubted Jody's story about the cafeteria worker was true, but she was right about the doctor. His belly protruded well over the waist of his pants. His walk reminded me of that of a penguin, and his arms had such trouble clearing the mountain of his stomach that I wondered how he managed to button his pants each morning.

"Hey, there," the doctor said to Jody, as if she were a five-year-old he was trying to soften up before a tetanus shot.

When the doctor stuck out his hand for a shake, I tried to squeeze his hand extra hard, but my fingers were smaller than his and couldn't eclipse the entirety of his monstrous hand. Jody's shake was worse than mine—only a slight curving of fingers.

The doctor read from Jody's chart, a small spit bubble wavering in the left corner of his mouth. He mentioned that her electrolytes were low and that her essential nutrients weren't what they should be. As he spoke, his thick chins bobbed up and down, moving like waves.

"Anorexia," he finally said.

But neither of us believed it. Jody ran cross-country, was an eighth grader that had made the varsity team when they'd needed more runners to fill out their squad. Jody had had to pass a physical fitness test in order to move up. Just last week, she'd set a new personal record. On the wall in our shared bedroom, a calendar portraying distance runners showed the image of Paula Radcliffe winning the New York City Marathon. She didn't look much more than skin and bone—her muscles small things hidden somewhere in between. Her eyes were still bright, and her body strong enough to plow through 26.2 miles.

"I run," Jody told the doctor. Then she added, "Fast. Have you seen me in the newspaper?"

"I've seen her in the newspaper," I said before he could answer. "She's *fast*." The newspaper from last week's meet was days old by then, or I would have run around the block to collect one from a corner deli.

The doctor crossed his arms over his chest. He breathed so deeply his stomach moved beneath his scrubs. He said he thought it'd be best if we waited for Mom to continue the discussion. Then, before he left, he set the hospital menu in Jody's lap.

❀ ❀ ❀

I was finishing off the green Jell-O the nurse had brought Jody when Mom walked in. She caught me with the plastic spoon in my hand, my tongue turning a faint green. I considered reminding her that she never made green Jell-O, never made any Jell-O at all. She basically thought artificial colorings and flavorings were poisons that would make tentacles grow out of the sides of my head. I swallowed the last gulp, the lime taste lingering on my tongue.

While Mom pulled a chair up beside me, Jody lifted her head off the pillow to sit up. The effort made muscles in her neck bulge, and she shifted herself back against her pillow, sitting a little higher this time.

"Don't worry. I'm fine," Jody said. She gave the IV bag an evil eye and covered her tubed arm with her sheets.

Mom let out a sigh that could have sent my plastic spoon skittering across the floor. She twirled the one long braid that ran down her back. She'd just come from the garden department at Lowe's and smelled of dirt. It showed underneath her fingernails and she picked at it while Jody and I explained to her how monstrous the doctor had been. We guessed he had his clothes tailor-made. We guessed his bed was reinforced. We guessed he went through an entire refrigerator of food every day. We gained energy as we went, the way a fire picks up with wind, and by the time the nurse returned, we had invented a car powered by his own body fat.

The nurse asked Jody if she wanted anything. Her voice was soft and her words finely punctuated. We could have fit ten of her inside of that doctor.

Jody requested some music. "It's freakishly quiet in here," she said, scrunching up her face so that it all curled toward her nose.

"Honey, I think she means something to eat," Mom said. She rubbed at Jody's arm and suggested vegetable soup.

Jody shook her head.

The nurse brought a boom box anyway. It was an old hulk of a thing and smelled like Pine Sol. I guessed the nurse had salvaged it from a janitor's closet and given it a good dusting. I pulled out the antenna and tuned it to the local rock station. Mom thrust the hospital menu toward Jody, and Jody brushed it away, pushing it out of Mom's hands so that it slipped under her bed. Jody pulled back her blanket and sheets, and, at first, I thought she was going to retrieve the menu. She stood, two pale skinny legs sticking out beneath her gown, her kneecaps looking two sizes too big for her body. She snapped her fingers and began to dance to the music, her bare feet jimmying across the floor, her hips making her gown dance from side to side. Out her one small window, the sun set in streaks of orange and red, its light sifting through the pane to offer Jody's skin a healthy hue.

I stood to dance with Jody. Because of her IV, we had to keep our dancing in a tight line. We moved from the head of her bed to a couple of feet from its end. Once, while Jody swung her arm back and forth, her IV touched my arm. It was smooth and warm—made goose bumps rise on my arm. Jody did the moonwalk in her bare feet while I tried for something close in my sneakers. I felt Mom's eyes on us, and it only made me dance harder, made me wish I'd paid more attention during our hip-hop unit in gym class. I pumped my arms and twirled my hips. I did a tap dance in my sneakers, and sweat burned on my back.

When a slow song came on, Jody took my hand. "Dance with me," she said.

Her hand was cold and soft. Mine easily encircled hers. She led us from floor tile to floor tile, expertly staying within the reach of her IV. Her gown fluttered like an evening dress as we moved. Her breath fell on my face in gentle puffs, like the air being pushed out from between a butterfly's wings as it flew.

"Girls," Mom finally said toward the end of the song while Jody dipped me toward the floor, "we didn't come here to dance."

I met Jody's gaze, her eyes the color of bluebells Mom had once brought home from work. Jody smiled. "We shouldn't have come here at all," she whispered to me.

By then, she was panting. I guided her back into bed, telling her that the DJ had to take a break. I replaced her sheets, looking at the sheets instead of her, then I slipped back into my own chair. Mom had pulled out her scheduler, had already begun to plan out the doctor appointments. She turned back a page, where our concert was circled in red and planned for that Friday—just three days away.

I squeezed my hands together, worried Jody might not be able to attend. She'd been the whole reason I had joined in the first place. Our move from seventh grade to eighth meant after-school band practices and concerts that required traveling. My time with Jody was slipping away, and because cross-country was a sport that would leave me in an asthmatic mess in the middle of the wilderness, or impaled on a tree branch after tripping down a hill, I'd chosen band.

Mr. Scotts had granted me a tryout that had ended with a mallet slipping out of my hand and hurtling toward the chalkboard, where it made a mark that couldn't be erased. He'd suggested I might spend a year practicing and then try out again. I politely nodded. Then I showed up during his free periods and lunch breaks. I told him I practiced my drumming skills with twigs from the back yard because my mom was too cheap to buy drumsticks and mallets until I had a real place in the band. Once, I'd even dropped to drumming on my stomach, telling him it made a different sound, depending on what I had just eaten. None of this convinced Mr. Scotts, so I made a call to my grandfather, who had some Cherokee in his roots, and he made a call to Mr. Scotts, giving him a speech about drumming and what it would mean for my soul.

Mr. Scotts let me join the band three days later, and I gave Grandpa the credit, but later learned that the band's previous bass drum player had been suspended for smoking pot in one of the practice rooms.

I'd had high hopes for my first concert with Jody. I thought, after her clarinet solo, she might look back at me, standing beside the bass drum, and offer up a wink. Mom would bring two bouquets this time; one for Jody and one for me. Mom would tell me how good I looked beside the drum.

Even then, in that hospital room, a nurse dabbing at the sweat on Jody's forehead from our dance, another taking her racing pulse, I couldn't help but ask Mom if she was going to make it to the concert.

"Eliza," she said. She closed her planner and gripped it tightly. Then she let out a breath of air. "This just isn't the time." She rose from her chair and went to sit at the edge of Jody's bed, running her fingers through Jody's hair.

"It's the damn IV," Jody said. "I felt just fine until I got here." She looked up toward the ceiling, where the lights were bright, but not as bright as the ones on stage.

Mom pushed the nurses away, asking for some time just for us. She leaned in toward Jody and wrapped her arms around her thin body. Mom spoke in whispers not meant for me while she massaged Jody's scalp. Although Jody couldn't see it from her angle, tears slowly flowed from Mom's face.

❀ ❀ ❀

Jody was assigned three doctors: a psychiatrist, a nutritionist, and a new physician accustomed to working with teens. Mom had the numbers to all of them hanging on the refrigerator, and I called each personally, mentioning that I was Jody's twin and the concert was of significant value to me, but especially to Jody. I added that, as Jody's twin, I really knew what was best for her, even if Jody hadn't mentioned the concert herself. The psychiatrist thanked me for calling, but said that files were confidential—even when it came to twins—and that if I wanted to talk, he'd be happy to sign me up for an appointment of my own, given my mom was willing to pay for it. The nutritionist said a concert wasn't really her area, but that if Jody did go it'd probably be best to avoid eating dairy before her solo. I never got through to the physician, but the receptionist said she'd leave a message.

Mr. Scotts assigned Jody's solo to Stephanie, a senior with breasts so large some guys traded in their lunch money just to touch one. She had to take care to position her clarinet directly between her breasts, or, I guessed, serious chafing occurred.

During our last practice before our concert, Mr. Scotts cut us off in the middle of a song. He looked back at me and rubbed at the collar of his shirt. "Eliza," he said, "you're not keeping the beat."

I wanted to blame Stephanie, who earned the attention of the entire row of trombone players each time she stood for her solo. While most percussionists could keep the beat, even if the rest of the band was off, I relied on each section of instruments to play almost perfectly so that I could stay on track. I didn't tell Mr. Scotts this. I shrugged my shoulders. He sent the band for a water break and when I returned, he handed me a softer mallet, said the snare drums could keep the beat and all I needed to do was provide a quiet accompaniment to their playing.

That evening, Mom served cooked asparagus, black rice, and lean grilled chicken. Jody had chosen the entire menu, yet she spun all of it around on her plate. She sliced the chicken into tiny pieces and mixed it with the rice. She scooted the asparagus to the other side of her plate.

Across the table from us, Mom spent more time watching Jody than eating. "Eventually, you'll have to lift your fork to your mouth," Mom said.

Jody pushed her chair back from the table, but Mom's gaze kept her from going too far. "Remember last weekend," Jody said.

Jody had won a race she wasn't even supposed to win. It was one of her favorite courses. The girls ran up the steep dam, disappeared into the woods for most of the race, and then weaved their way through the trees to run back across the dam and then down it before finishing. Jody liked running free from the crowd and even though she'd gone into the trees in fourth place, she'd come out of them in first. She had looked as strong as ever as she sprinted across the dam, her legs pushing forward in lengthy strides, despite her height topping out at a few inches over five feet. As she ran, her shadow slipped along the dam beside her. Its size, double that of Jody, seemed to say: *I'm bigger than I look.*

Jody's first steps down the side of that steep dam had been careful and slow—like an ice fisher working to step only on sturdy ice. Jody had always liked going up hills more than down them, and as she came down the dam, down the trail laden with mud that her racing spikes spat up onto her calves, there was a second in which her front foot caught in the mud. It began to slide forward, her knee bent toward the ground, and her back leg kicked out behind her. Two other racers were sprinting their way across the dam, casting their shadows toward Jody, who looked like she might fall at any moment. For a second, I actually wanted it to happen. I wanted Jody to fall face first into the mud. I wanted her to slide down that trail on her belly. I wanted to find out how quickly she could get back up and if she could keep running afterward.

But Jody didn't fall. She lost a little ground on those girls, but she still crossed the finish line first.

Mom sighed. She remembered the race.

"I'm not really sick," Jody said. She continued on before either of us could argue with her. "I think I need to go to the concert tomorrow." She sat up straighter and drove her fork through a piece of asparagus.

Due to her schedule of doctor appointments, Jody hadn't quite made it back to school yet, but that didn't stop me from believing Mom might let her go to the concert anyway. I looked over at Mom, trying to show her I, too, was eager for Jody to attend. I even pushed my plate—entirely cleaned—toward her.

Mom set down her fork and ran her hand over her mouth. She shook her head. "I don't think so," she said. "Not until you eat a full meal."

I looked over at Jody, but her fork didn't make a move toward her mouth. Then I looked over at Mom. "You're still coming, right?"

She pushed her chair back a few inches from the table, then pulled her napkin out of her lap and folded it beside her plate.

"I really want you to be there," I said.

She rested her head in her hand, and when she spoke, her voice was soft. "Eliza, I have a lot that needs figuring out right now. I need to get in time at work and then make a meal for Jody." She pulled her glasses off and set them on the table.

I knew the waterworks were coming, but I kicked my chair backward and stood up from the table anyway. I looked over at Jody and then back at Mom. "Weren't you the one who was supposed to keep this from happening?" I threw my arms up in the air, the same way Mr. Scotts had each time I had failed to keep the beat.

Mom's head dipped lower and her shoulders shook. Jody rested a hand on my forearm and looked up at me with eyes that longed for me to stop.

But I was already standing. My arms were already in the air. "You shouldn't miss my concert just because you didn't notice Jody getting sick. I shouldn't have to pay for that." My voice was so loud it didn't even feel like mine. I tossed my silverware onto my plate.

Mom didn't say anything, just ran a finger along the edge of her folded napkin.

Jody glared at me. "Enough, Eliza," she said. She shoved her plate away from her and then went to Mom, rubbing a hand along her back and whispering something I couldn't hear while I carried my plate to the kitchen.

❋ ❋ ❋

Hours after dinner, after I had drifted into an uneasy sleep, I awoke to a sound that reminded me of a dog we'd once had. When Ginger had grown old, she'd panted all the time. Even in her sleep. It had been light and airy. Mom had said it was Ginger's way of practicing her breathing; in heaven, she'd have to carefully time her breaths as she jumped from cloud to cloud.

The panting sound that evening was Jody. She stood in front of our full-length mirror, practicing her solo. She practiced without the reed, and she practiced in nothing but her bra and underwear. The small nightlight plugged into the wall made her thin body glow.

"Jody?" She didn't budge, and I went to her.

Even in the dim light, Jody's vertebrae seemed too knobby. Her ribs reminded me of the starving children shown in television commercials. Her shoulder blades looked like plates pushing their way out of her skin. Once, we had looked so similar people had told us we must be identical. I'd seen Jody every day of our lives, and I'd seen myself in the mirror, but I couldn't remember ever beginning to detect such stark differences.

Jody must have seen me standing beside her, but she didn't stop playing. Her fingers shuffled along her keys; she continued to pant into her clarinet.

"You could put in your reed," I finally said. "I'm awake and Mom sleeps like a log."

She looked over at me, her lips purple with the cold of the room.

I took a step closer and noticed the goose bumps that coated her body. "You could at least put on some clothes," I said.

Jody stared into the mirror. "Dr. Montrose says I don't see my body the way everybody else does. I don't see what's really there. She says every mirror I look into right now turns out to be like one of those silly mirrors in the funhouses at the fair."

"So you thought you'd play your clarinet naked?"

"I thought I'd stare at myself as long as I could. I got bored, and it only seemed right to play my clarinet."

Her hand began to shake, and I took the clarinet from her. I set it on her bed. I peeled out of my pajamas so that I stood in only my

underwear, an old purple pair the color of a plum. I stepped in front
of the mirror, allowing her to see both of our bodies at once, mine a
thicker, more curved version of hers. Then I took Jody's hands in mine.
Her fingers were tiny, slim things, and I gave them gentle squeezes as if
I could pump air back into them.

"Close your eyes," I said.

"It's already pretty dark in here."

"Just close your eyes."

She did, and with her eyes closed, I let myself really look at her
body: her barely there chest, her sunken-in cheeks, her stark ribs. When
my throat went hot with tears, I gave her hands another squeeze. Then
I guided one of her hands to her ribs, and the other to my ribs, pressing
her palms down so that she felt both of our bodies at once. Her fingers
were cold against my skin, and goose bumps rose on my body, too, starting where her hand had touched and spreading across my limbs. I held
her hands at our ribs a moment and then switched them to our collarbones. I ran her hand along the length of my collarbone, then I ran her
other hand along the length of hers.

When our hands reached the second half of hers, tears began to spiral out of the closed corners of her eyes. She dipped her head and then
held it high again. A deep groan, something like the call of a bullfrog,
began to rise from her throat. Her hands tried to slip out of mine.

I held them tight. I showed her her hips and then mine. I showed
her my biceps and then hers. I asked her to feel her elbow with her opposite hand. She began to fall toward the floor, and I hugged her just
under her shoulders, guiding her toward her bed, her feet managing
to carry enough of her weight that I wouldn't collapse underneath her.
She fell into her bed, her eyes wide open, tears trailing down the sides
of her face, heading for her pillowcase.

"Do you want your pajamas?" I asked. I looked around the room, but
couldn't find them.

She shook her head, and I pulled the comforter over her. In the
closet, I found another blanket. That went over her, too. I hid her sharp
edges—the ones I had somehow managed to miss and now wanted to
forget again.

When I took apart her clarinet and placed it back in its case, Jody
began to cry harder. She buried her face in her pillow.

"You'll get another solo," I told her.

Jody tugged a tissue off of the nightstand and wiped her face. "I
wish I could give it to you," she said.

"You don't really mean that," I said.

She cried even harder, and I sat at the edge of her bed, rubbing her head until her crying slowed. I sat on her bed an hour longer, watching her chest gently rise and fall, counting her breaths and timing my own to match hers.

❁ ❁ ❁

I considered not going to the concert at all. Then it occurred to me that no one would miss me, that Mr. Scotts might be happier to have no bass drum player at all rather than a poor one. I didn't want to let him off the hook that easily. And I thought Mom just might change her mind about attending the concert while she drove me there. She didn't. She barely came to a stop at the school's front curb, left me just enough time to escape the car, and then zipped back to Jody again.

When the curtains opened, the auditorium seemed smaller with so many people packed into it, and the stage felt more cramped than ever, even though there was the same number of us—minus Jody. Mr. Scotts wore a tuxedo with a tail that made him look like a beaver. Stephanie wore a dress so flamingo pink I wanted to vomit. My bass drum mallet felt heavier than ever.

While Mr. Scotts introduced our songs to the audience, I gazed up at the domed lights, imagining they were the butt end of a rocket that would launch at any moment, busting through the ceiling and granting us all more breathing room. Then he turned around, lifted his baton, and led us into our first song.

When Stephanie stood for her solo, when she plunged into that first low note, her heel tapping away on that old wooden stage, I strengthened my grip on the mallet. Sweat slipped down my back, under the fall sweater Mom had chosen for me, what she had said would be her own special way of attending the concert. It was a deep orange. When Mom had brought it home from the store, she'd presented it to me as if she'd found the one right sweater in the world for me, but I thought it only made me look like an odd pumpkin. I guessed no one in the audience knew me, or maybe only as Jody's twin. Maybe they whispered to each other, *that pale girl under the lights, she's Jody's twin.* Or maybe they didn't see me at all.

When Stephanie hit her third note, I began my own solo on the bass drum. An unused mallet sat on the tympani next to me, and I took it in my left hand so that I could beat on both sides of the drum at once. I'd never had a good sense of rhythm—Mr. Scotts had told me that before—and I guess I didn't then either, unless you count the sort of rhythm that doesn't follow any song at all. It crept up from my feet, moseyed its way into my hips, and shot from my shoulders to my wrists, where it traveled the length of the mallets. It was supposed to be a slow song, but I fit in as many poundings as I could. In the echo of the drum across the stage, and the vibrations rising from the floorboards and into my feet, it was hard to tell when I was hitting the drum and when I was just feeling the echoes of my hits. But I couldn't stop. I imagined myself as a frog calling out into the night, forcing my call as far as I could in the hope I might get a response. I drummed with such force that sweat dripped from my forehead and pooled in my palms. It took an extra tight grip to be sure the mallets didn't slip away. The snare drum player, who stood only a couple of feet from me, and whose grip on his sticks was not as tight as mine, had to fish one of his drumsticks from the floor after it slipped out from between his fingers.

Stephanie gave up part way through her solo. She spun around to look at me, and I met her stare. Tears welled in the corners of her eyes, and she hammered a heel into the floor. With her hand not gripping the clarinet, she squeezed the edge of her hideous dress. Then she bit her lower lip, doing her best not to cry on stage. I looked away from her and into the line of light cast by one of the overhead lamps. My poundings had made the light gently rock from side to side, and a shower of dust glowed in the light, drifting toward the heads of the trombone players. The stage was like a snow globe, the audience only outsiders incapable of cracking the glass and shrinking enough to fit inside. No one on stage could escape the glass walls we had erected together, and while I could, I controlled the rotation of our globe—made the snowfall.

❖ ❖ ❖

After the concert, Mom was ten minutes late picking me up. During those ten minutes, I worried that maybe Jody had been rushed off to the hospital again. Maybe Mom had lost it and force-fed Jody. The image of Mom pinning Jody to the floor with her knee, preparing to pour a smoothie down her throat, formed in my mind just as Mom's headlights appeared in the parking lot. She pulled into a spot, and I took my time getting to her. As I climbed into the car, I searched her face for signs as to how the night had gone. Her fingernails looked clean; there probably hadn't been any forced feeding.

"So, how'd it go with Jody?" I asked.

She told me in short, clipped phrases. She had made three separate dishes for dinner. Jody hadn't eaten more than a couple of bites of any of them.

Even after our pajama-less dance in the dark the night before.

I squeezed my hands together and swallowed hard. As I fastened my seatbelt and Mom weaved her way out of the parking lot, she asked if I had any ideas for something else she might try. She had skimmed every recipe book she had. She had brought up the library database and asked Jody to pick a book from there, but Jody hadn't given her any help. Mom noted my special twin connection, as if Jody's mind was a radio channel I could tune into whenever I wished. I shrugged my shoulders. If I had known what Jody would eat, I would have told Mom already.

"How was the concert?" Mom asked when we pulled to a stop at a red light.

"Fine," I said. It wasn't like I had ruined the entire concert, or even an entire song. Stephanie didn't get her solo, but Mr. Scotts directed the rest of the band back into the song, and together, their sound outlasted mine. After we had finished the last of our four songs, Mr. Scotts pulled me aside and told me he forgave me. He said it was probably hard times for me and my family. He asked if there was anything he could do, and I refrained from asking about another solo.

Mom smoothed her hands along the steering wheel and sung softly to a Beatles tune before looking over at me again. "Did Stephanie have enough time to learn Jody's solo?"

"She didn't show up," I said. "Mr. Scotts gave the solo to me," I lied.

Mom nodded, as if considering my answer, and then slid one hand from the steering wheel long enough to tap my knee. "Every band needs a bass drum player," she said. "Some things don't need to be shown off. They just need to be."

"I played the solo, Mom," I tried again. I kicked at my backpack, which sat at my feet.

"Okay," she said. She stared out the window at the stars beginning to show, at the streetlamps casting a glow on the sidewalks. "While we're at it, Jody ate dinner tonight, too." She ran her tongue along her front teeth. The light turned green. Mom took off. "Jody started with a tall glass of chocolate milk," Mom said. She turned the radio down and continued to fabricate the rich details of Jody's uneaten meal as she drove: steak topped with fried mushrooms and onions, garlic and herb mashed potatoes. Her eyes lit up, dancing in the light of the oncoming cars. Her fingers tapped on the steering wheel while she spoke. She drove ten miles over the speed limit.

When she came to the Caesar salad, she worried herself with the details of Parmesan cheese and croutons. "Do they make whole wheat croutons?" she asked me.

"I don't know," I said. "There doesn't have to be croutons on the salad."

Mom shook her head. "There has to be croutons. Jody used to love croutons."

She was right. Jody had loved croutons when she was five. She left them for last. She made them into a train that she ran around the bottom of her bowl, zigzagging through salad dressing puddles.

"I bet there would be whole wheat croutons at that natural foods store," Mom said. She squeezed the steering wheel. "But they're closed tomorrow." Her shoulders began to shake. She bit her lower lip in almost the same way Stephanie had. She swerved into the opposite lane, just crossing the yellow line, and then straightened the car again.

Afraid we might crash before I could tell Jody what I'd done with her solo, I said, "You forgot dessert. You had warm apple pie." It was my favorite, but for some reason, Mom always remembered it as Jody's. Maybe because Jody loved picking apples at the orchard each year, loved bringing a bag to cross-country meets so her teammates could bite into them after a race.

I told Mom about the pie's whole wheat crust, carefully rolled out on our counter at home, and the cinnamon and oats sprinkle she'd added to the top of the pie. She'd timed the baking of it perfectly so that it came out of the oven just minutes before she and Jody finished the meal. Steam rose from the pie as it was served. Even Jody hadn't been able to say no to the pie, and they'd eaten it while candles glowed on the table.

At the candles, I recalled the bag of Raisinets I had purchased from a vending machine before the concert, the bag that now rested in the front pocket of my backpack. I began to wonder if I could get Jody to eat any of the remaining raisins, and while I did, I went astray with details like where Mom and Jody were sitting at the table and whether or not the ceiling fan was on. Mom dipped closer to the steering wheel. We still had a few miles before we made it home. So I added a scoop of vanilla ice cream atop each of their slices of pie—ice cream that melted so quickly they had to be sure to eat it before it turned to milk.

Photo by Tula Morales

THERESA DUVE MORALES grew up in Des Moines and now lives in Woodland, California, with her husband and two daughters. She teaches middle school art and is working on a short story collection. "Jacinto's Teeth" is her first publication.

JACINTO'S TEETH
Theresa Duve Morales

Jacinto spent two years of his adolescence without his two front teeth. It would have been devastating had he lived elsewhere, surrounded by a different group of friends. As it was, they all wore the same T-shirts, passed through many hands, worn on many backs; small hole under the right sleeve, a frayed collar, printing in Spanish or English worn and unreadable. Their socks, if they wore them, had holes or were darned. They went barefoot or wore shoes with flapping soles or broken laces tied together in knots. That the shoes stayed on well enough to kick a soccer ball, to spin around an opponent and outrun him the length of the field was all that mattered. Today Jacinto had on the nicest shoes—new shoes, a gift sent from the States.

"Señor Tenis," his friends giggled proudly crowding around the gleaming white shoes, fingering the stripe on the side. "Cone-vare-say. *Sí*, All Stars Cone-vare-say," they repeated to each other, proud to recognize an American label. They tugged at his arm and pulled him out on the street, fighting over which team the faster shoes would play on.

It was 1978, Mazatenango, department of Suchitepequez, Guatemala. Jacinto was fourteen years old. At the same time he was playing soccer in the street, one hundred kilometers to the northwest in the highlands of Huehuetenango, Tomás Machic was returning home after attending a union meeting with fellow farm workers. He entered his front door to find three militia men at his kitchen table, eating the *tamales blancos con chile* that his wife had prepared for his dinner. She lay dead at their feet next to the bodies of his son and nephew.

As Jacinto spun the ball around a defender, a bus was being stopped at a checkpoint just outside Sololá, forty kilometers to the northeast. All the passengers were instructed to get off and line up facing the bus with their hands up. They were searched for identification at gunpoint and then returned to the bus with the exception of Ariel Peña, a student from the University of San Carlos in Guatemala City, who was put in the back of a Jeep and never seen again.

As Jacinto glanced over his shoulder at Magdalena on the sideline in Guatemala City, where he had traveled twice on the bus with his grandparents and both times eaten ice cream, Marisol Ortiz was approaching the back door of a boarding house where Hugo Sandoval and Angel Ordoñez were renting rooms. Both classmates of Ariel's, they had recently marched with him in a successful campaign to protest the government's increase in bus fares. Marisol knelt down next to the two bodies she found there in the dirt alleyway, took Angel's head in her hands, and turned it only enough to see the lips she had allowed to suckle the nipple of her left breast briefly just the night before, covered with blood and dirt.

But Jacinto's world was smaller than the country he lived in. In it there was a wood fire for him to set in the stove each morning before school. There were shoes to mend and sell in the *zapateria* after. There was sometimes aching hunger in his belly and other times, warm tortillas and black beans to fill it. There were nights of sweet sleep in his hammock that hung in the corner of the home he shared with his mother and uncle, and filling every moment that remained to him, there was soccer.

And right now there was a scissor kick which, if successfully performed, would clinch his team's victory and impress the beautiful Magdalena who looked on in anticipation from the sideline.

"*Dále, dále,*" the encouragement of his teammates reached his ears as he jerked his body horizontally, face-up into the air, arching his back while driving his right leg straight up to meet the ball that had just raced past his eyes. The laces of his shoe met the ball with a smack at the same time that the front of his thigh slammed into his cousin's right ear.

"*Ay, puta vos cerote.* You shithead. You hit me." Jacinto's back slammed against the dirt as Carlitos, who had tried to head the ball before the crash, landed on top of him, both hands clutching the right side of his face.

"*Tu madre, cerote.* You're the one who hit me." Carlitos rolled off his cousin moaning dramatically as he curled up into a fetal position.

Jacinto pulled his leg to his chest and clenched his eyes shut as he tried to wish away the pain. He felt a sharp kick in his ribs. "Damn it, Carlitos." He grabbed at what turned out to be a bare ankle and opened his eyes to see Magdalena staring down at him.

"Jacinto, Carlitos," she whispered urgently. "*La policía.*"

Both boys looked up just in time to see their soccer ball, which had drifted far to the right of the goal, being slashed with a knife and their teammates scattering. Carlitos, who was already up, and Magdalena each took Jacinto by an arm and pulled him upright. The three ran between a nearby bakery and *tortillería*.

"We'll get another ball, Carlitos," Jacinto reassured his cousin in a hushed voice as they rounded the back corner of the bakery and headed down an empty alleyway. "Here, this way." He took Magdalena by the hand and pulled her around another corner and past a long winding concrete wall. An empty but lush, green lot lay on the other side. Jacinto knew how to get in. Carlitos trailed behind them.

"No, Chinto, not through there!" Carlitos slowed as he approached the opening in the wall that Magdalena and Jacinto had just passed through. He stopped under the archway and fingered the rusted hinges that had once opened and closed the gate of the abandoned property.

"What? What is it Carlitos?" Magdalena asked anxiously. She was already hidden behind a large coffee bush, but came out to peek around the wall and make sure they hadn't been followed.

Carlitos pointed at the tangle of vines and trees behind them. "The old cemetery is underneath there."

"*No seas hueco,*" Jacinto scolded Carlitos as he stepped over a fallen branch and tugged Magdalena a little farther into the shadows. The possibility of frightening Magdalena a little excited him. "You're such a chicken."

But Carlitos stayed frozen. He looked down at his feet firmly planted at the edge of the alleyway, then slowly moved his gaze up to meet his cousin's. He pointed a trembling finger at Magdalena. "If your girl is bleeding right now," he said in a forced whisper, "and she goes through there, the spirits will take over her body."

Jacinto stepped backward, tugging Magdalena in a little farther. "You're nuts, Carlitos. *Es cuento de viejas.* The old ladies love to tell those stories."

"Yeah, and you ought to listen to them," Carlitos said. "You didn't see my sister. It was her time and we walked through there. She was talking crazy things. Some language I couldn't even understand. I held up my medallion to her face and she hissed at it." He grabbed the Virgin Mary hanging around his neck and held it up for effect.

Jacinto, forgetting his circumstances, howled out loud. "*Eres loco!* Your sister hates you. She just wanted to see you pee your pants."

"Go to hell, Chinto!" Carlitos, now more terrified of spirits than police, turned and ran back down the alleyway.

Jacinto took a step through the entryway in his cousin's direction, but then realizing his opportunity, turned back around and grabbed Magdalena by the arm. The two ran deeper into the forbidden tangle of green until they were well-hidden in the shadows. Jacinto stopped and leaned back against the trunk of a mango tree and pulled Magdalena toward him.

"What about you Maggie? You scared of this place?"

"Sounds like you're the one who should be scared, Chinto." She stepped in front of him; close enough that he felt her blouse brush against his shirt. Jacinto felt his face warm up and he looked over Maggie's shoulder to avoid contact with her eyes.

"Look at me Chinto." She touched his chin with her fingertips and guided his face back in her direction. "Do you think I'm possessed?"

Jacinto's first kiss tasted a little like the strawberry-flavored Fanta he drank out of plastic bags in the marketplace. He wasn't sure he liked it. As Magdalena's lips pushed against his, he felt the inside of his front lip buckle in the space where his teeth used to be. The exhaustion in his legs from the soccer game and the run through the streets overtook him and he thought his knees might give way. He thought he might throw up. His trembling fingers reached up his neck and searched for his crucifix as he squeezed himself out from between Magdalena and the tree trunk. He willed his tired legs to start moving, and a bewildered Magdalena watched him as he raced back out into the alleyway, following the route his cousin had taken only minutes before.

Jacinto ran until he was sure Magdalena could no longer see him. The sun was low in the sky. He should get home soon. It wasn't safe on the streets after dark and he didn't want to worry his mother. He slowed to a walk and then stopped and bent over to gulp in air. He was on Second Avenue across from el Estadio Carlos Salazar Hijo where the Suchi soccer team trained and played. He crossed the street, looking up at the stadium walls. They were covered with painted advertisements. His index finger traced the edge of the giant "B" in "El Banco Industrial." He would play in this stadium one day. He knew it. He dreamt it.

He would have a nickname like the Brazilian players. Manilla, Little Peanut. That's what his coach called him now. He was short. But he was fast. The fastest on his team. No, he needed a stronger name, a manlier name. Flecha Veloz, The Speeding Arrow. That was better.

"Flecha Veloz, Flecha Veloz," he repeated his new name in a whisper. His fists punched the air and his feet dribbled an invisible soccer ball. Yes, much better. That was a good name. He giggled and pressed his cheek against the cool cinderblock wall, closing his eyes.

He could hear the crowd shouting "Flecha, Flecha, Flecha" as he ran onto the field dressed in a blue uniform. The sound filled his ears. He looked into the stands, searching for Magadalena.

"Flecha, Flecha." She and Carlitos waved wildly.

The team took the field and the referee signaled the beginning of the game; the applause grew deafening. A storm of firecrackers shook the stadium; the sound so loud and real that it forced Jacinto's eyes open, shattering his daydream. He looked up in the direction of the noise. Not firecrackers. Propellers. A green army helicopter was landing on the field.

Jacinto sprinted toward the stadium gate.

Fwhit, fwhit.

Jacinto turned in the direction of the whistling and saw Don Pedrito, the ice cream vendor, wheeling his white cart toward him. Jacinto caught up with the old man before he went through the gate. "Don Pedrito, how many times have they landed today?"

"Three. Can you believe that?" Don Pedrito leaned close. "Three times Chinto. With this much disruption the players will never be ready for the match with Los Rojos this Sunday." He spit on the sidewalk. "And you know how much we hate those sons of bitches."

Don Pedrito rolled his cart into the stadium and Jacinto followed him. A Red Cross ambulance was parked at the field's edge. Jacinto scrambled up to the second set of bleachers and scanned the field. In a cloud of dust the Suchi team split itself in two, each group moving to opposite ends of the field. The helicopter hovered above the center of the field for a moment and then lightly touched down. Red Cross workers ran toward it with a stretcher. Jacinto scratched the space between his teeth with his tongue.

The helicopter doors swung open. A man dressed in camouflage jumped out with a rifle strapped across his back. He shouted something to the ambulance workers as he reached into the helicopter. Jacinto caught El Loco Flores, the Suchi goalie, crossing himself. Jacinto did the same.

The first soldier they carried across the field was dark-skinned like Jacinto.

Indio, Jacinto thought.

The soldier was dressed in camouflage like the man who helped carry him. His pant leg was ripped and blood-soaked. His fists waved in the air, opening and closing, clutching at nothing. As the stretcher passed near him, Jacinto could hear the soldier groaning. An odor rose from his body, horrible but familiar; like the air on Christmas morning bitter with the lingering smell of fireworks; like the burning flesh of a freshly plucked chicken set over a wood fire to singe away any remaining feathers.

The second soldier they pulled from the helicopter made no sound. A bandage wound around his head and covered one eye. As he passed, his arm dropped from the stretcher jerking his face toward the stands. It was a very young face; clear skin, no sign of a beard or moustache. Two perfectly straight white teeth shone between his parted lips.

Jacinto's eyes followed the stretcher until the Red Cross workers closed the ambulance doors. He turned to see the helicopter lift itself back into the heaven it had dropped from. The players retrieved their ball and moved back to the center to reclaim the field and finish their practice.

Jacinto nodded to his friend who already had a crowd around him waiting to buy ice cream and followed the ambulance out of the stadium. The sky was quickly turning to dusk around him. He broke into a run.

The buildings on Jacinto's street sprang straight up from the sidewalk and connected to each other in one endless wall. Each home or business along the wall was identified by its own door and street address and its own bright peeling paint color. Two doors along the wall belonged to his family. Jacinto tried the green door first, but his Uncle Beto's shoe shop was locked up for the night. The blue door beside it belonged to their one-room home. He opened it. One bare light bulb cast its light over the kitchen table where Jacinto's mother served coffee to his uncle and a man Jacinto did not know.

"Chinto, *m'ijo,* sit," his mother said. She took his arm gently and guided him toward the empty chair.

Jacinto looked warily at his uncle and the stranger before sitting. His mother took a cup from the shelf and set it in front of him.

"You're leaving tomorrow night," his uncle said, fixing his gaze on his coffee cup.

Jacinto shivered. He ran his tongue over his lips searching for strawberry, but Magdalena's kiss was long gone. "Why? Where? I don't understand."

"Don Bonifacio will take you," his uncle said, still not looking at him.

His mother filled Jacinto's cup and then set the kettle on the table. She stirred a spoonful of sugar into his coffee and then, as there was no chair for her, crouched down next to Jacinto and folded his hand in hers.

"M'ijo, your grandmother—she's sending for you. You will live in California. You will get a good education and learn English. When you get there, they will fix your teeth."

Jacinto pulled his hand away from his mother's. "I don't want to go." He stared at his coffee. "I like it here."

His uncle pushed a stack of bills toward Don Bonifacio.

The round-faced man counted the bills. His gold-rimmed teeth glinted through his smile. "I will return for the other half after my Tijuana contact gets the boy safely to Los Angeles. He will be safe with us—but, if for some unforeseen reason, we don't make it across," he tapped the stack of bills on the table, "I assure you that all of these will come back to you." The coyote rolled the bills between his hands like a tortilla and tucked them into his vest.

"Please, I don't want to go," Jacinto said.

His uncle took a gulp of his coffee. "You're an ungrateful little shit." He squinted at Jacinto. "Your grandmother won't do this for me, her own son, but she'll do it for you. What the hell will you do if you stay here?"

"I'll play soccer. I'll play for Suchi," Jacinto said, trying not to let his voice crack.

"A little indio like you?" His uncle's green eyes looked at him, cold and hard. "You're lucky the army truck hasn't come to drag you off. You'll be a soldier before you're sixteen."

Jacinto wrapped his trembling fingers around his cup to still them. "The army can't get me. I run fast. I'm the fastest on my team." *Flecha, Flecha, Flecha*, he repeated in his head and clenched his eyes closed, willing them to hold onto their tears.

His uncle slammed his cup spilling coffee on the table. "The money's been paid."

"Please," Jacinto said, "Don't make me go."

But his mother and uncle were already outside the door bidding Don Bonifacio goodbye.

That night, Jacinto's dreams shook him and rocked his hammock in the corner near the room's only window. In his dream, Don Bonifacio's round face was looking at him; his gold-lined teeth opening and closing, opening and closing. "You will go to California. You will learn English. I assure you, if we don't make it, all of these will come back to you." He repeated the same things over and over, tapping the bills on the table. "All of these will come back to you. You will go to California."

But as he spoke and tapped the bills, the light skin of the coyote's face began to darken. His hair grew long and coarse and braided itself into a gorgeous black rope. As his mouth opened and closed, the gold edging of his teeth disappeared and ceased to glint under the bare bulb above the kitchen table. His brown eyes widened and his voice turned softer, sweeter. "Are you scared of me, Chinto?"

Jacinto watched as the coyote turned into Magdalena. She held Carlitos' soccer ball. It was round and perfect as it was before the police had taken it. Jacinto smiled at her, relieved, and reached for the ball. "Maggie, how did you get it?"

But Magdalena pulled the ball to her stomach and wrapped her arms tightly around it. Jacinto was confused. He grabbed her sleeve. She was wearing camouflage.

"Magdalena, what's wrong?" He struggled to pull the ball out of her arms. "Give it to me, please. Magdalena, *por favor*."

But as he pulled at the ball, her soldier's uniform began to bleed. She hissed at him and spoke in words he didn't understand. The blood covered the ball; covered his hands.

"Please, Magdalena. I don't want to go. Por favor." He jerked the ball free and fell backward, backward, backward. The second before he hit the ground, he woke up.

His heart was pounding. *Only a dream. Only a dream.* He pulled himself up and swung his legs over the edge of the hammock. The wooden shutters on the window were slightly ajar, allowing a sliver of moonlight to shine through across his mother's cot. She was still asleep. His uncle's hammock was covered in darkness, but Jacinto could hear him snoring.

He gave his eyes a moment to adjust and then stood up quietly. He walked over to the window, pushed the shutters open and boosted himself up. The window opened onto a shared courtyard. It contained an outhouse, a well, a large tub for washing clothes, and in the center, a brick woodstove. Beside the stove was an old door set up on cinderblocks with a bench on either side. The women had tied a plastic tarp to tree branches above so they could sit below and sort beans and husk corn and gossip without being burnt by the sun or pelted with rain.

Jacinto hopped down and walked over to the makeshift table, sitting to face the almost-full moon.

The light shone on a post leaning against the trunk of the Jacaranda tree. His mother had set it there so her chickens could climb it at night and roost in the branches. They made soft, cooing sounds above Jacinto's head. Who would take care of the chickens when he was gone? Who would light the woodstove? He didn't want to leave his mother; he didn't understand why she couldn't go with him. She said there was no money for her right now and his safety needed to come first. He would do well in school, get a job and send her money. That would make her happy. But who would protect her? Someone must protect her.

Not his father. His father wasn't coming back. Jacinto was sure of that. "*Mujeriego*," his grandmother called him. A no-good womanizer who had never wanted his mother.

"Indio," his uncle called him. Too poor and useless to take on the responsibility of a family.

His mother insisted that none of it was true. She kept a picture of his father tucked in the pages of a Bible that she could not read. When no one was around she showed it to Jacinto.

"*Que guapo, verdad?*"

Jacinto agreed that his father was handsome. He recognized his own high forehead in the photo, the sharp sculpted cheekbones, the dark skin that was lacking on his mother's side of the family.

"Don't believe what they say *m'ijito*. Your father was sick. He left because he loved us, to protect us from the tuberculosis. If he could be here with us, he would be."

An owl passed overhead as Jacinto sat pondering. He waved a stick at it and looked up protectively at the chickens.

He wanted to believe his mother. He tried to think of his father as good and kind and loving. But despite his efforts he knew his uncle and grandmother were right. His father did not care about them. And underneath it all, he thought that is what his mother believed too.

How else was it that she allowed another man to enter her life? Don Meme, the *panadero*, had a stall at the market where he sold his fresh baked bread. Jacinto remembered seeing them stealing glances when he went with his mother to do the shopping. Jacinto thought she invented errands just to have a chance to see Don Meme. "The chickens didn't lay today." And she was off to the market for eggs, leaving her basket on the table. "We need oil for the plantains." But would return without oil and they would eat their plantains boiled instead of fried.

Sometimes Don Meme would stop by when he was out making deliveries. His mother would giggle, crack the door and teasingly send him off. "*Al ratito* . . . a little while, not now." And then go back to her mortar and pestle, but grinding now with a little more energy in rhythm to a secret song that played only in her head.

Jacinto scratched in the dirt with his stick. When the neighbor women sat at this table they scolded his mother.

"You are playing with fire," said Doña Elsa.

"You're a married woman," said Doña Consuelo.

"What are you thinking?" said Doña Monchita. "Any other woman in your situation would already be out on the street. Your brother's charity has its limits."

The doñas did not know that the house belonged to Jacinto's grandmother, and that his uncle could not throw them out without enduring her rage, but the gossip scared Jacinto, nonetheless. His uncle was a violent man and not happy sharing a home with his sister and fatherless nephew.

Did the doñas tell Tío Beto about Don Meme? Jacinto didn't know for sure. Only that there was anger in his step the evening he came back early from the cantina. Carlitos and Jacinto were kicking the soccer ball under the streetlights when he passed. Carlitos picked up the ball and gave his cousin an anxious look. They followed their uncle's giant strides through the house and into the courtyard where his mother was bent over the washtub, rinsing the last of the dinner dishes.

"*Puta, cerota*," Beto yelled. "You have a husband."

A plate slipped from his mother's hand as her brother approached her. His palm came down hard on the side of her face. Carlitos dropped the soccer ball. Jacinto threw himself at his uncle, fists pummeling, feet waling, but his uncle tossed him to the side, discarding him like an empty sack. Jacinto's knees hit the ground at the same time that his mouth hit the edge of the cinderblock table.

No, his father was not coming back. He dropped his stick to the ground and remembered how his teeth had lain there glistening in a pool of scarlet.

The next morning Jacinto and his mother took the bus to Samayac, a small town about an hour ride from Mazate. The *brujos* lived there—witches, healers. Good ones, his mother said. Jacinto had been to Samayac once many years ago, but only remembered sitting on a blue bench under a lemon tree. As they stood crammed in the aisle of the bus holding on to the seat backs, he asked his mother about it.

"Yes, the brujo's name is Don Valeriano," she said and, "Yes, there is a blue bench behind his house."

She explained that they had come to see Don Vale last when his grandmother needed a blessing before leaving for California. His mother told him that she had also gone to see him when she was pregnant. His grandmother had traveled safely to California; Jacinto had been born without problems. Don Valeriano was a good brujo. He could be trusted.

The bus let them off at the edge of the small village. It was not yet midday, but the sun was already hot and Jacinto's shirt stuck to his skin. Yesterday afternoon there had been a tremendous thunderstorm, which had cooled things briefly, but its relief had worn off and now the earth steamed like a freshly cooked pot of rice.

As in Jacinto's neighborhood, the houses were constructed of brightly painted cinderblocks, topped with corrugated tin roofs and connected together in long waving lines. Jacinto and his mother followed one of the colorful rows of homes and businesses up a long slow hill. They passed small stores advertising Cerveza Gallo and Cigarillos Casino and stepped over children playing marbles on the sidewalk. When the wall changed color to lime green his mother stopped and knocked. A small gray-haired woman answered.

"Good morning," his mother said. "Is this the house of Don Valeriano?"

"*Pasen adelante.* Come in, come in." The gray head bobbed as it turned and they followed it through the doorway.

Inside, a small man reached for his cane and pulled himself up from his chair. He did not look magical or wise. Brown, wrinkled, balding. He smiled at them and Jacinto noticed that the few teeth he had were black with rot. They followed him toward the home's only other room. On a wooden table in the center of the room sat a lit white candle, a small black pouch, a cigar and a bunch of *ruda*—the same herb-of-grace his mother grew in pots to protect their home—tied together with a cotton string. Jacinto and his mother sat down at one side of the table and the brujo at the other. Jacinto could see the lemon tree and blue bench through the window behind him.

"Now, how can I help you?" Don Valeriano asked.

"My son leaves tonight for California," his mother answered. "I want his journey to be a safe one. Can you help us with that?"

"I can help you." He lit his cigar on the candle, gave it two puffs and then blew the smoke in their faces. He stood up and hobbled over to a bookcase housing two statues. Jacinto looked at the statue of Jesus Christ seated in his throne; his red robe open, revealing his sacred heart. Thorns pierced his heart and head. Blood trickled down his mournful face, his hands, his bare legs. The statue of Maximón looked jollier. Many people called him San Simón, but Tío Beto said that that was wrong. He was not a real saint, just an Indian superstition, which was why he was not allowed inside Catholic churches, but instead greeted his faithful in church entryways and courtyards. Maximón sat in a wooden chair dressed like a gentleman in a black hat and suit coat. He had a black mustache and full beard. His mouth was open and he looked as if he were laughing. To his right lay a plate of corn tortillas and to his left a small glass of Guaro—Guatemalan rum—the saint's favorite drink.

The brujo stuck the smoking cigar in Maximón's mouth and returned to his seat. "I will help you," he laughed, "and now Jesus and Maximón will help you, too." He supported himself on the edge of the table and then let his body plop into his chair, letting out a grunt as he settled in.

He picked up the black pouch. "Now, let's see what the beans can tell us," he said. He held it to his heart and mumbled some words in Cakchikel.

Jacinto's mother did not speak the Mayan dialect, but Jacinto turned to her for understanding anyway. She shushed him with her eyes and puckered her lips into an arrow that she used to direct his attention back to the table.

Don Valeriano spilled the contents of the pouch into his open hand and then scattered the red beans in front of them. He studied them for a moment, took in a deep breath, and tapped his fingers on his chin.

"Hmmm." He looked over the beans carefully. "You will travel safety to the Mexican border."

He scooped up the beans, shook them and threw them a second time. He pondered. He grunted. He scanned all the beans and then settled his eyes for several seconds on one that had rolled apart from the others. He cleared his throat, hacked, and spit on the floor beside him.

"No problems in Mexico either. Two good souls will get you safely to the border."

A final time he gathered the beans and tossed them, studying them carefully. He looked at Maximón. Then at Jesus. Then back at Maximón. He looked at Jacinto and his mother.

"No problems," he said. "I see no problems. This will be a good journey." He chuckled as he looked at the young traveler. "You are in good hands son, very good hands."

The brujo stood up again and instructed Jacinto to do the same. "Here, let me clean you now." And using the ruda like a small broom he swept over every part of Jacinto's body chanting in the same mysterious language. When he finished he pulled an even smaller pouch from his vest pocket.

"An amulet." He handed it to Jacinto's mother. "Pin it to the inside of his clothing where no one can see it and he will travel safely."

"Bless you," she said with hopeful eyes. She walked to the bookshelf, kissed the feet of each saint and then tucked a few bills into the red coffee cup between them.

At the door, Jacinto's mother thanked Don Vale and gave him a quick hug. Jacinto shook his cold hand.

That evening, Jacinto's mother walked him to the bus terminal. They passed Carlitos's house, Jacinto's school, and the cemetery where his grandfather was buried.

As they walked, Jacinto thought about the education he would receive and the English he would learn in California. He wondered what his new school would look like and if there would be a girl there as beautiful as Magdalena. He thought about the new teeth the American dentist would make for him and moved his tongue around in the empty space in his mouth, imagining how it would feel when it was full. He practiced smiling. He carried two changes of clothing, a comb, and an autographed newspaper clipping of El Loco Flores in his backpack. He carried the dinner he'd been too nervous to eat in a small paper bag.

At the terminal, they found Don Bonifacio waiting beside the bus with the three men that would be traveling with them. Jacinto was the only child.

His mother hugged him. "M'ijo . . ." She didn't say anything else, but she didn't let go of him either.

A hungry dog sniffed at their feet and rubbed against their legs. Her ribs poked out through her matted red coat and her teats hung full and low. Jacinto peered down at her through the folds of his mother's skirt and wondered where the dog's puppies were. He broke off part of a tortilla from his food bag and let it drop to the ground. Then he tucked his amulet into his mother's apron pocket. She didn't notice. He didn't want to let go of her, but it was getting dark. It wouldn't be safe for her on the streets. She pulled herself away. The coyote put his hand on Jacinto's shoulder and nudged him toward the bus. His mother turned her back on them and headed home. Jacinto stepped up into the doorway of the bus and stopped. He turned and watched his mother walk away. He smelled the roasting corn of a nearby vendor and felt the sting from the wood smoke in his eyes. He heard women's voices singing, "*Quiere su cafecito? Tortillas con carne?*" and watched passengers hold coins and paper bills out the bus windows as they reached for steaming paper cups and dinners packaged up neatly in banana leaves. He saw young men jump from bus top to bus top, tying down baskets and brightly colored bags with long pieces of rope. A warm breeze blew from the north. The bus driver started the engine and marimba music blasted from the radio. A chicken in the front seat squawked. Jacinto raised his fingers to his mouth, felt the depression behind his lips and wondered what else he might lose.

Photo by Hieronymus Jones

CHRIS BELDEN is the author of the novel *Carry-on*, published by Rain Mountain Press in 2012. His stories have been published in *Skidrow Penthouse* and *VENU*, and he is co-author of the feature film *Amnesia*, starring Ally Sheedy. Belden teaches writing at Fairfield University and at a high-security men's prison. In 2011 he received his MFA from Fairfield University.

TALK
Chris Belden

Peter Morgan was on the phone getting the bad news: His mother had wrecked her car again, running it into a telephone pole on McKinley Avenue.

"*She's* fine, not a scratch on her," his wife, Cindy, told him as he stared out the office window at a freight train slowly rolling past. Every turn of the train's wheels gave off the high-pitched whine of metal on metal. "But the car," Cindy said, "It's pretty much done for." Morgan imagined the old Dodge Intrepid, already dented from various fender-benders and parking lot mishaps, with its hood accordioned against a telephone pole.

"That's it then," he said. "No more driving for her. I'll have to call Joe over at Smiling Taxi. Maybe we can set her up with an account."

Al Klar, the station manager at WTLK, stuck his jug-eared head in the door. "Three minutes," he said before moving on.

"Gotta go," Morgan told Cindy. "It's show time."

Morgan left his office and walked down a narrow hallway crammed with metal file cabinets, stray office chairs, and stacks of books. He entered Studio B and waved at Tommy Sanchez, his engineer, who sat in the control room on the other side of a large pane of glass. Beyond the control room, in Studio A, Nick Dander was reading the noon news update. Morgan sat down at a desk in front of a microphone and slipped on his headphones. He heard Dander's deep, radio-ready voice announce that somewhere halfway around the world an American serviceman had been killed by insurgents. The four incoming call lights were already blinking furiously.

While he waited for the newscast to end, Morgan thought again of his mother. It irked him that she had called Cindy about the accident and not him, her own flesh and blood. Here was this eighty-four-year-old woman behaving like some naughty teenager, delaying punishment by fessing up to the less threatening parent. And here *he* was, in the role of strict father, thinking, with some embarrassment: Well, she's not going to get away with it.

The news ended, there was a brief commercial, then, at precisely 12:05, Sanchez gave the signal.

"Happy afternoon," Morgan began, as he always did, continuing the unfortunate tradition begun by the previous host of the program. "Welcome to Lunchtime Chat."

✿✿✿

After the show, Morgan drove over to Shorb Street and parked his Hyundai in his mother's driveway. His parents had moved here eight years ago, and, even after all that time, he was still not used to the place. At the old house—the one he'd grown up in—there was a side door that led from driveway to kitchen, and it lent arrivals and departures an air of informality. But now, as he rang his mother's front doorbell, Morgan felt like a salesman. He scraped his shoes across the bristly AstroTurf welcome mat and coughed self-consciously.

The door swung open. "Look who's here," his mother said. She stood aside and added, as if she'd been waiting for him all day, "Well, come on in."

A few minutes later, they sat in the kitchen drinking peppermint tea. "Have you seen the car?" his mother asked. "It's totaled. At least that's what Carl told me." Carl—who, as far as Morgan knew, had no last name—ran the service station down the road. He wore oil-smeared coveralls and chewed big cigars and filled gas tanks till they overflowed.

"I called Joe Taglione over at Smiling Taxi," Morgan said. "He says he'll start up an account and give you the senior citizen rate."

His mother scowled. It was an expression Morgan had noticed only since his father, the original Peter Morgan, died five years ago. Sometimes he wondered whether she'd been holding it back all those years, or perhaps it had simply never registered with him. While he was growing up, his mother had always seemed so placid and eager to please. Now she was often curt and had no trouble expressing her less flattering opinions about things. He supposed he should be thankful she was still relatively healthy. Her hair was dyed a squirrelly brown color that didn't fool anybody, but other than that she looked good for an octogenarian. Slim, with an upright carriage, her arms remarkably toned. That and her good coloring were due, she claimed, to her hours spent in the garden. A bouquet of her own fresh flowers—he didn't know what they were called—burst from a vase on the kitchen table.

"Why can't I just get another car?" she asked. "I can afford it."

"We'll see." After thirteen years as a radio talk show host, Morgan had learned that, with certain people, there's no use arguing. "But for now," he told her, "you'll have to use the car service." He wrote the Smiling Taxi phone number on the chalkboard by the telephone, and, after hesitating, drew a smiley face next to the number.

"That's cute," his mother said. "I haven't seen one of those in years."

When she opened a box of cookies Morgan knew he was expected to stay a little while longer. He sat back down at the table and sipped at the lukewarm tea.

"Today's show went well, I thought," his mother said.

"Uh-huh." For reasons he refused to analyze, the idea of his mother listening to the show made Morgan nervous.

"I noticed that woman called again. What's her name?"

"What woman?"

"The woman who goes on. You know . . ."

"Carrie?"

"That's her. She calls a lot."

Carrie was indeed a regular, one of those people who called once or even twice a week to make sure, Morgan theorized, that the world knew they were still alive. But Carrie was different from the others: She had the sexiest voice Morgan had ever heard. She talked endlessly about the most mundane topics, but her voice had that raspy, booze-and-cigarette quality that Morgan associated with raw sex. Today's critique, for instance, of the city's public bus system sounded to Morgan like a pleasantly obscene phone call. He kept her on the air for a full five minutes, dragging the transportation issue well into the ground before Sanchez began signaling frantically, running an invisible blade across his throat, to cut her off.

"It's a free country, Mom," Morgan said. "People can call all they want."

"I'm just afraid people will turn their dial when she comes on, is all I'm saying."

The sun slid behind an oak tree in the backyard, bathing the kitchen in a metallic gray light. Morgan felt tired—but then he always felt tired in this house, with its funereal smell of flowers and rotting *House and Gardens* on the shelves.

"How's little Peter?" his mother asked. "I wish you'd bring him over more often."

Morgan told her that they'd be over the following weekend, but that his son was in the midst of the Terrible Twos and was a menace to society.

"I don't believe that nonsense," his mother said. "*You* never had the Terrible Twos. And you know why? Because your father and I weren't threatened by you."

"What are you talking about?"

"You parents are so crazy these days! You give an infant anything he wants—when he wants it—and then when he grows up a little bit, all of a sudden you expect him to disregard everything he's ever learned. It makes no sense!"

"Mom, have you been reading a book?"

"You have to be a parent, not a *friend*," she said.

"Mom."

"Maybe then he'd finally deign to talk."

Morgan's ears burned at the mention of this touchy subject. His son Peter, at twenty-seven months, had yet to say his first words—no "Mama," no "Dada," nothing. When asked to repeat a simple word or phrase, the child responded with a blank stare. He could *hear* perfectly well—ask him to retrieve the stuffed platypus Grandma bought him and he'd run right to it—but he patently refused to speak. Dr. Daruwala assured Morgan and Cindy that this was not all that uncommon, that the ones who start late are often very bright, but Morgan never quite bought it. He worried that maybe they had waited too long to have a child, that his son might be stunted in some way as a result. Still, he repeated the doctor's assurances to anyone who made inquiries.

"Thanks for the tea, Mom," he said. "I have to get back to the office now."

"Bring him over Sunday afternoon. I'll show you how it's done."

"We'll see." Morgan pecked his mother on the cheek and rushed out the front door.

❋ ❋ ❋

Back at WTLK, Morgan ran into Sanchez in the hallway. The engineer was short and square-ish with a thick black beard flaked with dandruff. His passions were electronics and dirty jokes. He'd recently had to publicly apologize to one of the female secretaries so traumatized by an obscene limerick that she'd threatened to file a harassment suit. Since then, Sanchez told his jokes only man to man.

"Hey, nice show today."

"So-so."

"No, it was good. You know how to talk to those people. I know *I* could never put up with them."

"Thanks. I guess."

"Listen: How are women and tornadoes alike?"

"Not now, Sanchez," Morgan said, opening his office door.

"Okay, I'll let you think about it. It's a good one."

There was a message on Morgan's desk that Cindy had called. His wife used to be an attorney but was now at home full time. The change had been profound. When Morgan came home from work he'd often find Cindy, with little Peter in her arms, dancing through the house to old records from the 1970s. "That's the way, uh-huh, uh-huh, I *like* it!" she'd sing, and Peter would giggle and shake in her arms. Once in a while she'd tell Morgan about having lunch with her old lawyer friends and she'd talk about them as if they were heroin addicts. "I can't believe I did that all those years," she'd say. "What was I *thinking*?" But Morgan had always admired her lawyering; her powers of attorney had turned him on. She used to wear pinstriped jackets and skirts that showed off her muscular calves and thin ankles. Her hair had been coiffed into a professional style, short and pleasantly bristly at the back of the neck, and she'd visit an electrologist regularly to remove the dark fuzz over her lip. Now she wore loose jeans and men's flannel shirts; her hair, turning gray in places, hung shapelessly to her shoulder blades; and kissing her was like making out with a bearded lady. "I've gone to pot," she used to say regularly after Peter was born, until the day when, fed up about something else, but at the same time really meaning it, Morgan said, "So *do* something about it." This led to a long night of angry lecturing about men's unrealistic expectations, the havoc wreaked by childbirth on the female body, and pornography, after which Cindy both stopped complaining about her appearance and did nothing about it.

When his wife answered the phone, Morgan could hear Peter bawling in the background.

"What's the matter with Peter?" he asked.

"Oh, hi. He's being impossible today. He refuses to wear his sweater to go outside."

"Don't give in to him."

"What?"

"My mother says we're threatened by Peter. We can't just let him do what he wants."

"I'm not threatened. Are you?"

"A shrink once told me I was threatened by anything I can't control."

"That includes just about everything, then, doesn't it?"

"Anything else exciting going on there this afternoon?"

This was Morgan's coded way of asking if Peter had spoken. He used to broach the subject more directly but he'd grown tired of the answer and now preferred a more general approach.

"Not really," Cindy said. "Hey, I gotta run. Peter's trying to go outside on his own."

"Make him put his sweater on!" Morgan shouted, but she had already hung up.

On his way to the men's room, Morgan ran into Al Klar.

"You like that Carrie girl," Klar said. "I can tell by the way you egg her on."

"She should have her own show. I'd listen to her talk about *anything*."

"And you do."

Klar stood there, on the verge of saying something else. This was a habit of his—he believed in the dramatic build-up. The problem was that the dramatic build-up usually led to nothing of much importance.

"Al," Morgan said, "I gotta go to the bathroom."

"Right. Oh—don't forget we're going remote tomorrow."

"That's tomorrow?"

"Yeah. Kempton Motors."

"Again?"

"They're a big advertiser, Pete. You'll do the program live from the show room. It'll be fun."

"Can't wait," Morgan said, retreating into the men's room. He hated remote broadcasts. He was a creature of habit. He liked coming to the office, he liked the familiarity of the studio, and most of all he liked the solitude. Remotes were open invitations for people to come and gawk at him in a public setting. Radio was for aural consumption, he argued. But then commerce always wins out.

❁ ❁ ❁

On his way home, Morgan tuned the car radio to WTLK. Jules Green was hosting the drive-time talk show. Morgan shook his head as Green chewed out, then hung up on, one of his callers. Green had a voice like boots on shattered glass and took joy in harassing his callers, but he was very popular. In fact, the drive-time show had the highest ratings of any on WTLK, and Green's salary was the largest in the market. Rudeness pays, Morgan thought, and he wondered what would happen if he got a little tougher on his own callers.

As he pulled into his driveway, Morgan heard another familiar voice on the radio. It was Carrie, calling Jules Green's show. She wanted to talk about property taxes. A wave of jealousy rolled over him. Carrie was *his* caller! Why on earth would she want to talk to Jules Green? Morgan sat in the driveway with the motor running while Carrie went on about the death of the inner city. Her voice—warm, moist, perhaps lubricated with alcohol—flooded the car. After about thirty seconds, Jules Green interrupted her.

"You're boring my listeners!" he shouted. "Get a life!" Then he hung up. Morgan cursed Jules Green and his high salary, and turned off the radio.

As he made his way to the front door, he heard music blaring inside: "Love Will Keep Us Together." He looked around at the neighbors' houses, hoping no one else could hear.

Inside, he found Cindy traipsing from one end of the living room to the other with Peter in her arms. The boy beamed when he saw his father and leaned forward with arms outstretched. He had dirty-blond bangs, blue eyes, and a bowed upper lip that lent him an expression of coyness.

"How's my boy?" Morgan asked, accepting the hand-off from Cindy.

"He's got a runny nose," she said. Then to the boy: "That's what happens when little boys go outside without a sweater."

"*Honey*," Morgan whined. "You weren't supposed to—" He held Peter at arm's length and pulled out a handkerchief to wipe the snotty sheen beneath the boy's nose. "Maybe you'll *want* to wear a sweater next time, eh, little man?"

He set Peter down and they both followed Cindy into the kitchen, where she began to tear leaves off a head of iceberg lettuce and hurl them into a colander. She wore a pair of baggy khaki trousers and a sweater. From behind, even with the graying ponytail, she might have been a chubby adolescent boy.

Peter plopped down in the corner with a book. He loved to look at the pictures and could amuse himself that way for hours on end. If pressed, Morgan would have had to admit, guiltily, that he preferred this to one of those motor-mouth children always asking questions. He wondered, even more guiltily, if Peter had somehow intuited this, and that's why he refused to talk.

"How was your day?" Cindy asked.

"Fine."

Cindy frowned, then started slicing a large ripe tomato. "Your mother was very lucky this morning. Her car took all the damage."

Morgan opened the refrigerator. The top shelf was jammed with bottles of milk and apple juice, but toward the back he spotted the thin green neck of a beer bottle. As he reached inside, he felt a tug on his pants leg. Peter stood beside him.

"Whatcha need, fella?" Morgan asked. The boy pointed vaguely into the fridge. "What? I can't know what you want unless you tell me."

Cindy watched, disapproving, from the sink.

"Come on, you can tell me, Peter," Morgan said. The boy looked up at him with large, wet eyes. He moved into the small space between Morgan and the fridge and set the tip of his little index finger on a bottle of juice.

"What *is* that stuff?" Morgan asked. "*Ap-ple juice.* You can have some if you tell me what it's called."

"Just give him the juice," Cindy said, and returned to slicing tomatoes. Morgan grabbed the juice bottle and the beer and slammed the refrigerator door shut.

❀ ❀ ❀

That night, as Morgan lay in bed trying to read a spy novel, Cindy fussed around the room, tossing dirty clothes into the hamper, slamming drawers, and sighing dramatically every ten seconds. Though his instincts told him to ignore her, Morgan knew he would have no peace tonight if he didn't deal with this right away.

"What is it?" he asked.

"Nothing." She had stripped down to panties and brassiere, and it pained Morgan to see the doughy rolls that collected above the elastic of her panties.

"Please, Cindy—don't insult my intelligence. There's a bee the size of a tennis ball up your ass. What's the problem?"

"My *problem*," Cindy said, stopping at the foot of the bed to look down on him, "is that I don't know who talks *less*—my son or my husband."

"I talk all day long. It's my job."

"Oh, right. I forgot. The big talk show host. He'd rather chat with his crazy callers than his own family."

"My callers aren't crazy," Morgan said, thinking of Carrie, and Jules Green's rude dismissal of her.

"You won't even tell me how your day was!" Cindy said.

"My day? My day was boring!"

"Your mother was nearly killed, Peter. You know, some husbands would come home and tell their wife every effing detail."

For some reason, ever since she'd given birth, Cindy had started using that ridiculous euphemism: "effing."

"You want every *effing* detail?" Morgan asked. "You'd be asleep in half a minute."

"Do you ever think about what my day is like? Stuck here all day with a person who doesn't utter a word? Not a single syllable of verbal communication? I was so happy when your mother called to tell me she'd nearly been killed in an accident. A voice! A human voice! And then when my husband comes home, is it any better? No! More silence."

"You can call your friends," Morgan said, feebly.

"Do you ever wonder why Peter doesn't talk? Do you think it might have something to do with the fact that his father hardly ever opens his mouth around here? Like maybe he's imitating you?"

"Maybe he doesn't have anything to say yet." This was another stupid thing to say, Morgan knew, but he needed a moment to organize a defense here. He hadn't expected this line of attack.

"Do *you* have anything to say?" Cindy countered. "*Do* you?"

"Cindy, I had a strenuous day. My mother, work, now *this* . . ."

"You know, when I married you, your mother warned me. She said you were off in your own world."

"She did?"

"She said it was the same with your father. She said I should get used to it, because the Morgan men do not change. 'You get what you see,' she said."

"Get outta here," Morgan said. "My mother really told you that?"

Cindy nodded. "And I suppose it'll be the same with Peter."

With that she adjourned to the bathroom.

Morgan felt a little uneasy knowing that his mother had said those things to his then-fiancée. At the same time, he was sort of proud to have been associated with a family tradition, even a flawed one. "The Morgan Men"—he liked the sound of it.

"Hear that, Peter?" he muttered. "You've got a tradition to uphold. Keep up the good work."

Then, as if the boy had heard him, there was a loud shout from across the hall.

"There he goes again," Morgan said.

Peter had been suffering from nightmares for a year now, often culminating in these unintelligible yelps and cries. Cindy ran from the bathroom and across the hall, but Morgan knew she'd find the boy lying there sound asleep, seemingly at peace. It was a mystery.

Sure enough, she returned a few moments later, and after casting a look of disgust at her husband, disappeared again into the bathroom.

❀ ❀ ❀

Morgan's mother favored pantsuits, which showed off her still-slim figure. Solid-colored slacks—khaki in the summer, and something dark, a navy blue maybe, in the winter—and colorfully striped or flowery print tops. It was this uniform that Morgan spotted first on the lot of Kempton Motors while he was still a block away. His mother was kicking the tires of a large sedan while Dick Kempton looked on. That figures, Morgan thought. Only his mother would kick the tires of a car before buying it. Determined to stop her, he swerved the Hyundai into the lot from a side entrance, failing to notice the heavy metal chain suspended from two short poles across the opening. Dick Kempton explained later that he kept the chain up to prevent anyone from leaving the lot by any exit but the front one. When Morgan's car hit the chain, it was as if it had run smack into a wall. There was a sickening thud, and he was thrown against the steering wheel.

He sat there for a moment watching a dark cloud float in front of his eyes. When it had passed, he shut off the engine and tried to figure out what had just happened to him. The chain was hidden by the car hood; as far as Morgan could tell he hadn't run into anything but air.

Faces appeared at the windows: Dick Kempton's at the driver's side, his mother's at the other. Both doors opened simultaneously.

"What the hell?" Kempton said, taking hold of Morgan's elbow. "Are you okay?"

"I think so."

"Be careful!" his mother shouted as Kempton helped him from the Hyundai.

Morgan leaned against the car roof and rubbed his head.

"Do you need an ambulance?" his mother asked as she rushed around the front of the car. She touched him gingerly, as if expecting him to break into pieces.

"No. I'm all right."

"Didn't you see the chain?" Kempton asked. He wore a turtleneck shirt and a suit jacket; a gold cross dangled against his chest.

"What chain?"

"What're you doing here?" his mother asked.

"I'm broadcasting the show from here today." His forehead felt cold, numb. A bump was growing by the second. "What are *you* doing here?"

"I was just looking. I'm allowed to *look*, aren't I? Besides, maybe it's *you* who shouldn't be driving."

The Hyundai wasn't too badly damaged. One headlight was shattered, and the grill was scratched. Kempton untied the chain and drove the car over to the service area to get the headlight replaced. Morgan and his mother walked to the glassed-in showroom. The place was festooned, specially for the live broadcast, with colorful helium balloons and streamers. There was a refreshment table with complimentary coffee and lemonade, and a hot dog stand run by a young blonde in a skimpy outfit. Salesmen and other workers milled around, eating hot dogs and sipping from Styrofoam cups. In the corner sat a long table covered with broadcasting equipment.

Sanchez, on his knees plugging in some cables, looked up and, upon seeing Morgan's face, exclaimed, "Jesus! What happened?"

"Nothing," Morgan said, sitting down on a metal-framed couch against the wall. "Just give me a minute."

Four shiny new cars were parked at various angles throughout the room, each one a different make and color. Morgan, rubbing the bump on his forehead, stared at a cherry-red sports car ten feet away. Cindy had been angling for a new car for months now, but their finances weren't in such great shape since she quit her job. With her old salary, Morgan thought, they could easily have afforded this nice little number.

"That's turning into a nasty bump," his mother said. "Are you sure you shouldn't go to the hospital?"

Morgan nodded. "I can't even feel it."

Sanchez was beside him now, bending down to look at the damage. "Wow. That's quite an egg you got there."

"He had an accident," Morgan's mother explained.

"Never mind," Morgan said. "How are we doing on time?"

"We're on in about twenty. You gonna be okay?"

"Don't worry about me. I just need a few minutes to collect myself."

As Sanchez returned to his work, Morgan could almost hear the gears and pulleys moving inside his mother's head. "I really wasn't going to buy a car today," she said. "I was just shopping around."

"Mother, you can't drive anymore. They're going to take your license away."

"Nonsense. I *need* a car." Suddenly, her face seemed to collapse, as if all this time the skin had been held taut by invisible pins that had just now been stripped away. "I can't stand the idea of being helpless," she said.

Morgan wriggled a few inches away on the vinyl couch and stared out the window. In the past few minutes the sky had turned an ominous gray.

His mother put a hand on his arm. "I'll only drive in the daytime. I promise."

"Mom, you hit a telephone pole at high noon. It was your third accident this year. They really will take your license away. You *cannot* drive."

She reacted as if he had shoved her, leaning back and staring at him with big tear-filmed eyes.

Dick Kempton, grinning like he'd just heard a good joke, came loping into the showroom. "You're all set, Pete. Just see Ray at the service garage when you're ready to go."

"Thanks."

"Can I call a cab for you, Mrs. Morgan?"

"Call Smiling Taxi," Morgan said. "She has an account there."

"I'll take the bus," his mother said.

"Mom."

"I'll be fine. How do you think I got here?"

Kempton looked at Morgan. "So should I call for the taxi?"

"Absolutely not," Morgan's mother said.

Morgan rubbed the knot on his head.

"Besides," his mother said, "it's a hell of a lot cheaper."

Morgan looked over at Sanchez, who sat fiddling with the portable soundboard. It wasn't long before airtime. "Fine," he said.

"Good," his mother said with a sharp nod. "That's settled."

Kempton stared at Morgan's head. "Are you going to be okay for the show?"

"I'll be fine."

"Cuz this thing is costing me a bundle."

"I'm *fine*," Morgan said.

Kempton backed away, holding up his palms as if to say, "Okay, okay," then turned and disappeared into his office.

"That man," Morgan's mother said, "could strut sitting down."

"Mom, I gotta get to work."

"Don't let me get in your way," she said, rising unsteadily to her feet.

"Please, Mom," Morgan said, rubbing his head again. He could almost feel the bump growing under his fingers. "We'll talk later."

"Fine."

She walked toward the showroom door, slowly, as if waiting for her son to stop her. He didn't. She opened the door with a show of struggle and went to wait for the bus out on Market Street.

Morgan stood and wobbled over to the desk. There were more people standing around now, not just car dealership employees, but the usual remote broadcast crowd, sad souls looking for free refreshments and the chance to see a minor local personality speak into a microphone. Still, he was spared the kind of horde that shows up for outdoor events such as last month's chili cook-off at the county fairgrounds, where hundreds of people hovered near his booth, staring at him with globs of chili dribbling down their chins.

Among the crowd he noticed a worn-out-looking woman in ragged jeans and a frilly blouse, her reddish hair pulled back severely into a ponytail. She stood back a ways, watching as Morgan chatted with Sanchez.

"Did you figure it out yet?" the engineer asked.

"Figure what out?"

"The joke. How are women and tornadoes alike?"

"No, I didn't figure it out."

"They both moan like hell when they come," Sanchez said, "and take the house when they leave."

"Uh-huh."

"Two minutes," Sanchez said.

Morgan put one side of his headphones on so he could hear Nick Dander back at Studio A reading the latest news, something about another school shooting down south. Meanwhile, a fat man in a Pink Floyd T-shirt sidled up to the red-haired woman and started to chat, but the woman didn't seem to know him. She looked wrung out, her skin pale, like old, faded rice paper. Maybe she was a junkie, Morgan thought. Or a hooker. They tended to congregate just a few blocks from here, pacing the jagged sidewalks in front of abandoned row houses.

Sanchez gave him the countdown. At precisely 12:05, Morgan leaned into his microphone. "Happy afternoon, and welcome to Lunchtime Chat."

✿ ✿ ✿

The first hour went smoothly enough, with the predictable calls about school shootings and the various causes of such violence—rap music, the ACLU, homosexuality. Caught up in the process, Morgan almost forgot about his head injury, though every once in a while he could feel it throbbing. For the second hour they would take comments from the live audience. Pink Floyd-man and a few others had departed, bored by the reality of live radio, but the red-head remained, and a few new faces had recently arrived.

One of those new faces belonged to Morgan's mother, who had re-entered the showroom just as Nick Dander was finishing up the top-of-the-hour news. Morgan gestured toward her with a "What happened?" expression. She shrugged, mouthed "No bus," and joined the crowd.

"Okay," Morgan said, "we're going to open this up to the audience here."

Sanchez carried a cordless microphone into the assembly, where the red-head had raised her hand.

"You there," Morgan said, "with the red hair."

Sanchez followed his lead and thrust the microphone in the woman's face.

"Hi," she said in a familiar, silky voice. "My name's Carrie, and I want to talk about the city council slashing funds for the local libraries."

There was an audible groan from the crowd. Sanchez looked back at Morgan with an amazed expression. This was Carrie?

Morgan was so surprised he had a difficult time responding. Conscious of the dead air ticking by, he glanced over at his mother, who rolled her eyes. "Carrie," Morgan finally said. "It's good to put a name to the face. I mean—"

Carrie launched into her speech. She was thoroughly disgusted with the city council's position on the library issue, she said, and wondered what the people could do to turn it around. While Morgan agreed with her, and said so, Sanchez was visibly itching to move on to another speaker. But Carrie kept talking, and Morgan kept on agreeing with her. It was her voice—it was just so slinky, so juicy. How could that amazing voice belong to this pale, scrawny, life-beaten migrant worker out of a Depression-era photograph, he wondered.

As she continued talking, a thuggish man at the edge of the small crowd said, not loudly but quite clearly, "Shut up, already."

There were a few snickers and murmurs of approval. When Carrie went on, saying something about the number of books that would not get purchased by the main library this year, another man on the other side of the crowd shouted, "Pull the plug on her!"

Voices called out, "Yeah!" and "Enough, already!" and one person cried out, "Shut that bitch up!" Morgan could hear all this over his headphones, which meant, of course, that it was going out over the air. A drop of cold sweat ran down his spine and into his underpants.

"All right, everybody," he said, interrupting Carrie's filibuster. "Let's show some respect."

"Respect this!" someone called out.

Sanchez attempted to move on to another person, but Carrie took hold of the microphone and continued speaking, as if nothing was wrong. Morgan could feel the blood pumping through the knot on his head. The engineer looked back at Morgan, wondering what to do. Morgan shrugged, and imagined what it must sound like over the air. He was just grateful no one out there could see the hateful looks on these people's faces.

"Shut up!" someone yelled.

"Someone turn her off!"

Morgan saw his mother at the edge of the throng, watching him. She mimed yanking the mic away from Carrie. "Go on," she seemed to be saying to him, "Do something." And he did consider jumping in, going to Carrie and putting an arm around her, somehow getting her to surrender the microphone, but then he would have had to abandon his desk, his post, leaving behind his own microphone and headphones. To do that, he felt, would be like running into a burning building with no protection. Meanwhile, Carrie went on to mention the need for more computers in the various library branches, and how our children's future depended on such things. Sanchez had given up at this point; Carrie had full control of the microphone.

It was then that Morgan realized she was tappy. His mother used that word when describing people who were a little off—not certifiable, maybe, but not quite right in the head either. That's all Morgan could think: *Carrie is tappy.* Her elevator didn't go to the top floor, as Sanchez would say. She was a few fries short of a Happy Meal. A boxcar short of a full train. He didn't know why this had never occurred to him.

"Thank you, Carrie," he said, interrupting, unsuccessfully.

"And one more thing," she said, and that was it, the crowd erupted into even more strident objections, much of it laced with profanity. Terrific, Morgan thought—now we'll be fined by the FCC. The audience had ceased to be a collection of separate individuals; it was now one thing, a throng, or a mob.

"Who cares?" someone hollered.

"Let someone else speak!"

"Booooring!"

A scuffle broke out. It took a moment, but Morgan realized then that his mother had grabbed hold of the microphone, that she and Carrie were now wrestling for control of it.

"No one wants to hear your nonsense," his mother said through gritted dentures.

"Right on, old lady!" someone shouted.

Morgan stood up and tore off his headphones. A circle of people had formed around the two women, chanting, "Shut her up! Shut her up! Shut her up!" As Morgan pushed through, Sanchez passed him en route to the soundboard, where he shut off the mic and brought up a commercial.

Morgan stepped between his mother and Carrie and took hold of the microphone. Both women's grips were gorilla-like, and it took several tugs to wrest it free.

"Yeah!" the mob cried.

"You," Morgan said to his mother, "wait for me over there." He pointed toward the couch they had sat on earlier.

"Someone had to do something," she said, half defiant, half pouting, as she walked away.

Morgan turned to Carrie. She was visibly upset, her eyes turning red at the rims, her lips quivering. Up close, she was small and frail, so unlike the way he'd always pictured her. Her voice was so muscular, voluptuous, larger than life.

"Are you okay?" he asked. "Can I get you anything?"

She rubbed her reddened nose and shook her head no. By now the others had wandered off, some to the hot dog stand, many more out the doors and into the parking lot. Sanchez gave Morgan a signal: one minute till they returned to the air.

"What's wrong with people?" Carrie asked.

He didn't know what to say. He put his hand on her bony shoulder and, with a sudden movement, she hugged him tightly, a real clutch that took the wind out of him.

"Thirty seconds," Morgan heard Sanchez call out behind him.

"Gotta go now, Carrie," he said.

She held fast to him, and he could sense now that she was sobbing, letting out big heaves against his chest.

"Twenty seconds, Pete."

"Carrie, I gotta go now."

She wouldn't let go. Her back was puffing in and out with sobs, her face buried in his chest. Sanchez came over to pry her off, but Morgan waved him away.

"But we've only got about ten seconds!" the engineer said.

"Play another ad for Kempton Motors. Dick'll be thrilled."

Sanchez grimaced, but went back to the controls.

"It's okay, Carrie," Morgan said as she held onto him. He glanced over at his mother on the couch. She had the same look she always had when little Peter came over, as if she were carefully cataloguing everything her son was doing wrong.

"Twenty seconds," Sanchez called out.

"Carrie, I really gotta go," Morgan said.

She finally pulled away and looked up at him with oily eyes. "Thank you." Then she turned and headed for the door.

Morgan got to his seat and put on his headphones, watching as Carrie stepped outside and walked across the car lot. Sanchez waved and mouthed, "We're on!"

"Okay," Morgan said, as if nothing had happened. "Welcome back to Lunchtime Chat."

❉ ❉ ❉

"Thank goodness that damn bus never showed," Morgan's mother said as he turned onto her street. Until then they had ridden in silence. "Else that woman would probably still be talking."

Morgan ignored her. He'd noticed the Hyundai wasn't handling quite right. Perhaps it had been seriously damaged by his little accident earlier today. Now he'd have to take it back to Kempton, which would cost a fortune. Or maybe it was *he* who was handling strangely. His head was killing him. He reached up and touched the bump there. Had it grown? Was it cancer?

He pulled into his mother's driveway and shifted into park.

"Well," his mother said, "thanks for the ride."

"Mom, did you tell Cindy that 'The Morgan Men' never talk?"

She seemed caught off guard by the question, but recovered quickly. "What if I did? It's true, isn't it?"

Morgan thought of his tight-lipped father, all those nights spent in silence at the dinner table. He'd always assumed it was normal.

"It must have been hard for you," he said. "All that dead air."

She waved, dismissing the idea that she had suffered. "It makes it easier when you're gone."

"Mother!"

She laughed, then looked thoughtful. "It's harder for you than it is for us."

Morgan stared up at the house that would never be his home. "Do you want me to come in?"

"Nope," she said, opening the car door. "You go home to your family."

❀ ❀ ❀

There was music playing in the house when he arrived, but he found Cindy at the kitchen counter, her hands buried in a bowl of chicken meat, while Peter sat at the table rubbing a red crayon in a coloring book. They hadn't heard him come in.

"I'm home," Morgan said.

Peter jumped up and ran to hug him. Morgan scooped him up and said, "Hiya, buddy."

Cindy turned around and said, "Whoa! What happened to your head?"

"It's a long story."

Time seemed to freeze as his family looked at him: Cindy, from the sink, her hair wispy around her face, her shirt untucked, her hands dripping with olive oil and soy sauce; Peter, his angelic face framed by feathery blond locks, his blue eyes wide and full of what Morgan could only call love.

The boy sat back in his father's arms and opened his mouth. For a second, Morgan thought he might be about to say something.

Photo by Sean Conaway

Sean Conaway writes and teaches in the Blue Ridge Mountains of Virginia, where he lives with his wife, two daughters, and a smelly dog. He is currently pawning off his just-completed novel to anyone brave enough to read it.

JOHN THE REVELATOR

Sean Conaway

Burley was taking his daily constitutional when the deputies came for JR. The constitutional was what his kitchen staff had come to call his thirty-minute forays into the woman's restroom—the men's didn't have a lock (nor did it smell quite as nice: like flowers)—always exactly thirty minutes, they noted in wonder, never more, never less. They were both intrigued and sickened that Burley emerged red-faced and sweating, and rumors abounded about what he could possibly do in there every day for exactly thirty minutes to leave him in such a state. No one yet had built up the courage, or become drunken enough on their monthly outings to the titty bar across the border, to come out and ask him. Something about the look in his eye when the door bolt unlatched and he stepped back on line—a quiet blend of grimness and desperation—squelched any boldness achieved during his absence.

He, of course, knew his boys were dreadfully curious. He called them that, his kitchen staff: his boys. Burley knew everything that went on his kitchen, even—or especially—during his constitutionals, and sometimes wondered if it wouldn't be better just to come out and spill the beans, and had nearly let it slip a number of times (usually after the boys had pitched in to buy him a lap dance—they hooted and hollered as his grimace devolved into adolescent bashfulness as he fretfully considered where he could safely place his hock-like hands or rest his hooded eyes as the thonged woman vigorously shook her various money-makers scant inches from his meaty, pockmarked nose). The fact was that Burley hadn't pissed in months; it'd been even longer since his last erection—or boner, in the parlance of his boys. Thirty minutes was the amount of time he allotted himself to stand before the toilet—he refused to sit, although his feet hurt something awful—and whisper pleas for his treacherously limp dick to release a thick and steady stream, receiving in return a few paltry drops that invariably dribbled out onto the porcelain seat. Wiping up his urine humiliated him enough to silence him forever on the subject, despite the rumors growing ever-more wild and deprecating. He was unwilling to broach the topic with a doctor for the same reason: a deep and throbbing fear about what invasive tests might find kept his mouth shut and his pants zipped as well.

Cops have a distinctive way of knocking on a door—an over-compensation, really—and cops especially loved banging on the service door of the Calvary Grill. The thick aluminum had enough give to encourage zealous thumps with balled fists or hardened heels of the hand—not to mention kicks of a boot—and resonated with satisfying noise and depth: a door made for pounding. Burley had been tapping his toe to a smooth and jazzy rendition of Jay-Z's *Izzo* when the three resounding booms echoed over the quiet Mu-zak piped throughout the front of the house into the women's toilet. Burley knew instantly that (1) the cops had come (he didn't yet know who for—always a wildcard with his staff) and (2) that the new kid, Peaches, would let them in without first looking through the peephole.

Cursing as he shoveled himself back into his checks—two lonely and dissolute beads of urine splashing against his wrist—he burst out of the stall (he figured he'd make Peaches clean up the dribble this time, and later, after the dish room was spotless, fire him), fumbled with the bolt before throwing it open, and shuffled out into the car-peted dining room—a man Burley's size could do little else but shuffle in kitchen clogs—through the swinging door, past the beverage sta-tion, the dish room, and around the corner to the prep line, and found the deputies—Murray and Flanders, today, he noticed—had already pulled their guns and were training them on JR, who at the moment had Pretty Bear in a stunned Gutwrench Waistlock. Burley instantly saw that JR must have been demonstrating The Seventh Seal, his fin-ishing move he'd been devising for the big match three weeks away, and assumed that the Waistlock would be inverted into a Crucifix, setting up a Spinning Crucifix Powerbomb, and Burley found himself terribly anxious to learn how JR planned to finish the move and the match. Burley himself had been lobbying for some variation of a Knee

Drop Bulldog—something in theme with the whole apocalyptic persona—but JR had wanted something flashier.

"Sorry to leave you short-staffed, Burley, but this piece of shit ain't fit to be walking among us," Deputy Murray sneered, his mustache twitching in disgust.

"I didn't do anything!" JR contested, his arms still wrapped almost lovingly around Pretty Bear's waist.

"You gotta go with them, JR," Burley said calmly, holding his hands aloft in a way not dissimilar to the results of a properly executed Crucifix. "We'll sort this out and have you back on the line before you know it." When he saw JR comply, he asked, "There anyone you need us to call, big boy?"

JR shook his head—barely a budge on the bulging pivot of his neck—as Flanders cuffed him from behind, eyeing Pretty Bear warily (Pretty Bear had been the last one to get picked up from the Grill).

"There's nobody," he said, and led the deputies out the door.

❊ ❊ ❊

Drug dealers, embezzlers, arsonists, domestic abusers, aggravated assaulters, mail frauders—even peeping Toms: Burley had hired them all. He felt most comfortable surrounded by convicted criminals. He himself had learned to cook in prison (drunk driving), and trusted people who'd been through the system once or twice, but JR had been his first sex offender. Carnal Knowledge of a Minor, aged 13-15, JR had scribbled in a resolute hand while filling out his application, and Burley had been impressed by the courage it must have taken to write those words. Courage, he realized later, or complete disregard for societal norms. The former he respected, the latter kept him watchful.

"Don't have anything open right now 'cept porter," Burley said, rubbing his bristly chin with his blistered fingers, unaware of the traces of béchamel he smeared across his jawline. *Porter* was Burley's diplomatic term for janitor. "Not the most glamorous job you're likely to find," he admitted, although silently he realized that a convicted sex offender might have problems finding anything better. "But I'll get you close to forty hours—I don't give overtime—and feed you at the end of each shift."

JR's eyes opened wide. "What kinda food?"

Burley shrugged. "Hell, nothing gourmet—but you'll get your protein, starch, and veggie. We'll fill you up." He eyed JR, noting his heavily defined muscles, the way the tendons on his neck bulged against the collar of his stained shirt, and realized this boy would be able to pack it away. "Within reason," he added.

"When can I start?"

"Right now—on the bathrooms. Make sure you polish the toilet seats, now."

JR left the office and Burley noted with approval that he went right to the slop sink and began preparing a mop bucket. Burley closed the office door and pulled out the employee files to make sure none of the hostesses were under eighteen.

One night, a month or two later, Burley lumbered out of his office to watch JR finish mopping the pit. Most dishwashers liked to dally at this final task to get a few extra minutes tacked onto their receipt, but JR went at it like he did every other job: with determined precision and speed. Thinking of his babysitter, curiosity gnawing at his faulty prostate, Burley asked, "So what was she? Thirteen or fifteen?"

JR continued to mop, not even bothering to look up. "Fifteen—but I didn't do anything to that girl," he said in a flat voice, as if reciting a script. "I was camping out at the lake, had my four-wheeler, and started talking to the folks in the next lot over—some lady and her daughter. The girl asked for a ride, so I gave her a ride. Two weeks later, the sheriff picked me up. Statutory rape—the lady said I'd got her girl drunk and . . ."

"But nothing happened?"

"Hell, no. But it don't matter with a charge like that. No innocence until proven guilty."

"Well, shee-it," Burley said in sympathy, but to himself he wondered. Although he couldn't ask for a better porter, Burley had begun to speculate about JR. A high level of bullshit is maintained in any professional kitchen—usually dealing with the sexual prowess of the bullshitter or the lack on the part of the bullshitted—but Burley had heard JR say some things with such earnestness that he suspected JR might be a pathological liar—or just plain crazy. He'd claimed that he'd never received a blow job because, in his words, "My dick's too big"; that his estranged father was Walter Hornbrow—known as Pig—former head of the local outlaw bike gang The Pagans; that he'd been courted by a scout for the Cleveland Browns ("told him I was holding out for the Raiders," he'd shrugged); that he'd been struck by lightening twice; and that his grandfather on his mother's side had invented ChapStick, but that his uncle had cheated them out of their inheritance.

After word got around that JR's dick actually *was* too big for a blow job—one of the Melanies had a picture on her cell phone to prove it—Burley put his suspicions to rest, but then he began hearing the myriad stories surrounding JR's incarceration, and Burley grew nervous. He prided himself on his ability to accurately read people—especially criminals, who he found, if not more honest, at least were usually more genuine after they'd found a decent job—but he couldn't get a handle on JR.

Rumors abounded: the Melanies claimed he'd dated the girl for months before her father found out and, after realizing he wouldn't be able to kick the shit out of muscle-bound JR, had called the cops instead. His boys alleged that the girl herself had dropped a dime after he dumped her for another, more mature woman (age seventeen). The age of the girl varied between thirteen and fifteen, and her level of attractiveness swayed between, in the parlance of his boys, dog-ugly and smoking hot. Others still said that it was his much younger cousin that he'd bestowed his gargantuan affections upon and that her older sister, jealous, had been the one to maintain she'd been deflowered.

❁ ❁ ❁

He'd already placed the produce and meat orders with his purveyors, poured himself two generous fingers of Top Shelf, squeezed half a lime into his glass of the sparkling mineral water, and kicked off his swampy clogs in the back office when the kitchen phone buzzed. Fearing it might be his wife—she had an uncanny sixth sense when it came to Burley and his consumption of whisky—Burley cursed, hoping Pretty Bear might pick up the line extension, but he saw him through the smoked glass flirting with one of the new Melanies. Burley couldn't keep any of the wait staff's names straight, and settled on calling them The Melanies. It was continually pointed out to him that there were usually more Brittanys and Ashleys on the payroll at any given time, but Burley merely shrugged: "They all look the same to me."

"Shoot . . ." he groaned, pushing the two fingers behind the computer monitor, just in case Brenda could see through the phone (he often wondered), slipping his feet back into his clogs, and shuffling over to the phone. "Kitchen," he answered.

"Burley. It's JR. They just let me out—is there someone there that can pick me up?"

"Well, damn, boy—didn't think we'd be hearing from you anytime soon." JR had been locked up for two weeks.

"Do I still have a job?" The unease in JR's voice was palpable.

"You still got it—don't worry—although I wouldn't have been able to hold onto it much longer. Give me a few minutes to, uh, catch my breath," Burley said, thinking of his scotch. "You at the courthouse?"

The first thing Burley noticed as he pulled his truck up to the courthouse, rubbing the back of his neck uneasily (he hated this part of town, with all its cop cars and judges and bondsmen) was how JR was covered in thick red fur, poking out around his wrists, bursting from under his shirt, stretching up his neck and over his jaw up to nearly his eyeballs. His hair—a strange configuration of receding hairline and thick curls—ran wild over his skull, like his head had caught fire.

"What the hell happened to you—they feeding you Rogaine in there?" Burley asked after JR had pulled himself up into the cab with a grunt of thanks. "You look like a goddamn sasquatch." Like someone he wouldn't allow near his daughters.

JR shrugged. "Couldn't shave like I usually do in the pen. You mind stopping at Tickles? I need some coffee and a biscuit."

"Tickles closed a few hours ago, boy—there's the Sonic up the road. You mean you shave your body?"

"Wrestler's gotta be smooth—you ever seen a hairy wrestler? How 'bout Sheetz—don't like Sonic."

"They kept you in the pen—why not here in County?"

Another shrug. JR couldn't keep his hands steady, and Burley wondered how JR's two weeks inside had gone. Didn't look good. "They didn't think they'd be letting me out."

"Well—why did they? Why they'd pick you up in the first place?"

"Not Sheetz—Arby's. Need some protein—I have to hit the gym tonight. Lost 'bout five pounds—they only let me work out an hour a day. Some busybody—court stenographer or something—saw me talking to a Melanie at the Y and called me in. Said she was a minor."

"Was she?"

"Hell, no, man—she graduated high school when I did. They finally appointed me a lawyer and he asked to see the evidence—they had to let me out."

"Shee-it—two weeks in the pen for nothing? You could sue, you know—for damages, loss of work." Burley wasn't entirely certain of this, but he liked being able to give advice.

"Yeah—then they'll put my picture back in the papers, with the words 'sex offender' beneath my face. Four days left on probation, six before the big match. I just want this over with."

Burley drove in silence, shifting to neutral down the big dip that led back to the retail zone of town (cost-effective, he liked to say about his driving strategy; like a grandma, said most of his passengers), and wondered what it must be like to know that anyone could access your address, occupation, and mugshot if they so desired. Shifting into third to chug up the hill, the roar of his truck's mistuned engine resembling a jet turbine that had picked up a few pebbles, Burley asked, "So tell me, big boy, what really happened out there at the lake?"

JR looked at Burley and cocked his head, his crazy hair catching the glow of the streetlamps, setting it ablaze. "What lake?"

❋ ❋ ❋

Smatterings of footsteps poked through the sticky film coating the inside of his head, and Burley opened one tentative eye to find his daughters two paces away, discussing him.

"Do you think he's dead?" his curly-haired four-year old, Apple, asked her big sister.

"He's not dead—look: His eye's open. And he's snoring." Dolly, seven, freckled and long-limbed, was sharp as a tack.

"How can he be snoring if his eye's open? I think that's just how Daddy breathes." Apple was pretty sharp, too. "Maybe we should poke him."

Through the open door of what he referred to as his office, his girls called his bear cave, and his wife had labeled, with a sneer, "the flop house," he heard Brenda stomp down the hallway, her sharp heels clicking on the hardwood in time with the throbbing jelly behind his eyeballs. "Just open the shade, girls—that'll get him up."

He groaned and reached a beseeching arm out from under the cocoon of his quilt. "No, honey—don't!"

Too late. Apple, with the self-important zeal only a four-year-old can muster, yanked down on the blackout blind and let it violently rip back to reveal the intrusive sun.

"Ughhh . . ." Burley moaned, covering his eyes with a thick hand smelling of Stilton and scallops—a terrible thing to smell first thing in the morning, but an aroma he'd awoken to all spring and most of the summer. He needed to change the menu, but that would only create another dastardly concoction of odors for him to deal with hungover.

"Morning, Daddy!" He had a scant second to shield his groin from sharp knees and elbows (razors to his beleaguered bladder) before his daughters administered their AM Big Splash. Burley was amazed at how both his daughters had so much energy first thing in the morning, but then squinted at the clock and realized that they'd probably been up for a few hours already.

"Morning, my little roasted squabs," he muttered in what he hoped to be a merry tone, but his voice got caught somewhere in the phlegm coating his throat and he croaked.

Apple pulled away from his hug and wrinkled her nose. "Your breath smells like dead poop."

Peeling his lips apart to run a bloated tongue around them, he couldn't help but agree. Something had died around here a long time ago. "Why don't you go pour your old dad a cup of coffee while he brushes his teeth, and then I'll make y'all some pancakes."

"We ate like two hours ago, Dad," Dolly said, rolling her eyes. Burley was terrified by how quickly she was becoming her mother. "You have to go pick up Candi—her car broke down again."

From the bathroom, where he imagined her painting her lips the color of freshly sucked blood, Brenda called, "Hurry up, *Burley*"—she'd been using his name as a curse for years. "I have an open house in less than an hour. Honestly—I told you last night."

Burley wanted to point out that she had told him directly after explaining to him how she was selling her old boss's house, the first man she'd slept with when she decided that she no longer wanted to sleep with him, hence his nest in his "office." She'd been completely honest about all the lovers she'd kept since—completely honest being the way she put it, a brutal bitch his own view of the matter. Brenda had laughed and told him he'd been cheating on her with every kitchen he'd opened since they'd met, and he'd had a hard time arguing (she was quite deft in choosing to open a discussion when he was otherwise indisposed: drunk, hung over, or—more recently—trying to piss).

And then there was Candi. "Can't she, uh, find a ride? Or walk—she only lives three miles away."

"Dammit, *Burley*—I don't have time for this. Do you realize how important it is for this open house to go smoothly? If I sell Howard's house, it'll put me at the top of the food chain in this town."

"Alright, alright. Just let me find my keys . . ." Dolly had wandered off, but Apple watched him expectantly. Hoping for a buffer between him and the babysitter, he asked, "You want to come pick up Candi with me, Dumpling?"

"Your feet stink, Daddy," she pointed out, then ran from the room giggling, her curls bouncing behind her like a taunt.

Burley couldn't figure out if Candi was a punishment sent down from a vengeful God or conjured up from the Old Testament spite of his wife's twisted brain—the two of them, God and Brenda, had become one in his befuddled mind—but he knew that the disloyalty of his dick and the hiring of Candi coincided. Whether the relationship was causal (Candi = disloyal dick) or coincidental (in which case it was either an unlikely blessing in disguise or a humorless irony even his wife couldn't knowingly manufacture), Burley didn't know, but whenever he tried to figure it out, he found himself wanting to roast his brain with veal bones.

His bladder tugged at his belly as he pulled up in front of her house, a little white cottage bracketed by apple trees his wife had sold to Candi's parents last fall ("great curb appeal," she'd winked knowingly). Burley tooted the horn twice, unwilling to leave the relative safety of his truck. After a minute and another toot, he sighed, opened the door, and walked up the manicured lawn, looking over his shoulder to make sure no one had seen him stumble over the ditch. Who had time to make grass look this green? he wondered, when Candi emerged from around the back, wearing nothing but tiny terrycloth shorts and a pink bikini top covering very little. The girl didn't even have shoes on!

"Hey, Burley Bear," Candi called, waving a long brown arm, smirking behind her oversized sunglasses. A giant tote bag with broad pastel stripes dangled from her thin shoulder, knocking against her hip in time with each slithery step she took towards him. "Well, shoot—did you just wake up? Lazy boy," she admonished, her glossy lips jutting into a pout.

"Eh. Hey, sweetheart. At least I found time to get dressed," Burley said with fake cheer, trying not to look at her breasts.

She slapped his arm. "Oh, stop. I'll throw on a shirt when we get to your place. Want to take advantage of this gorgeous sun," she said, throwing up her arms and spinning across the grass. Emblazoned across the seat of her tiny shorts in block letters: JUICY. Burley rubbed his eyes, hoping he'd read wrong—Junior, maybe? Juvenile?—but no: JUICY. Did her parents know she wore this kind of stuff?

Candi always insisted that he open the door for her, offering as thanks a smiling "My hero" or "Such a Gentleman." Sometimes she'd lock his door as he made his way around the truck, giggling as if it were still as funny as the first time, calling him a grump if he showed the smallest sign of annoyance. Thankfully, she was more interested in mashing buttons on her cell phone than teasing him, and as he pulled himself into the cab his head swam from the bouquet of cloying aromas lifting off her bronzed and shiny skin. What the hell is that? he wondered as he grinded the gears, stalling the truck. Magnolia? Chrysanthemum? Papaya? He didn't bother to ask.

"So," Candi said, arching her back as she yawned and stretched. Burley furtively looked out the windows, hoping that no one would see him with a half-naked minor. "Daddy finally gave me permission to go to the match on Monday—you still going?"

Burley's heart sank. He'd told Candi about his newfound interest in professional wrestling a month or so ago, trying to get the conversation away from Candi's rambling description of her boyfriend's physique. He hadn't expected her to take up an interest, too. In fact, he assumed that she'd realize they had nothing in common past the fact that she watched his girls when school was out, but her slightly pointed ears had perked up and she'd said, "Ew! I just love that stuff—those guys are hunks!"

"Oh, yeah—I'll be there," Burley said, his voice betraying anticipation despite his best efforts. "The promoter said that it's going to be JR's big breakthrough. They're working him into a face. Or maybe a tweeny. Can't remember—but he's going to win . . ." he trailed off, grimacing with the realization that he'd broken kayfabe.

"It's not rigged," JR always insisted. Pretty Bear (conspiracy to overthrow the government—dropped—and arson) and some of the other cooks—Noodles, Loggy, Stinktooth (larceny, destruction of public property, and mail fraud, respectively)—liked to get under JR's skin about the predetermined nature of professional wrestling. "It's choreographed!" Kayfabe, he'd explained solemnly while his fellow line cooks rolled their eyes, was the maintenance of the illusion that pro wrestling was real. "We must uphold the reality at all times," he intoned with a touch of pomposity, turning his nose up at his profession's detractors. "Those of you who can't suspend your disbelief long enough to be entertained—because that's what it's all about: entertainment—shouldn't bother coming to watch. We don't need your support."

"Or, anyway," Burley stammered, backtracking. "They say JR's got a good shot at this match—a big one, too. Televised on Pay-per-view!"

Candi laid a hand on his bicep; Burley shuddered. "Ew! That's great! I can't wait to meet him!" she squealed, and he almost snorted at the thought of JR, given his muddled sexual history, having to deal with Candi. "Can I get a ride?"

"Oh, no!" Burley said too loudly, and Candi slouched with a huff. Burley tried not to watch her hanging breasts sway as he turned the corner into his neighborhood. "I mean—not this time, sweetheart. Me and the boys, well, we'll be . . . making some extra stops after the match that . . . well, I just can't take you, honey. Sorry." Informing her that they'd be celebrating at the titty bar after the match didn't seem to be something that would dissuade her.

"Fine," she said as he pulled into the driveway. "I'll just find my own ride." She hopped out of the cab with a huff. He watched her yank on a T-shirt that covered her JUICY rear before walking through the front door.

❀ ❀ ❀

Burley's customers loved his Snapper Soup. Burley despised it: a vile concoction consisting of monstrous headless turtles simmered in their shells with roasted veal bones, lemons, and cooking sherry. Two days before the big match and his stomach lurched as he whisked in the roux, steam redolent of rancid fish and rubbery chicken basting his face as the inky liquid thickened to the consistency of glossy motor oil. Someone banged on the backdoor—not the triple boom of a cop knock, but close.

"Goddammit, Peaches—if you touch that door I'll drop your head in the fryer," Burley barked as he shuffled down the line, cradling his bladder. He'd decided, in the end, not to fire Peaches—with JR in the clink, he'd needed someone to mop the bathrooms—but the kid couldn't seem to understand that the doors were locked for a reason.

Peaches, a scrawny little rat of a kid with a thin, bristly mustache he was misguidedly prideful of (it looked, to Burley, like possum fur—possum with mange), stood on his tiptoes, peering through the peephole, a deranged grin on his face. As if this were the happiest day of his young life, he announced: "It's John the Revelator—in costume!" Peaches was JR's biggest fan.

"Oh, lord," Burley muttered, and kicked open the push-bar to reveal . . . Captain America.

Burley—who'd had a cellmate named Rasp (rape, sodomy—illegal in Virginia—and postal fraud) obsessed with the book of Revelations, reciting it verse by verse aloud every night after lights out, leaving Bur-

American Fiction

ley with some rather unpleasant dreams and a few interesting thoughts on predetermination to mull over in the daylight—had been the one to suggest the John the Revelator persona to JR, thinking it might be an interesting take on the concept of choreographed battle. JR had instantly taken to it, devising signature holds and aerial attacks he called such things as The Four Horsemen, The False Prophet, and The Vestal Virgins (Burley had dusted off his Bible but never found a reference to vestal virgins in Revelations; the implications of JR conjuring this out of his own possibly addled brain were something Burley opted not to dwell on). As JR strutted into the kitchen, freshly shaven and oiled, his chest heaving in practiced rhythm, Burley wondered if he had sufficiently explained to JR the details of John of Patmos—or at least the time period from which he'd prophesied.

Burley's initial impression was that JR looked like a Chippendale with a patriotic streak: His knee-high, patent leather boots glowed white and were fringed with red and blue tassels. To account for his relative shortness (he weighed 230 pounds, but rose only to 5'8") he teetered on two-inch heels, counteracting somewhat the bravado he hoped to achieve with height. American flag print bandanas cinched tightly around thighs and biceps. Burley couldn't help but stare at the lumps bulging from the crotch of JR's elastic Speedo—it *was* true!

Pretty Bear lumbered over from the Hobart, where he'd been emulsifying a vat of balsamic vinaigrette, shaking his head in disbelief. Noodles glanced over, crossed himself, adjusted the laboratory goggles he preferred when slicing onions, and returned to his work. Peaches bounced on his heels excitedly, frantically clapping his hands close to his chest. "Open the Seventh Seal! Open the Seventh Seal!"

JR raised his arms over his head—wobbling just a tad on his elevated boots—releasing a potpourri of Old Spice, a strange chemical burning scent that Burley recognized as Nair, and sour sweat, bellowing, "Shall I open The Seventh Seal?"

Peaches squealed.

JR flexed his arms and shoulders, straining slightly as he forced his veins to pop out, and asked again, "Shall I open The Seventh Seal?" Without waiting for a response, JR shoved his forearm into Peaches' stomach, grabbed him by the nape of the neck until his head was firmly lodged between JR's thighs, his lumpy nuts resting on Peaches' excitedly quivering shoulders. "Behold the Crucifix!" JR cried, reached under Peaches' waist to flip him over his shoulder so that he lay sprawled across JR's back, and then lifted him above his head, Peaches' arms spread out as if he dangled from a cross. "Whee!" Peaches moaned dizzily as JR spun slowly around, displaying his victim.

"Judgment is upon us!" JR declared, tightening his grip on Peaches spindly arms, and Burley, seeing the disaster unfold before it'd begun—predetermination!—yelled, "JR—No!"

But too late: JR lurched forward and thrust Peaches over his head to finish his Spinning Crucifix Powerbomb, and Burley foresaw the back of Peaches' head splattering like fruit across the hard tile floor, the call to the dead kid's mother explaining how her son was a casualty of overly-suspended disbelief. But JR, as if he'd planned it all along—perhaps he had—shifted Peaches' weight at the moment of release and deposited him safely onto the steel prep table, although momentum carried the little rat headfirst into a rubbery pile of calamari that Noodles had been trimming.

Tendrils of purple-veined squid clumped in his hair, dangling from his ear, plastering his neck: Peaches sat up and gaped in awe, still processing his revelatory moment.

"You have been redeemed!" JR declaimed triumphantly.

"Jesus Christ, JR—what do you think you're doing?" Burley yelled. "You could have killed him! And what the hell is that get-up? You look like a goddamn exotic dancer."

"Think you might be revelating a bit too much, there, JR," Pretty Bear said. Now that Pretty Bear had pointed it out, it did look to Burley like JR's outfit might be cutting off the circulation in his legs.

JR, still exultantly flexing his pecs, looked down. "Oh, yeah—that's from the waxing. Lady said that the swelling should go down by tomorrow."

The entire kitchen—save Peaches, who ogled JR admiringly—collectively shuddered.

"Guess what, Burley? Bobby got a call from the promoter—this is it! My first win! My big break! They're going to work me into a face—a good guy!" JR said, his muscles relaxing slightly as his excitement overtook kayfabe.

Peaches moaned again: "Whee!" Burley shook his head, uncertain why he was so disappointed with JR's costume. What had he expected: a robe and sandals? A long flowing beard? A candelabra? JR, perhaps sensing his boss's disappointment, offered, "Bobby thought since I'm going to be a face I should look, well, virtuous."

Pretty Bear snickered and wandered onto the front line. "Chump," he called over his shoulder, then, "Hey Burley—is your turtle soup supposed to be boiling over?"

❖ ❖ ❖

The Cox Memorial Sportatorium, tucked behind Rooster's Bar and Grill, resembled a cow barn on steroids. Burley pulled his truck into the parking lot—a rutted field of overgrown weeds and cow patties. Pretty Bear whistled from the passenger seat. "So this is the big show, huh?" The boys in the back, already half drunk, hopped out; the clinking of beer cans and airplane bottles followed them. Despite the shabbiness of the Sportatorium—Burley had looked the word up in three separate dictionaries before deciding it'd been pulled from thin air—two news vans sat close to the entrance, as did the local rock station, blaring music through a cargo van constructed of speakers. Two large spotlights bracketed the entrance, stretching high into the cool night air.

Burley walked slowly, clutching his stomach. He'd swilled vast volumes of beer, thinking at the very least it'd flush him out, but no satisfyingly rich stream seemed possible; every once in a while, though, such as when he ran his truck over a pothole or curb, a warm trickle ran down his thigh. What he hoped was his bladder but feared was his prostate felt hard, swollen, and wobbly beneath his gut. "You okay, boss?" Pretty Bear asked quietly. "You don't look so good."

Before he could lie, Burley was ambushed by the overpowering scent of chemical flowers followed quickly by Candi as she jumped heavily into Burley's surprised arms, forcing another paltry dribble into Burley's already damp undies.

"Burley Bear! I hoped I'd find you! This is great, isn't it? Like, totally exciting. I love wrestling!" she beamed, doing a phenomenal job of ignoring the irritation twisting Burley's face.

"Eh . . . how'd you get out here, sweetheart?" Burley asked, nervously scanning the crowd for her father while his boys gathered, lewdly eying his babysitter up and down.

Candi, reveling in the attention, pushed out her chest exactly the way JR did after tossing Peaches into the calamari. "Hello, boys—*who are you?*"

"Candi, sweetheart," Burley began, already knowing his attempts at dissuading her from sitting with them would fail, asked, "Who'd you come here with?—The show's about to start, you better find them before it's too late."

"Oh, I came with Louis—he thinks he's my boyfriend, but . . ." she shrugged, smiling coyly.

Noodles slid his arm under Candi's and began escorting her to the spotlighted entrance. "Well, darling, you'll just have to sit with us! We know all about wrestling—you're in good hands." He winked over his shoulder at Burley, then slid an airplane bottle of whisky into Candi's hand, eliciting a delighted squeak.

"Gosh—she's pretty," Peaches observed. "How old is she?"

Burley groaned, his kidneys throbbing sharply. "Save me a seat, Peaches—I need to take a leak," he muttered, stumbling to the side of the building. "Don't let them touch the girl."

Finding a secluded shadow past a row of chrome-heavy motorcycles, Burley unzipped his pants and offered up a mournful mix of prayer and curse, sweat dripping from his nose more steadily than any urination he could muster. Deep beneath his stomach, he felt a compressed roiling that both scared him to death and offered a vague sense of hope—the pressure was reaching critical mass and he'd either release his piss or explode with the effort.

"Burley—is that you?" a voice came from over his shoulder, and Burley moaned as his concentration flitted away.

"Oh, Jesus—thank God!" JR, wrapped in a satiny American flag, picked his way through the furrowed weeds, tottering on his heels. "Oh—you're pissing. Take your time, I'll wait."

Muttering under his breath, Burley tucked himself back into his pants, dismayed at the trickle running down his thigh. "Well, all finished up, now. What'cha doing out here, JR—shouldn't you be inside?"

"They got me up against Madame Babylon, Burley! My first big match—against a chick!" JR complained, pulling at his hair—in what Burley noted—a very biblical fashion.

Burley wanted to laugh, but his loins pulsed, impossible to ignore. "A woman, huh? I thought women wrestled other women."

"They do! At least, they're supposed to, but the promoter is trying to work us both. He wants Babylon to kick my ass, then I'll get a Superhuman comeback—like the Hulk used to do. Says that we're both biblical, that'll it'll fly."

Not wanting to point out the historical and religious implications arising from a pitched battle against a prophet and the mother of all whores—who, if Burley remembered correctly, got nice and drunk off prophets' blood—Burley instead said, "Well, hell, JR, least you'll be getting some coverage. Looks like a couple different TV crews are here. And, uh, like you said, you're . . . patriotic."

"Oh, yeah—thanks—but a chick, Burley! They'll laugh at me. And Madame Babylon—she's ... dirty. She's got a reputation, you know, for being, like, a bitch. I tried to talk to her about the match, work the moves a bit—she spit in my face! Called me a kiddy-fucker! How the fuck does she know I'm a kiddy-fucker? I mean—not that I am, but still."

❊ ❊ ❊

Stabs of pain accompanied each slow step up the bleachers to where his boys waved for him. Burley held his breath as he crept down the row of seats, muttering apologies for each stepped-upon foot. "Damn, Burley—where you been?" Loggy shouted, grabbing him by the shoulder in the overly affectionate way of a drunk. "JR's match is about to start," he yelled in Burley's ear, spraying spit and the stale reek of beer.

"You okay, Boss?" Pretty Bear asked again as Burley collapsed onto the hard plastic bench, sending another electric bolt through his sloshing innards.

"Fine, fine," Burley mumbled, waving to the ring below, where two women in bikinis circled, holding signs advertising the services of a divorce lawyer and a local variety of West Virginia's infamous grain alcohol, White Rabbit. "Where's Candi?"

"Who?" Pretty Bear asked around a mouthful of pork rinds.

"Candi—the girl, Candi! My goddamn babysitter! She came in with Noodles," Burley yelled, suddenly dizzy.

"Oh, yeah," Pretty Bear guffawed. "So her name's really Candi? That's hilarious. She was all over Noodles as soon as they sat down. We told them to go get a room. How old is that chick, anyway? Hey! Burley, sit down, man—where you going?"

The ring seemed to draw farther away with each step, and it took Burley a moment to realize that the lights had dimmed, not his vision. Hidden speakers roared in his ears, adding to the building vertigo, making the seats spin. "The penultimate match of the evening, Ladies and Gentleman," a voice announced, so deep that it set the fluid in his guts churning as red and yellow lights began to spin. "Introducing, his first time doing battle in West Virginia, a newcomer to Cox Sportatorium, please welcome, The Harbinger of the Apocalypse, The Forecaster of Doom and Despair, The Opener of the Seven Seals ... please bow your heads for ... John! The! Revelator!" A bell began to peal.

"For Christ's sake," Burley groaned as JR made his way down the center aisle, his arms held above his head. Perhaps the ringing tolls of the unseen bell drowned them out, but JR seemed uncaring or unhearing of the jeers and catcalls being spewed his way by the crowd. "The Lamb opens the seals," Burley shouted into the air. "The Lamb!"

"Do not be afraid—I am the first and the last!" JR yelled hoarsely into the microphone as Burley made it to the bottom of the stairs, his relief at returning to flat ground tempered by the sight of JR's ridiculous figure. The lady who had administered the waxing had been wrong about the redness fading: JR looked like a lobster boiled too long, his skin slightly swollen, the sharp edges of the muscles he'd tried so hard to achieve softened by bloat. The oil he'd greased himself with gave his skin a glossy, crustacean look, amplified by his stars and stripes motif. Someone had misguidedly applied makeup to his face, and Burley almost chuckled—JR looked more like the mother of whores than Madame Babylon ever would—but the gnawing pain and dawning realization that he very well might piss himself drowned his mirth.

"I am the living one," JR bellowed, his expression belying the bravado he mustered in the face of the obvious scorn of the crowd. A spectator cloaked in darkness kept shrieking, *Pederast, Pederast, Pederast!* "I hold the keys of death and Hades! I shalt smite thee!" JR hollered as he spun slowly on his elevated heels, buffeted by the open derision. His eyes caught Burley's and held them, but Burley turned away, searching for an exit, for Candi.

"And now . . . climbing her way out of the Abyss, returning undefeated to Cox Sportatorium, Rider of the Scarlet Beast, the Mother of Whores and All Abominations of the Earth, Madame Babylon!" the announcer called, and the crowd erupted. Strobe lights flickered as howls of suffering multitudes blared from the speakers. A knife twisted itself into his guts and as the air turned red he saw Candi stumbling towards him, thick mascara bleeding down her cheeks, mouth opened in a silent sob as she ran. Too late, Burley sighed, as she fell into his arms.

Photo by Rob Cook

STEPHANIE DICKINSON's poetry and fiction have appeared in *Cream City Review* and *Inkwell*. She is an associate editor at *Mudfish* and is publisher and editor of *Skidrow Penthouse*. Her poetry collection, *Corn Goddess,* and two short story collections, *Road of Five Churches* and *Straight Up and No Sky There,* were published by Rain Mountain Press. Dickinson lives in New York.

THE WHEELCHAIR GIRLS
Stephanie Dickinson

S tuck. I feel like one of those falcons with his wings clipped. Or a prairie dog in the last grassland the gas companies keep cutting roads through. A few hops in one direction and then back. No farther. We're ten miles south of Las Cruces looking for a town of two streets called Jump, New Mexico. The night is darker than I've ever seen, but when I turn off the headlights to save the battery, starlight pours down. Not like Sioux Falls or even Pierre where the stars can't outblink the Pizza Hut's neon lights or the tiny diamonds in the cashier's heart necklace. We wouldn't be out here if the phone hadn't gone dead just after Penny had called saying she had to get away from Wystan, we wouldn't even be out here.

I let the car rest, and then I start it again, shift into reverse, and step on the accelerator, but the tires just spin in the sandy soil. They spin and spin until I smell smoke and it's not just from my cigarette.

"Well, what are we going to do?" I ask Natalie, who sits half lying down in the passenger's seat.

"Turn there. See the lights back in the field? That looks like something back there."

It doesn't look like a whole town, even if the town we're searching for is supposed to be two streets. Where else would you expect a man named Wystan Ricker to live? I didn't see any other options so I turned. We should have asked directions at the roadhouse we passed—a bar-restaurant in the middle of nowhere—but that would have meant me getting the wheelchairs out of the backseat. And it was one of those entrances I hate, with steps and the promise of more stairs inside. I had seen all that in the sweep of the headlights. It made me think of the house where I grew up. In junior high, when I couldn't walk anymore, I hated the carpet, the piled pale blue that used to push soft against my toes. I hated the carpet because my wheels couldn't roll across it. Trapped. When my father suggested Crippled Children's Boarding School in Sioux Falls I shivered, glad to go.

"Are you awake, Natalie? We're stuck."

We met in college six years ago and she's followed me everywhere ever since. I moved to Las Cruces to go to graduate school and Natalie moved to Tucson, but eventually her visits here became permanent. I ended up only attending one class, two times.

Penny told us that Wystan comes from oil money. One of his ancestors was Haymond Ricker, a wildcatter who had a leasehold interest in the Permian Basin, the first huge Texas oilfield. His cousins still get royalty checks, but Wystan took his share in one lump sum and spent it all before he reached New Mexico. He claims he used to date Jennifer Jason Leigh and paint desert sunsets.

"Maybe you can try again," she says, unzipping her coin purse. "Try going forward not back."

I pump the gas, try forward again, then back. The wheels dig in. Natalie's always full of talk about nothing, but quiet as a ditch when something important needs to be decided. A blonde with bangs, blue eyes, and a big, slightly crooked nose. When I'm mad I can see all the things I don't like about her. Her uneven features remind me of her father's loud voice and her mother not paying attention. Natalie slumps, her head back, hardly seeing over the dashboard. "And try to sit up." She squirms this way and that, as much as her rheumatoid arthritis will let her. It's not like old people arthritis but the kind that invades every joint in your body from your little toe to the vertebrae of your neck. All your cartilage petrifies to stone with spikes sticking out of them. Still, she swallows enough pain killers. We all have it rough. I hold onto her sleeve and tug her up.

There's mesquite all around us and the jaggy branches seem to reach out in the blue moonlight. Those stars and still there's a full moon swollen in mist like something you want to stuff in your mouth. I wonder how everything could have seemed so dark before, how a light in the middle of a field seemed the brightest thing for miles. Must be Jump, New Mexico. Righto. The light was an oil tank in the middle of scrub brush—one of the fields they're stealing from the prairie dogs and falcons.

"Well, give me your onion, if you have one. What should we do?" I smooth the silky white shirt over the top of my jeans which are harder than hell to zip sitting up. I know I'm going to have to pee soon. There's a pee cup over by Natalie's feet.

"Nothing. Somebody will see the car and help us," she says, lifting the can of Coke that sits between her legs. "Jannie, want a drink?"

"I don't want to drink from your straw. And stop calling me Jannie."

She reaches for the box of straws she carries in her overstuffed purse. "I'll give Jannie her own straw." Then she goes back to digging in her purse. "I found something Jannie might like. How about a joint?"

It's long and skinny. I light the joint from my cigarette, inhale. It tastes more like the inside of Natalie's coin purse than pot, but I get another drag and pass it over, careful that she can manage it between her fingers. Natalie takes a toke, then another. She belches smoke and I offer my congratulations on a nice burp and we laugh. "We have three Cokes on the floor," she says, "We won't thirst to death."

"Penny might not be so lucky. What do you think Wystan has done to her? Do you have an onion?"

"He probably beat her up. Maybe she'll leave him this time. He could have hurt the baby. If he did that I'm sure she'll leave him."

My knuckles whiten. If Wystan touches the baby he's going to be sorry. I'll see to it.

When I moved to Las Cruces, who knew the Mesilla Valley with its cotton fields and the Organ Mountains would be such a draw? Penny was a college friend who wrote me the second month I was here and asked if she could stay with me while she looked for a job. She showed up off the Trailways with her clown collectibles. Figurines. Tumbling clowns with green triangle hats. Cloth doll clowns with red molded noses. Crying clowns. With her straight As in sociology, she found work right away at the Social Services office. That's how she met Wystan. She never had a date in high school, never had a date in college. She wore glasses and her cheeks were speckled with purple acne. When she talked she didn't realize she picked at her face.

❈ ❈ ❈

I toke on the joint and feel the ember sizzle against my lip. I imagine how it was for Penny sitting in the Social Services office, a square stucco building next to a strip shopping center. You could be in Sioux Falls for all the building told you, but then you glance up and see the mountains: snow-silver cathedrals. She moved here with all the important things; besides her clown collection, there were her Avon products, all the hand lotions in bottles that looked like lampshades and music boxes, all of the perfumes smelling like insect repellent. Penny thought she might sell Avon, but then the good job came through. And after all those sociology classes, those studies of deviant behavior, when Wystan showed up in her intake chair, she took him for misunderstood.

Penny kept writing her brother about how she liked New Mexico, the dry climate, and there was something about the elevation, about those mountains looking down or you looking up to them that made her acne vanish. I lightened her mousy brown hair to blonde, and when her glasses broke she discovered she didn't need them at all. And in the high altitude her weight dropped. She'd lost fifteen pounds without even trying. No one from college would recognize her. Her own parents would walk by her on the street and not say hello.

Penny was doing food stamp intake interviews, going seriously over the questionnaire line by line, how many dependent children in household, what relation, making sure only the truly needy were approved. She could see the mountains over the top of the intake chair filled today with a man: a youngish, white guy with brown hair combed back from his forehead and tucked behind his ears. He gave off an intensity like the overhead florescent light bearing down on her. His eyes were dark and never left her face. "Mr. Wystan Trevor Ricker," she said, reading his name off the application.

He cocked his head and crossed his leg, "Wystan. Please call me Wystan."

"You have three children, Mr. Ricker?" she asked, raising her eyes as she usually did to the window and the pewter-colored mountain. She felt uncomfortable asking direct questions and making eye contact.

He nodded, brushing the knee of his faded black jeans. He wore cowboy boots and, rather than making eye contact with him, she studied their spirals of hand-tooled patterns. He wore an indigo turtleneck and a suede jacket, and while his clothing looked lived in, it also gave off the air of having been expensive. "Wystan. I said call me Wystan." He smiled showing very even, white teeth. They reminded Penny somehow of a cat's. "I do have three children. Samuel, Tyler, and Patricia. I'm a single dad trying to do the best I can."

"What happened to their mother?"

"She left me. Finally I divorced her."

That was their beginning. When she started dating Wystan she had to hide it from the agency. It was forbidden to date clients. She hid a lot from us. About Wystan's three kids, about the wife who deserted him and he had declared dead, the woman named Magdalena who lived with them, the so-called babysitter, about the bedroom's mirrored ceiling, about the surveillance.

❁ ❁ ❁

The roach burns and I buzz the window down and flick it. Natalie slurps from her Coke and then parks the can between her legs. Wystan could be beating the shit out of Penny and here Natalie is cleaning her fingernails with a tweezers. I take the tweezers from her and jam them into her purse. "Can you believe Wystan says he's heir to an oil fortune? If his cousins cheated him out of his share on another oil lease, why is he receiving food stamps? He's a paranoid. A beater."

"Wystan is a rich lady's poodle's name. Here, Wystan. Bow wow," Natalie says in her low voice, then starts to bark.

"You're no help at all. What if we sit here for days, huh?" I rest my head on the window and look up. The stars shine down, bits of light so chiseled they would fit on the tip of a safety pin, and a sky filled with billions of safety pins. The night breeze smells like sage. How could anyone question the meaning of existence when everything vibrates with meaning—except people. Natalie and I hate most people.

If Wystan found out we called the police, he'd go crazy. We've called the Las Cruces police plenty of times. They tell us they don't have jurisdiction in Jump. The sheriff's department does. Then we tell them Penny works in Las Cruces and Wystan stalks her here in their municipality. *How can a man stalk a woman he's having a baby with? They live together for Christ's sake. Maybe you young ladies need to mind your own business.* We call the sheriff's department and they say they'll drive by. *Not much anyone can do unless your friend makes a complaint.*

"We'll just have to wait here until morning," Natalie says. "Someone will tow us out."

I bristle. "That's easy for you to say. You don't mind nodding off in Red Owls and being locked in until morning. You'd fall asleep anywhere."

Sometimes my words sound harsh even to my ears. Give Natalie a break. Her hands are gnarled and she's only twenty-four. Like frozen starfish, her stiffened fingers. I have muscular dystrophy and it's progressive. I could tell you the little ways I'm weaker than six months ago, how I have to sometimes use my right arm to hold my left arm up. I light another cigarette, a Benson & Hedges, a long, white elegant smoke. I'm playing with the most important organ of all—the lungs.

I take another puff on my cigarette and think of the picture Natalie tacked on the bulletin board in our kitchen. Natalie Deeter, four years old in a snow suit, a black and white Brownie camera snapshot of an apple-cheeked girl with a steady unsmiling gaze. Still, it's an intelligent, mischievous face. Behind her is a garage and house with picture window and shutters. Deeter block, three Deeter families populate a tiny suburb of Crystal, Minnesota. Nothing can hurt this world. In the house, Ruth, Natalie's mother, is planning a baby shower on the phone, her hair in those curly clusters that resemble dusty, plastic grape bunches. On TV the Vietnam War is humming along; a half-naked girl tries to outrun the white flames of her clothes and skin. Ruth changes the channel to local news. Snow is forecast in the black and white world, a heavy snow with biting winds. Button up. Whenever I look at little Natalie I feel the wind chill of thirty below. The cold is already inside the grim munchkin, a chunky-faced elf, juvenile arthritis that fucks with cartilage in the joints and causes it to grow spikes like the necks of chickens. She's no more than eighty-five pounds when it begins, missing sixth grade entirely, home with Ruth, later a special bus driving her to school where she's ignored, invisible. Shame on Natalie who isn't trying hard enough. Ruth takes Natalie's crutches just to see if she can walk across the room. "Come to Mom." Natalie falling.

"It'll be okay, Natalie," I say, "someone will come."

Then I see a pair of headlights, the beams poking through the arms of the mesquite. I don't know whether I should turn my brights on. I get a chill, nudge Natalie, who is cleaning her thumbnail. "Someone's coming," I warn, but she doesn't look up.

The headlights make an arc on the road and I buzz the window down an inch and listen. Tires crack asphalt, scaring the sleeping prairie dogs, headlights fishing through the creosote and tarbush. The high beams blink, becoming low beams and suddenly I puzzle out a truck behind those lights, not a huge truck but a medium-size one. Hesitating, crawling, now coming on.

"Natalie, hand me one of those Cokes."

"I thought you didn't want any, Jannie." She wedges her fingernail under the top about to pop it.

I reach over and snag the can from her. "Don't open it. I want a weapon," I hiss, locking the doors. All of this is Wystan's fault. I think of Penny two weeks ago stopping by to check her storage closet, wearing sunglasses, her lip split.

Serial killers particularly like to bring their dead girls to shallow desert graves. They shovel dirt and sand into the pale eyes of victims. Flowers bloom from them to accuse. I've read plenty of true crime books, usually shelved between the sociology textbooks, and always more interesting. I used to like to steal them and I taught Natalie how to steal too. Bookstore people saw us as wheelchairs and I guess they paid for that.

The pickup's headlights stay on and the driver's door opens. A small guy jumps out. He's wearing a fatigue jacket like he's been in the service, but some time ago because his hair is longish, about the length and style of Natalie's with bangs.

"He's got your hair," I say, starting to chuckle. "At least we can get him to call Triple A for us, if he doesn't slit our throats."

Natalie actually lifts her head. "He's kind of small don't you think? He reminds me of a wiener dog." She can't bother with being scared. I guess that's what endears her to me. One of her favorite people growing up was Skippy, the family's piebald dachshund, one blue, one brown eye.

The guy carries a flashlight that he'll use to break the windshield and bash our heads in. Little or not he walks toward the car, the driver's side. Through the glass I can hear sticks and dry grass snap under his feet. The flashlight peers into the backseat, which was taken out so I can slide our wheelchairs in there. The beam noses around the wheel and spokes, the folded blue seat. I feel it slip over my shoulders and I brush the light off my cheek. It has a lukewarm texture to it. Like cream of mushroom soup. What I use to make my favorite recipe: Bean gunk. I taste the light in my mouth.

He motions for me to lower the window. I buzz it down half an inch. His nose has a bump in the middle like Natalie's and his lips are hardly there at all. His long nose slopes, sniffing the top of his very thin upper lip—like a dachshund after a badger—and his eyes are bright like blue, moist muzzles.

"We're stuck." I tell him. "We were on our way to Jump. We have friends there."

"Jump's about five miles up the road. You turned off in the wrong direction." He walks around the hood of the car, crouches to get a better look. "Your tires are in pretty deep. I've got a winch and chain and I'll try to pull you out. My truck is pretty lightweight and you've got a heavy car. After I give it the gas you give it the gas too. Otherwise keep the car in neutral. I'm Manfred by the way." He hooks the chain around the grill of the Impala and fastens it to his winch.

"He does look like a wiener dog," Natalie remarks, interested now. "His legs are short and for a little man his body is long. Skippy was exactly that type."

"I think he could be your brother," I say, tartly. "Twins."

When he swings himself up into the driver's seat and gives it the gas, I feel the Impala shudder and try to lift itself. I pump the accelerator. The truck tries again, but the Impala holds fast to its new home in the field.

"Man Fred's not budging us," Natalie comments dryly. "Wystan has probably finished Penny off by now."

After three more tries our Good Samaritan gives up. He loosens the chain from his winch, loops it back into his truck, and then comes for us. "I'll ride you in my truck to your friend's over in Jump." He tells me to hang onto his neck and I do. He hoists me into his arms and his chest muscles strain. It's not that I'm fat—I'm not—but my flesh is unwieldy, my muscles losing their strength. Like carrying an almost dead girl. "Hang on," he says, "just hang on." But by the time he's got me near his truck his heart is pounding. I want to tell him to hang on. The seat of a truck is higher than a car and Manfred heaves me onto it. I grab the steering wheel and pull myself in. Natalie is a toothpick and he has no trouble with her. We're already on the highway before I realize we've left our wheelchairs in the Impala. A shiver runs through me. What if we get more lost or the car does? The truck is a stick shift and each time Manfred shifts he brushes my leg. And there's my hair that I can sit on, everywhere.

"What's your business in Jump?" he asks, twirling the radio until he hits country-western music. "I know a guy who lives there."

"Do you know Wystan Ricker?" Natalie asks.

"What's his last name? Ricker?"

"Yup, that's what he tells people," Natalie answers. She does most of the talking to outsiders, while I sit silent. "You'd know his house. There's a seven-foot wall surrounding it on three sides. I believe there's just a fence in back."

Manfred lets out a low whistle. "Wystan Ricker. Everyone calls him WR."

"We don't," Natalie pipes up. "He's Wystan to us with corned beef and sauerkraut."

I snicker.

"Sure, I know him. I went to high school with the girl who married him. In fact Verona was my fiancée until Wystan moved to town." He pulls out the ashtray for me, but then I decide not to smoke.

"Oh," she asks, "was your girlfriend black?" Because Wystan's children are bi-racial and he seems to be white.

"She was Spanish and black. So is Wystan your friend?" Manfred twists the volume to low, cutting off a steel guitar and banjo. He's taking another glance at us with his moist blue eyes. "Is WR your buddy?"

"Hardly, Man Fred," Natalie chuckles. "Our friend Penny lives there and has a baby with him. He takes her car keys on the weekends. During the week she can drive to work, but he follows her in his truck. We're worried."

"You should be." His fingers clench on the steering wheel and he grinds down on his teeth. "Verona disappeared five years ago. No one's seen her since."

"Really? But he says she left him for another man. That's why he divorced her."

"They're not divorced. He had her declared dead. What woman would leave three children behind? We're talking a first-class girl. Basketball player, track star, homecoming queen. She was adopted by the Gonzales family. They used to be big cotton growers."

❁ ❁ ❁

The moon shines down yellow-white like all of the desert's coyote yipping was wired together and thrown into the sky. Jump, New Mexico. Two strings of lit-up houses, everything unfinished. The streets don't have names. Manfred pulls into the driveway bordered by the wall of white concrete blocks seven feet high. I want to sit and just stare. I hear dogs madly barking. The headlights burn into the pale blue garage door, sparking the silver handles.

Above the white concrete the roof of the house looks out, shingled, gray-white like thousands of roofs all over America. The house where I grew up on North Huron Drive in Pierre, South Dakota, had a wood-shingled roof, a very expensive one I heard my father tell my mother. Actually, he shouted it. The first time I could remember. "That roof—those shingles pounded on one at a time!" He stopped to catch his breath. "I bought that roof for you and our children. For our love. And what did you do? An affair! God, what you did!" A roof like that can last two lifetimes, but their love wore out faster than the shingles. I admit I was part of what went wrong. One thing Natalie and I agree on is that there isn't any such thing as love. That's all selfishness, all self. However, we do believe in friendship.

"Wystan has a double garage. I wonder who paid for that," Natalie says, lifting her flash camera from her overflowing and bottomless purse.

"Verona paid for everything," Manfred answers, his fingers and toes tapping like he thought Verona might be still inside the walls. "She night-managed Luby's and had spic and span credit. Medical insurance, life insurance. Even after she married him we stayed friends. She came to me for advice. Should I take out a loan and buy the house? I advised her against it. Let Wystan take out a loan. See that he gets a job." Now his elbow is bumping the door, wanting badly to rescue his lost girlfriend. He clenches his fingers around the steering wheel, his nose twitching. "I'm going to see about knocking on that garage. I guess that's the front door." When he tries to open his own door the handle jams and he has to fiddle around pushing and pulling at the same time.

The yard light goes on and at the top of a ladder leaning against the wall, soon a head peers over. A small, sweet-faced boy with a medium afro. I nudge Natalie. "I bet that's Samuel—Verona's son." The boy disappears and the garage door slides up. A Rottweiler rushes out. Barking and lunging, he jumps with his front paws on the passenger door—Natalie's side, his glassy eyes on fire. He bites at the side mirror.

"Here doggy," Natalie chortles, "nice doggy. Look at those teeth. I wish I had a roast beef samwich to give him. I wish I had a roast beef samwich to feed Natalie."

A slender man who looks like he's trying to be Michael Douglas dressed in leather jacket and sunglasses swaggers from the darkness of the garage. "ZAPATA! DOWN!" he hisses. The Rottweiler's nails scratch the door as he slides down and trots to his master's side.

"Why is he wearing sunglassers?" Natalie giggles. "Where's the sun?"

I feel the laugh that moves from my stomach and pops from my mouth like a bird opening its beak wide. "He thinks he's stone-cool in sunglassers."

So this is Wystan. He's all olive-green shirt and black jeans. His boots have a two-inch heel. They remind me of Crippled Children's School—the auditorium days when the alumni showed up—the older generation there to pep talk us, wearing orthopedic shoes. The last of the polio kids, their feet encased in black bricks you had to lift along with thirty-pound leg braces.

He walks toward Manfred, passes him by, doesn't speak. He throws his shoulders from side to side, his head slightly rocking too. He's pleased with himself. This is his kingdom and he's happy. I reach for my abalone lighter. Wystan stands outside the passenger door making hand motions to lower the window. Natalie doesn't, and then the dog growls at Manfred who scrambles back into the truck. He buzzes down the window. Wystan knows us, I realize, he's seen us on his surveillance rounds, he knows exactly what we look like. Now we know him. The long, intense face. Like he would never raise a hand against a woman in anger. Too intelligent.

"What brings you here?" he asks, showing that he knows us.

"We came by to see Penny. We have mail for her, but we got the car stuck," Natalie tells him. I reach for the packet of letters that came for Penny at my address.

Manfred breaks in, his fingers tapping again. "They took the wrong turnoff and ended up in the field where the old gas meter used to be. About five miles south of here. I saw them out there. I've got a winch and tried to pull them out, but they're driving an old, heavy Impala. Maybe you can call a tow truck."

The corners of Wystan's mouth turn up in a half smile. "I've got a winch too. I'll get them out," he says in a dry, whispery voice. You have to lean toward him, almost read his lips to get his words. His eyes close up look jelly-black. Then Penny drifts from the garage in an orange floor-length nightgown with cream-colored lace around the neck. Her blue eyes widen with surprise, the arched brows lift. When she turns toward the truck the breath catches in my throat, a blue-red bruise blooms on her jawline, her cheek is swollen. My legs tremble. Her heart-shaped pink mouth is cut and specks of blood are dried in her lower lip.

"Natalie and Jana," she says in her breathy little girl's voice. "What are you guys doing here?" Her fingers reach up to grasp the window like she wants to climb in. Still naive. Innocent eyes, innocent like her secret storage closet with only more Avon products, and terrycloth clowns. But the storage is her freedom. If I have that, he doesn't have all of me. They've fought about the baby's name, she wanted Rita Rae, and he wanted L'Valarie. They settled on Valarie. The Rottweiler growls. Desert wind blows and billows Penny's orange robe. I want to signal her to go inside, get the baby and come with us.

Wystan turns to Penny and rasps, "Cover up. Can't you see him looking?"

I startle when a woman appears behind Penny, tall and slender with short black hair shaved along the sides, in turtleneck and wranglers. Her long arms drape a blanket around Penny's shoulders, covering her nightgown completely, then she takes a long look at me.

"Pull the truck out, Magdalena," Wystan says, squinting at Manfred suspiciously. "You look familiar. Do I know you?"

Manfred shakes his head. "I definitely don't think so."

I try to catch Penny's eye, tell her to get the baby, we've come for you.

"Go back to bed, baby," Wystan tells Penny. "I'll get them pulled out." Then he opens the truck door. "I'll take it from here. I know they can't walk and I'm going to carry them in my truck. Thanks for getting them here."

The wires around the yellow moon holding the coyote yipping tight are coming loose. Manfred bristles, argues the point—he brought us here, he'll drive us back. Wystan lowers his whispery voice that makes me wonder if his voice box is damaged and says, "I'm carrying them in my truck."

❀ ❀ ❀

The live-in housekeeper Magdalena drives the largest pick-up truck I've ever seen out of the garage. Painted purple-pink, the color of grape bubblegum, wheels the size of tractors, and the cab so far above the ground you need a ladder to climb in.

Natalie and I are cramped in the front seat of Manfred's tiny pick-up idling in the driveway. I sink my elbow in Natalie's side and watch the so-called housekeeper in the denim jacket slide out of the pink truck like she just finished a bull-ride. From the back, her black hair shorn to her head makes her look like a guy, and when she walks past Manfred's truck she looks my way, the tragic glance of a broken vanity mirror. I tell Natalie I've seen Magdalena before. "Is that your onion too?"

"That's definitely my onion. And I know where," Natalie says in her low voice, the one she doesn't have to actually open her mouth to speak with. "She works at Luby's Cafeteria. I've seen her carrying cornbread." We have one electric wheelchair at the apartment and Natalie likes to wander Las Cruces in it, eating at cafeterias. Magdalena and Penny and Wystan disappear into the darkened garage. Natalie raises her flash camera and snaps. "Man Fred," she says, "Do you think you could go stand by the wall and I'll take your pitcher? Hurry before they come back."

He pulls a brush from his jacket pocket and straightens out his hair, then gets out of the truck and slouches over to the wall. Natalie clicks her camera twice.

"It's 'picture,' Natalie, not 'pitcher.' You pour milk with a pitcher."

"No," she says, scratching her nose with her thumb. "I take pitchers."

I'm wondering what kind of man erects a wall seven foot high around his house, with only the garage as a front door in and out. I've seen Magdalena somewhere else, somewhere closer to home. Like a shadow I caught watching me from the parking lot.

Manfred gets back into the driver's seat, tapping the dash with his fingers. He tells us he really didn't have anything better to do tonight, except work on his model clipper ship. Some take a year to finish, and then he travels with them to competitions. He dreams he sails them in the middle of the landlocked desert and rescues his ex-girlfriend. "Would you like to see a picture of Verona? It was taken about ten years ago." He reaches over my knee to his glove compartment, flips it open, and pulls out an envelope.

An old newspaper article about a March of Dimes dance marathon. *Manfred Schmidt and Verona Perez, the winning couple after ten consecutive hours of dancing.* They both glow in the yellowed clipping: Manfred in a dress shirt, the number five pinned to his pocket, sleeves rolled up, his hair slicked back from his forehead like he'd been swimming. He holds Verona in a backward dip, her neck like a swan, her dark body overflowing the white dress molded to her. On her head she wears a white turban that reminds me of a drenched T-shirt. There's another photo of them receiving the trophy, couple number five, Manfred and Verona, about the same height, he white and she black, her large eyes glowing like those lights in the scrub field, her teeth a blaze of white. "I'm sure she's out there somewhere." Manfred's voice trembles with emotion. "He buried her in the desert. I bet he drove her across the border and buried her in Jornada del Muerto. Do you know what that means?"

"Journey of the Mother?" I guess.

Natalie guesses, "Juice of the Del Monte?"

"Single day's journey of a dead man," he answers. "She wanted to leave him, but he always kept one of the children with him. Always, so if she left she'd have to abandon one of her children. She wouldn't do that. I said the same thing when I reported her missing."

I'm still looking, trying to understand Verona, a desert princess. How could she have been seduced by Wystan Trevor Ricker? Penny, who never had a date, innocent pimpled Penny I understand. Maybe Verona wanted a firecracker white guy. Someone who could hold himself against the waves of body flooding the straps and bodice. I can feel her ready to take her name back, wanting to have legs and knees again, to run, and to see her children. Her eyes tell me I don't know how lucky I am to be breathing.

"Natalie, we're going to get Penny out of there," I vow, clenching my fists. "And the baby."

The pink truck looms like a tanker, like a tractor-trailer with a chain winch.

❀ ❀ ❀

Wystan and a fully dressed Penny emerge from the garage. She walks slowly over to Natalie's side of the truck like she's still listening to something her boyfriend is saying. "He says he'll follow you out there." Her blue-green eyes look blank. Natalie keeps her eyes peeled on the pink truck where Wystan, already in the driver's seat, checks the headlights.

"I want to see the baby," I say. "Where is the baby?"

"She's asleep," Penny says in her little girl's voice, looking down. Now touching the bruise on her cheek.

"Who's watching her?" Natalie asks.

"Magdalena."

"Why don't you go get her," I say, "we'll wait."

"Huh?" she asks.

❀ ❀ ❀

The field hasn't moved. The Impala looks like it's waiting patiently under the lights. Like a girl buried in the desert about to be dug up. Manfred stops the pick-up, tells us to hang on, he's going to open the car doors first and then carry us to the Impala. "He seems decent, don't you think, Natalie?" Natalie pushes her camera into her purse. "He's crazy, but not too bad." He brushes his blond bangs and large nose and carries Natalie and her purse first to the car. I shift closer to the passenger door and wait for my turn when the door opens and there stands Wystan. He reaches under my knees with his right arm and works his left under my back and lifts me off the seat. I feel him stagger once backing up, then steady himself, his low center of gravity adjusting to my weight, carrying me away from Manfred's truck. Now the stars fall into my face as I look past Wystan, his neck straining and the veins standing, his jacket smells of new leather and strong expensive cologne. He wears a gold pinkie ring. I wonder if that's what he cut Penny's lip with. Manfred has already opened the door of the Impala and I see my wheelchair in the back seat and feel relief. Wystan sets me down on the edge of the front seat. Home. I lift my feet and slide myself in.

"What's wrong with you? Why are you in a wheelchair?" he asks in his raspy voice that would be low even for a library.

"That's none of your business," I snap, my cheeks burning. An owl hoots. Prairie dogs huddle broken-heartedly. I sometimes wish I could stop being a person. It's dangerous to communicate with the enemy. He might try to beguile you into a conversation. His eyes open a little wider, and then the lids lower to that half-mast, half asleep expression. He bows slightly. "Do you play chess?"

"Yes," I say, wondering if he'll still pull us out with his winch.

"I'd like to play you sometime," he says, his lips pulling back into a kind of grimace. "Keep your car in neutral once I put the winch on." He pushes the driver's door closed.

What's wrong with you? If people don't ask that question directly, they think it. No, fool, what's wrong with *you*. You sleepy-eyed horned lizard. I'm one of Jerry's girls, who are you? Have you ever heard of the Jerry Lewis Telethon? I hate his movies, his idiot bucktoothed jokes, but the Muscular Dystrophy Association has money because of him. Not like Natalie's Arthritis Society. When I was in elementary school and still normal, my mother used to make me watch the telethon. It was torture.

I put the car in neutral and light a cigarette. "Natalie, did you hear Wystan? 'What's wrong with you?' Like he had a right to ask. And looking at me with those greasy eyes of his."

Natalie unzips her coin purse and slips an aspirin into her mouth. She chews and dry swallows it. "Check out the Wystan samwich now," she cackles. "He's carrying his chain over his shoulder like he's Hercules. He shouldn't have brought children into the world. Someone should have snipped him. Penny, too."

The front of the Impala shudders.

"Girl's don't get snipped," I tell her, putting the cigarette out. I blow out a cloud of smoke and wait for Wystan to get back into his pink truck. But he's fiddling around with the Impala's hood. There he stands under the desert stars holding his chain like a rattlesnake.

"Neutered then. But we have to get the baby out," she says.

"We will. I have an idea."

"Think he's drugging her?"

"With what?" I ask. "No, he's beating her. That's a drug."

What's wrong with you? When you're in a wheelchair everyone thinks they have the right to pry into your life. Jerry Lewis' March of Dimes spins around in my head. Muscular Dystrophy. The muscles atrophy. Some MD attacks the upper body muscles, some the lower. There's MD only boys get in infancy, the bad gene, the one that doesn't know how to process proteins, gets passed from the mother to her son. Five-year-old boys waddling and up on their tiptoes not able to use the heels of their feet. MD is rarer in girls. The gene I got came from my father, Richard, an engineer. He suffers from mild, almost invisible MD and kept it secret. He never told my mother until he had to—when I was diagnosed. I could never smile with my mouth. My facial muscles didn't let me. Maybe my father noticed, maybe that explains his coldness to me. When puberty arrived, the secret inside me began to bloom too. I think of how my eyes roll back when I'm asleep and the muscles in my lids don't work and can't close. So if you watched me sleep the whites of my eyeballs might frighten you. It was me not smiling that finally woke my father up.

I remember being ten years old in my camel-colored pleated skirt seated on the floor with legs to the side, as if riding the carpet side-saddle. The Siamese, Sasha, lies against my leg. For a moment the photographer focuses on me and the cat. He tells us we both have bewitching eyes. Ten is a peculiar age, awkward, but I had those long slanting lids and dark brown irises staring out so solemnly. A cat-girl. Behind me the stupid flocked Christmas tree and the blue stars and red satin covered balls. "Okay let's all smile. Big smile on the count of three. Cheese, say cheese," the photographer commanded. I could see him thinking he'd have to get the cat of a girl to smile, to stop staring at him with those slow river eyes; she knew he needed to get to his next house, his next appointment. Just get her to smile, like her two brothers Steve and Christian, honor society boys in cable-knit sweaters, like Sharon, the gap-toothed younger sister, grinning ear-to-ear. "Jana, would you look this way and say cheese?" Maybe my eyes flashed, irritated because I was smiling, at least I thought I was. I could feel it in my cheeks and chin. He wanted me to show teeth. "Spaghetti, Jana, relax. Think spaghetti and say cheese." I was looking his way, and then I said cheese but the word didn't turn my mouth into white-teeth. My father, sitting on the couch next to my mother, looked at me. In that moment he knew I had it. Earlier I'd seen him trip going up the steps into the living room. His leg gave out, then he immediately righted himself. I tore that photograph of my Christmas family into many pieces, I tore up the fireplace burning its gas log, the eggnog and fruit cake, a can of Redi-Whip, the ruby red goblets. I reminded my father of a Siamese cat too. I had the secret in me like he had it in him. I tore up the handsome father seated next to my fine-boned mother, who wore a turquoise skirt and cashmere sweater her lover had given her. I tore her up too. I tore up the tinsel tree with blue bulbs.

❀ ❀ ❀

We're back on the highway heading for Las Cruces. Natalie tries to laugh and says we showed Wystan that Penny has her protectors—the wheelchair girls. I think I believe her. I believe the dry earth weeps water. That birds never die and babies don't grow up into draggy adults. Then I turn up the radio and Natalie and I sing.

Photo by Alex Lloyd

CHIDELIA EDOCHIE's fiction and nonfiction appear in *Utne Reader, Gulf Coast Magazine, Michigan Quarterly Review*, and various other journals. Her work has also won numerous awards, including a grant from the Elizabeth George Foundation and Top 25-List honors in *Glimmer Train*'s Short Story Award for New Writers. She is the 2012 Writer-in-Residence at the Shanghai M-Residency, where she is currently working on a novel.

THINGS OF BEAUTY
Chidelia Edochie

I made up a song about the new Korean kid at school and got all the other black girls in my class to sing it, too. We spent the whole day practicing, whispering the song under our butterscotch breaths. We were supposed to be gluing rainbow-colored construction paper onto large white poster boards, and our teacher, Mr. Peters, commented on how well we were working together, so quiet and diligent. He couldn't have known that a secret plan of attack had bonded us for the day, so that we had begun to move unconsciously in unison. The snip of our scissors created a dry, sawing hum, and it was to this melody that we whispered our taunt. Maybe Mr. Peters heard us—we were only a few feet away from his desk after all—but who would believe such mean words could tumble from our sweet little-girl lips?

We were busy creating oversized maps of the continents in our eighth-grade homeroom. That evening we would put on a cultural performance called "Things of Beauty from Around the World" for our parents and the local community, where we would traipse out onto a stage and detail the natural glories and deliciousness that could be found in countries we'd never before heard of, and continents we'd thought of only in dreams. I had fought to be assigned to Asia when the teachers were picking the roles. I wanted to be the one to don the poofy black headpiece with chopsticks sticking out, and there'd been rumors that a long red kimono dress would be provided. I'd already decided that year: Red was my color. My momma had taken me to a department store for my thirteenth birthday months before and had allowed me to try on a short, red, frilly skirt, and twirl around in front of a three-sided mirror.

Even though my knees were too knobby for skirts, as my momma told me, I looked good in red.

So when the Korean kids showed up at *my* school, and Mr. Peters decided to give that Korean girl *my* part in the performance, it was like a punch in the gut. I was ready for war.

❈ ❈ ❈

We went to an Atlanta magnet school built in the 80s by the then-mayor who had promised a safe academic haven for the children of his black, middle-class voters. We were bussed in from rowdy suburbs—Stone Mountain, Lithonia, East Lake—and learned quickly to be proud of our new school that had teachers with Master's degrees and no outdoor trailers. It was a clever zoning trick, stipulating that only students from overpopulated districts could attend and that all students had to be tested in. Because of these policies, the school ended up filled with the children of upwardly mobile blacks who firmly believed that they were worlds apart from the working-class black folk down the street from themselves, just as the mayor had planned. Our parents thought it was funny—white folks had been doing stuff like this for years.

This was why the arrival of the two Korean kids—one girl, one boy—was so strange. Over the years the school had diversified a little. We had some whites and a few Latino students, but there had never been any Asians. The two showed up in the middle of the school year just after we'd gotten back from Christmas break. My friends and I were sitting in Mr. Peters' classroom, comparing gifts. I was showing off the jean pleated skirt that swished against my newly-grown butt, getting up to prance around the classroom under the guise of sharpening my pencil and throwing away crumbled balls of blank paper. My best friend, Leila, was trying to get me to *ooh* over the new purple bracelet she wore, and I was considering telling her how ugly it really was, when the school secretary walked in with the new kids in tow. We couldn't tell if they were cousins, or brother and sister, or what. The boy, a sixth-grader, clung to the girl's winter coat like she was his momma.

I sized her up. She wore faded corduroys, the same pink color as the rims of her glasses. She wasn't really fat, but had a chubby, smushed-up face, which made me think she *could* be a fat girl until she took off her coat.

Mr. Peters told her to introduce herself to the class. "Tell us your name, sweetheart, and speak up so we can hear you," he said.

She leaned her head to the side, so low that it almost rested on her shoulder; it was then that I noticed how long her neck was. My momma said a long neck made you look graceful. But my neck is short and thick. My momma told me once that it looked like a tree stump.

"I'm Kimmy," was all that the girl would say.

Mr. Peters sent her to a desk near mine. When she was close enough for me to see her face, to see the red skin under her nose, I stopped talking to Leila. My arms stiffened up and fell dead against my sides.

I knew her.

Leila leaned over and whispered into my ear. "Oooh, Alysha," she breathed. "Look at her hair."

※ ※ ※

Kimmy's family owned the Korean beauty supply store where my momma and I shopped. It was less than half a mile from our house in Stone Mountain, an all-black suburb outside of Atlanta. Their store was set inside the shopping plaza where we went to buy groceries, get our nails done, rent videos—everything. All the stores in that plaza used curved blue lettering for their name signs, but the beauty supply store sign was red and blocky, the words "Beauty" and "Supply" separated by a large cherry hanging down.

My momma and I both loved to shop there. She preferred it to the supermarket because it had everything her body needed: shea butter for her sandpapery feet, face lotion to lighten her complexion, peppermint oil for her underarms. I liked it because I could get away with stuff without being watched by some keen-eyed clerk. I would sample each bottle of body butter until my hands smelled like every tropical scent combined. I'd pour out drops of shampoo onto the floor to see if it soaked into the fibers of the carpet, telling me whether it really was moisturizing enough for my dry, nappy hair.

We usually went to the beauty supply store that Kimmy's family owned on Sunday afternoons, and my momma always headed straight for the wall lined with wigs. I'd follow close behind—eager—ready to help her fit a stocking cap onto her head and comb out the wigs' plasticky curls. She and I would stand at the store mirror for at least half an hour, both of us trying on different hair pieces in varying shades of reds and blondes that contrasted sharply with our cedar-colored skin.

My momma was a beauty. She liked to tell me stories about how, at a summer picnic hosted by her sorority, she had hooked my father with only a look.

109

I was standing on the line-up with the other Sorors, getting ready to do the call. Your daddy was standing away from the crowd under a tree, leaning back like he was just too cool, watching me. The other girls and I were calling out our trademark "skiii–woop!" and this man had the nerve to flick out his tongue at me! Humph, he probably thought I'd fall for him right then and there. But I knew how to play it. I never had to chase a man in my life, and I wasn't about to start. Just gave him this here look. Then she would show me the look, where she pursed her thick lips and lifted an eyebrow. Depending on the day, a shoulder shake was involved.

When I thought of my daddy flicking his soft pink tongue at my momma—a woman he barely even knew—it made my body heat up, like I was burning from the inside. It made me wonder if my daddy still did that, flicked his tongue at strange women. And watching my momma as she told the same story again and again, her head tilted to the side as if the very thought of herself as a young sorority girl made her drunk, I'd get the funny urge to kiss her on the mouth.

My momma and I had only seen Kimmy at the beauty supply store a few times. She'd be sitting behind one of the counters, cheek in her hand and elbow planted. I could tell she was around my age, but besides that I didn't find her too interesting. We never spoke to one another. The woman that I guessed was her mother was usually busy with a customer, and my own momma wasn't the type to force me to speak to other kids, especially not to chubby-mouthed Asian girls who slouched over counters and blocked our view of the wigs.

We did almost speak, but only once. It was the summer before eighth grade, when Kimmy would show up in my class.

Kimmy's momma was ringing us up. I was buying a bottle of red sparkle nail polish. I stood there, hand on my hip and leaning to one side like I was grown; buying things with my own money always did that to me. Her momma handed my purchase to Kimmy to put in a plastic bag, and when her pale little fingers wrapped around the bottle, I saw she was wearing the same red shade on her own nails that I'd just bought. She must have seen this too, because she looked up and smiled, and I smiled right back. We looked at each other this way for a moment, our lips puckered up and cheeks dimpled. Kimmy opened her mouth to say something to me, but stopped when my momma reached out to touch her hair.

"Oooh," my momma breathed, "your daughter has the most beautiful hair." My momma leaned over the counter, her elbow knocking over some lip glosses. She stroked Kimmy's head as if she were petting a family cat. Kimmy's momma just smiled, and my momma kept on.

"I wish my girl had hair like this. You probably don't have to do a thing to it."

Kimmy kept looking at me, her head titled toward my momma. Her eyes moved to the top of my head where my short, scraggly brown ponytail sat. Years of perming and hot-pressing had left my hair thin and fried, but it was still all right by black girls' standards. It was my momma herself who'd insisted on me getting a perm when I was only seven years old, hauling me into the salon and sitting me down on a black leather swivel chair that I took for some kind of throne. But now, my momma seemed to forget this, seemed to forget me, even. All I could do was stand there and watch my momma touch that girl's head.

She started at Kimmy's scalp, cupping her palm slightly. She weaved a thick strand of hair between her fingers. Kimmy's eyes had slid almost closed. The smirk turned into a full smile, so that the pudgy features broadened and stretched across her face. She almost looked pretty.

"What a beauty," my momma said, finally letting the girl's glossy strands drop from her fingers. She turned to me and smiled. "You ready to go?"

We left the store. In the parking lot it smelled like trash, and the dry cleaners attached to the beauty supply store gave out a wet warmth that made me sweat and want to throw up. My momma lifted her head toward the sky, smiled at nothing, and then looked down at me

"Pick up your face, Alysha," she said to me. "You look so ugly when you scrunch up your face like that." She waited. "What's wrong with you?"

"Nothing," was all I could say.

❀ ❀ ❀

It was half a year later when Kimmy walked into Mr. Peters' class, a week before the "Things of Beauty from Around the World" show. She sat down at her new desk, only a foot away from mine, and stared at her feet like she didn't know what to do.

I pushed my elbow into Leila's side. "Let's go talk to her." Leila nodded and we got up from our seats, a few other girls following our lead. We crowded around her desk.

"Hey," I said, drawing out the sound, my voice honeyed. Kimmy's head jerked up, and she took in the circle of dark faces surrounding her, smiles on all of our lips. She pulled her hands from the desk and into her lap, as if she wanted to hide them from us.

"I'm Alysha," I said. "Who was that little boy who came in here with you?"

Kimmy didn't answer. She just looked at us sort of dumbly, as if she didn't understand who *we* were, like she didn't know that she was in *our* school. She was acting like she didn't even recognize me, which I couldn't believe. How was she going to just sit there and pretend to forget *my* momma's hand on her head, *my* nail polish on her fingers?

Leila chimed in. "Was he your brother, or what?"

Another girl behind us, Thomasina, asked, "What school did you come from?" Kimmy wouldn't answer anybody, just kept staring at all of us. Then, her eyes settled on mine.

"She's stuck-up!" I screamed, and pointed my finger into her chest. My voice was so loud that even my friends backed away from me at first, their eyes widening, thinking I'd gone crazy.

I looked around at them wildly. "*She's stuck-up,*" I said again, this time in a whisper. But my voice held an urgency that made the girls eye Kimmy with new suspicion.

Mr. Peters came jogging over to us. My outburst had made him spill something green onto his favorite ugly sweater, and his normally pink face was now red with worry and surprise.

"What happened?" he asked in his weak, pleading way. Mr. Peters looked at Kimmy, who was still sitting there with her hands clenched in her lap. A red blotch had formed across her cheeks and nose so that it looked like she was about to cry. I was sure she wouldn't, though. I still stood frozen over her and must have been looking menacing and corrupt, because Mr. Peters sent me out into the hallway.

Mr. Peters—up until then—had been my favorite teacher. I liked the way a dark, bristly mustache covered up the pink of his lips, how you could only see that fleshy, moist bit. When he smiled he did so wanly, as if smiling actually hurt a little. He was skinny, almost knobby at the knees and elbows and jaw, but I'd still spent entire mornings imagining him flicking out his tongue in my direction. As I stood outside the classroom in the hallway I could see Kimmy behind Mr. Peters' desk, being listened to, comforted. I had my head poked through the doorway, but when Kimmy and Mr. Peters both glanced over at me, I pulled myself back outside so fast that I knocked my head up against the steel side of the door and fell, sliding down the walls of the hallway. My hands shot out to grab a hold of something and I ended up ripping down the paper mural we'd painted earlier in the year of all our faces, surrounded by a border of handprints in reds and yellows and browns.

I considered ripping up the rest of the mural, shredding it, but then Mr. Peters came outside.

"Alysha," he said, his voice wound tight as if he were scared of something, maybe of me. "Alysha, Alysha. What happened? Kimmy says you just started yelling at her for no reason." He tilted his head, pursed his lips. "Now, can you tell me why you did that?"

I didn't say anything. I couldn't explain to Mr. Peters—or to myself—what it was about Kimmy that had gotten under my skin so much. But even so, I was ready to apologize. If he told me to, I would go back inside and say sorry and do a handshake or hug or whatever it was he wanted. But before I could tell him so, he looked down at my hands. A torn off piece of the mural—a project that I now remembered had been Mr. Peters's brainchild—with half a brown face and half a yellow hand painted on it was still clutched between my fingers.

"Alysha, what is this? Did you do this?" he asked.

I actually considered saying *No*. But he didn't wait for an answer. He took on the stance he used when he was trying to be firm with his students, holding his arms to his stomach and clutching his fingers together the way young singers in a choir do. He wouldn't tell me what Kimmy had said about me. Only that, since I was "being so unwelcoming," I could not be in the "Things of Beauty from Around the World" show. The next day I found out that Kimmy would take my spot.

❀ ❀ ❀

I taught my friends the song on the day of the show. Our gym teacher—a scrawny Italian transplant from the Midwest who did not believe in the existence of Georgia winters—made the class go outside for morning PE even though it was cold. We sat in a group on the blacktop, lying on our stomachs and picking off the gravel that stuck to the elbows of our coats. There, we plotted.

I'd told Leila that Kimmy had lied on me and gotten me kicked out of the "Things of Beauty from Around the World" show on purpose, just so she could steal my part as the presenter of Asia. Leila, being a friend, went and told everyone else. As far as they were concerned, Kimmy had lived up to my accusation of haughtiness. She refused to speak to anyone at school except for teachers and the little boy that she'd shown up with on the first day.

The boy's class had gym at the same time as us, and Kimmy would stand at the edge of the blacktop and watch him. He wasn't a thing like the coat-hugging baby from that first day. I knew this because I watched her watch him, and I watched him, too. He hung with the other boys easily, as if he'd spent his entire life exchanging teases and shoves with little black boys without fear. I almost felt bad for Kimmy, having to watch her little brother—or cousin, or whatever—arriving at a place that she'd never get to.

All during PE we practiced the song, changing up the cadence from a rap to a ballad, then back to a rap. The nasty words rose up from our mouths, hitting the dry air in fat steamy puffs.

One of the girls, Thomasina, didn't understand why the song would be insulting to Kimmy.

"I mean," Thomasina said, wiping her nose with the back of her hand, "how is *this* supposed to make her cry? Aren't we trying to make her cry?" Leila answered her, sparing me having to explain.

"She'll cry," Leila said as if Thomasina were the stupidest child she'd ever come across, "because we're saying that she looks like a cat. A dumb, *ugly* cat." And then she looked directly at Thomasina and muttered, "Fool."

We all laughed at Thomasina for asking such a dumb question. And Thomasina, like a fool, laughed, too.

I had told my momma and my daddy that I wasn't going to be one of the presenters after all, but a set director instead. The lie slid from my mouth easily, though I didn't even know what a set director was. They didn't question me, and said they'd just sit in the back then, to get a jump on the traffic when it was time to leave. The song ran like a river through my mind all evening, ready to seep from my mouth like dirty water right up until the start of the show when folks piled into the auditorium. I sat in the front row teaching the song to the white girl in our class, Bianca, who'd also been kicked out of the show for getting caught kissing the presenter of Mexico. I felt a warm pleasure at my genius for coming up with the words.

Chinese, Japanese,
Lookin' like a Siamese!
Chi-nese, Jap-a-nese,
Loo-kin' like a Si-a-mese!

The show began. Thomasina's role was to do the introduction—walking across the stage holding a long sheet of white paper that had "Things of Beauty from Around the World" printed across it. Leila's presentation on Jamaica came first. She did a Jamaican dance, swinging her arms low and high then low again, then threw some Jamaican hard candy out into the crowd. A boy presenting Brazil sang a song in Portuguese in a deep, operatic voice that shocked the whole audience, the baritone in his voice seeming to make the walls shake. Then it was Kimmy's turn.

She wore the kimono, which turned out to be purple, not red like I thought. I crouched down low in my seat, ready. She was carrying a brown teapot that didn't even look all that Asian to me—my grandmama had one just like it. Kimmy started her presentation, talking about the history of tea and how it started in China. She looked afraid.

The plan was this: While Kimmy was presenting the mountains and the rivers and all the other beautiful things that Asia had, Leila and Thomasina would start whispering the song from offstage, so that only Kimmy could hear. In the front row, Bianca and I would start to sing it softly, too, then louder and louder until the other kids joined in. We were sure they would.

"So tea's from China?" Bianca whispered, nudging me. "But I thought Kimmy was Korean."

I didn't correct her. I didn't say *No, she's not from China or Korea, she's from somewhere in Atlanta and wears my same color nail polish and would look pretty if she smiled more instead of pinching up her fat little face so much and she really is stuck-up.* I didn't say any of this because I had turned around in my seat, looking to make sure my momma and my daddy couldn't see me.

They were sitting right next to the exit, waiting for the show to end so that they could make a run for the car. Someone must've passed my momma a piece of the Jamaican candy, because her mouth was working up and down, and she looked happy. My daddy sat next to her, looking bored, both their coats piled on his lap. I was about to turn back around, back to the plan, when something stopped me. It was my daddy's tongue, flicking across his lips, light pink moving across dark brown. It was then, sitting on a folding chair in my school's little gymnasium, that it hit me: My daddy did this all the time. When I really thought about it, I couldn't remember a day going by without catching him massaging his bottom lip with a quick brush of his tongue.

My body began to heat up again, like how it did when my momma told me stories of catching my daddy with just a look, just her beauty. But now I was hot for a different reason. I knew something my momma didn't: She hadn't really been all that special after all. That flick of the tongue at a summer picnic, a little gesture she'd thought meant everything, was really just my daddy, now her husband, doing something he always had and always would.

Bianca was digging her elbow into my side. It was our turn to sing. I turned back to the stage and saw Kimmy standing there, her cheeks shiny, already crying. She was looking off to the left side of the stage, where Leila and Thomasina were probably crouched down, evil words dripping from their lips in a whisper. I could not hear them. But Kimmy could.

Bianca began to sing beside me. She was doing it wrong, she was saying *Siamese, Siamese, looking like a Japanese.* Again, I didn't correct her. I was too busy watching my momma. She was spitting the candy back into its wrapper. Even as the thrill of having some secret knowledge over my momma passed through me, I still knew that she must have figured this all out by now. She must know that my daddy had only been a man wetting his lips on a dry Atlanta day. It was a tic, just some physical quirk done without thinking. A woman like my momma—a beauty—must have known that men's bodies just *do* things sometimes, without reason. But as Kimmy stood before me on stage, tears streaming down her pudgy cheeks, I wondered when exactly had my momma figured this all out, and had it broken her heart?

Photo by Sarah R. Putnam

PETER W. FONG is a freelance editor and a flyfishing guide. His stories have appeared in *Carve, In Hemingway's Meadow, The New York Times Sophisticated Traveler,* and many other magazines and anthologies. Over the past fifteen years, he and his family have lived and worked in Montana, Vermont, Tokyo, Shanghai, and Aruba.

THE LIFE OF HUAI LI

Peter Fong

The government reported that two men fell from the sky that winter, but Grandmother could only confirm one. He was a foreigner, tall and handsome in the same way that a peach tree, split by lightning, remains pleasant to the eye. His passing tore an irregular hole in Grandmother's tile roof, and some of the cracked black slates landed beside him on the dirt floor of the kitchen where the old woman had been boiling water for tea.

Kuan Di said later that Grandmother could not remember if the man was wearing red or orange, but that his eyebrows were frozen— she was sure of that. Ice crystals glittered among the dark, curling hairs; it was the first thing she noticed in the unfamiliar light—that, and the white patches on his pale skin, like frost on a potato.

Huai Li could not forget the way that Kuan Di had told the story, with her strong legs tucked beneath her on the thin mattress of their Shanghai lodgings.

"Little brother," she had said, holding the throat of her nightgown closed with a fist, "these foreigners are—"

And then she'd waved both hands in the air, so that the gown fell partly open—so distressingly open that he had forced himself to watch her painted fingernails, fluttering in mad arcs of intolerable beauty.

She had laughed too, so freely that he'd wondered if his own excitement should rightly be called joy or sorrow. Everything had seemed strange to him during that first anxious month in the city: the buildings, the air, the people—and not just the outlanders with their odd customs and otherworldly hair, but even Kuan Di, who had bathed him as a child. He could not understand how she had become so different during his four years at Hangzhou Foreign Language High School. Her face, which had been ruddy and cheerful, was now pale and smooth as a winter melon. And her manner, while recognizable, had become infinitely more interesting, a multilayered puzzle of symbols and gestures that might inspire years of devoted study.

At that moment, if you had asked him what he wanted most in the world, America might have fallen from its customary position, replaced by the desire to press his cheek against the skin between Kuan Di's collarbones, to taste the air that escaped, spent, from her lips.

It was a shameful feeling, and the shame warmed him in the drafty, high-ceilinged room, the smallest of twelve apartments in what had once been a single family's home. Behind a false partition, the judge's old wife coughed, then struck a match. Huai Li waited for the sharp tobacco smell to overpower the stale scents of last night's sleep and yesterday's fried dumplings. Kuan Di stretched both arms above her head and yawned without the least inhibition, showing so much pink in the back of her throat that he had to look away.

The judge's old wife coughed again. No one in the building, including Comrade Gong, had ever met the new wife, or the judge himself for that matter. It was said that they disappeared separately, no more than a few days apart, soon after the revolution. But that was sixty years ago and more. The Comrade didn't look old enough for firsthand information. Huai Li wondered if Gong had read the story in a newspaper, or heard it whispered in the alleys, although he himself did not know which should be considered the less reliable source. The *Shanghai Daily*, for instance, had echoed the government's account of the frozen men, describing their fall from the landing gear of a Boeing 777 that had arrived in China after ten hours in the air from, of all places, Paris.

Still, it was possible, he thought, looking up at the pressed tin ceiling of what had once been the judge's elegant ballroom. Anything was possible in Shanghai, the Paris of the East, but all things were possible in America.

Kuan Di stood suddenly up, leaving him alone on the mattress. "It's time," she sighed.

Huai Li knew what she meant, but resented it all the same. When she held out a hand to him, he took it cautiously. They were the same height now, but he—who had always been smaller—still felt himself at a disadvantage.

As usual, he had slept in his gym clothes. Kuan Di tugged briefly at the neck of his wrinkled T-shirt. "You can't go out like that," she said.

Huai Li drew a deep breath, hands at his sides, as if to fill himself with purpose, although even he knew that purpose was not what he lacked. Kuan Di had already turned away, and stood now at the melon-crate desk that doubled as her dressing table, contemplating her lipsticks. He watched as one of her hands combed distractedly through her hair, cropped short in the manner of this season's television idol, while the other twisted a knot of fabric against her hip. With her back to him, it was easier to pretend that they did not share a family drama, complete with absent mothers and a bit-part gangster father. He had forgiven his father for many things over the years, but this accident of blood was beyond absolution.

He felt a childish misery rise in him, a nameless anguish that was nothing like the pain imparted by his monumental failure on the university entrance exam. In those first weeks after receiving his inadequate scores, Grandmother had been afraid to leave him alone with the kitchen knives. "Never mind, boy," she'd said. "Defeat isn't bitter if you don't swallow it." But try as he might, he could not understand what had gone wrong. He could remember the quiet certainty with which he had answered each question, the weary confidence he had felt at the end of the third day of testing, surveying the scene outside the exam center, crowded with anxious parents, some tight-lipped, others weeping. It had been an unusually stifling July, and the sweetish stink of rotting vegetables wafted across the fetid canal. He had not been expecting anyone to meet him and yet there was his father, wearing a knock-off suit cut for a bigger man, his bare forehead dampened by the summer heat.

"So, Professor," his father had said, grasping him by the elbow, "soon you will be teaching everyone about America." Huai Li had smiled back at him, surprised at the gratitude that welled like hope in his breast. He had almost forgotten what it was like to be glad to see his father.

"Hey dream boy," Kuan Di said, turning from the dressing table. "Are you listening to me?" She tightened the belt of the nightgown before placing her hands on his shoulders.

Huai Li struggled to retrieve himself from the confusing memories of assurance and pain, to return to the everyday desolation of unknowing. He forced himself to look into Kuan Di's unfathomable eyes.

"Today we need money," she said.

❊ ❊ ❊

The funny thing, Huai Li would think later—in one of those repetitive loops that added meaning to his life in the same way that waves added detritus to the shore—the funny thing was that he never even tasted the cheesecake. He had seen it from the street at first, through the window, on the plate of a foreign woman, an American or larger European, where it glistened like an emperor's bauble, bejeweled with fruit: small dark berries that were bluer and rounder than grapes.

He had noticed the café before, one of the many Nanjing Road establishments that displayed its clientele as prominently as its wares. Always he had made the requisite covetous glances, then moved on to the next exhibit of wealth and finery: Italian handbags, French pastry, American athletic shoes. He was no longer intimidated by such places, he told himself, and at that moment someone had touched his arm.

"Excuse me," a woman had said in English. "Can you help me find this address?" Her gloved finger pointed to an entry in a guidebook: "The Former Residence of Mao Zedong."

"Yes," he had replied, pausing to take stock of her knitted cashmere cap, the dangling jade earrings, the mature constellations of freckles on her cheeks and nose. Was it really cold enough for hats and gloves, if he had any? "I think so," he continued, while the woman openly returned his gaze, not in a challenging way, but as if she were genuinely interested in the tenor of his reply. Remarkably enough, he knew the place—Kuan Di had walked him past the gate on his first day in the city. She had not taken him inside of course—the entrance fee was five yuan—but it was only a few blocks away.

He glanced at his reflection in the café window, marked his image as dressed by Kuan Di, in blue oxford shirt and khaki cargo pants from the Xiang Yang market, notorious for cheap and occasionally skillful counterfeits. Because of the hunch-shouldered way that his hands slotted into his pockets, he did look a bit chilled, if not actually cold. He saw himself smile and nod, then noticed the other woman standing behind him, anxiously clutching her shoulder bag, another American.

"Hello," he said, politely extending his right hand, as if he greeted foreigners every day.

"Hello," she replied, moving closer to her friend with the jade earrings, but visibly relaxing. "I'm Megan, and this is Hannah."

Both women appeared to be of the same indeterminate American age, neither fourteen nor forty, though much closer to the latter, Huai Li thought, judging from Megan's faded denim jacket. That style, he knew, had been popular in the 1970s, after *The Last Picture Show* but before *Annie Hall.* For a moment, he felt that old inevitability return. It was time for a test, and he would know all the correct answers. His head echoed with Kuan Di's voice: stand straight, take off your sunglasses, don't waste your time with exchange students, lift your chin, introduce yourself with an English name.

"Pleased to meet you," he said. "My name is Huai Li."

❊ ❊ ❊

Mao had lived in the lane house for nine months in 1924, with the second of his four wives, Yang Kaihui, their two young sons, and Yang's mother. Huai Li followed Megan and Hannah through the young family's drawing room and bedroom, populated by thoughtful wax mannequins. The two Americans were respectful, if not openly awed. They took off their hats and gloves, then snapped pictures of Mao's figure seated behind a desk, his writing brush poised at the edge of the paper. Hannah asked how old Mao had been at the time, and Huai Li answered "Thirty-one," adding, "very young."

As they proceeded through the second-floor galleries, Hannah paused before each display of photographs and artifacts, lightly touching his arm again and again, her fingertips cool against his skin. As they regarded the leather sofa on which the Chairman had sat when visiting the Shanghai Machine Tool Works, Huai Li began to seriously wonder what might happen next. He had read on the Internet that sex with a stranger was the most erotic subject of American women's fantasies. Of course, he had also read that swallowing ten thousand milligrams of vitamin C a day would prevent cancer and that the Chinese central government planned to build a city of one million people which would be entirely self-sustaining, with no need of food, water, or energy from beyond its borders, like an island ark. How could he know which of these statements were true?

"Seventy million," Megan murmured, shaking her head.

"Pardon?" said Huai Li.

Hannah smiled thinly. "I'm sure that's exaggerated," she shrugged, her fingers again finding his forearm.

He knew then that the two women were referring to the widely cited number of deaths attributable to Mao, and considered reminding them of the Iraqi body count, but instead his mind leaped oddly to Mao's second wife, Yang, who could easily have been included in that number. She was arrested in Changsha by a local warlord and executed on November 14, 1930. Mao, who was by then the leader of the Red Army (and involved with another "revolutionary wife"), made no move to save her. No doubt it would have been impossible, Huai Li thought, or perhaps even unwise. His enemies would have been watching for just such a sign. This portion of the story remained untold in the museum, and Huai Li could not, at that moment, recall where he had learned it himself. No doubt on a Google search via some proxy server, but what did it matter in the end? As far as the museum-going public was concerned, Yang's mannequin—trim and modest, wearing a chaste white turtleneck, seated alongside a plumply waxen boy—was evidence of the Chairman's common humanity, his ability to form the ordinary family attachments. Mao *loved*. And he was loved in return.

Huai Li allowed himself to look closely at Hannah for the first time since she'd asked for directions. She reminded him of a certain American actress, the one who vacuums an empty living room wearing nothing but a slip and high heels, a scene that he'd cued up over and over on the school library's DVD player while researching a paper on "Images of Honorable Labor in the Post-Capitalist Cinema." He smiled at her, and she responded by saying, "I'm hungry," as if that were the most uncomplicated statement in the world. Her teeth looked very sharp and bright. For some reason, he thought of the blueberry cheesecake gleaming on its pedestal of clean white porcelain.

They followed the signs to the exit, no longer paying attention either to the exhibits or their typeset placards. The route led them toward the requisite gift shop, with Huai Li walking behind the Americans, asking questions about their lunchtime likes and dislikes, until he suddenly stuttered on the word "dumpling."

Ahead, to his surprise, sitting straight-backed on a folding stool, was Comrade Gong. Or was it? Huai Li hadn't realized that Gong was the beneficiary of gainful employment; the man always seemed to be hanging around the old judge's house, playing cards with the neighbors at a folding table, smoking cigarettes on the dirty stone steps that fronted the entryway. He didn't seem to have the motivation to keep a caged bird or even a pet cricket, much less a steady job. Huai Li peered down the hall at the man's profile: the wide-winged nose and smooth-shaven cheek, the delicately mouse-like ear, the receding thatch of gray hair leaking from the band of his security guard's cap. If only he could see the bald scalp, scaly with eczema—but that was no longer necessary.

The guard turned his head at the sound of their voices. Huai Li met his gaze. He would've spoken a greeting if Gong hadn't flicked his eyes from Huai Li to Hannah and then quickly away again, to some vague middle distance. Huai Li felt an unaccountable warmth suffuse the back of his neck, the palms of his hands—not shame exactly, but something like guilt. Without recognizing the source of his resentment, he scowled at Gong's placid face.

The Comrade held a Chinese-English dictionary in his hands, not reading it, but apparently contemplating its weight. He nodded at Huai Li in noncommittal fashion, as if they shared some secret that Megan and Hannah were not privy to. The American women took no notice of Gong at all, moving through the gift shop with practiced discrimination, ignoring the standard paraphernalia of Mao's divinity: bronzed medallions, crystal paperweights, a palm-sized gilt-framed portrait that cost more than Kuan Di's monthly rent.

Huai Li edged closer to Hannah, turning his back on Gong. He leaned over her shoulder, pretending to be interested in a Foreign Press edition of the treasured Red Book. He held his breath, listening to the blood beating in his brain as she rustled the pages, then read aloud in her guileless voice: "We must first be clear on what is meant by 'the people' and what is meant by 'the enemy.'"

Gradually, he became more aware of the nearness of her person, of the warm expanse of skin beneath the dangling earring and the hemmed neckline of her blouse. When he allowed himself to breathe again, a stifled intake of the air close between them, bearing a ration of her scent into his lungs, the image that formed in his mind was of Kuan Di descending the steps of the judge's residence while Gong's gaze turned, focused, then turned again to that middle distance, the practiced stare of a card player who already knows what's in his hand. In that moment, Huai Li's attention had also been on Kuan Di, on her face shining in the dull light of a Shanghai dusk, on the casual smile that lifted his heart like a leaf. It had seemed petty to take notice of Gong at the time, and yet here was the man again, commanding attention in the manner of a wayward piece of furniture, like a kitchen stool in a parking lot.

He couldn't think of anything to do except follow Hannah out of the museum and into the brick courtyard. There, free of Gong's abstracted scrutiny, his mind returned to the present task. To his astonishment, Huai Li saw that both Hannah and Megan now held small bags from the gift shop. He stared at the pair of them, wondering when they had found the opportunity to make these purchases, and marveling at the ease and quickness with which they had parted with their money. Hadn't he been in the same room, breathing the same air?

"What's next?" asked Hannah, rubbing her hands together, although the sun had warmed considerably while they'd been inside. She smiled at him—wasn't she always smiling?—and at that moment Huai Li understood that she was not desperately beautiful like the American actress, and not achingly beautiful like Kuan Di. Her face was too generous with optimism and good cheer. Hannah, he realized, would give him anything that he asked, within reason.

He stepped forward and took her hand. "I'm sorry," he said, "but I have another appointment."

"Oh no," said Hannah, still gripping his hand. "But what about our lunch?"

Huai Li was again close enough to register the scent of her skin, a distinctly sweet smell in the sundry atmosphere of the city, tainted with a trace of body lotion and the faint odor of baked goods.

"Please let us take you to lunch," Hannah continued, looking into his eyes as ardently as some people gaze into mirrors.

"Something for your time, at least," said Megan, stepping between them, a ruddy hundred-yuan note in her hand.

Huai Li glanced away from the money, but the calculations came unbidden: fifteen bowls of beef noodles, twenty-five plates of pork dumplings, fifty bus fares, one thousand text messages—if he'd owned a hand phone, which he did not. "No," he said resolutely, shaking his head to banish the image of Kuan Di's disapproval. "Really. It was my pleasure."

He walked away from them, out of the gate and onto Maoming Road. He kept on ahead, furiously resisting the urge to turn back, sidling across busy Weihai Road and its shops of dusty autoparts, a drab commercial block destined, he had read, for repurposing as luxury apartments. At the next gate he turned into a quiet lane, where a remnant of Shanghai's traditional rows of stone-framed housing had survived the latest real-estate boom. Between the high walls of red and gray stones, his thoughts slowed to match his steps. Kuan Di was wrong about this; he was sure of it. Money was as indispensable as criticism—that went without saying—but what good would it be to arrive in America with his heart frozen inside him?

In Huai Li's estimation, the two foreigners who fell from the sky had made at least two mistakes. First, they had botched the choice of destination: It was absolutely no trouble to get to Shanghai. Millions of undocumented peasants had done it, by bus or by train, and with little risk of frostbite. More importantly, the two had failed to insulate themselves from the rigors of the journey. They had dressed like construction workers ready for an ordinary day on the job, when in fact this occupation was nothing like a job. It was neither a living nor a livelihood, but more like a rehabilitation, the deliberate recovery from a grievous injury, inflicted at birth.

He himself had heard of a boy from Chengdu who had walked to America, literally walked from his parents' tea house, out of the provincial capital and over a succession of mountain passes, walking whenever he felt tired or hungry (which was all the time), walking vaguely south and east until the low hills gave way under his feet, walking until the river became a delta and the delta became a port, walking undeterred aboard a freighter bound for Lima, Peru, laden with laptop computers and children's toys, walking watches around the deck, miles and miles across the indifferent ocean, walking long after his persistence had been proved.

Photo by Phillip Tobin

EMILY HOWSON received her MFA from North Carolina State University in 2012. She won the Brenda L. Smart Fiction Prize in 2011 and received an honorable mention for a 2010 Academy of American Poets prize. Her work has appeared in *Raleigh Review, Orpheus,* and *St. Anthony Messenger.* For the next year, Howson will be living in Tel Aviv, Israel, with her husband and her dog, writing, editing, and searching for the Ark of the Covenant.

COUNTRY CLUB PEOPLE
Emily Howson

The photograph shows an open, flower-draped room filled with young men and women dancing. It is black and white but fading, really more slate and beige. The young men face away from the camera, dark pillars of tuxedos with turned faces, slicked hair, stiff shoulders. Along the wall a line of older men in suits, not dancing, stand holding glasses of scotch, winking I-was-young-once and, I imagine, saying things like, *How'd you play the back nine today?*

There are no wives standing beside these men, or along the adjacent wall in their own comfortable row. Perhaps they had gone to get more punch, or to sit at a table, quieter, further from the exhilaration of the dancers, to exchange a new recipe or gossip. *What did he do to get detention? Why would she plant hydrangeas out of season? For years he's been screwing that girl at the lumber yard.* Or perhaps, after all, they are standing just outside the camera's range, watching the dancers, their hair curled and pinned tight, their feet remembering and tapping I-was-young-once, too. The mothers, the ones with daughters dancing, must've helped prepare for this night with perfume and hairspray and warnings like, *Wait till he's through with law school.*

These daughters—young, young women—are whirling. Their faces, as they look in the direction of the camera, are pale and smooth—pretty in a way that can be trapped in an old photograph. A few are laughing. Most are smiling as they stare up at the young men, their dance partners. Their eyes are almost devious, hinting, *Maybe if you promise to love me* or, *Later when your mother won't see* or even, *After you're through with law school.* Behind the dark columns of the men's backs, their skirts flare in wide, white, imperfect circles.

❀ ❀ ❀

My grandmother is one of the dancers in the photograph. I know because when I was fourteen, the balding bartender at the Westwood Hills Country Club told me while handing me a Diet Coke and pointing behind him to where the photo—large, matted, and mahogany-framed, hangs above the bottles of Tanqueray and Gilbey's. He said, "Wasn't your grandma pretty?" He thought I knew. He thought, like anyone would, that, having passed by this bar and its photograph with my parents hundreds of times, one of them would have stopped, and pointed, and said, "Look, right there. That's your grandma. Wasn't she pretty?" So I didn't tell him I didn't know which dancer was my grandmother. I just nodded, and smiled, and tipped him five dollars of my parents' money.

Later, another day, when I was supposed to be swimming and there was no bartender to observe me, I sat at the bar and stared at the photograph and wondered which woman was my pretty grandmother. *Shouldn't I be able to recognize part of my own face? Was she happy that night, dancing?*

Long before I was born she had disappeared—banished from my family's lives—remaining only in that photo and the scandal she left behind. For the people at Westwood, scandal was art—to be studied, preserved, kept on display. My parents were part of it, and I became part of it as well. We were firmly, religiously country club people—though it wasn't until after I went off to college that I learned what that meant and developed contempt for it. My dad sold real estate, the kind of large gorgeous mansions that make you whisper when you enter and wonder what to do with your shoes. He was a fat man with a fat mustache who was constantly sweating through his golf shirts. First under the arms, then down the back, and finally, around the chest—patches of dark damp curving under his breasts, soaking the brightly colored polyester. I liked to pick out patterns on him: sometimes a butterfly, sometimes a jet pack. He insisted on giving hugs before showering, greeting my mother and me in a press of moisture and warmth. I figured it was an unconscious thing, an elemental carry-on, throwback to the days of stone clubs and scent marking. It was to be put up with.

Worse were my mother's wispy clasps, a flutter of hands and perfume, a cool cheek that usually met my own but sometimes missed and hit my neck, or my ear. She was short and her skin always managed to feel as though she'd just applied lotion, though I never learned why and she never passed on the secret. She helped my father sell his mansions; though in another life, she said, she played piano, thinking of being a music teacher. I found this difficult to believe, considering I hadn't been allowed to go near the piano in our house, preserved as it was in the front room, where nothing was touched.

My mother was a sleepwalker and had been ever since girlhood. It was especially bad when she was worked up about something. Usually she just walked the house, talked to the picture frames, or went looking for the cat. Once, she'd peeled six lemons. My dad was a heavy sleeper. He didn't always notice when she was up sleepwalking, and they'd figure it out later when a trash can had been moved, or she had a new paper cut on her hand that left her thin skin parted.

As a kid, I could never understand what brought my parents together, the two having absolutely nothing in common that I could see except that neither of them liked to mention their own parents. Both of Dad's were dead and he grew flustered when talking about them, which I took to mean he either loved them, was embarrassed by them, or both. Around country clubs, love and shame are hard to separate. My mother never spoke of hers but in silences—sharp and sometimes so awkward it was hard to breathe around them if you're like me and feel responsible for the discomfort of any given moment.

I knew that my mother's father had committed suicide two months after my parents' wedding—a full year before I was born. *He'd been sick for a long time,* my dad had explained. The two of us were sitting in a golf cart, sweating in the sun, alone before a wide open fairway. He told me about hospitals and long battles and diseases like marching armies, how sometimes people grew sad and tired, but my grandfather was not a bad man; he'd stuck around to see my mother in good hands. She hadn't taken his death well—*how would you feel if I died,* Dad reminded—and that was why I was not ever, ever under any circumstances to ask her about him. All of this I took in, but I wasn't satisfied about why I couldn't know my grandmother, my one remaining grandparent.

I remember asking my mother when I was young, ten at the most: "What's my grandmother like?" I never called her Grandma; she wasn't a person to me or even a signature on a card in the mail. She was my grandmother, a reference point only.

My mother could have said anything, any of that semi-instructional nonsense parents tell their kids: "She's very, very smart, and you will be too, just like that, if you eat the rest of your spinach." Instead she didn't say anything, and after I repeated the question twice, my voice plaintive and bewildered, Dad had to answer: "She's not a very nice grandmother, Honey. Some people just aren't nice. So be a lady, hmm? Don't bother your mother about her."

I stopped asking.

Then, when I was fourteen the bartender pointed out that photo, and I started to figure out what happened on my own. There was Mrs. Liebholtz, drunk at swim practice, when I pushed Joey Katz in for telling me I had a unibrow. It was August and the sun was glittering on the blue water and reflecting off the ranks of white plastic lounge chairs lined up along the concrete edge of the pool. I was always unnerved by the empty, towel-less chairs; their plastic bars made them look like skeletons, like rib cages. Mrs. Liebholtz was a loud, leathery woman, and she was never without a gin and tonic, poured into one of the Styrofoam cups allowed at the pool. She pointed it at me then, slopping some over the rim: "Watch it, Miss Hayes."

I thought she was going to yell at me for pushing Joey. Instead she gave me a slanted, knowing look that I instantly hated. "You're starting to get yourself quite a pair of boobies." Ten other kids standing around and she had to say "boobies." She gestured to her own. "Got to keep an eye on them or they'll lead you to trouble. End up like your grandma."

If I'd been a braver kid, I would have said, "How?" and demanded to know what she meant. But I was never a brave kid. Instead I spent the next few months distrusting my breasts, guilty for liking the way they looked and aware that at any moment they put me one false move away from trouble.

There was also Dr. Mackey, a retired dentist. He had a habit of calling me Susan even though my name is Gloria. I would hold the door open for him sometimes. He was a shaky mover and walked with a cane. "You're a good girl," he'd say. "Your mother's daughter. Not your grandmother's, eh?" Like we were both in on a joke, he'd start wheezing laughter. "You see her, you tell her Bobby Mackey says hi, eh?"

Of course, I didn't see her. I didn't know then if she was even still alive. But there was Dr. Mackey's watery eyes and the smell of his breath—like old tuna—when he made me lean in close to hear him, and so I lied and told him I'd be sure to pass his greeting along.

It was one of the clubhouse waitresses who eventually let me in on my grandmother's story. The waitress's name was Clara. She'd been working there since she was a girl, serving sandwiches to golfers, salads to their wives, and re-filling the bridge club widows' peanut bowls. Her birthday was two days after mine, and she turned seventy-two the year I turned fourteen.

The night she told me what happened, I'd escaped from a wedding reception in the clubhouse ballroom and wandered in on her sitting alone at the main bar overlooking the eighteenth hole, which had closed early. The wedding was a polite affair—everyone smiling too much—and I didn't know any of the other kids my age. I didn't even know the bride and groom. We'd only been invited, Dad said, because he was on the board this year, and worth sucking up to. We'd only attended, Mom said, because some of her friends were going, and they'd had to cancel the ladies nine-hole this week. She needed to catch up.

In the bar, Clara was folding bright red linen napkins, spotlighted by a single lamp in an otherwise dark room. Her shoes and her apron lay in a pile next to her on the ground, and by her elbow there was a plate of half-eaten lasagna that I recognized as a leftover version of what I'd been served at the wedding. I thought I'd be scolded and sent back to the party, but instead she let me use the fountain gun behind the counter and fix myself a Diet Coke with cherries in it. I was allowed to stay and sit next to her.

"Oh, just look at your grandma," she said after a while. We both stared at the photograph above the bar.

"She was gorgeous. A gorgeous woman." The skin on Clara's face was heavily lined and thick-looking, like yogurt. "But you know these people," she said. Her hands were swollen at the knuckles, and bent, like claws. She paused in her folding and waved one in the direction of the ballroom. "Bunch of bored asshole perverts."

I don't know if she talked like that to everyone, or if she'd sensed, or hoped, that I was different. Old age had given squeakiness to her voice, like the pedaling of a rusted bicycle.

"What happened?" I asked.

"Didn't your folks tell you?" Clara leaned in closer to me. "They used to have stag nights here, in the old clubhouse. Bring in prostitutes; whores from Cincinnati." She pronounced it *Cin-suh-nati*, spitting out the city's name like I'd heard other old locals say New York *Citay*—fabled, monstrous, contemptible. "Used to screw 'em in the locker room, make 'em dance, take off their clothes while the men watched. Here, in this very room."

Clara cackled at the look I gave her. "This is way back, back thirty years. They don't have no more stag nights." She patted my wrist with her strong, ugly hand. "Bunch of perverts. Had these things once a month. Stags were men's only. Yes, just the men. The women who worked at the club we'd get sent home at five o'clock. Not even allowed in the building. Hell no. Sheriff's men would guard the doors.

"They had a bunch of themes for the stags, like for galas, but it was just men and whores. They let the golf boys serve. Get all drunk. Let Walt—he was the club manager—tend the bar. But your grandma Millie got in. It was Mardi Gras, with masks and feathers, dances, sick little toys.

"Your grandpa was sick at home. He'd got cancer by then and dried-out, and Millie was still a pretty young thing, gorgeous. Should never have married a man so old—her daddy's partner, you know that? Leonard. What was his name? Leonard Gregory. Of course, you know that. Made a fortune investing other folks' money but I don't think I ever saw that man smile. And like I say, Millie was so young.

"So you know what she did? She paid off the whores. They say she bribed those Cincinnati whores. Have you ever heard such a thing? And they let her wear one of their costumes, so she could dance and screw in the locker room for money. For money. When you folks got plenty of money.

"They say she screwed half the members in one night. You listen though, that's a bunch of asshole talk. That's tale-telling. She did all sorts of things in that locker room though, with those old perverts.

"But you see, Doc Mackey pulled off her mask. Pulled it right off. So then there was this huge ruckus: They voted, she got kicked out of Westwood—they let your grandpa stay because of course it wasn't his fault—he divorced her and she left town. Good thing too. Half the members' wives would have seen her dead."

She cackled at me again then raised an index finger, crooked at the knuckle, and pointed it at me. "Can't blame her for leaving. You'd have thought your grandpa'd leave too, but business is business to these people—only club in town—and besides that he didn't get blamed for what Millie'd done. He was sick. Your mom was just a little thing when it happened, maybe seven years old, raised up here with all that talk chasing itself around."

I stared up at that photograph, into each of the pale, captured faces, and finally asked, "Which one is my grandmother?"

❊ ❊ ❊

For months after Clara's story, I avoided looking at the photograph and felt nauseated every time a man smiled at me. When I undressed in the locker room, I would think of what she'd done and picture someone watching me—through a vent, from around the corner, with a camera. At first this made me change hurriedly. Yet the more I thought about it, the more it became a kind of game. When no one was around, I'd pull off my clothes slowly, lingering over my own bra strap, and feel my skin pebble with goose bumps. Sometimes I'd hum to myself. I knew from practicing in the mirror how to stretch and twist my body in flattering ways. I was always embarrassed afterwards, confused at my own behavior, but that didn't stop me from meeting the eyes of the some of my dad's golfing buddies and imagining, maybe, that we had shared something forbidden.

Over time I discovered that what my grandmother had done was not really a secret, that most of the adults at Westwood seemed to know the truth and most of the kids knew an overblown mythical version in which my grandmother was anything from a rapist to the leader of her own whorehouse. Boys my age teased me about it; girls whispered behind cupped hands.

Pat was the first one to confront me directly. I was seventeen and he was twenty-two, a senior at Ohio State. He got a job at the halfway house that summer selling beer, Gatorade, and hot dogs so he could save up to buy a car. I thought he was poor, but he wasn't; his parents were both pharmacists. They just weren't country club members. He had Ed-Harris-blue eyes, long-fingered hands, and a way of talking to members that flirted with the line between respect and mockery. He chain-smoked cigarettes on his breaks, and on Mondays, when the clubhouse was closed and the course was quiet, I would smoke with him in the air-conditioned stockroom when I was supposed to be at the driving range. Pat had perfected a permanent look of boredom, making it clear that he barely tolerated my presence. He spent most of the time telling me I better not get him fired and the rest teaching me how to blow a smoke ring.

One afternoon, when we were sitting side by side on the floor, smoking in silence, leaning our backs against a metal shelving unit stocked with ketchup and mustard and boxes of M&Ms, and watching our gray-white breath mingle and rise and disperse, Pat said, "I heard a story about your grandma the other day."

When I didn't say anything, he leaned in closer. I could see the near-black ring surrounding the steel blue circle of his eyes.

"I heard, she was a whore," he said. He lingered over the word "whore"—testing, tentative, fascinated.

My hand was shaking a little from the nicotine.

"I guess what I was wondering," Pat said, "is if that kind of thing runs in your family." He took a drag off his cigarette with one hand and brought the other to my hair, toying with a strand that slipped like dark water between his fingers.

I laughed, but he didn't, only kept his fingers in my hair. I carefully put down my cigarette and I asked, "What do you think?"

His hand—long, cool fingers—moved to my hip and then slid under my pale yellow golf shirt, up my ribs to my bra. He kept his eyes on mine the whole time, watching for my reaction. I tried to smile.

He said, "It's okay. I won't tell."

❁ ❁ ❁

We met in the stockroom for that entire summer, and when he went back to college in September, we both said we'd call, visit, keep in touch. We didn't. He had made me feel different about myself, but after he left, I found that other boys could do the same. The only part of him I held onto was the American Spirits. I kept smoking until my dad caught me. It was January and I was in my room, using a fan to blow it out the open window, but when he walked outside on the patio to cool off in the winter air, he smelled the smoke. He lost it, cornered me in my room and lectured me about young ladies' conduct, yellow teeth, a larynx so scarred that at eighteen my voice would come out sounding like Liza Minnelli's. He worked himself up into a sweat, beads of salt and water forming at his hairline, racing each other to his eyebrows, then down his cheeks.

"We don't have to—we shouldn't tell your mother," he said finally. This was a long-standing arrangement between us; the lines of communication kept closed so as not to upset my mother. At all times, this was my father's protection for her—from me, from being upset.

For the cigarettes I was grounded, forced to spend the night of Westwood's Christmas dance on the sofa watching a tape-recorded PGA tournament with my dad while my mother locked herself in her bathroom for one of her self-prescribed at-home spa treatments. She'd been worn thin all week, she said, and couldn't be expected to chaperone the dance so it was just as well I had decided not to go. I spent most of the night fuming silently. I wanted a cigarette. I kept seeing Pat's lips curved around a smoke ring, curved as he said the word "whore." In the middle of one of Jack Nicklaus's putts, I worked up enough courage to ask, "Were you ever going to tell me about my grandmother?"

A long second stretched and hung. Dad paused the TV on a zoom shot of the ball trundling toward the hole. "Where did you hear about that?"

"It's everywhere."

"Keep your voice down."

"I'm whispering." We stared at the slightly blurred, unmoving screen. "Have you ever met her?" I asked.

"No."

"Did you ever want to?"

"Drop it, Glor."

"But why? You don't think it's odd? Mom pretends like nothing's wrong. She actually *likes* Westwood."

"Of course."

"'Of course'? There's no 'of course' in this. Everybody knew."

Dad glanced over his shoulder and pitched his voice even lower. "It's not something we should be discussing."

"We're the only ones who aren't discussing it."

"You have to look at it the way she does."

"Right. The way she does—which I have to intuit telepathically. She's in total denial."

"I think she has a right to it."

"To live in pretend-land? And, what, that's it—all she wrote? Why? That's what I want to know. Why stay?"

"Why does it matter?"

"C'mon."

"You're out of line. I'll say this once and then we're done with this conversation: Your grandpa's business was at the club, just like mine—Westwood is part of doing that business, spending time with the right people. We need those connections."

For years my mother had been a pathetic figure, but my dad had been different. I remember sitting up straighter on the sofa then and looking, really looking, at the wrinkles growing like branches, the retreating hairline, the Nilla Wafer crumb caught in the hairs of his mustache. "The right people?" I repeated.

"He wanted your mother to be well taken care of. Same as I do."

"He had money, I thought, boat loads. They could have moved. Westwood isn't the only country club in the world."

"You're an expert on this? He needed the community."

"Because it's such a loving place?" I couldn't look at my dad. "They call her a whore."

"She was a whore."

I looked up at him, caught his face as he said "whore"—the way his mustache curved with his lips. I turned away, stared at the lamp next to the sofa. The word settled between us, expanding, pressing against my chest with an unexpected tightness. "I thought you didn't know her."

"I didn't need to." He shifted on the armchair, drawing a noise from the leather, like a whimper. "I knew Leo. He did what he had to for his business and he took care of your mom until someone else could."

I had a vision of my dad, younger—slimmer waistline, slimmer mustache—shaking hands with my grandfather, a pale, suited figure, unsmiling. Business.

When I didn't say anything for a full minute, Dad unpaused the tape. The ball sped forward, curved down into the hole. Applause broke.

"I'm going to bed," I said.

Dad didn't take his eyes off the golf tape. "If you bring this up with your mother, you'll be grounded for a lot more than two weeks. You got it?"

"Yeah."

"I mean it. I don't want her to know that you found out; everybody else, fine. You? You keep it to yourself."

❋ ❋ ❋

In college, I tried to look her up. I found three Camilla Hutchinsons. One had died in an apartment fire; another was teaching web design at Kansas State. The last lived in the UK. Nobody fit the age, the type. None of them was the person I was looking for—the one I imagined, in her seventies and fierce, still attractive. That's how I thought of her: wearing tight dresses and pearls, smiling knowingly, hardened and fascinating, sleeping with men who wanted her and moving on, giving no promises. Other times I thought of her as quieter, exhausted from her one terrible rebellion, and given over to housework or soap operas with her hair tied back, no kids but a good man and secrets in her eyes.

I carried her with me, wrote her letters in my head sometimes and received her responses, her pride, her joy that I was so unlike *them*. She was still my reference point, wilder than I, harsher but wiser too. A couple years after college, I met my own good man, Mark. He asked me to marry him after eight blurred weeks, and he laughed when I asked whether he was going to take care of me. "You're not that kind of woman," he said. So I said yes.

My mother's first words at hearing the news were, "Why that's per-fect! I've been looking for a reason to throw a big party and look at that, now we've got one. We'll do the reception at Westwood, of course."

Mark and I had driven three hundred miles to share the news, to let them meet my future husband, and that was what she said. It turned into a full-on fight.

"Well, I don't see why not except for you're selfish; selfish and preju-diced," Mom declared.

"Prejudiced? *I'm* prejudiced?"

"Against good people, too."

"Country club people are *not* good people."

She fled the dinner table, chased away by my anger. I looked over at Mark. He was staring at me in a way he never had before, with wide eyes, face pale and unmoving—a look of animal surprise. Looking at him, seeing myself in miniature in his eyes, I almost cried in front of someone for the first time since the fifth grade, when I'd gotten my period at school and thought I was dying.

After dinner, I leaned against the granite-countered island, lis-tening to Dad and Mark talk in the living room and sipping a strong scotch and water. Dad had made it for me in the kitchen earlier saying, "Why'd you upset her over this? Is it worth it? Your mother needs this."

She called me upstairs around the time I finished the scotch. She was in her bed, collapsed against the white and gold brocade pillows. I stopped in the doorway. "I really don't want to fight," I said.

"You're my only child," she said, blinking at me with red-rimmed eyes. "And I—I may not be around much longer. I want to celebrate with my friends."

"You're not dying. And, I won't even know half the people you invite."

"If I'm paying for it—"

"Dad's the wallet, not you." I leaned against the wall just inside the door. "All right, look, I've been thinking. How about a trade—we'll compromise?"

Her eyes narrowed a fraction. "What's the trade?"

"I'll agree to have the reception at Westwood. *If*," I said, watching her carefully, "you tell me how to get in touch with my grandmother."

Her lips parted. Whatever she might have expected, I could tell it wasn't this. I took a step forward, worried she might fake a faint, but she didn't. All things considered, she looked calm. Pale, but controlled. I thought, *I should have asked her this years ago.*

But then she said, "No. I won't do it."

"Even for this reception."

"No."

"The reception you called your dearest dream half an hour ago?"

"Leave me alone."

I had only meant to dissuade her from Westwood—for this exact thing to happen—but now that I had, I didn't care so much about the reception. "Was it so bad," I asked quietly, "that you can't even handle the idea of me meeting her, talking to her on the phone?"

My mother stared resolutely away.

"Is she even alive?"

No response.

"Mom," I demanded, wanting her to at least look at me. "Fine. You can listen."

I had never been much of a drinker, and the scotch's leathery heat made the words tumble out unresisted. "Look, your mom, I know what she did. I've known since I was a kid. She left you, and you never talk about her. But it's all Westwood. That place is sick. Sick. I don't know how you don't see it. She was right to leave. Or she was forced to leave, but it was good that she did. You know what I mean."

I crossed my arms. "I know you don't listen, but you should leave too. Burn Westwood to the ground. Get out of here. Make Dad retire. Go to Florida, go to California. Go anywhere, just leave."

"Go like her?" My mother was looking at her hands. "Just leave."

"Yes."

"She's your role model now, is that what this is?" Her top lip was curled up, trembling a little—an almost-smile.

"I think what she did was brave."

My mother's nostrils flared. She looked up at me and then away, running her tongue under her top lip. "She was a whore. Left a whore; died a whore. You want to be a whore?"

I looked at her—red eyes, runny nose, the snarl of her lips. "Maybe it's in our blood."

"Excuse me?"

"She screwed maybe six or seven country club members, one night. The way I see it, you've been letting the whole club fuck you for years."

The words hit her like a slap—a staggered glaze slid over her eyes. Her chest fluttered, the shallow, erratic breaths of a child about to cry herself sick. But she didn't. There were no tears. Nothing. Only her breathing, and the sudden swelter in my throat and face, and a torn space between us—parted, gaping open. I waited for a long time for her to say something. When I left, she was back to staring at her hands. They were cupped loosely together in her lap, holding air.

Later that night, curled up in the bed in my old room and listening to Mark's snoring through the vent connecting to the guest room, I couldn't sleep. The room was nearly black, but I could see it without light, with just memory: a wall of swimming trophies, a desk stacked with framed pictures of old friends—some, at Westwood parties—and a bay window seat whose gray-green cushions I'd worn thin, sitting and staring at the line of pine trees separating our lot from the one behind it. I was thinking of those trees, of the high school running back who'd pressed me down in the sharp, scented needles, telling me how pretty I was, over and over, while he fumbled with his belt. I heard a creak in the hallway, and then the light tread of step on the stairs.

Mom was sleepwalking.

Growing up, I'd often heard her and guided her back to bed, though plenty of times I'd simply rolled over. That night, unable to sleep, I slipped out of bed and down the stairs after her. I found her in the front room, petting the piano bench. She was wearing a long lace-necked nightgown. She looked crazy, stroking that bench and muttering about bouquets. I watched her from the foyer. I knew I should approach her, talk her into wakefulness, or at least up the stairs and back into bed. I didn't.

After a moment more of attention to the piano bench, my mother suddenly reached down and pinched the hem of her nightgown, lifting it up, over her head, and dropping it at her feet. Then she stood still for a moment, naked but for a pair of slippers. Though it was dark, moonlight slanted in through the tall window next to the piano, catching on her silhouette, painting her body in shades of pale icy blue and shadow. I couldn't look away.

She was getting old. She had always been a small woman, but compact, curvy. Now her hipbones looked too prominent and her thighs were thin and weak, almost the same size as her calves. Her skin was showing her age, bunching in wrinkles at her waist, her butt, around her arms. Her breasts, looking thin and empty, sloped down her chest, sagging to pointed tips.

I stared, transfixed. My mother was lifting her arms, curving them upward into a circle, the shape of Pat's lips blowing a smoke ring, of hers and my father's both forming the word "whore." I thought she was dancing. Then she bent her elbows, palms together as though praying; she was doing yoga. The muscles in her back quivered, unsteady under the weight of her arms.

When a warm hand descended on my shoulder, my whole body flinched. Dad was standing behind me, his eyes on my mother. I wondered how long he'd been there. He squeezed my shoulder. His voice was low. "Back to bed. I'll take care of her."

I tried to read his expression, but his face was shadowed. "I didn't know she still did this," I said.

"Only when she's upset."

The familiar accusation settled heavily between heart and stomach. I looked at him, and then at my mother, and felt a prickling pain rise up my throat, binding it shut. I couldn't get any words out.

"I told you to keep it to yourself," Dad said.

I nodded, blinking. I faked a yawn.

"Well. What's done is done," he said.

I nodded again. Mom had lowered her arms. She was wrapping them around herself.

Finally I said, "She never changed in front of me," and I made a noise—a laugh, but choked, half out my nose. "I barely remember seeing her in a swimsuit."

"She's never been easy with herself," Dad said, and he sighed after, a heavy gust, as though some great secret had been let out.

"She'll be embarrassed tomorrow."

"Only if she remembers."

"You won't say something?"

Dad tilted his head, looking at me sideways. "Why upset her?"

❀ ❀ ❀

Mark was waiting at the top of the stairs. "What's going on?"

"My mother." The words came out croaky. I cleared my throat. "She sleepwalks."

"Is she okay?"

I thought, *Who could know?* I said, "Dad's with her."

"Are you okay?" Mark's eyes were losing their sleepy confusion, roaming my face, my neck, the loose T-shirt that brushed my skin mid-thigh. He was always turned on right after he woke—whether it was eight or two in the morning. I let him guide me back to bed and tried to share his thrill in slow strokes and whispers and the forbidden heat of being in my old room, of breaking my dad's old-fashioned rules. But I couldn't get into it, couldn't focus, and I ended up rushing his tenderness into a kind of violent rocking exercise, though Mark didn't complain. He was soon snoring again. I lay awake, feeling the sweat cool on my skin. I thought of my mother sleeping, standing by the piano she never played. I thought of her body and my father's eyes on it.

I thought of my grandmother in that photograph, the third dancer from the left, a slim-waisted girl with light hair, dark lipstick, a wide, artless smile. She was beautiful, but not in the way I'd pictured her. She had freckles and strong, stockinged calves that peeked out from beneath the flare of her skirt. Her dance partner was tall, taller than the others and narrow, almost lanky. He wasn't my grandfather. She was looking up into his face, her smile trapped in the moment just before laughter. I thought of that photograph and I wondered if they had been sweethearts, if they would have been husband and wife but for a car accident, or polio, or Korea. I wondered if that night in the locker room her thoughts had been of him while she whispered and sweated and tried to keep her mask from slipping. Him, dead and gone, or maybe just out of reach, and her, married too young to her father's too-old partner, with a daughter she didn't want, and this one night, this one chance for raw escape.

Or, I thought, maybe after all she was not so artless as her smile said, and she danced to string that lanky young man along as she would with so many others, until finally there was nothing left untried, no excitement humming in her blood when she brought a new stranger out to the ninth hole and exhausted them both on the bright green grass. Then all that was left was masks, and feathers, and the thrill of a crumpled fifty-dollar bill pressed into her palm in haste and fear and breathy eagerness.

I grew cold thinking this, and shut my eyes on the room of my childhood, and buried my face in Mark's shoulder. He mumbled something in his sleep, something I didn't understand. I found his hand, pressed it between my legs. Then, for a while, I felt warm.

Photo by Naira Kuzmich

VEDRAN HUSIĆ was born in Mostar, Bosnia and Herzegovina, and currently lives in Tempe, Arizona, where he is pursuing an MFA in Fiction at Arizona State University. His fiction is forthcoming in *Witness* and *North American Review*.

DEATHWINKED
Vedran Husić

I hear, the axe has bloomed,
I hear, the place is not nameable,
I hear, they call life
our only refuge.

Paul Celan, "I hear, the axe has bloomed"

We called Sniper Alley the Alley of Wolves. We were young and boys and had nicknames for everything, first of all the girls. There was the Nanny, the Epilogue, and the Soulcrusher. We thought these nicknames very clever, breathless with truth. We were thirteen and easily excited. To be killed by a sniper meant to be deathwinked, a verb. I came up with that. I had a minimum understanding of poetry, a maximum amount of fear.

We ran across the Alley of Wolves to test our recent manhood, among other things. We ran because there was nothing better to do. We ran because it was more bearable than standing still. We were young and anxious to be brave. We were practicing martyrs. Our fathers were gone; mine gone forever, heaven-swallowed one winter night at the front. Miralem's father was still at the front, firing his gun at the threatening distance. All three of us dreamed of soldierhood and feared that the war would soon run out. Edin's father had come back from the front and was gone in yet another way, halfway between the gone of Miralem's father and the never coming back of my father. He was crazy, half-crazy, according to the completely not insane. He spoke the names of the dead, but not in his sleep, like normal people. He confused the living for the dead, which sombered the living. He did not always know where he was, or in what year, which was a mixed blessing. We all smiled at him when we saw him and pitied him the best we could. Edin took it all in stride, in run actually, explaining it away through philosophy, intellectualizing the problem until the problem grew wings. His father's dead-waking rants did not bother him, but it bothered his family, who wanted to institutionalize the father. But there were no institutions left. Edin argued that to call somebody insane, or almostinsane, was ridiculous in time of war. Nobody in his family listened to him; he was thirteen, which is its own form of almostinsanity. But Edin's father was too crazy for war; that was why the army had sent him back, holy and broken. Or maybe he wasn't crazy enough?

A poet is looked at funny, too, pitied and misunderstood and patted on the head. But the poet rants with a pen, and softly. That is the only difference. To the poet, the world is one big psychopathic ward, full of unwanted visitors to pity and belittle you, to speak slowly as though you are the one who doesn't understand, to measure their sanity against your honesty, to look down on you, hiding a life's worth of precious ignorance behind their knowing smiles. I was a poet at thirteen; I'm a half-poet now.

Our fathers were gone, and our mothers had no authority over us. We loved them, our unreluctant Slavic mothers, but we loved our courage more. "War is our true mother," Edin once said, inspired and dumbfounded. "Unable to give birth, men make war," he said another time, quoting surly. Was there a contradiction in these two utterings, or is the contradiction in the remembering? Edin was the oldest by a month, a small lifetime, had slow blue eyes, and spoke deliberately, like a drunk wanting to be understood. He liked Kierkegaard; he liked the idea of Kierkegaard. He argued about religion, for and against it. His father had taught philosophy and was now insane, or within untiring reach of insanity. His family had been wealthy, but now money did not matter, had lost meaning. It was wartime and everything was free, if you wanted it enough, and everybody on the eastern side of Mostar was equal as the dead are equal. The dream of Communism bloomed among casual shell bursts and articulate sniper fire on the eastern side of a town without bridges. Eastsiders have nothing to lose but their lives, and an afterworld to gain. Alley-runners of all countries unite!

The family library lay in rubble, but some of the books had been saved, and being the only books left, they were many times read and meticulously understood by Edin. Edin came up with the name "Alley of Wolves," and it had been his idea to run across it. To impress the Epilogue more than anything else. Larger reasons became apparent only later, and by virtue of their late arrival sounded like excuses. Ideas were Edin's guardian angels; he had a whole tear-bright choir of them. Beyond the grave there will be singing. He had bulletproof testosterone. A missionary's courage. There were doubters to convert to something less than doubt. There were detractors to prove wrong. And death proved everybody wrong, eventually, always. Now that I think about it, he may have been younger than me, if not the youngest of us.

We congregated near a spilling set of trash cans, behind buildings bruised by mortar fire. Houses in every state of uninhabitable lined the alley on one side, walls left to stand as monuments to futility, while on the other side stood nothing, open space and a gravel path leading down to the river. And up ahead, the nothing-goal, more desolated houses and the mute storefronts of empty shops, the stone remains of a mosque, with its third of a minaret, and the promise of intermission, and the burden, almost motherly, of the run back. A small and narrow street, strewn with garbage and garbage scented: our ground of play. These adjectives come all too easy, self-compounded at birth, not unearned, though, not at all.

Mostar, my city, you are far from me now, but I peek through the spyglass and you appear so near. In my third floor apartment, in the neverdesperate America of my childhood dreams, at my desk, armed with pencil and paper, sensitive as a landmine, fumbling similes like live grenades, I, the young, triple-tongued poet, write down the name of my birthcity like the name of a former lover. Mostar. Mostar, my city, stunned quiet. They took the Most, threw it into the river and made you unnamable. My city, one night you went dark all around me. You trembled and could not be embraced. The bombs fell on you, near-constant and heartbeatloud. Each night strangely amplified, the lullaby of artillery. The shudder and light of false dawns. The shrill, the senseless, the bizarre and inescapable sirens. I recommend war-tourism to any artist, poet especially, a month or so of up-close-death, a month, or twenty-three, of dark-houred explosions in a world maddened by sirens. You'll never lack material, or have to account for sudden mood swings, and you'll almost never lose at those drunken games between friends, intimate games, those poetic games of whosufferedmost.

Three floors are enough to kill a man. The truthhearing poet gives the truthsharpened tip of his pencil a lick, he writes:

Three floors are enough to kill a man
There can be no hate without memory

To love is to imagine
In the white noise of other feelings
Hope is outshouted
In the prayer-answering silence
Faith blooms.

That, with his pencil, the poet writes the truth is implied, was implied, is implied no longer. He gives the pencil another swift lick, he writes:

All brave men are stupid
But not all stupid men are brave
All children pretend
Their games are serious
All games have rules
Even the games of animals
Have rules.

Our game had but a few rules. If you ran last yesterday, you must run first today. That was one rule. If you ran across the alley to the other side, you must run back. That was rule number two, for there was another way to get back, sniper-less but long. And there were rules of which we were ignorant, the secret rules of the sniper. But whether the sniper followed any rules was left to debate. Sundays we did not run. Yesterday, Miralem had run last; he would run first today. Who would run second was decided by a coin toss. Edin headed and I tailed and Edin would run second. I would run last. Tomorrow I would run first. Tomorrow I would not run.

The time leading up to the first run was the happiest time of the day, our concentration lax, our muscles fearful and limber, the words between us intimate, unexpected, binding. Sometimes we sang. It was morning, Tuesday or Wednesday, during the week of lentil soup. Miralem stretched his arms and legs, while Edin and I sat on opposing stubs of stone arguing in war-hushed tones. The blue sky promised no rain, and the sun looked blotchy, a vague yellow. Miralem threw one arm behind his back and pressed the bent elbow with his other hand, his legs wide apart, his torso stout and unfamiliarly armless. The amber sheen of autumn leaves, the gazelle-like wind, the abashed leaf-rustle, they all spoke in different languages about the same things. Beauty. Nature. Truth. Poetry. We spoke of philosophy, Edin and I, while Miralem quietly and thoughtfully stretched, and in the new dawn's unraveling silence, under a sky morningpureblue, the sniper fired the first shot of a long day. Bullet, trash can, a metal *ping* almost adorable, almost loud.

We turned our heads toward the sound, then toward each other, then back. We resumed our conversation and Miralem joined us, having nothing more to stretch. He was arguably pretty, one of those who narrowed their eyes when they grinned, one of those who gestured with their fists. His eyes were green, a little blue, and he had a full Slavic forehead, broad and thought-pale. He was short but athletic; he was short and had a temper. He did not like tall girls. He did not like the Soulcrusher, with whom I played games in death-proof basements. There we spoiled each other for our future selves. He brought daily lilies for the Nanny and kissed her deeply, with a more meaningful tongue, with more daring and saliva than I ever did Selma. I write her name like the name of something lost. She knew how to swing the hips she did not have. She knew how to haggle good enough and long enough to make you give up everything. With her smile she fooled you into laughing at yourself. With her laughing eyes she crushed your soul. She dreamed of a husband with money. She dreamed of big hips. A skirtful of memories, everything I have, for a handful of her skirt.

Miralem had played soccer before the war, before the cemetery turn of every idle field, before the dead-packed stadiums; he was fast, his run was urgent and blind, it was a sprint, and he ran with his head down. And yesterday he'd tripped and fallen a yard or so from safety. The sniper had fired and missed. He did not fire again. A little dust rose, it settled. Miralem was on the other side by then, bent over, with his hands on his knees, breathing greedily. The sniper did not fire again, as if to let us take in the full magnitude of his miss, or as if to impress us with his patience. The confidence of those with death on their side, how could we ever understand it? Miralem said nothing when we got to him, his tender calm edging on some kind of bewilderment, and after the run back, we walked home in silence, and parted from each other in silence, the silence of raised stakes.

Now Miralem ridiculed the sniper, saying that he missed because he was a bad shot, and not on purpose, saying he was some fat, pimply boy playing at war, and not a man of many battles, not a man at all, just a novice at death and not worth the fantasy of our revenge. But Edin wouldn't have it. No, to him he was a man and a master, a Machiavellian sniper-prince, with a nihilist's love of beauty; his aim is steady and true, he shoots you with a shot made of lead, his slit eye is Catholic blue. Edin had read his Celan, saved from the rubble. Death is a master from the Balkans. But it is more intimate than that. He is a close relation, the mysterious uncle bearing strange gifts at each prophetic visit, the one who winks at you behind your parents' back. We were brought up on his knee, on the black milk of his wisdom. Our blood is his blood. The one who waltzes you across the Alley of Wolves, the one who lets you stand on his feet as you move against each other in this gently wicked dance. Our songs are his songs. He sings into your hair as you dance. He whispers in your ear, forbids you to stop.

Miralem ran across the alley, with his head down, lifting it only slightly toward the end. Alive on the other side, he grinned at us, his eyes almost closed. Then it was gone, the grin, memory-wiped, collapsed into a thinking pout. The sniper had not fired. Sometimes he didn't. And when he didn't he blessed our run with innocence, like running before the war. Sometimes that was what we wanted. We had run for a month now, had been in this war for years, and weren't getting any wiser. Death was still strange, but it had shown too much of itself, had become part of the landscape. So why not go back? To a time of sparrow-enswirled minarets and non-firewood lindens, to a time of packed café terraces and their murmur like rushing water, when death and its mirror image, life in war, were as distant as nightmares after waking.

In front of our buildings, punched blue and black by rockets, there was a large, grassy courtyard, and this courtyard had been the setting of our first game, a game of collection. Under the spell of sunlight and tall grass, we'd search for bullet shells and find also glinting syringes, uncapped bottles of pills, an occasional limb abstracted from the body. One day, we found a rocket shell the size of a baby seal, unexploded. We dared each other to touch it. Edin moved toward it, extending an unsteady finger. "BOOM," Miralem yelled at the point of contact, and Edin jumped back. Miralem laughed and Edin fumed. They fought it out, and afterwards both fumed. And as they sat on opposite sides of the projectile, not looking at each other, I got up from my seat and placed my palm against its belly. The metal was scorched by the sun and felt smooth and naked to the touch. I let my fingers linger haughtily, waiting for them to notice. A shiver spidered up my spine. I felt an upward rush of courage, like a declaration. Miralem and Edin joined me, our three hands pressed against the hot metal in a silent oath; they felt the courage, too, and that was when we knew we wanted to be soldiers and never die.

Beyond the broken-down stores and houses, beyond the kneeling minaret, on the side that we first ran to reach, was their headquarters, in the sandbagged gymnasium of a shell-bitten, practically roofless elementary school. We peeked on three soldiers, all three young: We watched them gather by a corner table; watched two of them sit on upturned milk crates and the other stand; watched them eat lentil soup from a can that was warmed by old-fashioned fire; watched them listen to a portable radio as they ate with no hope of satiation; watched their hands busily scratch and their lips seldom move; watched all three turn toward the radio when the human voice got lost behind an unrelenting tearing of sandpaper. The soldiers went back to patrol the rubble and we watched them walk away, toward danger, unafraid and half-amused. There was something solemn about their amusement, something sensual and elusive about the way they carried themselves, in their warstained boots and burden-heavy uniforms, something eerily casual about the guns slung over their shoulders, lustful and sentimental about their lack of helmets. What bleak respect we had for them, all God-like and dusty-loined. They were not so much defenders of our city as defenders of our dream of the city. The odds were against them, but the crowd on their side, the cheer of the wind in the trees.

We wandered about for a while, wasting time before our run back. It was getting to be noon, the shadows growing long and ragged. Women appeared on the street, braving their way to market, located makeshift in one of the rear classrooms, smuggled goods, gifts of Western arrogance. Once, we had looked for ingredients to make a cake for my birthday and found nothing but a nestful of eggs. We had the party in a basement, with no cake, but with many candles, more than was my age. In another yard, a new breed of child explorers rummaged for shells in the overgrown grass, their pockets full of singing metal. Further east, toward Stolac, a blue-gray tower of smoke had risen, straying from its origin, swallowing houses whole along its path.

We saw the absence of the bridge and a gentle curve of river below. The Old Bridge was gone, but the Neretva River was still here, flowing bright and prewar green. The river doesn't care. The river had seen worse. The river is not concerned with what we throw in it: debris, bodies, blood, and stone; the water stitches it all to a mend, never stopping to wonder what we send downriverflowing. We climbed a garage and flopped down on our bellies. With our voices love-timid, our stares remote, we looked over our half of the city, shielding our eyes from the sun's knives. Behind us, the boughs of a large tree whose name we had not yet learned shielded us from danger. Green mountains enclosed us on all sides, separating us from our enemies but not from ourselves. The piled smoke rose still higher, spread out greater than a cathedral, more clouded than the idea of God. Sparrows chirped, crests chirped, gunfire chirped. The waxwing had flown south, summer was over. The dandelions had been beheaded; the lilies had hanged themselves. It was autumn now and nothing bloomed, except the year-long ax.

Miralem was on the starting side again, alive and well and one day braver, while Edin stood on the edge of safety, waiting to run. He stood just behind a little shop, its interior gray and plundered. Before the war, I'd run there to get emergency Vegeta for my mother, and sometimes its owner, old and Hellenic Mr. Salemović, would call me into the back and ask me to stack some items for him, rewarding my impromptu work with free candy. I remember red jars of Ajvar, tall glass bottles of Lero Juice, and those compact silver cans of Eva sardines, with a waving walrus dressed as a sailor on the blue cover. I remember Dorina Chocolates and Bananko bars, Bajadera pralines and Napolitanke Wafers, and Jaffa cookies with their chocolate skins and orange jelly hearts. I remember an old-fashioned balance scale on the counter, with numerous dust-colored weights in increasing sizes of mass; I remember the slow sway of its thin shoulders, the delicate movements of its plates, their eventual, hard-earned symmetry.

One surging whiff of Vegeta and I'm back in a light-filled kitchen, beside my mother who smells of red vegetables and spices, not doing anything helpful in particular, just standing innocently in the way, marveling at her instinctual measurements. Just one guilty, helpless whiff and I remember my mother, half-orphaned by one war, wholly divorced by another, tasting the sauce and smiling down at me her expert opinion. Music comes from the living room, where my father is taking his afternoon nap. This tells me that we already ate, that the food being made is for tomorrow, that despite the Sunday texture of this memory, this is more likely a work day, a day my mother will end at the hospital, where she will begin the new day, working at her typewriter, administering injections, changing sheets. The number of coffee cups on the table tells me there will be guests, our next-door neighbors, a Muslim man who always guessed the card in my hand and his Catholic wife who could read the future in the muddy remnants of the coffee.

Edin stood on the brink of danger, waiting to prove his bravery. But in war everybody is brave, even the coward. Even the sniper at his post, beguiling the fates. The three soldiers patrolling the rubble, pretending to be who they are. They were braving another day of boredom, their courage doomed. Huddled around the radio, they waited for the news to tell them what they already knew. The war will not end today. The children in the tall grass, in the bloom of their inexperience, they were brave without knowing. The women in search of food, carrying their unburiable grief inside them like a long pregnancy, their bravery no conciliation for their loss. Everybody is brave in wartime. Everybody wise, even the fool with his warning. We were just braver, the answered prayers of our patient tormenters. Victims of our own death-mined wisdom. Strange prideful lambs, we made our courage our God. Like every rose is a flower, every Slav boy is an Icarus.

Edin was on the verge of his run, waiting for a favorable sign that only he knew how to tell. Then, suddenly, he was off, his footsteps echoing bluntly in the empty street, his thin vicious elbows stabbing the air behind him. The sniper fired and Edin crashed to the soundless asphalt. Deathwinked.

I thought I screamed, I thought I tore my mouth with my voice, but my cry, its angular fury, was only imagined. I took a couple of steps toward Edin, to soothe the distance between us, but Miralem raised his flattened palm and I obeyed. We looked on from the disbelief of safety at his unflinching body, waiting for loyalty to move us, for fear to release us, for courage to break us free. I wiped my tears on my sleeve; I looked at Miralem and knew. He lowered his hand and we ran. A new game had begun: a game of retrieval. I grabbed him under his armpits and Miralem grabbed him by his ankles, and together we carried Edin home, running. I remember the sun in my eyes as I ran, I remember thinking I would trip. I felt the weight of his body like never before. The sniper did not fire.

And now? What now? Why stop one's war story in mid-exhalation? Why bring in the present to take revenge on the past? The past, which is our only refuge. Now my sleep is fragmented by nightmares. Now I'm ghost-weary, my tongue a cripple. Now I lean out of my window and think about ending this chance-riddled life, but can never keep my eyes closed long enough. Now I walk barefoot in my apartment trying to catch in a mason jar every flicker of insanity. Now I sit at my desk and write.

The sniper did not fire.

Now that the war is over we laugh that it ever began. But even now we hunger for the right man to lead us down the wrong path again. For even now, in some small, divided village, a Milošević is waiting to be stubbornly born.

Now the exhumed graves are again silenced with our soil.

Now the past is burned like sheets of infidelity.

Now, in comfortable prisons, under supervision kind and condescending, sworn enemies bond over a game of cards.

SHERRIL JAFFE's latest novel, *Expiration Date,* was published in April 2011. She is author of six other works of fiction, including *Scars Make Your Body More Interesting & Other Stories,* and two memoirs, including *One God Clapping.* She is winner of the 2000 PEN Josephine Miles Award for Literary Excellence, and is a 2010 MacDowell Fellow and professor of creative writing at Sonoma State University.

A WIDOW'S STORY
Sherril Jaffe

Marion, six months a widow, comes to this place over a winding mountain highway that ascends in hairpin turns. Blocking the impulse to drive straight off an edge and into the sea, she turns instead onto the driveway, leaving her car on a parking platform that seems precariously cantilevered over an abyss. Eucalyptus and cypress shadow the hillside and the weathered wooden stairs that slope up to the front door. She is overcome by a sickening-sweet odor. Something's dead nearby. Marion blocks the thought.

The entrance to the house is like a passage through the hull of an ark. She crosses the threshold, noting that from every window is a view of the ocean. Instructions have been laid out for her on the kitchen island. She will read from this list of tasks later.

Marion walks from room to room, studying the furniture and wall displays: a basket of snake skins, an urn full of ashes, a mask. Last, she climbs the tower stairs in the center of the house.

The corner windows of the north room reveal the rocky cliff the house nestles into. Despite the windows, this room is dark, the Zen Master's study. Above his desk is a painting of a blue Buddha in full lotus position, floating on his cushion in a celestial realm. On Buddha's lap is the white form of an ecstatic naked woman, locked with him in eternal sexual congress, her legs wrapped around his waist and her hands clasped behind her head. She tilts her head slightly so that her lips are positioned precisely upon his. Marian imagines the blue Buddha inside the woman, feels his mouth upon hers, a ribbon of unending pleasure running through her body. Marion remembers her husband's thousand embraces still alive inside of her. This is a sensation she does not want to block.

Or does she?

A stalk of bougainvillea pushes against the window panes, pressing its brilliant blossoms against the glass. Wild sage waves beyond it, visible in the middle distance, and then there is the stubble hillside, falling away to a dark stand of cypress on the edge of nothingness, the sea below rapidly flowing south. What if it could take her with it?

The sky is gray; the house is wrapped in mist. The wind lifts the branches of the cypress, waving the rattlesnake grass. The small bedroom in the south side of the tower has panoramic ocean views. On the wall over the bureau is a painting of a woodland scene, positioned to be viewed from the narrow, single bed built into the east wall.

This is where Marion will eventually decide to sleep. But first she will take the woodland picture off the bedroom wall and replace it with the blue Buddha and his alabaster lover. The woodland scene is more appropriate over a desk, where thoughts might look for shelter under the trees. She wants to see the blue Buddha and his white mistress when she lies in bed. She promises herself that she will switch the paintings back before he returns. He will never know, she thinks, but then she realizes he will know for sure; he has planned for her to do this.

Marion hears cats meowing at the kitchen door that leads to the brick patio. She comes down from the tower and opens the door. One cat rushes in, but the other refuses to enter the house. From the doorway Marion sees the reptile shed, where she knows a snake is waiting for her to bring it a frozen dead mouse.

She decides not to think about that now.

Marion has come to this place on a cliff to housesit for friends. The husband is the Zen Master, the wife a middle-school science teacher. The husband thinks it will be spiritually healing for Marion to spend some time here, alone; the wife thinks Marion can care for their garden and pets and all the creatures she has brought home from her classroom for the summer.

One of those creatures is a corn snake in the process of shedding her skin, Marion learned when she came for dinner and instructions before the husband and wife left on their trip. "It can't eat while it's molting," the wife explained. "As soon as it's done it will need to eat."

Marion could tell she was leading up to something big.

"A frozen dead mouse, which you will find in the freezer, should then be placed on top of the hollowed-out half shell of a log under which the snake likes to hide," she said at last, getting to the meat of the matter.

No, this can't be, Marion thought to herself. I can't do this.

The science teacher continued to explain in a half-amused tone how Marion would need to be careful not to wiggle her fingers in any gesture even vaguely resembling the movement of a mouse, for the snake might mistake her hand for a mouse, strike out, and bite her. Marion should be reassured by the fact that the snake has never bitten anyone in the science teacher's classroom, but should the snake bite her, she should not worry, for the snake is not venomous; however, should the snake clamp onto Marion's hand with her jaws and refuse to let go, Marion should simply put her hand with the snake attached to it under cold running water.

"The snake will be very afraid," the science teacher added, as if this were the most important consideration.

Marion goes out to the shed, which is where her friend the Zen Master has interviews with his disciples during the winter months. It is full of reptiles. There is a dead mouse on top of the hollowed-out log inside the snake's tank. The science teacher must have placed it there before leaving for the airport that morning, Marion deduces. She remembers what the science teacher told her: After the mouse defrosts, the snake will smell it and eat it. The science teacher must have decided that the snake was finished molting, or finished enough, Marion thinks. She must have thought she would save Marion from the unsavory task of removing a dead mouse from the freezer, unwrapping it, and then offering it to the snake, a task she is certainly not looking forward to. But if the snake were finished molting, it would have eaten the mouse by now.

Or perhaps both husband and wife had colluded on this, thinking the whole problem of the dead mouse would be useful at this point—six months in—for Marion to begin solving.

Back in the house she goes into the master bedroom. Clean sheets have been laid out for her on the bed. The bed is huge, as are the pillows. It is not an easy task stuffing the long pillows into their tight cases. The blanket is gray, the same color and texture as one of their cats, the old one who meows constantly. Facing the bed is a TV with wires coming out of it from every direction. The husband and wife have explained to her that there is no reception.

The Zen Master's weights and exercise machine are in one corner. Marion remembers her beloved's particular smell; it still lingers in his bathrobe hanging with hers on the hook in their bathroom at home. This is when she decides she doesn't want to stay in the master bedroom after all, when she goes upstairs to sleep in the tower room instead.

That night, she sleeps fitfully in the little bed in the tower, where the blue Buddha and the white woman float locked together. At last Marion drifts off, but she is awakened in the middle of the night by the gray cat meowing outside the door. She has closed the bedroom door to keep the cat out.

She knows it is the gray cat, and not the black and white one, because that one hadn't been in the house when she went to sleep. It is a scaredy-cat. It came meowing to the patio door, but when she opened it, it ran away. That was exactly what her friend had said it would do, so it must be all right, she thinks, though it makes her uneasy. What conditions must prevail for everything to be all right?

❧ ❧ ❧

In the morning Marion sits with her coffee on the brick patio bordered by red, salmon, and purple flowers. The half crescent of the beach opens up way down below. Here in the clear light of day she has to acknowledge that she is going to have to go back out to the reptile shed to remove the mouse from the snake's cage, or else it will rot. She finishes her breakfast and dresses in jeans, sweatshirt, and clogs. She goes out the front door and down the hill to the shed, praying that the snake has eaten the mouse and sure that it hasn't. She kicks open the door, stands on the threshold, peering inside. The mouse is still there, in the snake tank, laid out on top of the hollowed-out log. It is crawling with flies.

She steps into the shed and takes the forceps from the counter by the turtles' tank, kitty-corner to the gecko's tank, and she walks slowly toward the snake's tank, opens the lid, and reaches inside. Should she pick it up by its tail, she wonders? No, she thinks, the tail might just break off, casting the body of the mouse back into the tank, from which she will have to retrieve it, not wiggling her fingers, etc., etc. With no time to lose, she picks up the mouse by its belly and slowly withdraws it from the tank. The snake does not stir. She closes the lid with her left hand, already relieved; then, holding the mouse aloft with the forceps, she walks out of the shed and flings the mouse over the railing as far as she can down the hill.

But she is horrible at throwing, and it doesn't go far. She remembers when she first arrived, the sickly smell of decaying flesh. She looks up as a shadow passes before her. The buzzards are circling.

But now Marion must tend to all the other creatures. She looks at her pages of instructions. In a crate on the porch of the reptile hut live two box turtles and a tortoise. The tortoise is a vegetarian and needs to be fed some fruit, which has been cut up with some lettuce. The box turtles need to be hand fed, with pincers, three to six live meal worms each, which Marion is to fish out of a plastic tub with holes punched in its top. She has to make sure the turtles actually eat the worms and that the worms don't fall into the cage, because they will turn into beetles.

She opens the jar labeled "meal worms." At first she sees nothing inside, only dirt. Then she sees the dirt heaving. She reaches in with the pincers and grasps a fat, writhing white worm with spikes coming out of it. She leans over the turtle pen and offers the worm to one of the turtles, trying not to look at it, this white thing that lives in the dark and feeds on dead matter. The turtle takes it between his strong toothless jaws and begins to slowly ingest it, alive. Half of the worm protrudes from its mouth, waving in alarm. Marion has to watch this slow process to make sure the worm doesn't fall out of the turtle's beak into the sawdust on the bottom of the pen and turn into a beetle.

All the gecko needs is fresh water, because the wife fed him fifty live crickets before she left. Marion takes the heat lamp off the top of his tank so she can slide back the lid to get to his water dish. The two turtles swimming in the tank inside the hut also need to be fed live grubs with the pincers. The thought of feeding more live grubs to amphibians is abhorrent to Marion, so like an endless long nightmare that she doesn't know how she is going to tolerate it. Yet she does. She has promised her friends that she would, and she knows they would not ask her to do this without a good reason.

The hermit crabs are the only creatures left that need attending now, and after she gives them some lettuce she runs back into the house and washes her hands with soap for as long as it takes her to sing happy birthday to herself, just as the instructions specified.

❀ ❀ ❀

Her friends have told her it is a fifteen-minute walk down the road to the steps that run directly down the side of the cliff to the beach. She is ready to go. As soon as she leaves the house and garden where flowers bloom in profusion in every color, she enters a world of olive-green and gray native shrubs, some with cone-shaped wands of flowers growing out of them, others silver and glinting in the sun. Each of these shrubs, the Manzanita, the broom, the sage, is equidistant from each other, as if they have been intentionally planted. At last she comes to the steps. There are hundreds.

Marion bounds from step to step, as that seems to be what she must do, and soon she's gliding, almost flying down the cliff. At the bottom is a wooden bridge under a tunnel of foliage that leads out to the beach where pink starfish and green anemones cling to the rocks.

Marion must leap over a small stream to get to the end of the beach, and she does. Then she climbs to the top of a rock and lets the wind blow her clothes against her body. She doesn't know why she is here or why she is seeing any of this, why she is experiencing anything at all. Climbing back up all the stairs, it is with a surprising sense of satisfaction that Marion finds her stride again and maintains it, the swinging of the arms, the lunge of the legs, the solid placement of the feet, the chest held up, opening. And then she is back in the house, in her retreat upstairs in the tower once again, the ocean all around, vast and indifferent.

She gazes out the window. A shadow of a fog cloud moves over the bluff opposite, though the view is otherwise still bathed in late afternoon light. The waves beat against the rocks that line the shore. The fog is moving rapidly down the coast, but the tips of the cove are holding the fog out to sea, and inside the cove the sun shines.

Night falls. She lies awake in the dark once again, afraid to let go.

In the morning when she walks into the reptile hut, the Zen Master's winter office, she sees the snake's transparent skin, wound around its water dish, which it must have used as a rubbing post. The empty skin trails off to the inside of the hollowed-out log where the snake lurks. She can see him gleaming in his new skin, wet looking and dark pinky-red, when she crouches down and peers into the other end of the log. It is not a subtle thing when a snake sheds its skin. Marion wonders why her friend didn't wait to see a snake skin before putting out the dead mouse. After all, there is a whole basket of snake skins on her bookcase. She knew what they looked like.

Marion can't see the end of the snake skin. It disappears inside the tunnel where the snake is coiled, and she doesn't want to put her hand into the tank and lift up the hollow log to see if the snake is completely out of its skin yet. She decides to endure another day of the dread of having to take the dead mouse out of the freezer, having to somehow unwrap it, and having to place it into the snake's tank. At the same time, she can't bear the thought of a dead mouse in the freezer, and she knows she will feel better when it is out of there.

✹ ✹ ✹

She returns to the reptile hut and takes a closer look at the snake skin. It is still in the perfect shape of a snake. She can see the diamond shape of the snake's head. Then she sees the end of the snake's tail. The snake has finished molting! Now she can't put it off any longer: It is time to feed the snake its frozen dead mouse.

On her way out of the hut she notices that the heat lamp that normally sits on top the gecko tank is face down on the laminate counter top. She lifts the lamp and puts it on top of the wires of the lid to the gecko tank. The countertop is smoldering where the lamp has been resting on it. She takes a cup of water from the sink and pours water onto the black circle growing in the white laminate. This isn't happening, she says to herself. She can see right through the laminate now to the cupboard below. She pours a second cup of water over the blackened hole for good measure, and puts her fingers on it. The fire is out. There is a charred circle about two inches in diameter in the white Formica. How could this have happened?

She goes into the house and takes the mouse from the freezer. It is in a small brown paper bag labeled "mouse," wrapped tightly in a clear plastic bag. She is going to have to cut this bag open. She takes a pair of scissors from the kitchen drawer, but not the nicest pair. She is going to have to leave these scissors outside after she does the deed, she thinks. The scissors will be polluted.

Marion goes out to the reptile hut, lays the bag on the counter, and cuts it open. Holding her breath, she picks up the long-handled pincers and carefully removes the mouse from the paper by the tail even though she worries that it may be frozen brittle and break off. But she does not want to feel the body of the mouse through the pincers. The mouse is pale-gray and its fur looks dry. She can't bear to look at it. She opens the lid of the snake's tank with her left hand. This is terrible, but it is not as terrible as the fact that she has burned a hole in the laminate of her friend's countertop. Luckily, the snake is hiding in its tunnel, and she lays the mouse on top of the log to defrost. Then she lets out her breath. The rest of the day she is busy watering the flowers and cleaning out the cat box. How fast the ocean is speeding by, the evening falling, all the birds soaring and dipping! But if there is no one in the forest when the tree falls, does it make a sound? If she is alone, does anything matter?

                    ❊ ❊ ❊

The heat goes on in the middle of the night, blasting into the room. Turning the thermostat to *off* does nothing. She sweats through the night and in the morning calls her friend the Zen Master. He and the science teacher are across the country babysitting their infant grandson. The baby doesn't like them, the Zen Master tells her. Their grandson is crying all the time. As the Zen Master is telling her this, she stands in his kitchen by the open door to the patio where the black and white cat is meowing but refusing to come in. The Zen Master tells her to flip all the switches in the electrical box. That's what he did once when they had this problem. He can't remember which switch is the right one. She finds the electrical box and flips the switch, and the blower goes off. She doesn't know, of course, if it will stay off.

She confesses to the Zen Master that she has burned a hole in his laminate, assuring him, even though he doesn't ask her, that she will pay for its repair. He graciously reminds her that she could have burned down the whole cabin.

She slips on her clogs and walks out to the reptile shed to see if the snake has eaten the mouse, phone to her ear. She opens the door and peers in.

She can't believe her luck. The mouse is gone, and there is no trace. The snake is tightly coiled beneath its hollowed out log. "The snake ate the mouse!" she tells the Zen Master, and he says, "You must be so happy!" and she is, because now she won't have to deal with dead mice any more.

For her whole life, Marion has had a phobia about mice. She and her husband had lived in New York City for a while, and every time workers started digging up the streets, which was all the time, mice would invade their apartment. Marion had vivid nightmares of mice even before she spotted them in the apartment and started shrieking. She couldn't bear the way they appeared in the periphery of her vision, running along the sideboards, something she knew on some level was there, but didn't want to see. She always made her husband deal with them for her. He was not afraid of anything, certainly not a mouse. He was glad to come to her rescue. One day she came home and found that her husband's back had gone out. He had helped some folks push a car, he told her. Then she saw a mouse run across the floor, and he confessed that his back had gone out when he saw a mouse run under the heavy hide-a-bed couch and he had tried to lift it to get the mouse before Marion came home and saw it.

But her husband is not here now. Now she is the one who must deal with all the mice. She will make terrible mistakes, costly mistakes, but this is her task and she has no other.

MECCA JAMILAH SULLIVAN's fiction has appeared in *Callaloo*, *Best New Writing*, and other places. She is winner of the Charles Johnson Student Fiction Award, the William Gunn Fiction Award, and the James Baldwin Memorial Playwriting Award. A 2011 Center for Fiction Fellow, she holds a PhD from the University of Pennsylvania and is currently completing her first novel. She is from Harlem, New York.

BLUE TALK AND LOVE
Mecca Jamilah Sullivan

In the halls of Madison Avenue Country Day School, she was known as long Xiomara—Xiomara of the wispy bean-sprout hair, the rubber-band arms, and manila-folder skin, forever slurping soda through a striped and bending straw. Before she sat on Earnestine's bed, Earnestine watched her as everyone did—through a film of awe and envy, pressing their faces toward her like children fixed to the glass wall of an aquarium, marveling at the majesty of a family of whales, begrudging them the simplicity of the lives they seemed to live.

If Xiomara Padilla was a legume, Earnestine—born Rakisha Earnestine Davis-Sanchez—was the brown, bulbous potato that smart Upper East Side women pushed to the sides of their plates before crunching into the simple green goodness the legumes would bestow. Earnestine was big and black and boring. She lived in the Hamilton Heights section of Harlem, in a brownstone the color of plain construction paper whose surfaces were ever-crumpled, ever-fading. The house looked nice enough from the front, but would reveal quickly, to anyone who entered, that its walls were peeling in papier-mâché scraps and that its old, tired floors were taking their sweet time falling apart. Earnestine's parents were unable to do much in terms of upkeep. Her mother was a minister and her father was a musician, which meant her mother's life was very busy and her father's was a mystery of absence. Earnestine left the house every morning with her already blockish body tensed and pinched, her shoulders hunched, and her arms fanning out from her middle like the limbs of a frightened camper, always on the ready to intimidate a creature bigger and more desperate than herself.

Earnestine was the color and shape of oobleck, a lifeless science class concoction made of cornstarch, water, and coffee grounds, used to demonstrate the properties of plasma and to prove that some things were hopelessly sturdy, even if they were liquid inside. She understood oobleck's place in the chain of elements right away. Early in the fifth grade, months before the Xiomara sat on her bed, Mr. Halstring, the science teacher, had told her she should sit beside Xiomara during the Life Sciences lessons. Xiomara was delicate, he explained. Her pores were sensitive to synthetic light. Earnestine could *do good work* by protecting her from the sunlamp he'd set beside the tropical milkweed plant that the class was to grow that term. And since she was interested in seeing things change—and for that reason alone—Earnestine obliged.

Despite the quaking loneliness she felt in Xiomara's presence, the two girls had some things in common, even before the Sunday in the middle of the year when Xiomara sat on her bed. Both were brown-girl cheese-bussers who lived fathoms away from the elementary school in the tight, hot crevice between Harlem and Washington Heights. Xiomara and her mother lived two doors down from the Sanchez-Davis home in the mammoth-sized tenement building that towered over the block's quick row of five proud but portly brownstones, of which Earnestine's family's was the last. Whenever Earnestine's parents fought about the family's bills or Earnestine's grades or her father's joblessness, or anything else, she would steal four cigarettes from her father's coat pocket and creep down to the tiny plot of fenced-in pavement behind the brownstone that passed for a yard. She would stand on a broken yard chair and call Xiomara's name, pelting her window with plastic hairbeads or sunflower seeds. Eventually, if Xiomara was not out with a boy or busy on the phone, or painting her toenails, she would come over. Earnestine would lead her quickly through her bedroom and into the yard, where the two girls would smoke under the emerald-green weed trees and talk about boys.

In the yard, she felt that she and Xiomara were together in a secret tropical cave hidden beneath a post-apocalyptic city sometime around the year 2020, an impossible distance away. The brownstone walls on their side of the street were all dilapidated, their gray paint falling in jagged chunks like stalagmites, their windows either boarded up like drawbridge doors or gaping open like the mouths of intergalactic portals to unthinkable worlds. On the opposite side of their yard was another huge tenement covered with neon-green weeds that overlooked a sprawling lot full of wild trees, overgrown grass, and Technicolor trash.

The city's sanitation services did not manage to keep up with the neighborhood's waste production, so the rusty orange trashcans that peppered the avenues were always overflowing with bottles, newspapers, and dirty slouch socks. With nowhere else to put their trash, people would appear at the windows of the tenement at all hours, smoking weed, declaring love to their mothers, waging complaints about that up-stairs neighbors' heavy footsteps or the shrieking baby three doors down the hall. Always, they dropped something—a cigarette butt, a soda can, a dirty diaper—as if to punctuate their joy or ire. Occasionally, Earnestine would hear a large stairwell window slide open, its metals rubbing like a brandished sword, and a great crash would follow as a broken salon-sized hair dryer or an overused sofa fell down against the trash heap.

On one warm day, a few weeks before the bed, the girls sat on Myrna Davis' warping yard table, their feet dangling down over the wooden chairs, all but two of which were missing a leg or a rung. Xio-mara leaned back, propped on the pads of her palms, and Earnestine sat beside her, her wrists a jumble of brown in her lap. Occasionally, Xiomara put her cigarette down and stooped to pick a loose hunk of concrete from the ground, tracing its grooves with her nails. Then she looked up, her body loose as a thin-stretched cloud.

"Alex Orwell is kinda fly," she said, her voice spraying over the pave-ment like a playground sprinkler in the summertime. "And anyway, he can help me do math, which is dope." She leaned her head to the side and let her hair lick at Earnestine's elbows, arching her eyebrows in Earnestine's direction.

Quickly, Earnestine inched away. She scratched her elbows, made magnets of her knees, pressed her fingers tighter around her cigarette.

"Why you acting like that?" Xiomara said. She rolled her eyes and looked into the trash mound while Earnestine sat frozen in a dumb shrug. "You act like we're at school or something, like you trying to be all proper for your boyfriend, Mr. Halstring," she sighed and blew a funnel of smoke into the air. "I hate how Madison Country people act. Like if their mom-mies are there all the time, hiding in their pocket, 'bout to jump out and smack them if they do anything too loud or too hard. So *immature*."

She closed her eyes, her verdict delivered, and swayed her small, round head to the sound of a song Earnestine could not hear, and Ear-nestine knew she was gone. When this happened, which it almost al-ways did, Earnestine felt like the last person left alone in a movie theater, traces of sound and scent the only evidence that anyone else had ever been in the room. If Xiomara was not too bored or too busy to stay, they would continue to smoke until the cigarettes were done, and then throw the butts over the fence into the trash-filled lot. If Xiomara left, which she did often, abruptly, and without explanation, they would put the cigarettes out on the bottoms of their sneakers and lodge the stubs under one of the loose concrete slabs, saving them in case of some future emergency, which only Earnestine seemed to believe might ever come.

Xiomara was indefatigably bright, despite tragedies of her own life. Her father was a young Dominican immigrant, like Earnestine's, but unlike Ernesto Sanchez, Fernando Padilla had died in a drug-related gunfight on the block back in the eighties, when the girls were six. Sharon Farming-Padilla, Xiomara's mother, was a thin white woman from New Jersey whose face reminded Earnestine of a cartoon ghost mask, and who was always at the City Municipal Services building, where she worked as a clerk. When she did come home, she went straight into the kitchen to drink amaretto sours until she was dancing cheek-to-cheek with the plastic folding table. Still, by all indications, Xiomara did more than alright for herself. Her elastic smile and unwavering ease seemed to win her most of what she wanted—the choice spot in science class from Mr. Halstring, scraggly grins and homework help from the Madison Avenue Country boys, a solid half of Earnestine's stolen cigarettes.

When Xiomara talked about her many admirers, Earnestine listened, chimed in when she could, and pretended to be more interested than she was. In truth, Earnestine liked boys like she liked anybody else. If they were nice to her or had round, symmetrical features, she liked them. If they were very funny or very sad, she liked them. If they gave her cigarettes or invited her over to drink from their parents' wine cellars, as did James Schaffran, the sixth-grade goth whose every word rode the loose end of a sigh, Earnestine liked them. The real excitement of talking about boys with Xiomara was not in the thought of the boys themselves, but in the way the talking made her feel. In these conversations, Earnestine became a different version of herself, like a paper doll putting on a newly traced and cut out dress for each fantasy play. When she kindled up a crush on Perry Stoltz, a Jewish boy with hair the color of toast, she imagined herself a light-skinned black Barbie, her face the shape of an almond and her body as long and straight as Xiomara's hair. When her attentions turned to Owen McDonough, a loud-mouthed alterna-geek, she saw herself as a punk rocker with a slim patch of fruit-punch-red braids and a waist that curved in like the slope of an electric guitar. Xiomara, of course, did not need to push her imagination so far. While Earnestine prattled on about the dreams she'd had about Perry or Owen or So-and-

So, Xiomara talked about the book reports they'd written for her, the notes they'd passed to her, how their teeth tasted under her tongue.

Earnestine should have hated Xiomara, and if you caught her on a bad day, she would have said she did hate her—deeply, with a fullheartedness not unlike glee. When Jacob Morton, a screw-faced boy with a fancy calculator and a movie star father, accosted her with the question one afternoon in September, she pushed sour thoughts through her face and frowned.

"Why does Xiomara hang out with you?" The boy shouted at her on the courtyard, swooping down into her face like a bat. He leaned so close to her that she thought he might touch her, but of course he didn't; almost no one ever did.

"She doesn't even like you," he said. "She told Samantha Fitzpatrick that she hates you. She thinks you have B.O."

"Good," Earnestine said plainly, barely looking up from her Social Studies homework. "'Cause I hate her, and I *know* she has B.O."

"You're just jealous because you look like a guy," he said, opening his backpack and producing a pack of coveted Sour Power candies. He piled the sparkling gummy strings into his mouth and continued talking, his teeth gleaming with green slime.

"What you should do," he said, "is stop wearing those stupid dresses and just pretend you're a guy. Then you can be her boyfriend."

Earnestine sharpened her mouth to shoot an insult, but found she had nothing to say. So she grabbed the Sour Powers from Jacob and hustled to her feet. She poured all the gummy cords in her mouth and hurled the crumpled paper bag over her shoulder at him as she walked away.

Earnestine's clothes were stupid; it was true. Her mother, the only black woman ordained at the Columbia University School of Theology in 1992, had begun to read up on African religious syncretism just before the beginning of the school year, and decided to dress the entire family in homemade African-inspired getups from that point on. Earnestine liked the fabrics her mother used—they sang colors that reminded her of Easter eggs and outer space at once, rich plums and deep cerulean in geometric patterns so complex she could sit for hours studying a single square inch. But the clothes themselves were awful. Skirts as round as basketballs, billowing yards of fabric that seemed to add layers to Earnestine's onion-shaped frame. Pants whose legs clung in anguish to her calves, and low crotches which swung wildly between her legs like a cow's udders. These fashions were popular up in Harlem, and Earnestine liked the idea of Africa well enough. She listened happily to her parents' stories about Marcus Garvey and Liberian settlement, W.E.B. Du Bois, and Jean-Jacques Dessalines, dreaming of the things she might do and change when her own life began. Still, things had their times and their places, she felt, and lunchtime with Xiomara in the minty halls of the Madison Avenue Country was neither the time nor the place for a Back-to-Africa movement. She already felt as big and black as a Dark Continent. Kente crowns and cowrie shells were the last things she needed.

Xiomara did not have this problem, of course. She sailed into school every day like a lucky feather, waiting to be caught and wished on. After Earnestine stole Jacob's Sour Powers in that gruff display, Xiomara floated up beside him smiling, whispered something in his ear, and drifted away with the remainder of his allowance in her pocket. Her smile was like Alice's pack of magical sweetcakes, growing and shrinking her haphazardly, though always to positive effect. The "eat me" smile she launched at Jacob was as wide as a bowl of milk, and made her beanstalk body seem to stretch so high upward that she could grab a chunk of sun and smear it on her cheeks like blush. But then, to the Madison Avenue Country teachers, she gave a demure smile as tight and quiet as a yellow raisin, reducing herself down to an unfinished hope, a glimmer of pale brown potential. They liked that.

So if you asked Earnestine on a bad day what she really thought of Xiomara, she would have drawn her eyebrows up into her hairline, rolled her neck halfway around its orbit, and said, "I hate that ho." And she may nearly have convinced you, not because it was true, but because her bad days were very bad. On days when she was bleeding, or when she left the house too late to stuff her bag with cookies while her mother wasn't watching, she had nothing but shrill looks and sour words for anyone. And when her parents' fights kept her up into the slim hours of the morning, she spent all of the following day in what her mother would call *a funk*, her face set in a pit-bull glare from the first sirens of the day until the streetlight went out at night.

Her least favorite day was Sunday, when she would usually be forced to go to her mother's church or to spend the day feigning sickness, the only acceptable excuse for missing the service. It was on Sunday mornings that she began to dread the start of the week, which meant facing not only Madison Avenue Country but also ARYSE—short for African Rites for Young Sisters' Evolution—the rites-of-passage program that she had to attend every Monday in order to have her own big twelve-year-old coming-of-age party and not miss out on all her classmates' bat mitzvah fun. She hated ARYSE, not only because she resented having to learn about housekeeping and feminine hygiene along with self-defense and financial planning, but also because ARYSE was filled with girls like Xiomara and worse: They were all prettier than Earnestine could ever hope to be, and yet, unlike Xiomara, they were *like her*—black girls with black mothers who worked too hard to give them everything they themselves hadn't had coming up—including pride in their roots—and with fathers who were, in some fashion, gone. Her failure to fit in with these girls could not be attributed to her blackness or her mother's taste or anything other than the endless vacuum of space and synapse that was simply *Earnestine*. At Madison Avenue Country, she was an anomaly. At ARYSE she was a mistake.

She hated Sundays actively, and that active hating was how she spent most of the morning hours before Xiomara sat on her bed. That morning, Earnestine dripped down from sleep into a familiar pit of dread, horrified to see the weekend thin away. It pained to think that she would have to deal with Jacob Morton, Samantha Fitzpatrick, *and* the ARYSE girls the following day. When she awoke more fully, she heard her parents fighting, their voices splashing against each other two floors up. From the weight of the voices, she knew this fight would last a while. She lingered in the bed for a few minutes, pulling the covers up to her chin and imagining herself sinking deep into the fibers of the mattress. When this didn't work, she crept to the kitchen, poured a small mixing bowl full of Cocoa Krispies, and set herself up in the living room to put on *Saved By the Bell* and listen to the argument from under the blue-and-white flicker of the television.

"I'm all for exposing her to African culture," her father said. "But tell me why I have to be there when those women swoop in to scoop up their little Nubian princess chickadees. You never been there as me, Myrna. You don't know what it's like." The floor sighed. "*Diablo.*"

"She's twelve, Ernesto," her mother retorted. "We can't have her walking the city alone at night. This isn't the safe little place you want it to be." Her many bracelets chimed. "Sorry."

Spoon in hand, tongue adrift in chocolate mush, Earnestine sympathized with her father. It was true that the ARYSE mothers morphed frighteningly into overgrown cartoon witches around him, grinning and cooing over Earnestine's outfit as though she were a six-year-old, some even toting pans of bread pudding for him to sample, smiling sheepishly as they explained that they'd just made *too much food* for their own little families of two. But Myrna Davis had to work, she told Ernesto, and it was selfish for him to complain about watching Earnestine when she was the one who put food on the table and private-school-caliber insight into Earnestine's head while he sat around doing God-knew-what and playing his music, which, Earnestine knew, everyone in the family loved more than they'd say.

"And you haven't played a gig in months," her mother added, her voice claw-sharp. "What do you do up there all day anyway? Will I ever get to know?" But Ernesto gave no reply.

Earnestine closed her ears to this part of the conversation. She tried not to think about how he spent his days, fearing small betrayals as much as large ones, or more. A dead body, a secret family, even a sex change would have been easy enough to manage, Earnestine thought. Her parents would divorce, the house would be sold, and she would begin a new life as a new girl elsewhere. New Jersey, maybe. Or Long Island. But subtler insurgencies made her feel jittery. It was the small, hidden questions of her parents' lives—whether they picked their noses, how carefully they washed between their legs, how long each sat on his or her side of their bed before putting their socks on each morning—these were the things that scared her. Her biggest fear was that her father's secrets were not disastrous, not cruel, but sad.

When the show was over, Earnestine finished her cereal, dumped the bowl in the kitchen sink, and plodded back to her room where she waited for her father's music to spring up as it always did after a fight. He was a brilliant musician, though not a particularly talented artist. His gift was not in producing great expressions of feeling, but in recasting familiar songs so that their meanings transformed. He turned Michael Jackson's "Can't Help It" into a blues-saturated dirge and Donnie Hathaway's "A Song for You" into a raucous church hymn. Earnestine knew that this fight would end as most of her parents' fights did, with slammed doors, unfinished sentences, and her father's steady baritone lacing someone else's words through the halls of the brownstone, tying the loose ends as best it could.

Soon she heard her mother leave, tossing a weary "goodbye" into the air to be smacked into the house by the slamming front door. Then she heard her father's keyboard, its notes closer than usual. He was playing Earth, Wind & Fire's "September," one of her mother's favorite songs. She sat on her bed and listened, letting the song fill the space around her. She had heard it many times before, and even thought she could remember seeing her parents dance to it once or twice in the kitchen while her father cooked dinner, he whisking her mother into his arms and swirling her around the counter, a greasy spatula glistening in his free hand. Earnestine liked the song well enough, though she did not know if the memory was to be trusted. The original version was quick and catchy, and carried with it a breathlessness that did remind Earnestine of the month of September, the smell of freshly Cloroxed school lockers and unused erasers cut with the quiet pain of a blank year sprawling ahead. But her father's "September" today was different. It was a ballad, a relentless tale of loss that brought to mind all of the things she feared most about love, and made her wonder how people managed to grow up at all.

> Our hearts were ringing
> In the key that our souls were singing . . .
> Only blue talk and love,
> Remember how we knew love was here to stay.

The music paused as she made her way to the first floor, eager to grab the cigarettes and smoke in the sparkle of the weeds and waste until ARYSE and the Mothers Africa were things of the past, or at least of a future that had finally slipped her mind. Stopping at the hall tree, she peered around the corners to be sure her father was not around, then fished through his pocket for the smokes. Finding nothing but gum wrappers, paper clips, and dimes, she gathered the change and headed back down to the garden floor, planning to salvage a stub from her concrete stash. But at the bottom of the stairs, she found the yard door open and her slab upturned. Her father's keyboard lay on the table, its white keys flickering gray under the shade of the weeds. He sat at one of the two working yard chairs, his back toward her, a large Cerveza Presidente on the table. A cigarette dangled from his lips like an old-school soothsayer's chew stick. Every few seconds, he reached down and released a puff of ashes into the concrete pit.

Earnestine lingered in the doorway, wondering if he had heard her and whether she still had time to disappear. Just as she resolved to make a run for it, he spoke.

"*Qué tú'ta buscando, mija?*" he said. "You looking for me?"

She stuffed the change into her pocket and moved closer.

"No," she said. "Just wanted some air."

He turned toward her and pulled out the other upright chair, motioning for her to join him. His face was flat and pliant like a marshmallow, and the black centers of his eyes were as soft as smears of melted fudge. Had she not heard him play just seconds before, she would have thought he had been sitting there in quiet contemplation for hours.

"What is it about this sister-passage thing anyway?" he said, looking past her as though through the bottom of a glass bottle. "Do they really tell you anything your mama and I don't tell you? Anything you need to know?"

She paused. The smell of fresh biscuits from a neighboring building laid a sweet film over the garbage-thick air.

"Not really," she said. "I hate it. School, too."

He nodded, his eyes tracing the picket fence that circled the yard, its missing planks giving it the worn but hopeful look of a six-year-old's smile.

"The girls," he said slowly. "Right? The pretty ones."

Earnestine didn't answer.

"*Amor mío*," he said, his voice heavy with smoke and tenderness. "Fine—those girls *son lindas*, with their long hair and their boyfriends. But you have something they will never have, whatever they do. You have pain, *Duende*. Your mama calls it soul."

Earnestine considered the words, rolling them around in her mouth as she had seen her mother do with blood-thick wines at restaurants downtown. Soul seemed simple, something everyone had, though few knew how to work it. It reminded her of the gritty voices of the blues singers her mother liked, and the hard, heavy breasts of the women at church. But *duende* was new. The word curved around itself softly, took its own brief but delicious twists and turns. She reached for the pack of Marlboros on the table and held one to her lips, eyeing her father for a response. He looked into the neighboring yard, where a pair of pigeons had begun to peck at each other's necks. He turned his head and slid the matchbook toward her with an ashy elbow.

Earnestine lit herself a smoke and held it in the air as casually as she could, her wrist bent like a bird of paradise flower, the way Xiomara did when she was bored or thinking hard. She took a pull and coughed loudly. Ernesto whipped his face back toward her, then slid the beer across the table. She sipped only enough to clear her throat, then pushed the bottle back.

"*Mira esos pájaros,*" he said, his voice beginning to stagger. "They're not *swans* or *doves*, or fuckin' *nightingales*. They're pigeons. They're gray and they waddle and they all have *tetas grandotas*, even the male ones. It could be embarrassing, what people might say about them. They go through shit. They fight the rats for candy wrappers. They get little snot-nosed children running after them, chasing them from their food and shooting them with pissy water guns. But *míralos*," he said, his back still toward her. "They got their own thing. Let shit go down, let the world end, man, and it's them, and the rats, and the roaches gonna take over. They're not even worried about us. They do what they feel."

Earnestine took another pull and watched her father's neck sway under his head like a string beneath a helium balloon. Then she watched the pigeons, their bulging gray breasts flashing diamonds of muted purple and turquoise as they necked. She inhaled the smoke, the trash, the beer, the baking bread, the mild coconut smell of her father's hair grease, and the smell of urine that had sprung up from a yard nearby. She watched her father watch the pigeons, understanding, as though for the first time, how alone he seemed, perhaps always.

As an unformed sound began to wring itself from her throat, Ernesto turned toward her. He eased the cigarette from her hand and dropped it in the pit, then slid the loose slab of concrete back into place.

"Take a shower, míja, before your mama comes home," he said. "And brush your teeth," he added. "Twice."

He rubbed his hands on his knees and settled in before his keyboard, pulling the microphone up toward his face and clearing his throat to sing again.

> My thoughts are with you,
> Holding hands with your heart to see you
> Only blue talk and love,
> Remember how we knew love was here to stay.

In the bathroom, Earnestine pulled her T-shirt over her head and let her pajama shorts fall to the floor. She kicked the clothes into a pile and moved toward the shower, then paused. She looked at her parents' toiletries—her father's shaving cream and her mother's razor, her mother's designer body wash and her father's plain white soap. She imagined Xiomara's bathroom, full of amber-colored bath gel and the kinds of thin, fragile combs that broke as soon as Myrna brought them within an inch of Earnestine's hair. She imagined Xiomara spending her Sunday in a brightly colored room with angular furniture and electric-green clocks, sitting with her legs crossed, her shoulders as straight and slender as the ends of a clothes hanger, laughing on the phone with Jacob Morton as he offered to write her Social Studies paper. She imagined them chirping together for hours, lounging happily in the easy arms of a Sunday afternoon. Then she wondered what her father had been doing with his days, what he did all the time up in that room where she and her mother did not go, where there were no neon phones and no bright colors and no one to share his smokes and his thoughts.

She closed the curtain, pulled her bathrobe around her middle, and padded up to the third floor. The smell of cheap fried chicken was thick on the street in front of the brownstone, and her father's song had begun to play louder, crawling up the walls and spilling down from the ceilings.

She pressed lightly on the studio door and watched it slide open. The wood-paneled room opened before her like a broken pumpernickel loaf, its grains lit under the shafts of sun that oozed from beneath the curtains. She surveyed the space—the gleaming drum and cymbal set, the old, broken keyboards, the empty bottles, the guitar picks, the petrified rinds of limes. She settled herself into her father's chair and swiveled around, afraid, at first, that he would discover her, then not afraid at all.

Leaning back in the chair as she imagined he did all day, she turned to the small TV-VCR set and pressed play. A tall, thin, dirty-blonde woman rode a bicycle down a nearly empty street, her hair gusting behind her like a pile of turning leaves swept up in the wind. The tape was old, and the screen seemed covered in a gray film, making the woman's skin look as flat and thin as tissue paper. Then the scene changed. Now she was looking at a naked man with dingy black socks and a triangular nose. The man sat in a small living room on a large, brown sofa, reading a magazine and rubbing the space between his knees. Soon a doorbell rang, and the man rose, flopping, to the door, where he greeted the leaf woman with a kiss on the cheek and buried his hands in her hair. The woman gave a smile and began dancing around him, peeling her clothes off in layers and flinging them carelessly into the air like bits of confetti. Then their kisses grew slower and longer. Music began to play from the TV speakers, and the smell of hot chicken clung to Earnestine's face. Soon, the woman was bent over before the man like a candy rabbit, sputtering laughter and whipping her hair over her shoulder as he pounded into her from behind.

The woman screeched and began to shout out words like "yeah" and "go" as though she were a gym teacher making calls in a game of dodge ball. Earnestine's stomach lurched. She scrambled for the volume button and muted the television, then watched as the woman jerked like a string puppet in front of the man, her face frozen in a smile. Earnestine held her middle as she watched, pressing her hand beneath the belt of her bathrobe, waiting for her stomach to settle so she could move. She pressed on the low part of her stomach, the place her father used to call her *barriguita*, pushing down there until she started to feel better, then pushing deeper, until she started to feel good.

When the scene changed again, the woman sat naked on a sofa, alone, fanning herself with the magazine and smoking a cigarette. Her face had changed. Now it was hard and sour as one of her father's old limes, even as she gave the camera a wink. Earnestine watched the woman's hair flop against her shoulders to the rhythm of the fan. Soon, the woman set the magazine down and began kneading into her own flesh with her free hand. Every few seconds, she glanced at the camera distantly, as though she did not really believe that anyone would be watching her.

Earnestine paid extra-close attention then, fixing herself to the woman's body as it jumped and shivered above her hands, watching her skin go red with heat while her eyes stayed clear as marbles. After a while, the woman's face sank into a curious, pleasant ease. Slowly, her eyes and mouth opened wide, drinking the camera in, all her muscles working toward a sigh. And Earnestine found herself opening too, joining the woman, lying with her and fluttering into herself like a small bird into a puddle. When the woman was done and her body lay like an empty pillowcase on the sofa, she smiled gratefully at Earnestine. And this made Earnestine think, again, of Xiomara.

When Xiomara came over that evening, Earnestine did not lead her out to the backyard. Instead, she sat on the bed as soon as Xiomara came in and asked her to tell her stories there.

"So what's wrong with you?" Xiomara said. "Don't you wanna go smoke?" She smelled like bubble gum and sweat.

"No," Earnestine said, stiff on the mattress. "Not really."

Xiomara nodded and sat beside Earnestine, laying her open palm on her fist. "So what do you want to do?"

"I don't know," Earnestine said. She urged herself not to move away. "Did you talk to any guys today?"

"Of course," Xiomara said. She gathered her hair on top of her head, held it there for a second, then let it waft out behind her like the bicycle woman's. Earnestine felt the hair warm on her shoulders, and she was surprised.

Beginning a story about a boy she did not bother to name, Xiomara pressed Earnestine's hand down into the bedsprings. She told a tale Earnestine could not believe, about how the boy had promised to buy her a car and to take her to Santo Domingo, where twelve-year-olds could drive. How he had bought her mother a house there and had offered her a good job, and how whenever her family went there in her childhood, her mother would drink only water and strawberry *batidas*. Earnestine watched her talk, her eyes closing slowly like the bicycle woman's, her hair coiling, her chest ebbing, her smile curving like the woman's legs as she spoke.

"We're moving there soon," Xiomara said, passing her nose along Earnestine's neck. "I'm going to dance *bachata* with my cousins in the mountains. It's my favorite dance. You feel like you're in water when you do it. It can be loud or it can be soft, but you always feel free."

Still talking, she ran her lips along Earnestine's chin, and Earnestine softened her face, tilted her neck forward in response. She felt her chest jump, then slow, and she wondered if she should say something, too. But the story continued, and, after a while, she was not sure if it was her voice she heard or Xiomara's, her skin, her hands, her tongue or Xiomara's, whose lips, whose eyes. Pressed together, they shared the air, stomachs rumbling, trash falling through the sky on the far side of the window. The length, and the leanness, and the longing were theirs as her father's song poured its sad notes through the halls.

Photo by David Ruhlman

RACHEL MARSTON's fiction and nonfiction have appeared in *Puerto del Sol*, *Versal*, and *DIAGRAM*. She recently completed her PhD in literature and creative writing at the University of Utah, and she is finishing her first novel, about nuclear testing in the American West. Marston is from Las Vegas, Nevada, and she now lives in Salt Lake City.

HOW TO SPEAK TO GOD
Rachel Marston

If the radiance of a thousand suns were to burst into the sky that would be like the splendor of the Mighty One and I am become Death, the destroyer of worlds.

—J. Robert Oppenheimer, quoting the *Bhagavad Gita*
after witnessing the first test of a nuclear bomb

It is the sunlight streaming on her desk. It is the sun on her arms and her hands. It is the way the sun warms her skin and lights her hands as if in a painting. She sets the birds on the desk, settles them in a nest of shredded paper, lets the light shine over them, so white, those feathers smooth. It is really such a white.

the very intense flash of light, and a sensation of heat on the parts of my body that were exposed

She wonders if their whiteness runs right through them.

The birds are still small, small enough that each fits inside the curve of her palm, her fingers wrapped around, a nail tapping on the beaks, holding down their wings. She presses just a little harder, those smooth white feathers, those sharp little beaks, and their slender white necks.

✿ ✿ ✿

The birds are pigeons, not doves, but Annie tells Henry, when he calls from work, that she rescued two doves from the tree.

"How long were you out there?" he asks.

"You should see them," she says. "Just so tiny." She taps their heads. The birds look around.

"Annie."

"Doves," she says, "Henry, just imagine it. Doves."

But really they are pigeons and she does not tell Henry because he would worry about pigeons in the house, pigeons in her hands. He would say to her, "But Annie, pigeons don't need rescuing."

Annie knows that sometimes they do and that the difference between the pigeon and the dove, after all, is only in the name.

❀ ❀ ❀

Annie sat in her grandfather's dusty yard in Mercury, Nevada, playing dolls in the grass, so dry in the desert, yellow bladed; her grandfather refused to water it.

He sometimes sat Annie on his knee and bounced her, up and down; all that mattered was the motion and the next word from his mouth. But it was usually in the garden, his hands in the earth, showing her seeds and sprouts, giving her names for things—she, just like Adam—the wonder of the words, of naming the world. Las Vegas beanpoppy, soft lupine, silverleaf sunray, rosyking sandword, Bodie Hills rockcress, and the desert sunflower—her favorite, more delicate than the sunflowers she knew, absent that heavy center, a much brighter yellow, a wider and more supple petal.

He told her about birds, digging into the caliche earth, hunting for seeds. He told her how he changed the earth, the compacted soil, adding organic matter and taking it away, creating a space where things could grow.

His day job was much the same, changing matter, science in the desert, atoms splitting and splitting again.

❀ ❀ ❀

Henry calls himself a carrier of heavy things, a job description, but he always tells Annie that it's a better description for her. She repeats the phrase to the little birds on her desk, weighing them in turn with her hand.

"Carriers of heavy things," she says. She sets them back on their nest of paper, places them near the dish of water she has put on the desk. They shuffle toward it, dip, dipping those beaks.

already will largely have been reduced to ashes . . .

It is the things without actual weight that are the hardest for Annie to discard, those spectral shapes, the ghosts in their shiny skins. She waits for the birds to stop drinking, her pigeons, her doves, those heads buried deep in the feathers on their chests, the downy fluff, the little clack of their clawed feet on the desktop. The sun patterns her arm—a thin series of shadow details.

❄❄❄

Annie saw desert and highway and open sky. The skies were wide with thin streaming clouds, periodic, penciled across that blue—not the sprouting, growing clouds, so red in the middle, opening up like a flower, petals dipping into the sky. *Trillium*—her grandfather showed her its three-petaled loveliness with its elemental name.

Henry watched the road and she watched the road and him. They were driving back from three days camping in Cathedral Gorge and tomorrow she will find the birds and bring them home.

Earlier, while she drove, he slept and she watched him then, too, short looks between him and the road ahead, the sky pinkening, a filmy slip of gauze. She could never quite get enough, the line of his jaw, the red of the alluvial fans, the sweetness of his mouth with his plumy lower lip, the distant dark plateaus, the dark hair fallen on his forehead and cheek, the Joshua trees and the cacti, these things and so many more.

❄❄❄

In the world of tiny flowers and even tinier seeds, grains of earth and particles and molecules, atoms and nuclei, protons and electrons, Annie sat and sifted her hand through the soil in her grandfather's garden.

He said to her, "See this one. This one, Annie, will be a poppy." And she could see it, that plumy red fullness, falling over itself with all that heady weight, bending its slender stalk, dipping back to the ground.

At this moment, though, she sits all alone in the corner by the grapevines, the grapes small and succulent, tiny pops in her mouth, pulled straight from between the leaves, the air full of sweetness. She didn't understand this land with its dusty fields and green corners, yielding up such sweet fruit, and these piercing skies, but it is also all she knows.

Her grandfather lived alone in his small house near Blue Diamond Road. He sold the home in Mercury when she was fourteen, the year her grandmother fell and broke her hip and two days into the hospital died, the cancer having spread to her bones. Her father had said to him, "Dad, I worry about you out there all by yourself."

So now she's in the smaller garden, in the yard of the house out in the desert, but with the subdivisions quickly closing in, the stucco squares topped with thousands of red roof tiles.

She sits in the dirt, feeling the earth beneath her fingers, and while she still can, watches the stretches of unpeopled dusty landscape and the mountains. Her grandfather comes out with two mugs and lowers himself, such carefulness in his body, such deliberate movements, to sit next to her.

She takes the tea and together they sit, until long after the sun goes down.

❀ ❀ ❀

This is what she heard—God loves you, God loves you, God loves. So she started standing under the tree in their front yard, her arms raised toward the branches, her face expectant. She waits for God to speak. She thinks that she will hear him—even though she no longer believes in God.

Suddenly I felt heat on the side of my head, opened my eyes and saw a brilliant yellow-white light all around. The heat and light were as though the sun had just come out with unusual brilliance.

Henry finds her under the tree when he returns from work. She has been there for over an hour. Her face is red, her dress sticky with sweat on this 110-degree summer day.

He says, "You need to drink some water."

She says, "I've been waiting all day, Henry. I've just been waiting."

He touches her shoulder. "Come inside, Annie."

"I'd never really looked at this tree before. You know?" She looks up again. "You know, Henry. A sign."

He does know, just like he knows the slightly sour sweetness of her mouth in the mornings, the shape of her brow, furrowed in, that V-shape between her eyes when she slept, he knows this looking for signs.

"You don't believe in God." This comes out harsher than he means it. She looks over at him and frowns. He shakes his hand gently, a half-wave in front of his face.

She lowers her arms and stands on her toes. She kisses Henry on the cheek.

"I hadn't realized how hot it was."

She lets him lead her inside the house. He sees that she is not wearing shoes.

"You know, Henry. I don't think it is so much not believing in God, but it is much more disappointing to not believe in the devil. A world with the devil is made more simple by having one identifiable source of evil or badness."

But when she looks at the dry landscape spreading before her, she knows that such divisions are not only too simple but impossible. That good and bad in the world come from people, not a place outside. That it all exists on a spectrum, such a beautiful range, like all the shades between red and yellow, and that often what was meant as good became something so much more.

Annie looked out the window. The neighbor left the porch light on again and it pooled on their flowerbeds. Henry breathed deeply, sleeping on his side. She felt his chest move up and down. She rested her hand on his side, her leg on his leg. She shifted and he moved closer to her, wrapped his fingers around her wrist.

She wondered about the things which fell fast and hard to the earth, a meteor, a plane, a man with wings made of wax and feathers flying too close to the sun, oh, for another way to escape gravity, these gray sidewalks and purple lampposts and the constant chatter of the world.

covered with a violet luminescence, like that produced by the electrical excitation of the air

There was no threat here. This was just sleep.

She wanted to run her tongue from his hip to his jawbone, up that skin. She wanted to dig her fingers into his back. She rested her head on his shoulder, fitting right in the curve. She pressed against his back, felt the skin, that small fleshy line of her stomach on his.

Henry shifted again, pulled her hand over his chest, placed it on his other shoulder. This nightly figuring out how to fit together.

Just that evening, she sat next to a couple, the equation-working couple, with their graphing calculators. Her red head next to his dark one, both slender, and he tapped the paper with his pencil and she checked his fractions. Annie missed Henry at that moment.

She put her nose on his shoulder. He smelled so good, in his clean skin, which she wanted to peel right into, just pull it back, layer after layer, through to the molten core.

❀❀❀

The egg clings to Henry's lip, just a little bit of yellow, and she wants to climb over the table to lick it off him. Then just bite a little bit, that lower lip of his, dipping into his face, a sinuous curve against the angles of chin and nose and cheek. In fifteen minutes, Henry will leave for work and Annie will sit at her desk and then go outside and stand under the tree.

If Annie could make a movie of their life, film one brief scene, it would be the two of them in a car. They are driving through the desert, past those beautiful stretches of flat land, bounded by the mountains, sharp and smooth, just road and road and road, and the smell of sagebrush in flower and the dust in the air. It is dusk and the red in the sky slips behind the mountains, orange-shadowed landscape, with the promise of something lurking in the earth.

For a brief period there was a lighting effect within a radius of twenty miles equal to several suns in midday; a huge ball of fire was formed that lasted for several seconds. This ball mushroomed and rose to a height of over ten thousand feet before it dimmed.

And in this film, she sits, heels on the dashboard, toes spread against the windshield, watching the sky change as they drive, neither of them speaking because at that particular moment they shouldn't; in that way speaking would make it impossible to take in the world.

Instead here they sit, at a table in a breakfast nook in a suburban house on the road to Red Rock. She looks out the window and she can just see Lone Mountain.

Henry pats her hand.

She knows she can't leave herself behind but she wants solutions to problems, theorems, and proofs—a world of proof and proving—a little less about arbitrary signification.

Henry touches her hand again.

❁ ❁ ❁

When it is done, Annie will put it all in a box, a tiny box, those stacks of cardboard and glue, filled and filled, those tiny scraps of paper. The clippings, the day's news, the small-boned bodies.

Beginning to be eaten into from below by dark obscuring matter

The birds wander over the desk, pecking at papers and paper clips. They toddle around, their bodies a little awkward for their legs. She nudges them back when they get too close to the edge.

❁ ❁ ❁

The summer before her grandmother died, Annie broke her right leg jumping ditches behind her grandparents' house with her friend, Samantha. The bone came clean right through the skin, so white, that jagged piece, white like Annie's face, watching her blood pool and her skin flap against her shin, and that gleaming white, so shaped like the surrounding mountains. Samantha just stood and cried, "What do I do? What do I do?"

Annie couldn't move or she would have slapped her, a nice red hand across Sam's shiny little mouth. Annie couldn't speak either, but she did throw up, bent right over, and threw up on the spiny ground cover—a rockcress.

At some point, her grandmother heard Samantha, and she and Annie's grandfather came running, but everything seemed slow—the way her grandmother's hair suspended in the air, that one steady piece, just above her ear, and her grandfather, wiping his hands, left then right, then over and over again, working his jaw but not saying a word. He bent to pick her up, saying, "Elsa, hold her foot." Both so careful in their handling of her, carrying her together, going to piece her all back together again.

❈ ❈ ❈

Annie opens the paper and she reads, "uncertain as to the nature of the threat, only serves to raise tensions, this brighter future, the oppressed and impoverished peoples of." She knows now that the world is just living how it always lives—half-life after half-life. She sets the paper on the table and stands under the tree, waiting for God to speak, waiting for her sign.

She is cracked right open again, that chest, those ribs, that heart, beating, beating in her chest, nestled in, curled up against so much pink.

I was momentarily blinded, much as one would be in emerging suddenly from a dark room into bright sunlight. After a couple of seconds I regained sufficient sight to see the entire sky.

And that this is what Annie will see, after she gathers up those little birds, those birds she sees waiting for her in the lower branches of the tree, speaking to her so softly, those tiny breathing bodies. She will take them in her hands. She will sit with them at her desk. She will rub their feathers from beak to scaly toes, pinching at her skin. She will see these tiny lives in her hands, fragile, steady, just two, easy numbers. She will let them wander on her desk and peck at her fingertips as she tries to feed them. Then she will take them in her hands and she will push just a little harder, let those beaks scratch at her. She will push and they will push back, beaks into her fingers, into her fleshy palms, but she will hold them and hold them. She will rub her fingers over their lovely softness, hold just a little tighter, and their beaks will scratch her skin, but she will hold them close. She will carry them back outside and press a little harder. She will hear the tiny pops, a different type of sweetness, a different way of peeling back the world, to see how things work, and look up through the tree to see the entire sky.

Photo by Scott Salus

ROBIN MCLEAN was a lawyer then a potter in Alaska until she left to get her MFA at UMass Amherst. In 2011 her story collection, *Reptile House*, was a finalist for the Flannery O'Connor Short Story Award. She lives by Newfound Lake in New Hampshire in the winter and in the summer on a farm in western Massachusetts.

SLIP
Robin McLean

" Everything falls apart," said Mac from the bed. He lay, round and gray, tilted up on pillows. A nurse wrote numbers on a paper. The window was big and blue and a long way down. Below, the parade in the street was just beginning. The kids lined up in capes. The doctor took Mac's pulse with two fingers and a wristwatch. He thought of his mower at home. His wife, his kids.

"Everything breaks in the end," said Mac.

"Not everything breaks," said Dorothy. She held her head with her hands. Dorothy was round and gray and stood by the saline drip. She clasped Mac's foot, as if it belonged to her, at the foot of the bed with its mate.

"And the rest goes all to hell," Mac said, and laughed, but not a real laugh. "Look at me: new hip, new knee, now this." The young doctor also laughed to join his patient.

"And none of his own teeth at all," Dorothy said. "Those there, they were made in Chicago."

"Quiet about that and you know it," Mac said.

"It's just the doctor," Dorothy said to Mac. "He gets embarrassed," she said to the young doctor.

"Shush," said Mac.

"We've been married forty-nine years," Dorothy said.

"Let him talk, let him talk," said Mac.

"No apples or corn or tennis anymore," she said.

"He doesn't care about that, sweetheart. Hush," Mac said.

"Or taffy at all," Dorothy said.

"He's a busy man," Mac said.

Then the young doctor talked and talked of cutting and stitching and plumbing blood. Anything for living. He waved his hands like a knife, careful, like a needle and thread. She couldn't watch. The building rumbled. Iron lungs hummed, germs buzzed, scalpels whined. The washers thumped in the basement eight floors down, ten feet tall, getting everything clean. She needed to bathe, to brush her hair, to brush her teeth. The bags under her eyes needed tending. She squeezed Mac's foot.

The young doctor had the haircut of Superman, small hands; his mother must be proud. The lab coat was clean, the tip of his tongue clicked, the stethoscope was like any on TV.

"Your mother must be proud," said Dorothy.

"Honey, the man was talking."

The parade below was green, green, and more green and sliced through the city. The window needed a scaffold and someone brave. A parking deck was going up across the drive and a sign said, COMING SOON. The men in the hard hats stopped and leaned on new steel posts to watch a juggler walk by and a girl with a baton twirling. The band pounded. The fire truck inched forward with girls, caped and crowned; they waved at the people with their ankles crossed. A banner said LUCK OF THE but turned the corner and Dorothy never learned the rest of what it said.

"St. Patrick's Day," she said. She had just thought of it.

"She's overtaxed," Mac said to the young doctor, who nodded. "She doesn't rest."

"You need to rest," said the young doctor.

"Oh, I will," she said. "I do. I just didn't realize."

Trumpets and tubas shined and turned with the drumbeats. Fingers pumped on faith. The girl tripped and the baton flew off between the boots and shoes of the crowd and was gone till later when she came looking. The girl twirled on without the baton, with an imaginary baton that she flung up and turned and caught behind her back. As if batons were hardly needed. People clapped and waved at the girl. A cement truck waited to cross the street and get on with things.

This doctor was still talking. He was of the talking generation; Mac and Dorothy had once agreed about that on a morning walk by the river. This doctor had Superman hair, yes, and a Superman jaw, too, but he did not look particularly strong. Mac had been stronger. This doctor talked of valves and atriums such and such, ventricles, and ribs. He showed them his wife in his billfold smiling, because they asked.

"A sweet face," said Dorothy. "She drinks her milk."

"Thank you," said the young doctor. "I'm very lucky."

The baby fat above his belt was for pinching. A petting animal in a barn for a sweet-faced milkmaid. This doctor's kids got straight As. They played in the pool in summer. The rose garden was in the back. This doctor pruned the roses with his small strong hands and his large strong brain full of books and organs and that was enough. The doctor would take his wife to Europe to see the gardens and the castles. They would hire a boat up the canals with wine and go to the bullfights, too, but rush from ringside before the bull was dead. The concrete steps and dusty street. "Too horrible to watch," the wife would say. "You're right, of course," the doctor would answer. From a vendor's cart, the wife would buy soft cheese that would melt on her fingers. She would chew the rind like a melon on a bench by a foreign river and talk to him, and talk and talk. After that, the doctor and wife would return to the pool and the kids who stayed with her sister. Dorothy would get a pool like that one this summer; Mac had said so.

The doctor backed from the bed to go. He waved and said, "See you in the morning. Get some rest."

"You too," Dorothy said. "Hello to your wife. Is she at the parade?"

"I don't think so."

"Everyone loves parades," Dorothy said. She stood at the window even after the young doctor was gone. The band was just a hundred caps bobbing. Dorothy might have dropped an apple by its tail. People below would think a kid did it.

When Mac was in the john, an orderly came to change the sheets. Dorothy hawked this young man to be sure he tucked the corners properly.

"You're sweet-faced, too, you know," said Mac to Dorothy when the orderly left, and she petted his ear. She helped him into bed.

❀ ❀ ❀

She was the kind who looked both ways at crosswalks and trolley tracks.

On the day Dorothy met Mac she had worn a pretty new skirt. It was snug and slim and showed her figure. Her mother was making meatloaf at her sister's on Wabash, her grandmother's recipe, and Dorothy was walking out for breadcrumbs. It was a pretty spring day with blooms and lollipops.

The skirt was thin and white to her calves. She'd forgotten her slip so borrowed one from her sister who was two sizes bigger. The slip kept falling down her legs as she walked, showing the lacy hem. She considered canceling the meatloaf. Once, she stopped at a bench and rolled the slip's waistband twice over the waist of her skirt. Next, she tried a knot that looked silly and still the slip fell to her ankles. She ducked in an alley. She tucked the waist of the slip in the waist of her underpants, the old cotton kind with faulty elastic. At Thirty-Fifth and Wabash she hid between a stranded bus and a phone booth. She tried the tuck and the knot in combination; it seemed a good plan. She looked around for watchers. In the phone booth was a big handsome man in hat with a gold tooth, back then. He waved and grinned about the slip. She smoothed her skirt and crossed into the green light.

When the yellow light turned the slip was below the skirt hem and falling fast. The trolley car was gliding closer. Dorothy looked both ways and began to run. Cars were honking when the red light turned and she fell and was tangled kicking in the trolley tracks.

"There are no accidents," Mac would say for forty-nine years.

"He came from absolutely nowhere," she would say. "He left the receiver absolutely hanging." They married. He went to war across the world. He lost his teeth much later. He retired. The army paid for the partials, the root canals, and for the final complete set. He snipped the articles from the paper on gardening, important deaths, and advances in dentistry. He stacked the best of them in a drawer in his desk.

A nurse came. A nurse went. The world had gotten so small. The bed was small. Dorothy was shrinking.

Hours passed. Dorothy brushed his hair over his ears till he said, "No, please no more." She set the brush by the taffy on the sill. The church ladies came and talked and talked. They brought tulips in a pot and set them on the sill for Dorothy to water. From the Sunday school, they brought fish in a bowl that sat on the sill. The minister was leaving for Kansas, some scandal with a girl, the crocuses were up, the chocolate egg order had arrived. The ladies went away. Mac had read the obits out loud across the room at Dorothy in the chair, but that was always how she got her news.

Later, a nurse stared in his ears with a light. The fish swam in circles. Mac snoozed. The neighbors came, his brother came, the man who fixed their car. Night came. The car horns argued in the street below among the green detritus. The flag in the middle of the circle drive whipped in the March wind. In like a lion out like a lamb. The clouds moved behind the aspiring parking deck. They opened and closed. The moon rose orange waiting for morning, or some old orange trick.

Once, after their station wagon was sideswiped downtown, Mac had almost lost his leg. He wrote the following to say goodbye:

> We've had some years together
> Have walked some miles or two
> I hate to see you go just now
> But what's a man to do?

❉ ❉ ❉

They saved the leg. He got the knee and hip instead. She folded the verse in the bottom of her jewelry box. They read it on the leg's anniversary.

His teeth were lost more often. Once, in a motel in Erie, Mac and Dorothy searched in the grass by the office for an hour for them. It was where they had walked the dog. They had searched under the bed and through the sticky trash. He was silent till Rochester where the teeth were found in the cooler with the lunchmeat. "Never again," he said, "the fittings are torture." Next, on a lake vacation, the teeth were lost briefly but found by a kid with a snorkel and fins. The kid got twenty dollars in a sealed envelope, and last Thanksgiving a set was ground up in the disposal with the turkey carcass. Only the gums and some wire survived.

"We're taking out the disposal," Mac said. "I'm calling the plumber."

"I can't live without a disposal," Dorothy said.

❉ ❉ ❉

In the dark, while he slept, Dorothy packed his bag for going home when it was all over: a pair of tennis shoes, a jumble of underpants, a slip, a pair of propellers, a magazine with a lake on the cover, goodbye. A mastodon, a shaving kit, a portable tic-tac-toe with the ribbon still on it, a hard hat, the goldfish, the young doctor with keys in his backdoor. A light in the fridge. A book with a hip and a gun on the cover, a toothbrush and toothpaste, an empty case where his teeth could go. A watercolor set, unopened. A book about Richard Nixon, a card from a cousin in Maine, a card with a cross from the church, a card from his brother Bob in Florida, a stuffed turtle with the ribbon, the box of chocolates mostly eaten, a window sill, the doctor's backstairs to his wife and his bed, four pairs of socks and an undershirt, a V-neck sweater, the khakis he wore at check-in, the sand on the sill piled up with no one to tend it, a chunk of kryptonite from the alley, a drive-in movie theater, a buffalo rug, a pack of gum, a witchdoctor and his wife and no rest at all, a hard green apple, a pack of dogs, a fancy horse, a marching band.

She zipped it all up.

In the dark, Mac yawned. The orange moon cleared the last cloud and she forgot.

"Have you seen your plaid pajamas?" she said.

"What do they look like?"

"Plaid."

"I haven't seen anything."

"Your stubble is like a wild hog."

"Take the teeth then if I'm so bad." He pulled his teeth from his mouth and held them out to her. His lip sagged, his cheeks sunk, his eyes drooped. Mac was gone.

"Put them back in," she said. "I was joking."

"Take them anyway now. It's better. We can't forget," he said and waved the set of teeth at her.

"Put them back in, please," Dorothy said and would not take them.

He would have put his teeth back in then, she said later, but for the orderly's cart that banged the hall door.

"Good evening, Mac," called the orderly in the hall. "Coming in now. Hello, Missus." The orderly struggled to turn in the doorway.

"Get your purse," whispered Mac. "Before someone comes."

The wheels squeaked. A new caster was needed.

"Not yet," she whispered. "Keep them in till morning. Not yet."

"Take them now. Put them in your purse," Mac whispered. "We might forget them tomorrow. Take them."

He waved the teeth across the bed for the handoff. Their hands met in midair, crashed, and their old fingers tangled. The teeth fell in among the white sheets and plastic tubes that spanned the dark peaks and valleys made by knees propped up and shins declining to the foot of several blue frozen ponds, a subterranean paperback, a flock of cards roosting near hills of balled up pajamas.

"Oh, my word," she whispered. She pawed the bed. The cart passed the bathroom light that cast a shadow of a giant orderly.

"What?" Mac whispered.

"I had them," she whispered. She glanced at the bouncing light of his heart monitor. "I had them."

Her hands slid among the sheets, legs, and the terrain shifted. "Where are they?" he whispered. "Where are they?"

"Don't move so much," she whispered as the orderly's shadow came in.

"I found them," she whispered, but it was very dark. She picked up something exactly like teeth, stuffed it in her purse, and zipped it with shaking hands.

The cart bumped the rolling meal tray.

"Pardon me," said the orderly.

"Good evening," said Dorothy. She set her purse on the meal tray.

The orderly poured fresh ice in Mac's pitcher. They would take the sheets away in the morning bed change.

❀ ❀ ❀

Dorothy slept in the chair with her feet on the sill. The moon jumped up while no one was looking. A nurse tucked the blankets. Mac snored. The children ran in circles and the hogs bit at trees. The flags flapped every second. The sand tumbled and piled everything everywhere.

In the morning, the sun rose and staff came in scrubs. They lifted Mac onto the gurney. They rolled Mac away.

"My hero," she said to an orderly passing by into off duty.

The cafeteria was full. Mac and Dorothy's son and daughter came and sipped tea. They talked and Dorothy thought of Superman's blue tights, how strange, red trunks and how Lois Lane never changed her name. How Lois could get away with it, given career and danger. How yellow was his favorite color. She asked him once and that's what he had said, "yellow like the sun," a poetic answer she thought at the time.

"Mother, are you alright? Hanging in there?"

"Of course, dear. What were we saying? I should wash my hair."

She should have worn a skirt. A slip and stockings, and clipped up her hair. She should have brought the trolley car.

"A bird or plane?"

"What mother?"

She'd let someone else finish the sentence. Someone else can pluck the tabby cats from trees on the third shift. She needed the heat off his big hide in the bed at night.

The son and daughter talked of "Dad." The tea was warm and strong. Dorothy might have slept on the table, but for all the shakers and cups and saucers, and she was not that kind of tired since the buildings got bigger and crumbled even faster than before. The earth tipped off her axis so easily nowadays, bad guys and earthquakes, tsunamis swallowing mines caving in left and right. A hero's work is never done. Who's to carve the roast? Who's to share her bar of soap?

"I need to go to bathroom" and the daughter took her there, down the hall, to the right, then left, right again.

❈ ❈ ❈

The surgery was a great success. He had ten more years at least, they said. They sewed him up and brought him out on the gurney.

"It will be a very hard night," they said and dabbed his face.

He mumbled and groaned. His cheeks sagged. His eyes drooped. He retched by turning his head. His lips slumped. His tongue searched for the wet like a worm. He vomited. His chest looked exactly like a zipper. The young doctor came and the doctor's replacement. The room froze and baked, the nurses drifted and pecked, a gray man died who they rolled down the hall, where the moon came up. There was no need for windows. The clock said nothing much useful.

In the basement, the washing machines thumped and sloshed eternally. The laundry gals wore smocks and shook their heads, "No," at Dorothy, "We never did find them."

"Are you absolutely sure?"

"Very sure."

"What do they look like?" asked the second shift

"Just like regular teeth." Dorothy showed her perfect set. "My husband, he doesn't know yet. He's still in the I.C.U. We still have time."

The second shift refolded the sheets and towels and swept the floor and searched the enormous lint bin. Dorothy dumped her purse on an ironing board. The gals turned out Dorothy's pockets to see for themselves. They played cards when Dorothy left. They took the elevator to the roof for the air and chewed gum together.

❈ ❈ ❈

The young doctor took his wife to dinner. They fed each other cheesecake. The babysitter was worth every penny.

❈ ❈ ❈

Dorothy waited for Mac to wake up, but Mac snoozed. She stood and sat and watered the plant. She changed the pot to match their kitchen. She gave the plant to an incoming family down the hall.

Mac's tubes were disconnected one by one. Mac breathed on his own, then drank, then peed.

"You are making such progress," she said in his ear.

The orderlies took the bedpans.

The gurney finally delivered Mac back to the ward. The windows were being washed when he arrived.

"Now that's one brave man," whispered Mac and saluted the window washer, who saluted with his oversized squeegee. They lifted Mac to bed. They plugged him into the wall at various places.

The young doctor came and the church and children and the family down the hall for instructions on the plant. While Dorothy was sleeping in an empty bed a few doors down, Mac told his daughter how he once saw two small planes collide in mid-air. He'd been duck hunting in the bog, but he never did again. "They fell like two spinning bricks," he said, "and a wing sailed off to the trees like this."

The wing flew away again. His hand settled in his lap.

The daughter could have completed the story herself, "The firemen came but did nothing much. What could they do with hoses? Everyone died. Several children, so tragic, and an old man, and several people in their prime. I don't recall how many. I saved the clippings with pictures and captions and the quotes of what people said. I was a friend of one of the grandfathers. Everyone was a friend of someone's someone."

"You guys are going home soon," said the daughter.

"I went to all the funerals," he said. "Some were doubled up." The daughter nodded.

The daughter helped Mac to the bathroom sink. He washed his hands. Mac sat in his chair.

❀ ❀ ❀

It was sunny and getting green out the window. An orderly poured some juice. A nurse took his pulse with two fingers and wristwatch. The doctor wasn't on call. The day went by and at the end of it, Dorothy stood at the foot of the bed. Mac was propped up on pillows.

"I'm sorry," Dorothy said. "I don't know what happened to them."

"They were in your purse," he said. "How could this happen?"

"I looked and looked, I'm sorry." When he refused to sip from his straw, she said, "Please drink."

"And the washers in the laundry?"

"I checked there," she said.

"And the dryers?"

"Of course. They somehow got away from me."

"Did you check in the chute to the laundry room?"

"How would I check it?"

An orderly and a nurse came to change the sheets. They rolled Mac both directions and peeled the old sheets off and peeled the new sheets down. They went away. Mac took up the paper and scissors. He began to read.

"I can't believe it," he said. "How could you?"

"They make them in Chicago," she said.

"Or the hampers." He said. "Or the trash in the back."

"They will be perfect and new," she said.

❀ ❀ ❀

Once, when the young doctor was much older, he lay with his wife in their bed. He drew a line between her breasts.

"Just like that?" she said. She moved her hip.

"A very old pair. Forty-nine years."

"Ouch," she said. "Oh my."

The doctor's hand floated over this wife. He blew on her face like a whistle. Her lids shut then opened. He whistled again, so on.

The wind whined. The sand tumbled on the sill. A caped thing flew past the window.

Photo by Morgan Little

ERIK PARKER HOEL's fiction has been published in *Our Stories, Strange Horizons,* and the *2012 Writer's Digest Anthology,* and he was 2011 winner of a Writer's Digest short story prize. Parker Hoel is a PhD candidate in neuroscience at The Sleep and Consciousness Lab at the University of Wisconsin–Madison, where he studies information theory, causality, neuroscience, and emergence.

THE SUBSTANCE
I AM MADE OF
Erik Parker Hoel

In the years before the incident, when I did not yet dream of things which would come to pass, all events contained a lightness I failed to appreciate. Time seemed buoyant then, each moment singular, specific, and immeasurably fragile. Even Samara was known only in passing to me, for she had not yet pulled me from possibility to form. When she finally did, the transformation forged in me an acute awareness of proprioception, similar to standing on the lip of a sharp drop and looking straight up at the siren blue of the sky.

Samara and I at first just passed from one grade to another, but over time my eyes stopped sliding over her and instead lingered as she took a drink of water, laughed at recess, or tied her shoes. Later the moment came, in the hushed ballrooms of an early winter, when I looked over at her during history class and realized I was in love. Despite my quietly building consciousness of her I had no warning to this vertiginous fall. My awareness had not contained a hint of itself inside its growth. So when she looked back at the clock from the first row of desks as the teacher wrote on the blackboard I was provoked into a sudden, violent bloom. Samara had on her face a look that would cause many men over the years to tilt into a blind kind of worship. She would never know its precise, devastating effect, only be bewildered by the fervor it aroused. If you've ever seen a photograph of Anne Frank, with her hair flipped back and her eyes as black as stones, there is a similarity. Not a physical resemblance, no, Samara's parents were from India. Instead it was that Samara, looking back at that clock, her body turned, her lips slightly open, seemed on the verge of some terrible sadness, a great but quiet revelation concerning a thing outside the world. At these far away moments she was as erotic as a woman armored in faith. I imagine that Joan of Arc, on waking to the fog-blue of a cold French morning, had the same look.

So at 1:57 p.m. on a winter day in 2014 I was not in love, and later that minute, when she brushed her hair from her face and turned back to the front of the class after checking the clock, I was.

For a long time after I maintained a fearful distance, unable to approach her. Our first real conversation happened two years later, when we were in seventh grade. She had begun to grow the barest nubs of breasts, which she hid under men's T-shirts. To impress her I made rips in my jeans with a pair of scissors, learned to skateboard, and tried to act as casual as possible around her even as trembles ran through me, rewiring me. In biology our teacher told us that thought is electricity, and that idea, so beautiful, mentioned in passing, drove me slowly and quietly into a melancholy that lasted my entire life.

That same year my mother introduced me to Robert, whom she started dating. He had knocked over her cart in the grocery store, sending cans rolling down the white tiles. As they both rooted around on their hands and knees, he asked her if he could buy her dinner to apologize, and she, crouched, a can of SpaghettiOs in her hand, smiled and said yes.

He was a physicist, one of the many who had moved to Madison to work on the project, just like Samara's father. The town was flooded with them, and each morning they drove to the edge of the city, where the ground trembled with the heavy machinery needed to construct the underground chambers. The exits from the highway became clogged on weekdays with trucks carrying giant pieces of strange, reflective metals. Lights in town constantly flickered, and power outages were common during the school day. Each time that black depth descended we felt as if it were the interventions of the divine, and in the dark we prayed, even if we did not realize our silence was a form of prayer.

Robert was tall and skinny and pushed his glasses up to the bridge of his nose with his middle finger habitually. He radiated a kind of hawkish cognition. I could see him attempt to suppress it when I was around, as if his intelligence was so sharp I might cut myself on it. My mother massaged his hands instinctively whenever he was in reach. She also cooked for him, something she almost never did for me. At times she seemed more a mother than a lover to him, always making sure his clothes and briefcase were laid out each morning, finding his keys or charging his cell phone. One night as I was walking to the bathroom I heard them in her room; him breathing as if he was running a marathon and her moaning voice urging him on, encouraging him, cooing and congratulating. I was sickened with his attempts to insert himself into our life. My lips would curl into a grimace behind his back, revealing a set of teeth in need of braces.

The first time Robert ate dinner with us he told me about the project that had caused Madison to buzz with physicists, engineers, and journalists. My mother burned the pot roast and the house became smoky and my throat itched. Robert coughed as we waited at the table while she opened the windows, letting in an early spring breeze that fluttered the tablecloth.

"So Kevin, your mother tells me you're interested in the sciences at school."

"They're okay."

"Have you taken physics yet?" Robert asked as my mother served both of us. I shook my head as she sat down to serve herself.

"Have you heard of entropy?"

"No."

"It's the only law in the whole universe that accounts for time. It's what I study. Every other law can go backwards or forwards, and there's no difference in the equations. Entropy governs the arrow of time. It's why there's a past and a future."

"So what's the big chamber for?"

"The big chamber is for trying to stop it, for just a moment, in a very small area. We're going to create a little field in which entropy no longer occurs, contained by really big magnets."

I nodded and let him lecture, chewing instead of responding. It was at that dinner that I decided I was neutral about Robert because I realized he was harmless, and in a sense, despite his intelligence, obvious. Later my mother sat me down and told me I should be more respectful to Robert, that he was a great man, that he lived in a world that neither of us could comprehend.

I had guarded my love for Samara for three years by then. Finally, in seventh grade, we had slowly begun to talk; she started saying "Hi" in the hallways and smiling at me when I asked her if I could borrow a pencil. Once a group of her friends looked at me as I opened my locker, collectively giggled, and walked away. The signs were present, so events unfolded as they always do at that age. I told my friend Gary that I was desperately and secretly in love and Gary immediately told a friend of Samara's named Julie and Julie told Samara and as much as I yelled at Gary this was exactly what I had wanted to happen. Now it seemed like Samara and I were locked in a dance in which each simple greeting, each day-to-day request and interaction was done quietly and with vast meaning. We circled around each other like suns, testing and elliptical, sweeping out distances in the hallways, in the classrooms, in the smallest of motions. On our school bus she sat in the front and I sat in the back and I walked past her down the aisle each day and my knees trembled as our glances caught and locked and then flitted away, like the courtships of moths.

Our class took a tour of the underground chambers during April, just a few weeks before they finished construction. A bus took us through a large loading dock and then down a sleek tunnel lit by large halogen lamps. We assembled in a white office room with hard-backed chairs and watched a Nova Science Special on the construction of the chamber and the project. Our teacher then introduced us to a scientist who wore both a lab coat and a hardhat. He started by asking us to notice whether or not the day went faster or slower than it normally did at school, and he predicted that it would go slower for us, because it was exciting and new. He told us that the brain's "subjective horizon" would expand to meet it. Then he talked to us about entropy and the project. On the whiteboard he drew stick figures: little men who were always shuffling decks of cards and getting them back perfectly ordered, or unscrambling eggs. People for whom entropy didn't exist.

They took us down to ride in golf-cart like devices, which sped around the chambers. I sat one kid away from Samara and watched her watch the chambers move past us, like we were descending into the architectures of archangels. We weaved through traffic cones and occasionally workers were forced to step quickly out of our way. I thought I saw Robert from a distance wearing a bright yellow hardhat, gesturing with a piece of paper and pointing to the ceiling. Our cart got too close to a shower of sparks and Samara screamed as they landed like dying bugs in the metal bed. I laughed and she smiled at me, perhaps blushing.

After we stopped we climbed up a staircase and looked out at the succession of chambers blown together like soap bubbles. It seemed as if great gears were in motion; the bustle and sparks and yells were an organized cacophony as strange metals were forged together. Be-

hind us, Gary tried to draw a penis on the side of one of the gleaming surfaces in magic marker, and was immediately dragged kicking
by the teacher into a soundproof office. Samara had wandered off to
a side balcony during the commotion and I followed, shaking, and
time seemed to speed up and I was soon standing beside her looking out onto the construction. Our hands met on the railing, pinky
fingers touching slowly and exploring, telling us all we both needed
to know.

For the next month each day was reflective and full of itself as we
both tried to find the way to perform this serious play. It was the utter
honesty of each action that gave us this sense of gravity. Each time we
rode together in the back of my mother's car to get dropped off at the
movie theater, or held hands on our bikes as we wound down spring
roads, or went to the library together and sat back to back, thrilling at
the flesh pressing against us, we were aware of an inchoate narrative.
For some reason I had the idea then that a kiss could only be performed
after the delivery of a Hollywood-like romantic line. I had to work hard
for each kiss, mining movies and books for suitable proclamations. I did
not know the casual intimacy that adult relations possessed. When we
did kiss, electricity, both in our bodies and as our thoughts, ran through
us and galvanized us to a tremble.

Near the end of the school year Robert joined my mother and I for
dinner, and it was then that I brought up my father. I had been waiting
for this, as if constructing an intricate trap. I was feeling strong, and
I was sure then that Robert was secretly weak. I asked what Robert
would do when he met my father, what he would say, how he would
explain himself. There was a long silence after I spoke. My mother told
me that it was none of my business and that when I was an adult I
would understand, which of course was true. I told her that I wanted to
go live with my father. My mother then said he didn't care about either
of us, and wouldn't want me, which caused my world to blur and I stood
up and ran to my room. I slammed the door and lay on my bed looking
at my old stuffed animals. They stared at me until I threw them against
the wall, one after another, and then snuck back to the railing to listen.
At first I couldn't hear Robert and my mother, but then they went to
wash the dishes right underneath me.

"Marth, I really think we'll be able to do it. I mean, this has cost
us as much as the Large Hadron Collider. It's going to be huge. We're
finally going to figure it out. God, I wish professor Sagan was here for
this. And I wish you could have met him when he was still around the

best advisor and the smartest man I've met. I could've introduced him to Kevin, Carl was always great with kids, and you know, it would've been a big deal, to meet someone famous."

"I would have liked to meet him," I heard my mother say.

"I know."

The water stopped and when I peaked down I saw my mother leaning back into the crown of Robert's arms. I felt a rush of guilt as they swayed slightly, my mother short and squat and Robert tall and gangly. Robert spoke quietly.

"We're flipping the switch either tomorrow afternoon or night, depending on what the power grid looks like. It'll be a full field. We're going to stop time, Marth."

I fell asleep with that declaration ringing in my head, thinking of my father who had left so long ago that I told myself I remembered his face but in truth I didn't. There were no pictures of him in the house, so my memories of him were faceless and consisted entirely of his hands, which I knew had been large, rough, and moved about in slow circles as he talked.

The next day Samara and I got off at a bus stop that was not our own by a field with a vast gray water tower. We tramped across a warm expanse of wheatgrass and solitary oaks, toward an old junkyard orange with rust. The small trickle of a stream that ran through its center held in its banks the bones of a carriage, the bent wheels half-buried in whetted rocks. Weeds climbed around the ribcage of it. Farther upstream there were cars, and we walked up the muddy banks with the field at our backs. It was as if we were moving through time, from carriages to cars to a final pile of stereos broken and smashed amid the arching roots of a tree. Samara wore a dress the color of robin eggs, with her onyx hair spilling down her back. She matched the sky. We held hands as we walked and didn't need to speak, somehow both aware that the roles we were acting did not require words.

I took her back into the field where I picked her dandelions, like a fool. I pulled her down and kissed her and she told me that she loved me, and I thought she did, although what she loved was perhaps the idea of me. The world was perfectly still, the few clouds unmoving. The sky flooded over us, unmercifully inclusive, forcing us to swim, to find one another in the bluest of waters.

"You know how time goes slower when you are doing new things, like the scientist guy said?" I asked after a while.

She nodded, adjusting her dress and wiggling in the greening stalks.

"Well like, vacations are like that, right? Vacations always seem to go on forever, but a day at school goes by really quickly. What we'll do, from now on, is we'll only do things, all day, all the time. We'll go on vacations and learn to scuba dive and sky dive and go to foreign countries and learn different languages, and we'll be doing new things all the time. And we'll live ten times as long as everybody else. Ten times as long."

We lay in the grass more, inching closer with each yawn and little movement, cloud gazing. She told me about her family, how her father was never home. She told me about the small dramas of school, dramas that were then no less important than the play of nations. Eventually our hands met, curling around each other, interlocking into an embrace.

When we began to walk home we stopped underneath the water tower to hold a lingering, shaking kiss. Three miles away, the chamber was cooling down, huge streams of super cold liquid hydrogen pumping through coils kilometers long. Doors were sealed and systems were checked and then a button was pressed. Under the water tower, still kissing, the bones of time fell like a house around us.

It took a while to work out exactly what happened, although that is oxymoronic in that immediately, each one of us, the entire human race, knew what happened. Entropy stopped and for an instant, until the machine shorted out, the anti-entropic field pushed past the magnets and expanded at the speed of light and we lived in a world in which there was no arrow of time.

When it ended, if it ever ended, Samara and I pulled apart and looked into each other's eyes, both surprised and unsurprised. We stood in that field and cried, still holding hands, at the enormity of our lives, which we had just lived in their entirety. Later we would learn that the machine had been on for fewer than eighty milliseconds, but during that brief period I experienced everything I ever would, as had every other person on earth.

After the incident they disassembled the chamber piece by piece, filling in the metal caverns, the enormous gear work, with concrete. Slowly physicists left Madison, moving away in U-haul trucks which arrived and left in steady streams during the length of the summer. Robert stayed, finding work at the University. He never asked my mother to marry him, perhaps because he knew that their relationship was a constant act of recovery, a recurrent saving of one another.

It is a strange kind of knowing romance our generation has been doomed to. For Samara and I the nostalgia for each day was present during its occurrence, each long bouquet of moments was humbling and uncanny. Our freshman year of high school we called each other every night and listened to the same radio station, commenting on the songs and singing, humming, building eaves of shared secrets. She showed me the cuts she sometimes made, at the delicate curve of her ankle or in crisscrosses on her left arm. At the time I thought it to be a signifier, a portent of some darker curvature of the universe. Instead it was just a phase that slowly faded away, the same way she stopped sprinkling sparkles in her hair in the morning or later wearing fishnet.

Our sophomore year I skateboarded to school in the morning so that I wouldn't have to take the bus or show up with my mother. Samara would wear wide sunglasses and chew bubblegum throughout the day. In the painted hours before her mother came home from work we would wrestle through the house and then fall, trapped in each other's arms, onto the couch, where my hand would sneak up her blouse and our lips would bruise from kissing.

After school one day, with the afternoon dreaming long squares of light across the floorboards of her room, we undressed and awkwardly found one another amid the sheaves of exhalations and gasps. She lay sweaty and laughing underneath me, squirming like a nymph, with the sheets tossed around in an unfamiliar and titillating tangle of limbs. As I lay between the laurel of her legs I knew all forces, all roads converged here, to this exact center of the universe.

Samara's father was one of the last physicists to depart, the summer before our senior year, but by then she had already left me. She wanted to be a normal teenager, for that was in vogue. After the incident we all just wanted to forget that we had lived forever in that small bubble of time, that we had experienced each agony, each moment of euphoria, eternally. We wanted to forget our infinity but also to forget our sudden impermanence when it had ended, to ignore that now we had to shoulder the abysmal problem of time. Each moment slipped past us irrevocably, horribly, and it felt as if we lived among the ghosts of ourselves.

So in our junior year Samara told me she couldn't do it anymore, that she just wanted to do the things that everyone else did and I, by my mere presence, prevented that. I was an inverted reflection of those aspirations. I have always been one of the few who want to remember the incident, to hold on to it. I was instilled with a deep, oceanic awe when I thought of that expanding anti-entropic bubble moving away from earth at the speed of light, following our radio waves, our strange and devastating message to other civilizations that would be as caught unawares as we were.

It was because of my unwillingness to forget that by the time Samara moved away we had been separated for a year. We nodded to each other in the hallways and spoke occasionally, always politely, and each time we did a deep hollow would ache inside my chest. I imagine that by then she felt nothing for me, or perhaps the smallest of constant pulls, a soft inkling, like the earth feels for the moon.

❀ ❀ ❀

It is our ten-year reunion and I go because of her, and I'd like to think she goes because of me. We sit together awkwardly, and I am still, somehow, pathetically, in love, but she is clearly not. Her suit is well cut, her hair is professional, her make-up well done. A wedding ring flashes gold in the dimmed lights of the gymnasium. I wonder if she still wears only long-sleeved shirts or if the scars have faded and her arms are no longer ribbed with delicate patchworks. I am looking for the girl I was in love with, a girl who doodled dinosaurs on her sneakers, who made origami out of graded tests. I want to tell her I was in love with her because of those petite movements, a series of small revelations throughout the day, something she seems to have lost, something I am sure that this business woman would make light of. Instead I stir my drink and realize that while she has changed I have not. She is wearing a suit, while my T-shirt is un-tucked and there is a worn hole in the right knee of my jeans. I still feel thirteen. I often can't tell when I'm awake, as each night I dream scenes of my life in perfect detail, things that have happened or will happen. She though, she cuts through the conversation with her laugh, a sharp kind of laugh from a mouth filled with perfect teeth. I have nothing to say to her, as I am still carved open to the universe and she has hardened, toughened into adulthood. I leave that evening and as I am lying in bed that night I realize I haven't written anything in a year, and am unsurprised.

This calm acceptance is common. We all know whom we marry, what books we read, with whom we have our affairs, what our children are like, if we become murderers or rapists, and we know especially when and how we will die. I know how it will feel the night a car comes from the blind spot on my right side as I make a turn onto Third Avenue. I know how it feels to see such bright lights and how it pulls me gently, as if rousing me from sleep, away from my drunken thoughts of her.

This is the last run of a life of repetition. Each choice we make has been made a thousand, a million, times before. We have lived our lives as we would have lived after knowing our lives intimately, so there is no rebellion, because the rebellion has already played itself out—the vision included itself. The struggle against fate is as familiar and known as shrugging on an old coat and finding, to great surprise, it still fits. Choice has not been robbed from us; instead it feels as if we wrote a play, have performed it a thousand times, and are now performing it one final time.

We know that this is the final iteration because all events have taken on new meanings—although each word spoken, each action performed, is identical to the last recurrence, there is an intonation that was not previously noticed, a sadness and finality. So when I watch Robert try to teach my mother how to tie her shoes again, years after she has been diagnosed with Alzheimer's, I know what he will say. I have seen this scene many times and at each I think there is something new, a slant of light on her white hair, or a change in the lines of my mother's face as her brow furrows, as she tries to understand, to please.

"The rabbit goes around the tree, once, twice . . ."

I wonder what this generation would have done if not for the incident. Déjà vu is a constant pull in our lives, and in response we have been both louder and quieter than other generations. We leave parties to stand out on balconies and look at the New York City lights and imagine them running, tracing backwards, like they used to for us. Linearity is still shocking after the compressed bubble of narrative in which we lived for so long. Sometimes when I am riding the subway I lock eyes with someone and know that I have seen them before, right at this moment. There are no true strangers. In those brief moments of eye contact I can see a terrible depression that I myself feel. The past is impenetrable, and each moment that passes is lost forever to us now. Thus there is a slowness to our movements, a delicacy, and of course, a final sadness, especially on the greeting of a friend or lover whom you know will someday leave you. Goodbyes are expected, but greetings break our hearts and are often done in tears.

So when the car slams into the driver's side and the impact sends a shockwave through me, I am both expecting and surprised. Lying beside the broken steering wheel, the sharp metal and plastic wreck of a crushed car, I think that I have finally found my way out of this labyrinth, outside the madness of time. At the end of this eternal return I am moved to an incredible lightness, as if every event has regained its clarity, as if it were true now, that I have only died once, only loved once.

Photo by Rafael Fuchs

PAUL VIDICH's fiction and nonfiction have appeared in *Fugue, the Nation, Narrative Magazine* and other places. Junot Diaz selected his story "Jump Shot" as a winner of the 2010 *Fugue* Short Story Contest. His stories have been finalists in *Glimmer Train*'s short story contests, the Flannery O'Connor Award for Short Fiction, and nominated for a 2011 Pushcart Prize. Vidich received his MFA from Rutgers—Newark, and he is co-founder and editor of *Storyville*. He lives in lower Manhattan.

FALLING GIRL
Paul Vidich

She said the experience was ecstatic. In its retelling, the girl described her fall as dazzling, breathtaking, and beautiful. Her toes curled the edge of the high scaffold. She counted down from three, tipped forward slightly, and fell. Her job was to stay perfectly horizontal with her arms by her side, legs pressed together. The wind made her long black hair stream behind. Her belly flop slowed to a pause accompanied by intense light and weightlessness as she felt momentarily suspended above the gym mat. Then a bright splintering crack and her body smacked the dense foam, helpless and limp.

The truth is she didn't remember anything. The eighteen-foot drop took less than two seconds. Each time the audience gasped when she was halfway to the ground.

It was a phenomenon then. No one does it anymore. People would drive for an hour, or come by the F train, when they heard she was going to perform. The event was never advertised, but word got out and the time and place spread virally through private chat rooms, instant messaging, or texts. Her performances started in narrow industrial alleys by the Gowanus Canal where she'd stand in the open window of an abandoned building and wait for a crowd to gather. They watched her, always curious what a girl standing in a second-floor window intended. She'd wait for the crowd to get large, and when it did, there was always one bargeman who encouraged her, yelling "jump!" but mostly the crowds were worried and concerned, and frankly, curious. Those early performances were special because crowds didn't know what to expect. She was able to make a raid on their feelings—a syllable of speech, an embargoed memory, a story they'd tell later in the day.

There came a time when the large crowds forced her to move indoors. She found a boarded-up brick warehouse a block from the canal. She placed scavenged wood planks between old painter scaffolds that she pulled from the canal's mud. It took a little effort, and some cleaning, but she assembled the tubing into a workable structure that she stabilized with heavy sandbags. Her makeshift platform rose up to the ceiling's metal trusses. During the day shafts of sunlight that streamed through panels of broken windowpanes illuminated it.

Audiences came to the warehouse expecting to see her fall, and this was the biggest difference to the street art, where people who walked by at a particular time became caught up in the ambiguous anxiety evoked by seeing a young woman standing in an open window. The new audiences came expecting something.

With each performance she raised the height of the platform one inch. This increment was large enough to create some anticipation in the audience, but it wasn't so large that she'd quickly run out of height. She came to believe that there was no actual limit to how far she could fall. Eighteen feet? Twenty feet? Why not twenty-five? Or thirty?

The crowd wanted to see how far she would go.

Regardless of height, she fell on the same vinyl-covered foam-core gym mat. It was two feet thick, as wide as a queen-size mattress, and sat directly on the concrete floor. There was only one rule to her falls: Never land on the head. She could land on any surface of her body except the top of her head. The fall she most often performed, which always made the audience squirm and tense up, was the belly flop. She explained to art bloggers who had begun to notice her work that her goal wasn't to put herself in harm's way. It was the other way around. To effect certain emotions in the audience, and in herself, she put herself at risk. Danger was a means to an end. To produce certain consequences with her performance she had to get out of her comfort zone.

"I'm a normal person," she told one critic. "I'm scared of the same things other people are scared of. I just have an appetite to dig into my fear of heights and explore it at a deeper level. One day I'll be twenty-two feet up and I know I'm going to tip off and fall, and I know my job is to stay horizontal as the ground comes up to me. And some days it's no big deal to do that. The next time I'm just terrified and I don't think I can do it. How far am I willing to go? I don't know. There's a limit, I suppose. I haven't found it yet."

Audiences drawn to falling art were mostly young, predominantly teenage girls, who visited the private chat rooms and texted times of the performances, and in that way word got out. Crowds began to gather an hour before. Teenagers waited in a long roped queue that double-backed on itself before reaching the six steps up the loading dock that led inside. When it was time, a volunteer directed the crowd single file through a massive hinged steel door cracked wide enough for one person to enter.

Teenage girls came into the warehouse in groups of three or four wearing eyeliner, mascara, and dark purple or black nail polish. Their ears were pierced with laddered rings, and some had pierced lips or eyebrows. They were self-conscious of their bodies and to look older they wore sweat pants low, shirts that revealed a strip of skin just above their pubic hair, and purses they'd slung over shoulders. They glanced at the teenage boys who came in groups of three or four. Girls wore glitter in their eyebrows and some also brought glow-stick bracelets that they raised overhead when the warehouse lights dimmed.

Once inside, the crowd snaked through a dark corridor that opened onto a cavernous empty space with high ceilings. Scrap metal, old baking trays, and a jumble of junk left over from the time this had been an Oreo cookie factory was piled in front of sealed brick ovens. It was a dusty ruin of a place, a monument of scrap iron and industrial neglect. Audiences quietly gathered at the scaffold and around the gym mat. There were no chairs so the audience assembled in a groaning mass and while they waited they gazed at each other and at the height. Her fans pushed to the front, and the people who didn't know how they'd react to the performance stayed back at the wall. Hushed disbelief settled on the crowd as they gazed at the top of the scaffold.

Music was never part of the performance. Quiet was required. The audience's tension, its collective gasp, and the sound her body made when it smacked the mat, were integral to the performance. Only with silence did she feel she could create a shared experience and remove the boundary between life and art. Audiences experienced her fear and she said that was the gift she gave to the people who came. Critics had fun with her theory of the fourth wall, but it didn't stop them from showing up, and there was one wordy, self-righteous blogger who said there was nothing original in her work because hunger art had been there before, and anyway, he dismissed her technique for its staged sensationalism.

Her entry into the room was made through a black curtain, which she pushed aside as she stepped forward. She was petite, and seemed even more so when she stood under the tall scaffold. She had smooth, porcelain skin, a pretty face, and long black hair knotted in a bun. She wore a flesh-colored leotard, open in the back to show a bird tattoo. She was feather-light and her small breasts were compressed flat by the spandex. She scampered up the scaffold like an enthusiastic rock climber attacking a ridge.

At the top of the platform she shook her hair so that it fell loosely over shoulders to her waist. She stepped forward and gauged the distance. Her toes curled the edge, eyes settled on a vague point on the far wall, and she tipped forward. A collective gasp rose from the crowd. People in the rear pushed forward to get a better view of her on the mat. She bowed once to the people in front and made respectful nods to those on the left and right. She skipped off to the closed curtain. Sometimes a person in the crowd called out, "Doesn't it hurt?" or, "Are you okay?" She would turn and grimace. "The more I do it the better it feels. It's always quite satisfying when the floor comes up and I take it. You have to train yourself, though."

Audiences often lingered in the space. First-timers who expected a longer performance mingled with strangers to chat and speculate. The entire event lasted about three minutes. Some people lingered under the scaffold and eyed the height. It was not uncommon for young men to say they experienced a sensation of weightlessness after her fall, and often they were overcome by a desire to try it themselves, believing that vigorous arm movements would slow their descent. After one performance a drunk kid climbed the scaffold and leaped. He frantically flapped his arms, but it did no good, and he broke his wrist and collarbone. The EMT who arrived with the ambulance said the boy's elevated blood alcohol level relaxed his muscles and probably saved his life. This accident brought her performances to the attention of the police who cracked down on the event as an unlicensed assembly. Apparently there was no law against public jumping. She found another boarded-up warehouse, and after a short hiatus, resumed.

Notoriety from press reports of the accident, and the debate that accompanied discovery that there was no law against public jumping ("At what height does it become illegal?") changed her show. Her work, and her life, took a direction that she was not prepared for. She found the unwanted celebrity unsettling and strange. It crossed her mind to pack up and leave Brooklyn, but she didn't know what else she would do. She also enjoyed the attention, and she liked reading about herself on websites. Her boyfriend showed her how to Google herself.

One downtown blogger began to chronicle each performance with fuzzy time-lapse photos of her fall, which showed up as a long dim smudge. Before each performance the blogger announced the height she would attempt. Her boyfriend looked at the unsolicited sponsorship offers she received, and he was excited by what it meant for them. He brought her a proposal to put a Nike logo on her leotard, something small, hardly visible, just a token. They'd make some money, he said. Buy a toaster oven. Take a weekend trip to the Catskills. "What was wrong having what other people had?" he asked. "What was wrong with money?"

The commercial attention surprised her. Her boyfriend annoyed her. The money depressed her. She was aggravated by the predictable hunger of the art world to turn beauty into shit. This took a toll on her.

Audiences attracted to her shows changed too. Limousines from Manhattan pulled up to the warehouse and fashionably dressed people stepped out and presumed their spot near the front of the queue. Limousines double-parked for the brief performance and the drivers held open their car doors when passengers hustled out. The new crowd was wealthier, slightly older, less patient, but drawn to the idea that here was a person who basically jumped off a platform and could get hurt. Women dressed in heels, pearls, and sequin dresses. Their male companions wore tuxedos because the shortness of the performance meant that they could stop by, catch her fall, and still make the theater, or a dinner date. They had no interest in what falling girl intended with her art. They came because other people had gone, and they were told to go so they could say they'd been. This was made easier with a limousine driver who could find the warehouse without getting lost.

Once inside, these people became inconspicuous in the dark, and they stuck near the back so they could make a quick exit if the event didn't live up to its promised brevity. There were no announcements about the show. No one came out and asked for cellphones to be silenced, or pointed out the nearest exit. There was none of that. There was only a casual, curious milling and waiting and looking around for clues about what would happen. Some people missed her fall because they were on their BlackBerrys. "That's it?" one woman asked, looking up, mid e-mail. These people came for the novelty, not the art, and they came and left without being affected. "Be more interesting if she were fat," one man remarked. Sometimes an audience member didn't know what he'd come to see, except that he'd been told, "You've got to see it. And don't ask, just go. It's short. You'll be in and out in five minutes." These poorly informed people entered the warehouse, saw the scaffolding and even then, after being told that a young woman jumped from the top on to a small mat, belly-flop style, asked only, "Why?" Inevitably, that was followed by, "Does it hurt?"

Falling girl's mood changed as her performance attracted men and women who came for the novelty, or to say they'd seen it, or to cheer her on. The quiet that was integral to her performance was harder to find. Standing above the crowd she could hear people whisper, or speak on cell phones, or slowly unwrap hard candy. Twice she had gone to the edge, curled her toes, and had begun her slow tilt forward when a ring tone went off. Each time she stepped back to compose herself. This involved centering her spine and holding her hands by her side to visualize the flow of crud from her fingers into pails dangling from her wrists. Resetting her composure was difficult when she faced a restless audience who came expecting a safety-harnessed Circ du Soleil trapeze act.

Falling girl took long walks along the Gowanus Canal alone. She was disappointed in her boyfriend's attitude toward money, but not really surprised, because he'd always been the one who wanted to take taxis when she was happy to go by subway. She walked on the narrow stone wall that lined the edge of the canal, hands shoved in her pockets. These late afternoon strolls took her past the cable bridge and the rusted barges half-sunk in the polluted water, and sometimes she'd see a lone kayaker paddling along the oily surface surveying the remnants of the area's lively industrial past. She'd pick up an old bolt, or a doll's head, if size or shape caught her eye, and if it was special enough she'd keep it. Otherwise she'd pitch it into the canal. She liked the canal because it was an old ruin that wasn't worth much to anyone except artists like herself, or the kayaker. She invented stories about the canal and about the men who had worked on the sunken barges. She'd sit on top of the stone parapet, legs dangling over the side, and watch life go by.

Over several weeks audiences saw a change in her. Her bold enthusiastic entry from the curtain became a hesitant, self-conscious appearance, and she no longer powered up the scaffold like a climber breeching a summit. She climbed slowly, purposely, but not confidently, and her eyes averted the crowd. Baited by her tentativeness, the crowd grew quiet and respectful, but there was always one jerk who whistled or yelled a stupid remark. She told her boyfriend that she had a lot of confused feelings swirling inside that she didn't fully understand. He said this was a natural progression and she'd get over it. He explained that she wasn't a young nobody who surprised strangers on the street by standing in an open window. Whether she liked it or not those spontaneous moments were gone for good. Strangers on the street had felt an obligation to intervene, but the new audiences were satisfied whatever happened. "They don't know how difficult it is. They don't care. They're not with you when you're falling. They'd love it if you got hurt. Some of them, at least."

This also depressed her.

One night she was injured. She had climbed the scaffold, which stood at thirty-three feet. Her head was level with the roof trusses and she had to duck to reach the jumping point. It was a Saturday night in July and summer heat hung thick in the air making the audience restless. People in back pushed forward against those in front, who tried to hold their spot, and there was tension. A cell phone went off. Flash cameras popped. She stepped to the edge and braved her sadness.

The crowd gasped. There was the sound of feet rushing across the concrete floor, and urgent whispers of concern. Her fall hadn't been right. Hands covered open mouths wide in dismay and there was a cry of collective horror. She'd tipped too far forward and instead of falling horizontal, she'd angled forward. She'd landed on her head.

A man in front thought she'd had the wind knocked out of her. Her eyes were open, but they didn't move. Her legs were awkwardly positioned to the side, one shoulder jutted out and looked displaced, and her neck was twisted. When she continued to lie still and motionless the man in front leaned close and declared that she looked dead. And she was.

The warehouse door was padlocked with chains that fitted between an empty door cylinder and the jam. The *Times* reported the incident as a small item at the bottom of a back page. In the weeks that followed a few fans performed her technique from garages and trees, but public interest in falling largely died out.

The building owner discarded the scaffolding on the street, where it was promptly taken by a pickup truck that prowled the area for scrap. Her boyfriend had her cremated. On a clear, chilly Saturday morning in November, under a pale blue sky, the boyfriend and a companion took her cremains in a cardboard box to the observation deck on the Empire State Building. While his companion flirted with the security guard, he emptied her ashes over the side. It was windy that morning, and gusts lifted the swirling dust and bone fragments and blew them back on a group of tourists.

Photo by Thaddeus Austin

AURELIA WILLS was raised in Colorado and attended college at University of Wisconsin—Madison, where she studied philosophy and Russian. She taught ESL and creative writing through The Loft and Saint Paul Public Libraries. Her stories have been published in *The Kenyon Review*, *Hayden's Ferry Review*, *New Orleans Review*, *Salt Hill*, and forthcoming in *CALYX Journal*. Two of her stories were nominated for the Pushcart Prize. Wills lives in Saint Paul, Minnesota, with her family.

THE SQUIRREL PRINCE
Aurelia Wills

On his way to the bus, Brian walked past trees with new sticky leaves and grass that looked squeaky and juicy, and the squirrels talked to him. The robins and sparrows watched as the squirrels whispered in little squirrel voices he could barely hear, "Brian, Brian, Brian." When he walked home, a squirrel leaping through a yard would pause and stare.

Brian, seemingly alone among humanity, appreciated their powers. Squirrels were escape artists. A squirrel could run straight up a tree trunk, fly through the air between garage roofs, dangle upside down from a twig, sprint straight at a fence, and disappear through a hole, its fluffy tail vanishing like a puff of smoke.

Whenever Brian found a squirrel smashed in the street, he'd solemnly pick up the body with two sticks and carry it to a nearby bush for burial beneath leaves and dirt. He christened these fallen squirrels *Houdini*. Houdini I, Houdini II . . . He'd recently buried Houdini XX.

❀ ❀ ❀

He climbed the old steps of the front porch—one of these days they would paint them—unlocked the door, and dumped his backpack by the stairs. He peed for ten minutes—he never used the bathrooms at school—filled a mixing bowl with Cap'n Crunch and settled down on the Guatemalan rug beneath the TV.

He watched talk shows, reality shows, cartoons, snippets of the news, infomercials, chanting nuns with huge moles on their cheeks, more cartoons, a special on serial killers. After three hours, he was so sick from cereal and TV that he lay on the floor like a noodle. He was the only kid he knew of who still watched TV.

Suddenly his mom burst through the door, all hyped. "Baby, get up! As soon as I change, we're heading to the camping store. We still need a few items . . ." She clattered up the stairs.

Brian lay on the floor with his head tipped back like he was dead. His hair fell away; he could feel air on his high pale forehead. The light had gone from yellow to gray and the ceiling pulsated.

Then there she was standing upside-down in the doorway in her blue jeans and a pink tank top. "Baby, get up. We need to get this done. There's a show I want to watch at eight."

"What do we need?" It came out like a moan.

"I'm not exactly sure. We're inexperienced campers and there may be something critical we've overlooked. I can ask a guy who works there for advice. He's super nice. His name's Farley . . ."

"Oh, God." Brian groaned and rolled away from her.

"Get your ass up and moving, little boy, or your allowance is history for this week and next and, moreover, I'll give you extra chores to boot." His mother's junior executive side was kicking in.

Brian wandered down the steps. He was listening for the squirrels when his mom gripped his shoulders and stopped him short. "We're going to have a bitchin' time camping," she whispered.

❀ ❀ ❀

As he'd suspected, his mom headed straight for the counter and the young guy behind it. The guy was an outdoorsy hippie, lean and tan, with frizzy, puffy hair that ended in a tiny braid at the back of his head. He looked up and smiled like a lizard.

Brian sidled over to the case of Swiss Army knives. He was captivated by the glossy red enamel, the way the tools fanned out: a knife, tiny scissors, a file, a wrench. Everything you'd ever need could slip into your pocket. He was partial to the Evolution S17, though he'd have settled for the S10 in a pinch.

His mom whistled. "Brian, get your butt over here and meet Farley." Brian sighed like an old man and walked to the counter.

"Brian, this is Farley. Farley's advising us on last minute items we might need. Farley, my brilliant son Brian."

"Hey, Brian," said Farley. He was the kind who wore silver and leather bracelets and rings on every finger.

Brian squinched up his eye like he was looking at Farley through a telescope. "Mom, can I get a Swiss Army knife?"

She glowered and shoved out her lip. "No. Now go away."

As Brian drifted off, it all spun out in his mind like a cable TV show. Maybe this Farley would agree to meet his mom for a beer, and they might even have a good time at first, his mom could be really funny, but then she'd drink too much and she'd start to cry. She'd tell Farley that until very recently, she'd had a wonderful boyfriend, a decent man, she thought, who suddenly up and left her for a young girl with big tits . . .

And then this Farley might look at his mom more carefully. He'd notice that her bra was industrial strength, and that there was funny bunched-up skin on her neck that would suddenly appear when she moved a certain way, and about a hundred lines fanning out from her eyes. If you ran your fingers through her thin yellow hair, you could see black and gray roots and pink scalp with all its little hair holes.

When his mom went into the ladies' room to freshen up after her little crying jag, which she'd profusely—new spelling word—apologize for, old Farley might just take off. She'd come out with new lip gloss on and find two empty stools. Brian just could not stand it.

He trotted to the book section and hunted for a book into which he could disappear. He seized *Horrifying Deaths in Yellowstone* and opened it to the chapter that told the tale of a boy who was chewed up by a grizzly bear while his friend watched from a nearby tree. As he was being eaten, the boy called out for his mother.

Brian immediately calmed down.

❖ ❖ ❖

The girl of his dreams sat in front of him in both Advanced English and Pre-Algebra. Her name was Deidra—three syllables. Brian paid close attention when Mr. Spitzer wrote equations on the board—he'd never want to fail in front of Deidra Parker—but when he allowed his mind and eyes to rest, they rested on her sheet of brown hair that glinted with gold and copper. When she turned to pass him a paper, his eyes dropped for a millisecond from her green eyes and lightly freckled cheeks to the tiny lacy bra he could see through her white shirt. She was perfect. She had a mom and a dad and a brother and Brian was quite sure her mother did not use the word "tit."

In English, Mrs. Swanson called him to her desk. "Brian, have a seat," she said in a stage whisper. She crinkled her nose in a friendly way.

She smelled of Doublemint; he watched as her tongue transferred the small white wad from one cheek to the other.

She held out his spelling paper and tapped sentence number seven with her long orange nail. *The mother apologized profusely for her crying jag.* "Brian, is everything alright at home?"

Brian gazed at her as calmly and simply as a chipmunk. "It was something I saw on TV. On a talk show."

Mrs. Swanson blinked, then bonked her forehead with the palm of her hand. "Oh, stupid me. Well, I had to check. Go back to your seat, Sweetie."

Sweetie. Brian rose from the chair and walked back to his desk like a prisoner approaching the gallows. As expected, Peter Rominsky and John Holt, their faces reddening with hatred, strained against their desktops. Brian could hear a low growl.

Rominsky's eyes were so close together that if Brian squinted, Rominsky appeared to be one-eyed. Both boys had grimy fingernails as if they scratched in the dirt. They spent their free time killing each other with automatic gunfire on video game consoles.

"You're going to die, Houdini," whispered Rominsky.

The summer before, Rominsky had caught Brian in a cape and black hat giving a magic show for a party of six-year-olds in the neighborhood park. Brian still shuddered at the memory of trying to concentrate on Cups and Balls while Rominsky's gang sniggered on a nearby bench. And the aftermath—choked by the strings of his cape, his wand snapped in half, his black hat snatched and squashed on Peter's huge head. Brian was thrown onto the grass and landed on a dog turd.

Although he'd been paid ten dollars to perform, he'd shoved the costume and magic kit under his bed with the dead gerbil's cage. He had not looked at it since.

❊ ❊ ❊

As he closed his locker after last period, Brian was grabbed from behind and dragged to the dark alcove by the band room.

After blows that exploded crackling light throughout his body, a crazily shifting perspective, the indignity of having an arm twisted and pinned to his back while spit dripped onto his face, they gave him one last shove and left. Brian lay with his eye pressed against dirty linoleum that resembled a vast gigantic landscape.

Shreds of his inner cheeks were caught in his braces. He could feel a swelling under his eye and couldn't bend his throbbing left index finger.

He lay for a while in the quiet of the emptied hallways then forced himself off the floor. He picked up his scattered books, folders, notebooks, papers, broken pencils— they'd stolen his pens—and made it outside long after the last bus had left.

Throughout the long walk home, squirrels stopped in their tracks and solemnly acknowledged him.

❀ ❀ ❀

The door was unlocked, the air full of coffee smell. His mom sat at the desk with her ankles pertly crossed. She wore her glasses, her hair in a business-like bun. She was on the computer looking for a new boyfriend. He stood behind and watched her click from picture to picture.

"What are you doing?" he said, though he knew.

"Just looking, Baby. Just want to know what's out there."

"Why don't you . . . rest?" Brain flopped on the floor against the tent and sleeping bags.

"Because, Brian," she stuck a pen behind her ear, "I don't have any time to lose. Once I go through menopause, I'm going to lose all my skin tone."

"Oh God." He covered his eyes with his wrist; he always felt like throwing up when she used the word "menopause."

"Joke." She nudged him with her bare foot. "What's that beneath your eye?"

Then she was out of her chair and crouched over him. "What happened to you? What's this? Move your hand! My God, did you get beat up again? You've got blood on your lip! Show me your hand!"

"Ow, Mom." She'd bent his swollen index finger.

"Did they break your finger? Okay, I'm calling the principal this minute before he hauls his fat ass into his Lincoln and drives home to Wayzata."

She was up. With his uninjured hand, Brian grabbed her ankle; it was rather prickly. "Mom," he said. "Do you want me to die? The only thing that will happen if you call is that every day will become a living hell and I will die."

She paused, looking down on him, considering. The skin between her bright blue eyes wedged up with concern.

"Mom, it's okay." He tugged on her leg. "I don't think they meant to hurt me. Let's talk about our camping trip."

She blinked; one eye narrowed. He'd caught her interest, he could see that. "But, Baby, what about your finger? Do you think you need to go to urgent care?"

"Mom, when are we going camping?" Brian turned his head and stared out the window at the fading blue of the afternoon sky.

"We leave the day after school gets out. We have five nights at Flanagan State Park."

"Mom, five nights? What are we going to do for five nights?"

She shook her head as if waking from a dream and smiled brightly. "We're going to have the most wonderful time we've ever had."

She pranced to the desk and got a spiral notebook from a drawer, then sat cross-legged like they were already camping and read from her list. She was bringing the camera, painting supplies, a Frisbee, baseball mitts and a baseball, a kite, and swimsuits. They would go hiking, play charades, and tell ghost stories around the campfire. It was going to be fantastic!

She licked the tip of her finger and turned the page. "For dinner the first night, we have beans and wieners . . ."

Brian flinched; he hated the word "wiener." He rolled away and gazed out the window. A squirrel leapt from nowhere, clung to the end of a branch, and stared straight at Brian. Brian received the squirrel's telepathic communication: "Courage, comrade."

❊ ❊ ❊

His final project for Advanced English was to write a fantasy story. Brian wrote a story about a squirrel prince. It was the story of a prince who'd been turned into a squirrel by a queen who wasn't exactly evil, just a little mentally ill and self-absorbed; she wanted a pet. The only way the prince could break the spell was to make his way through a vast dark forest full of thorns and a violent cyclops. His reward would be marriage to the beautiful, kind, and decorous Princess Dianda. The last day of school, Mrs. Swanson handed back their work.

Brian sat dreaming, mesmerized by the red ink words of praise—"Brian, you have a great future ahead of you!"—when Deidra Parker suddenly turned around and looked at him and shocked the blood out of his face.

"What did you write about?" she asked in a not particularly friendly way.

"It's about, um, a sort of squirrel prince." He could think of no other way to phrase it.

"Can I read it?" She sneezed like a kitten, but held him with her green gaze.

"I guess . . ."

She snatched up his story and hunched over it. Her hair, attached by static cling, fanned across her pale blue, short-sleeve sweater. Her back softly rose and fell with each breath. Brian felt suspended from time, from history, as he awaited her judgment.

Rominsky strode past and grabbed the story from Deidra.

"The Squirrel Fag Prince," Rominsky announced, wheeling back on the heel of his Timberland boot. His ugly purple lip curled down as he began to read, though some part of Brian's horrified brain noted that he was hooked by the second sentence.

Chaos was breaking out all over the room. Mrs. Swanson had left to get "treats" she'd stashed in the teachers' lounge. Deidra Parker slipped out of her seat and stood very close to Peter Rominsky. Her little fuzzy front was only two inches from Rominsky's Metallica T-shirt.

"Come on, Peter, give it back," she said coaxingly, as if talking to a dog. Then, to Brian's horror, she hooked her pinky around Rominsky's pinky—they were a couple.

Rominsky suddenly looked bewildered, frightened, startled as if he'd been splashed by a wave; he backed away from Deidra. She ripped the story out of his hands and tossed it on Brian's desk.

"It's really good, Brian," she said with her lip hiked over her teeth.

Mrs. Swanson tiptoed in with a bakery box.

Brian stared at the pages, now crumpled and smudged with black thumbprints. He didn't give a crap what Deidra Parker thought. She was a girl with bad taste who liked to touch boys with dirty hands.

❀ ❀ ❀

When Peter and John captured him for his last-day-of-school mauling, Brian fought like a maniac and caught the underside of John Holt's chin with his elbow; he watched John's eyes pop with surprise. He spun down the hallway with his lungs tearing and made it to the front door of the school in fifteen seconds. He even had his backpack.

❀ ❀ ❀

Brian lay on the couch under a blanket eating from a two-pound bag of Starbursts. In a deep state of sugar sedation, he was watching a movie about teenagers getting slaughtered, one after the other, by a maniac with an electric bread knife. His mom burst through the door.

"What are you doing? Isn't this the last day of school? This is the first day of summer! Turn that TV off. Get your butt outside."

She yanked the blanket off of him and ran around the room opening curtains. Half an hour later, she came down the stairs in shorts and a halter top; she'd been hitting the tanning salon and was a deep nutty brown.

She said, "Baby, I ordered you a pizza to celebrate the last day of school. Do you remember that nice guy Farley from the camping store? He and I are going to get a burger and have a last minute discussion about camping, but I won't be out late because we're leaving bright and early. Okey dokey, Smokey?"

Brian had a terrible stomachache.

Jingling her keys, she stopped and laid a hand on his forehead. "You're kind of hot. Why not go sit on the porch in the nice air—it'll clear the germs out. Bye, Baby." She kissed his sweaty forehead with her sticky lips.

He had to get off the couch to pay for the pizza. "Say hi to your mom," said the tattooed pizza guy, his evil grin displaying teeth like tiny waffles.

Brian sat on the porch steps that were peeling like they had leprosy with the pizza box heating up his knees. He looked out at the first-day-of-summer evening and the first-day-of-summer street.

A squirrel, slipping across the grass, stopped and stared. "Yes, it's me," said Brian. He opened the box, tore off a piece of crust, and placed it on the bottom step. Neither of them moved. Then the squirrel darted forward, inch by inch, until it held the bread in its tiny paws and sat busily chewing. He never took his eyes off Brian.

"She's out with the guy from the camping store," he whispered.

The crickety air was disturbed by a frightening racket—the laughter and voices of what sounded horrifyingly like Brian's contemporaries. The squirrel vanished.

A mob was approaching from the end of the block. Brian bent low and ran like a wraith with a pizza into the house. He double-bolted the door, then crawled to the living room, eased the curtains shut, and knelt with his eye to the slit.

The early evening sun shone on Deidra Parker's hair as she calmly swung hands with Peter Rominsky. A crowd of girls clustered behind, chattering and stepping on the backs of John Holt's sneakers. "Sorry, John!"

Brian's breathing constricted; his heart was a piston ramming his chest wall. He waited for them to swarm, egg his house with a thousand eggs, TP the tree, break the windows. But they continued on without a glance, obviously on their way to the park.

They did not, Brian realized as he crouched in the shadows beneath the curtain, even know where he lived. There was one last high-pitched shriek of laughter and the voices were gone.

❋ ❋ ❋

His mom, looking yellowish and tired, sat in the kitchen drinking coffee and staring out at the yard. The lilac bush bloomed over a heap of bulgy plastic sacks—potting soil from two summers before. She pushed up from the table and said under her breath, "Why did I agree to this?" She yawned and sat back down. "Brian, next time I want to go out with a guy from the camping store, shoot me first."

Around three o'clock—"There's no rush. We have the whole damn week there!"—she came up from the basement with a dusty box that was torn and looked pretty flimsy. She started loading it up. "We've got beans, ketchup for the wieners, wiener buns, hot chocolate . . . shit, Baby, we got to load the cooler. Can you get it out?"

A hard lemonade from the summer before had spilled and dried inside the cooler. Brian stood at the sink and scrubbed it with a rag.

"I forgot to freeze the blue things! We'll buy ice on the way . . ." She squatted and lifted the dusty box. The bottom tore out and, in a big clatter and crunch, the boxes and cans fell onto her foot. "God damn it! Jeez Louise." She hopped on one leg.

"Mom, are you okay?"

"Leave me alone, Brian! Pack up the cooler and start loading the car."

He carried the tent, sleeping bags, and cooler to the Sunbird. She hobbled out with the food repacked in the box the computer had come in, then limped back in and returned with a black garbage bag filled with fun supplies—a pair of new badminton rackets poked from the top.

"Let's just go!" she said, blowing the hair out of her face. "We can buy anything we need on the way."

Within an hour, they were speeding past fields. Little corn plants stood in endless rows with their glossy leaves flapping out. The road, a wavy black ribbon, went over a hill and into the horizon. Brian had been in the country on a few school trips, but never before with his mom. She pulled to the shoulder of the road and squinted at a map. He'd had no idea she was capable of navigating through the world like this.

"About twenty more miles." She took off, spraying gravel.

On hillsides covered with scrubby tufts of grass, cows stood with their huge heads bent low and chewed. A black horse's long, glossy side shivered. In a toy-like town, a boy bounced on a little tractor across a huge lawn. A woman tipped back her head as she took clothes from a line. The sunny green fields stretched in every direction.

Brian was overcome with joy, with an overwhelming euphoria. There was a world, a real actual world, and he and his mom had burst out into it.

His mom turned toward him and lit a cigarette. She tipped her head back and the wind blew through her yellow hair and the lines around her eyes relaxed. In a light, girlish voice, she sang a song about mountains and hills and daffodils.

"I learned it when I was a little girl." She looked at him sideways through her blowing hair.

They sang the song fifteen times and were just starting again when they pulled up to the state park. She said, "High-five," and they slapped hands. She told him to wait in the car and guard their stuff, and she walked to the little park building. Brian stared out the window at sparrows fighting over seed at a feeder.

It seemed to take a long time. When she finally came out, she was smiling at the ground and shaking her head. A ranger with a bushy white mustache caught the door before it closed and pointed at a shed. "Honey, don't forget your firewood."

His mom put her hands on her hips and said, "Stupid me."

Brian felt his joy die out a little bit, like a fire that's been lightly rained on. But she got into the car and looked right at him with her blue eyes flecked with gold. "Here we go!"

She drove up a hill and parked in a gravel lot. They had a cart-in site, the ranger had persuaded her that this was the most wonderful option, but she couldn't get the cart's padlock undone and she wouldn't let Brian try. She swore while she spun the little dial. "Jesus, damn, cracker, poop."

The ranger came puttering up the road in a tiny truck. "Need any assistance?" he called. Just then his mom got it.

"Tell him no, then turn your back," she whispered. "He's a dirty old man."

With the bag of splintery firewood, the cooler, computer box, and garbage bag barely fit in the cart. His mom lifted the handle and rolled the cart across the gravel. "Mom, let me," said Brian. He was eleven, after all.

"Okay, Baby."

The cart was heavy and unwieldy and he struggled to keep it from tipping. The pillows kept falling on the ground. They headed across the road and down a path through a meadow of tall, deep green grass and yellow flowers. In the distance were filmy blue hills. His mom limped beside him. She started to sing.

As they descended toward trees with white bark and little green leaves, the path became steep and rutted. The cart's weight pulled Brian into a jog. The pillows flew off. "I can't hold on, Mom! It's too heavy."

"Just try, Baby!" she called. "Just try your very damnedest."

But he had to let go. The cart rolled away and crashed at the bottom.

"Whoops," said his mom. "Whoops!" She tottered down the hill after him. She was laughing so hard she had to sit on the grass. She dropped her head between her legs and shook. Brian sat beside her; he was laughing, too. She looked at him with her eyes full of water. Her face was all red and shiny. The garbage bag had spilled and the Frisbee and kite and paint set were scattered around the overturned cart. The wiener buns were squashed. The can of beans had rolled away.

They were pretty near in hysterics when a college boy with black eyebrows and spiky hair came along. "Can I help you?"

"Well, you may," said his mom, calming a little, though she still had tears in her eyes. "You certainly may. If you're free."

"I'm free," the college boy said, and righted their cart. He quickly packed the food back in the food box. "The trick is to put the heavy stuff in back."

Brian picked up and handed the college boy the pillows and scattered plates. His mom watched with her head tilted to the side. "Are you a Mormon?"

"Lutheran," said the boy as he wedged in the sleeping bags. He looked around. "I think that's it. See ya."

"See ya," said his mom. "Thanks a ton. I've got an injured foot. Long story." She delicately held out her foot.

"Sorry to hear it. Have fun." The college boy headed up the hill and muscles as big as goose eggs popped out over his woolen socks.

Brian picked up the cart handles and they continued on. His mom peeked in the outhouse and sniffed. As they came to the signpost for their site, a woman came down the path from site number three. She wore baby blue culottes and jingled with Christmas bells.

"I like your bells," said his mom.

The woman looked like the savage librarian at Brian's school. "They're bear bells," she said haughtily and walked on to the outhouse.

His mom shifted her jaw around as if she had an attack of TMJ. She said, "Interesting," and bravely hobbled in her bright pink running shoes down the path to their site.

Site number two was a square of shaved grass with a picnic table, a fire ring with a blackened grate, and a large latched box marked FOOD ONLY. It was surrounded by tall weeds and wild flowers, spindly trees, and plants with skinny stems and glossy pointed leaves.

"Sumac," his mom said decisively.

She sat at the picnic table, crossed her legs, and lit a cigarette. She jammed a knuckle into her nostril and sneezed. "I'm going to have a terrible attack of hay fever." She stared at the box set back beyond the fire ring. "Baby, what do you think that's for?"

"I think it keeps the animals out."

"Animals," she said, swinging her foot.

She abruptly stood and peered through the plants. "Look, Brian, we can see the other sites. There's that nice boy . . . he's all alone at his table. How sad." At the site above theirs, the librarian sat chewing carrots and reading a fat paperback.

"Baby, it's getting late. We'll divide the duties. First, get every scrap of food in the bear box, then you set up the tent and I'll start a fire."

The first time Brian put the tent together, it resembled a trapezoid. He pulled it apart, tried again, and this time it looked like a tiny yurt. It was so light, he could hold it over his head. "Look, Mom!"

She hunched over a thick, smoky cloud and coughed; her eyes were watery and red. "Baby, I can't get this to catch and I've used up half the matches and most of the toilet paper. Screw it." She slowly stood as if her knees hurt and sat at the picnic table. Her face had a dangerous stillness as she watched the librarian, who was still eating carrots.

Brian approached slowly. "Mom, sorry to bother you, but do we have any water?"

She closed her eyes and sneezed. "I knew there was something. We forgot to buy a water jug. I don't even know where the water is. Grab the pot and water bottles and let's go find it."

She limped ahead swinging the aluminum pot. "Maybe it's by the outhouse." She had three blood-swollen mosquitoes attached to her bare back.

"Mom, hold on." He smashed them with his hand.

"Brian, stop that!" she said, smacking at him.

There was no water by the outhouse. They stood uncertainly in the falling light and slapped at mosquitoes. It was eight fifteen and the late sun was a deep orange.

"Let's go ask that nice boy."

"No, Mom. No."

"What else are we supposed to do, Brian?" She glared at him, tipped her baseball cap at a jaunty angle, tugged down a few blonde wisps, and hobbled down the trail to site number one.

The boy with the spiky brown hair sat on the picnic table whittling a stick. He had a thermos and a bottle of bug repellant lined up on the table next to him. A fire crackled and popped in his fire ring. He looked up and smiled.

"Wow, you have a beautiful smile."

"You do, too," said the college boy.

"Sorry to bother you, but we don't know where the water is. My little son"—Brian closed his eyes—"and I have never gone camping before and we just don't know the ropes."

"Well, the water," said the boy, squinting at her, "is up by the cars."

"Oh," said his mom. "Oh, all the way back there."

"Yep," said the boy. He picked up the stick and started whittling again. He had a thumbnail like a pink moon.

"Okay, hmm. Well, that's bad luck. Have a great time camping! Say, before we go, could I ask a huge favor?"

"Sure." The boy's smile was strained.

"Could you spray us down with your bug repellant? I forgot ours and Brian is getting eaten alive. He's allergic and gets gigantic welts."

"Sure," said the boy. "Sure I can spray you down. No problem." He set down the stick and closed the knife. He stood up and sighed deep in his chest.

She pushed Brian out first and twirled him in a circle. He was misted with a damp chemical he tasted on his lips. It was horrible and bitter—the taste of his humiliation.

Then his mom stepped forward, closed her eyes, and turned while the college boy sprayed her. Brian saw how the boy stared at her chest and her bottom and her legs—she had blood all over her back. "Wow, you sure needed this," said the college boy, but his mom didn't know what he was talking about.

She didn't open her eyes for a second and smiled gently as if she'd been blessed.

"Thanks a ton. Hopefully, we won't have to bother you again," she said, sighing. She trailed her arm in goodbye as she limped up the path. The boy sat watching her.

"Let's go get the water." She looked up the hill.

Brian had an inexplicable, overpowering need to run as far and fast as he was able. If he couldn't run, he'd bust apart, fly to pieces.

"Mom, I'll get the water. Your foot's hurt. You go sit by the fire pit and rest. Try to start it again." He grabbed the pot from her.

Brian ran straight up the hill and felt sweat break across his forehead. The pot bumped against his thigh.

It was dusk, the day bowing to the night. The field glimmered in the blue air. The little yellow flowers were like explosions. Bright blue birds darted and swooped. A white haze rose from the river. At the top of the hill, he stopped and leaned on his knees, his breath torn and ragged. He looked at the blue air and hills and shimmering grasses and saw for the first time a place in the world that matched his dreams. His lungs burned like he'd burst from a barrel full of water and chains.

He found the pump next to the parking lot. He drank two bottles, then filled the pot. A shabby SUV pulled in. College kids climbed out and unloaded backpacks, sleeping bags and pillows. One of the girls had long yellow hair.

On the way back, the magic field had disappeared. The world had grown dim and gray and shadowy. Brian hurried down the bumpy trail and slopped water on the ground. His mom might be thirsty and she was afraid of bears.

She sat at the table smoking in the darkening campsite; there was no fire. He handed her a water bottle.

"I couldn't start a fire, Brian, and bad news—we forgot the can opener. So it's graham crackers and marshmallows for dinner. We forgot so many things . . ." She closed her eyes and slowly scratched her forehead. "I made a list in case we go to a store tomorrow." She talked of it as if of an impossible dream.

They had forgotten a can opener, bug spray, flashlights, her cell phone, antihistamine, extra matches and lighters, creamer for the coffee, extra cigarettes, wine, soap, towels, a first aid kit, an ace bandage for her foot, her glasses, contact solution, soup, spoons and forks, the traveling chess kit Brian wanted to bring, dish soap, rain coats, and ice.

Brian was frightened by how much they'd forgotten. "Why didn't you let me get a Swiss Army knife?" he said. "Then we'd at least have a can opener."

"God damn it, Brian." She violently rubbed her chin. "Why do you always nitpick? Why do you always point out my mistakes and make me feel bad? True, if I had bought you that expensive little knife, we could be eating cold beans with our fingers. Don't be an asshole."

She hunched toward the cold fire. They sat silently for ten minutes. Laughter floated through the air.

"Oh God," groaned his mom. "Invasion of the college students."

The voices traveled down from site number one where the college boy had been whittling his stick.

"Sounds like a dozen kids. That's against park regulations, unless I'm mistaken." His mom stood up and looked through the trees. She stood absolutely still watching for five minutes, then she sat back down.

Brian got up and looked. The boys and girls milled around and set up tents. The girl with the long yellow hair sat on the picnic table next to the boy with black eyebrows who had picked up their things and sprayed them with bug spray. The girl lifted her sheet of hair and the boy kissed her neck. Brian turned and found his mom standing behind him.

They both sat back down. His mom leaned on her elbows and looked at the picnic table with a puzzled and troubled expression, as if the table shouldn't have cracks, the paint shouldn't be peeling, as if it shouldn't be made of wood. She looked at Brian, then quickly away. Her hand went to her neck and stroked it. She looked like she'd never be happy again.

The college kids howled and giggled. They just couldn't stop laughing.

She pressed her fingers against her ears. "They're going to party all night. I won't get any sleep."

Beneath the laughter, Brian heard something else. The world chirped, the world whispered and rustled. He heard a loud crackle in the bushes behind the tent. "Mom. Mom?"

She laid her head on the table.

The crackle grew louder. Brian heard its approach with every hair on his neck, with the tiny hairs inside his ears, with the pink bumpy surface of his brain. He felt cold and brave, prepared to release his life like a dove from a black hat. He forced himself to turn around and face what was coming.

A squirrel darted from behind the tent and sniffed the door.

"I'm over here," Brian whispered, but the squirrel slipped back into the silvery grass.

His mom was silent and wouldn't lift her head. Mosquitoes hovered over them. He waited and the world got darker.

"Mom." He shook her soft freckled shoulder. She just lay there and let him shake her like she was dead.

Brian lifted his hand. "You're not my mother," he said. "You think you are, but I don't think you are."

He carefully watched her. His stomach was weighted with dread, but she didn't cry. She didn't say a word. Her shoulders heaved a big sigh. She was asleep.

The college students had quieted. The air was blue. The Big Dipper surfaced out of the blueness above them. The world murmured and rustled. Fires flickered through the trees.

Brian climbed on the table and sat cross-legged in front of her. He dribbled water on her arm. After a few minutes, she whispered, "What are you doing?"

"I'm going to tell you my story." He took a breath and looked up at the scramble of stars.

"Once there was a young prince who was turned into a squirrel by a misguided queen with magic powers. One day, the prince simply woke up in a ball of leaves at the top of a tree. He craved nuts. He never got used to the weight of his tail, but he learned to love leaping through the air . . ."

As if he was a magician pulling invisible strings, his mother slowly raised her lovely head.

Photo by Maury Zeff

MAURY ZEFF's fiction has appeared in *Southern California Review* and *Switch-back*. He has an MFA from the University of San Francisco, a San Francisco Writers' Grotto Fellowship, and is in the Writers Pool for PlayGround, a playwright incubator that stages monthly plays at the Berkeley Repertory Theatre. He is currently seeking representation for his Silicon Valley-based novel, *Love in the Time of Stock Options*.

THE BEAUTIFUL MOMENT
Maury Zeff

We position ourselves as we have practiced countless times before: Chul at the edge of the pitch, ready for the corner kick, eyeing me and Park, who stands at the point outside the goal box. Yoon-Soo places himself a few feet in front of the goalkeeper, ready for the bending shot, which he will divert to a corner of the goal. And me at the far end of the goal box, there as back-up if Yoon-Soo can't connect. The referee blows the whistle and Chul runs up on the ball.

❀ ❀ ❀

I recall running up the field, the turf soft under my cleats, my teammates—and Chae-Ku, our government minder from the National Security Bureau in a rare moment of emotion—swarming me, on top of me, lifting me on their shoulders. Much of this image is made up of memories I drew from watching replays in the hotel lobby and the airport waiting area on CNN, which I'd heard about but had never seen before that week. (Minutes after we checked into our rooms, Chae-Ku oversaw the removal of the hotel televisions.) The white and black faces, as rare to me as a zebra on the streets of Pyongyang, spoke in sharp-cornered English. I recognized a few words—*football, Brazil, goal*—but the televised images of that one glorious moment were what underpinned my memories.

❀ ❀ ❀

Our keeper, Min, stops eighteen shots. Every time Brazil comes within shooting distance, he transforms himself into a rectangular creature that obscures every corner of open net. Early in the first half, he denies three shots within the same minute. An angled kick from the left, burning toward the far right of the net, glances off his gloved fingers and bounces harmlessly into the penalty kick area directly in front of him. The Brazilian striker takes this opportunity with a high shot to the left side of our net. Min, who I have rarely seen eat more than a small bowl of rice and kimchi at any sitting, makes an impossible leap and thwacks the ball over the top of the goal. And then on the corner kick, he throws himself in front of the opposing midfielder, stopping a dead-on shot cold. The Brazilians are getting much more of a challenge than they expected and turn up their game accordingly.

❀ ❀ ❀

As kids, we all did gymnastics, partially for sport, but also in preparation for the mass celebrations around holidays like the Dear Leader's birthday and Liberation Day. My school happened to have an inflatable ball and a meadow next to the main building, so many of the boys took up football. Thanks to the Great Leader's glorious guidance of our national team to victory over Italy in the 1966 World Cup, we were all familiar with the basics of the game. With four coats laid out as goalposts at each end of the pitch, two roughly divided teams of boys chased the ball up and down the mildly sloping field. From the start I had never experienced anything quite as singular. All I had to focus on was moving the ball with my feet toward the other team's goal. Nothing and no one else mattered. Other boys pushed and went for each other, and, yes, I wasn't afraid to give the occasional elbow, but it seemed that if it was just me and the ball—keeping control of its movement between my feet—and I could get it close enough to the opposing goal, I could score every time. Even the unconditional comfort of my family hadn't been able to provide this level of escape from a life that seemed foretold.

I began to sneak out to practice my dribbling or to kick the ball against the school building. I would get into trouble, being denied the lunch I had brought from home some days or held after at the end of the day. But I'd be out there the next day. In a few months, around the time that I began to become bored with dribbling around and scoring on the other boys, they stopped punishing me for playing football. Sometimes men I didn't know came to watch me, which unnerved me.

Attention such as this from strangers could only mean trouble for my family and me. But they would smile reassuringly when I searched their faces and motion for me to continue playing. A new ball—this one a proper football with black and white patches and Roman characters—appeared, along with two fixed, wood-frame nets. The headmaster began to dismiss me from math and science classes so that I could practice my dribbling.

Then Mr. Park started coming every day to teach me the game. More and more, I was pulled out of classes and, extraordinarily, excused from the daily gymnastics practice in which every schoolchild had to take part in advance of the Mass Games, so that I could dribble the ball around Mr. Park and take shots while he manned the net. He would, at first, bark instructions at me with the impersonal tone of authority that I had come to expect from all of my teachers. He told me to connect my shoelaces with the ball on my shots, what part of my head to use for maximum accuracy on a header, and how to minimize the number of touches I made before I passed or shot. As I began to more frequently win the tackles with Mr. Park, his tone softened in a way that I had only known from my family.

❖ ❖ ❖

An outcome other than our team being eliminated hinges on two impossible eventualities: We will have to beat or tie Brazil, and Spain will have to lose against Switzerland. But after Min's rally of saves, our team crystallizes around the possibility that we might make a showing in this game. For eighty-eight minutes we play hard defense. Not being scored upon is our goal. I run harder and farther up and down the field than I ever have. I am everywhere and, as a midfielder, that is my job. Every time the ball is at our end of the field, I am there, crowding their forward, supporting Min, who plays as if he's fighting for his life. Brazil (Brazil!) can't place the ball past him.

We get off four dainty shots on the Brazilian goal without results. Then, after a Brazilian defender kicks the ball out at his end of the field to stop Yoon-Soo's momentum on a breakaway, we get the corner kick. The point of this shot, which is probably where art and athleticism are most conjoined in football, is to pass it the forty yards from the corner of the field to a teammate in front of the net. The rare corner kicker can bend it into the net, but the best odds are to get it to a well-positioned offender to dink with a cleverly placed foot or forehead past the goalkeeper. There are, of course, defenders on every man, so ball placement is everything.

We have practiced the corner kick thousands and thousands of times. They have had us out in the worst of winter in just our shorts and jerseys working on these plays. It is on these shots and the penalty kicks that we have the greatest chance of scoring.

Chul lets the ball fly. It's high. Yoon-Soo is in too close to the net to do anything with the shot. I feint around Brazil's number twelve—or "Bronze," as we've taken to calling him, because of the similarity between his skin color and the hue of the giant statue of Dear Leader in People's Park Number four—but it will still be over my head. I bend my knees and tighten my body. Like a recoiling spring, I explode the tension from my feet upward through my legs and torso. I extend myself into the air with as much force as I can. The ball is here. It is flying away from the net and it will take ferocious force to change its course. I am at the apex of my leap, almost level with the cross-bar. I whip my head forward and downward, catching the ball between my forehead and the bridge of my nose. The connect is true. The pain from the impact on my nose is nothing next to the sharp spike in the base of my neck. I am down and on my feet again. The keeper is looking back at the ball in the net. Bronze is staring at me in astonishment. The stadium combusts. I am running down the field. My teammates are on me.

❀ ❀ ❀

When I was fifteen, I became a starting right wing for the Rimyongsu football club in the capital, where I stayed in a dormitory. My father, who had been a coal miner, as all the men in our village were, was given a desk job in a provincial office. Our family had undergone a sudden change in its status. At the time, I didn't believe that this development had anything to do with my ball-playing, but when I arrived in Pyongyang, football went from being something fun to a thing more like work. I had no choice but to get it right.

Two years later, I was placed on the training squad for the national team. We played eight hours every day. Injured players were treated by two doctors or, if they didn't heal in due time, were sent away. What astounded me was the variety and quantity of food. Although the menus changed, unlimited servings of rice and sesame oil-soaked beef were a fixture at every meal. The first time I became full from eating I thought I would die. I lay in my cold bunk, waiting for each wave of cramps to strike and then pass. My mother would have known how to ease the pain, but then the shame of having eaten so much food, maybe more food than I had ever had or even knew existed, made me put her out of my mind.

I learned to control my appetite, but got into trouble for hiding food in my room. The dried fish went foul after a day and the smell gave it away. When the coach called for me, I knew I had ruined everything. I pictured the shame of returning to my family after a month, my father wheezing his way back into the mines. I resolved not to cry. But instead, he asked me if I was hungry. Then he told me that there would always be enough food as long as I kept playing the way I did. He sent me back to my bunk. For weeks I waited for something else to come of it, but that was the end of the matter.

Min, who came from Undok in the forlorn northeastern extremity of the country, where, in harsh winters, people had been known to pick undigested kernels of corn from the excrement of farm animals for sustenance, looked at the vast spreads of food they served us with an expression that bordered on revulsion. He was like a man who had never known hunger and was suddenly faced with privation, except, in his case, it was the reverse. While we fortunate sons of coal miners, factory-workers, and party officials gorged three times a day on this muscle-building array of meats and vegetables, he would sit quietly away from us, eating his rice and pickled cabbage. His spare body manifested its fitness with a closely connected network of sinews. From the opening and closing of his jaw down to the flexing of his foot, his every movement caused a ripple of components visible under his tight skin to move in concert. In the shower he looked not so much like a young man than a biologist's musculature chart, and, when he played goal, he looked like something engineered.

❈ ❈ ❈

I run toward our bench and become the nucleus of a group embrace. Chul is squeezing my shoulders, exacerbating the pain in my neck that hasn't quite registered. Min has run down from our goal, but he is off to the side on his knees, weeping. Yoon-Soo is screaming at me, "You did it!" or something like this. Chae-Ku has regained his composure, but he is still smiling off to the side. Constant flashes are emanating from the stands. I am projected onto the large screen, a vision of me watching the screen while I am being swarmed.

We kill the clock for the remaining two minutes, passing the ball up and back, anywhere the Brazilians are not. Park feigns an injury, writhing on the ground. At the whistle, the referee calls no extra time and the match ends with us as the winner.

The whole team comes onto the field once more, but the stands are strangely silent. Chae-Ku and the other government men keep the reporters at a distance from us. As we walk toward our locker room, by accident or design, our paths cross with some of the Brazilian players. Bronze walks up to me. In this ecstatic moment, I am suddenly fearful. Speaking to a foreigner could put me in a labor camp.

He is smiling, which is strange, since we just bested his team. The crowd parts so that we are in the center, facing each other.

He says something in Brazilian, or maybe it is English. I recognize the English word "beautiful." He takes my head with two large hands and bends forward to kiss my forehead. "Beautiful," he says again and beams at me. Then he runs off.

❁ ❁ ❁

Our win over Brazil was not enough to keep us in the tournament. Switzerland's loss sent us home. Early the next morning, a bus took us from our hotel to the airport. While we were waiting to board the military plane, television monitors at the airport replayed my goal. My neck ached, so I held my head at an angle to watch the screen. My face, levered by my body, smashed the ball into the net time and again as the announcers—one dark, one light—talked excitedly.

Chul walked over to me. "You are just like Pak Doo-Ik," he said, referring to our national hero who scored the singular goal that gave us victory over the Italians in 1966.

I smiled. "No, it was your shot. I just helped it."

In a few minutes, they replayed the goal. The announcers were laughing as they cut to my run down the field, followed by the bizarre encounter with Bronze. He had just lost, but he walked into the scrum of my team as if he was the victor. I didn't know much about Brazil except that most of the country had HIV. Yet this man didn't look ill. If anything, he was health on two legs. He had long brown hair and skin the color of chestnuts that must have come from a different, much brighter sun than the flickering, coal-encrusted one that hung in the sky at home.

His smile was sheer warmth as he approached me. The camera turned to me, the hero, yet I looked anything but. I had a stony-faced shock—maybe even fear—across my face as I stood in front of Bronze. His open smile, his wild hair, his thick arms and full chest that made me seem like a young boy next to him. He had no fear about how he would look or who might be watching him. Then he ran back toward his locker room, leaving me standing bemused with my ecstatic team in our greatest moment. The announcers were laughing again—I was beginning to believe—at me, as if I was not worthy of such a large moment.

By the time we got home, the whole country knew. The game itself had not been broadcast, but the state radios in every home and village center played out the details of our glorious win. I was honored with a meeting with the Dear Leader, where he decorated Chul, Min, and me for service to our country. For the next two weeks, I was allowed to take off and spend time with my family. They were proud of me, but could not begin to grasp the scope of what had happened. I did not tell them about Bronze.

My neck didn't heal right and when I returned to the capital, my playing wasn't the same. I also had lost some of my excitement for the game, for no reason I could understand. My single-minded forward movement of the ball waned. The coaches asked me about it, worked with me, but younger players were coming up. In time I was placed on the second string. And then, after I married Sang-Hee, my girlfriend, I was rewarded with a desk job in the capital. This was no small thing. By rights I should have been back in my village, working in a mine.

Now there are days when, at my desk, reviewing and summarizing communiqués from the Physical Culture and Sports Guidance Commission, wondering if I will be able to provide meat for the baby growing inside Sang-Hee, I put my head down and massage the dull ache in my upper vertebrae. I replay in my mind during those moments (during every moment) the goal and what followed; Bronze strides up to me with all the happiness there is and shares a moment of that light with me. And as this scene winds through my internal vision again and again, I come to the inexorable conclusion that the freedom that the goal and its aftermath represented was meaningless to the rest of my life and I wish they had never happened.

Editors

Kristen J. Tsetsi is an award-winning fiction writer and Pushcart Prize nominee who has taught creative writing, screenwriting, and playwriting at the Trollwood Performing Arts School in Fargo, ND. She received her MFA from Minnesota State University Moorhead in 2003 and has since found work as a college English instructor, a cab driver, and, recently, as a feature writer for a Connecticut daily newspaper. For fun, she co-writes and films episodes for a comic-relief YouTube series created for (and by) writers called Inside the Writers' Studio. Her debut novel, *Pretty Much True . . .*, released this year. For more information: http://kristenjtsetsi.com

Bruce Pratt's novel *The Serpents of Blissfull* was published by Mountain State Press in 2011. He was nominated in 2008 for a Pushcart Award in fiction, and his poetry collection *Boreal* is available from Antrim House Books. His fiction, poetry, essays, and plays have appeared in more than forty literary magazines and journals in the United States, Canada, Ireland, and Wales, and they have won several awards. In addition to working as an editor with *American Fiction*, Pratt serves on the editorial board of *Hawk and Handsaw*. A graduate of the Stonecoast MFA at The University of Southern Maine, he teaches undergraduate creative writing at the University of Maine. Pratt lives with his wife, Janet, in Eddington Maine.

Assistant Editor

Bayard Godsave is an assistant professor of English at Cameron University in Oklahoma. His fiction has appeared in the *Cream City Review*, *Confrontation*, *Another Chicago Magazine*, *Bryant Literary Review*, and the *Evansville Review*. Godsave was born in Pawtucket, Rhode Island, and raised in Western New York. He has an MFA from Minnesota State University Moorhead, and he received his PhD in English from the University of Wisconsin–Milwaukee. Godsave and his wife live on a small farm out in the country.

Judge

Josip Novakovich moved from Croatia to the United States at the age of twenty. He has published a novel, *April Fool's Day* (in ten languages), three story collections (*Infidelities: Stories of War and Lust, Yolk,* and *Salvation and Other Disasters*), and three collections of narrative essays. His work has appeared in Best American Poetry, the Pushcart Prize collection, and O. Henry Prize Stories. He received the Whiting Writer's Award, a Guggenheim fellowship, two National Endowment for the Arts fellowships, the Ingram Merrill Award, and an American Book Award, and he has been a writing fellow of the New York Public Library. Novakovich teaches creative writing at Concordia University in Montreal.